Woman of the Hour

JANE LYTHELL

First published in the UK in 2016 by Head of Zeus Ltd

This paperback edition first published in the UK in 2016
by Head of Zeus Ltd

9 7 5 3 1 2 4 6 8

A CIP catalogue record for this book is available from the British Library.

Paperback ISBN 9781784971212
Ebook ISBN 9781784971199

Typeset by Ben Cracknell Studios

Printed and bound in Great Britain by CPI Group (UK) Ltd,
Croydon CR0 4YY

Head of Zeus Ltd
Clerkenwell House
45–47 Clerkenwell Green
London EC1R 0HT

WWW.HEADOFZEUS.COM

Woman
of the
Hour

JANE LYTHELL worked as a television
producer and commissioning editor
for fifteen years. She has been
Deputy Director of the BFI and
Chief Executive of BAFTA. This
is her third novel, and the first
title in the StoryWorld series.

Jane loves to hear from her readers.
You can contact her on:
Facebook: Jane Lythell Author
Twitter: @janelythell
Instagram: jane_lythell_writer

ALSO BY JANE LYTHELL

The Lie of You
After the Storm

To my daughter Amelia Trevette, my rosebud

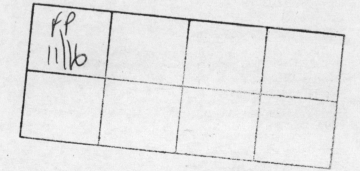

Woman
of the
Hour

CHAPTER ONE

'It's not true, is it?'

Simon was standing by my door and I beckoned him in. I know you shouldn't have favourites but Simon is the best researcher I've ever worked with. He's a finisher, never overlooks any detail and is great both with members of the public and presenters. He closed the door behind him.

'There's an ugly rumour circulating that the new job's gone to a daughter of the great and the good,' he said.

You can't keep anything secret in a TV station. It's the leakiest place on earth. I sighed but said nothing.

'Liz?' he persisted.

'I'm afraid so. Thumbscrews were applied.'

I was being indiscreet saying that. I should have held the management line and pretended that I had given the researcher role to Harriet Dodd on merit. But I was fed up about it too. Harriet is the daughter of Edward Dodd who edits a national newspaper and is a friend of our MD Saul Relph. What I didn't tell Simon was that Saul had called me into his office and told me that his friend Edward Dodd was worried about his daughter and he wanted her to be taught the meaning of hard work. It would be a major favour if we would take her on and train her up. I had resisted but Saul had added that my taking her on would help the whole station. Simon was giving me an old-fashioned look.

'It's a three month attachment. I've made it clear that if

1

she doesn't make the grade she's out,' I said.

Simon leaned forward and picked up the glass paperweight that Ben, my ex-husband, bought me on our falling-in-love trip to Venice. We had gone over to Murano to choose it. Simon gazed at the colourful swirls that orbited inside the glass sphere.

'How do you bear it?' he said.

'Because I have to.'

He put the glass globe down delicately.

'OK.'

I knew Simon wouldn't shop me to the others. Given the amount of TV we have to produce, I have a ridiculously small team of three researchers and a runner. I used to have three experienced researchers and we could manage our output, although we were working at full stretch. But Roomana had left recently to work at a rival company as an assistant producer. I had expected to appoint a seasoned researcher in her place. Instead, we were going to have to train up Harriet, a complete novice, and I knew this would put a strain on us all. My team is small because most of what we produce is sofa television. This entails getting a range of guests into the studio to be interviewed by Fizzy Wentworth, our star presenter. We also run pre-recorded stories on our show, but many of these are supplied by independent production companies; hence my tiny team. The phone on my desk rang and it was Henry, the floor manager.

'You'd better get down here quick. Dianne Lucas won't come out of make-up. Says her hair looks a fright,' he said.

I hurried downstairs to the make-up room on the ground floor. I had booked the actor Dianne Lucas as our interview of the day. She's no longer an A-lister but she is still a name and she's written this steamy memoir about a love affair she had with a much younger man at the height of her fame. She kept the affair secret at the time. Maybe she needs the money now because she's been extremely graphic about the affair and it is being serialised in one of the tabloids. I slipped into make-up and the moment I saw Dianne's fraught face in the mirror I knew this was a woman on the edge. Her eyes moved up and met mine in the mirror. I saw anger in her eyes, an anger she was barely containing. Why the hell had the publishers put her up for this interview? Live television is a tough gig and I've noticed before how actors can go to pieces when they don't have their scripts to hide behind.

'I can't go on with my hair like this,' she said, making a tragic grimace which made me think of one of those theatre masks with the lips turned down dramatically.

Make-up mirrors can be unforgiving with all the light they throw on the face and Dianne's hair, which had been over-dyed, hung limply around her cheeks and drained her face of colour. Ellen, our head of make-up, was applying blusher to her cheekbones.

'Maybe if we pinned your hair up?' Ellen suggested.

She and I both made soothing, complimentary noises as Dianne's hair was teased up into a bun and false hair was added to give it more body. I slipped into flattery mode. I hate the way I am able to do this so easily.

'Now we can see your lovely cheekbones much better,' I said.

I watched Ellen working fast and expertly and tried not to panic as I thought of Fizzy sitting on the sofa with no one to talk to. Fizzy could only spend so much time going through the newspapers.

'Your book was such a revelation; so authentic. I'd hate our viewers to miss the chance of hearing from you,' I said, touching her on the arm and helping her to her feet. I knew I was laying it on thick but if it got Dianne Lucas out of make-up and into the studio I was doing my job. She gave a parting look at the mirror, pulled her shoulders back and raised her chin; I could imagine her doing that as she stood backstage in a theatre just before she made an entrance. I hoped her professionalism as an actor would carry her through as I walked with her to the studio door. Henry the floor manager took her in to be miked up. I hurried to the gallery to watch the interview. We are in voice contact with Fizzy from the gallery via an earpiece and I whispered to her to take this gently as Dianne was fragile. Fizzy gave a tiny nod to show that she had got my message. As Dianne sat down on the sofa Fizzy leaned towards her, holding her book face out to camera, and said in a warm voice:

'Welcome to StoryWorld, Dianne, and thank you so much for coming in this morning. What a great read this is. I found it a very honest account of love.'

'Love!' Dianne Lucas hissed at her. 'What does that word even mean?'

Fizzy did not react to Dianne's aggression and ploughed on.

'Well, I agree that there are many different types of love, but what you seem to be talking about here, very candidly I thought, is a deep physical attraction between two people, an attraction that transcended the age difference.'

'No! That is prurient nonsense. It was a meeting of souls,' Dianne said very coldly.

I thought that was a bit rich as the book describes their first kiss and their first shag with relish and later goes on about how rejuvenating it was to have a much younger lover.

'Ask her what her happiest memory of the relationship is,'

I whispered to Fizzy who was now flicking through the book to give herself a moment.

'I was wondering what your happiest memory is of the relationship, Dianne, as clearly there were deep emotions.'

Dianne narrowed her eyes and I felt sorry for Fizzy.

'Did you read the book?'

'Yes indeed, wonderful.'

She hadn't. We had summarised it for her.

'The relationship was torment from beginning to end,' Dianne Lucas said, putting on the tragic face for which she is famous.

It was a car crash of an interview and I asked the director to come out of it early. He shot me a sympathetic look. He knew I was in for a mauling from Julius.

Every morning there is a post-mortem meeting on that day's show chaired by Julius Jones who is our director of programmes. He makes notes on each item and the show is pulled apart, and occasionally praised, in front of assembled senior colleagues. We have all come to expect more shredding than praise at these meetings. I knew Julius would have a go at me for booking Dianne Lucas because it had been one of the most uncomfortable interviews we'd broadcast in ages. I got myself a coffee from the staff café and joined the others in the conference room. Julius kept us waiting. Fizzy was already in there and I sat down next to her. One thing I've learned over the years is to be careful how you treat presenters when they've just come off air. For all their apparent confidence in front of the camera most presenters are deeply insecure and needy people. They need the love of the viewers to make them feel alive. When they come off air they are still full of adrenalin and cannot take any criticism. It is best to praise them and take it up later if an interview has gone wrong.

'Well done for handling Dianne. I know she was a night-mare,' I said.

'She's aged very badly,' Fizzy replied with a slight shudder.

Fizzy is a woman who sets great store by how people look. She is thirty-eight but she looks younger. She is pretty rather than beautiful, with her strawberry-blonde hair and pointed chin, more of a girl-next-door type who viewers can relate to, rather than drop-dead gorgeous. Julius entered the room and there was a palpable change in the atmosphere. No one says anything until they've had an indication of which way he is going to jump. Sometimes you can tell what his mood is going to be simply by the way he sits down and spreads his arms on the table.

Julius is handsome, though in a rather bland way. He's got light brown hair cut short, hazel eyes, a straight nose and full lips. He looks clean-cut and preppy but he is unpredictable, a chameleon, and his face can change from pleasant to menacing in a moment. Even his name is a sham. He was born and raised Nigel Jones but changed his name to Julius Jones when he started working in television. He's the man who spotted Fizzy when she was a PA and he has moulded her into the queen of live TV. He is a difficult man but I have learned a great deal from him about how to produce hit shows. He has a genuine talent for popular TV and knows what issues and personalities will connect with the audience. Now his full lips were stretching in a humourless line as he looked directly at me.

'What did we get out of Dianne Lucas today? Three sentences? Our interview of the day!'

'I'm sorry. She was a disaster and I think Fizzy did really well under the circumstances,' I said.

'That's a given. But doesn't Lucas have a reputation for being a nut job?'

'Neurotic certainly, but her book is getting a lot of attention and—'

'Why didn't you pre-record her?' he snapped.

'That's the wisdom of hindsight,' I said.

To my surprise Bob, the news editor, spoke up in my defence.

'To be fair, we do always say that live TV is better than pre-recorded,' he said.

Julius gave him a dangerous look.

'Rubbish. Liz should have predicted we would have trouble with her,' he said.

Bob wouldn't let it go.

'I'm just saying that we pride ourselves on our immediacy, don't we?'

This was true. Live TV is more risky than pre-recorded TV because you can't control what will happen and we are encouraged to go live whenever possible. It was Julius who came up with our slogan: *Real people, real life, real stories live.*

'Someone with your experience; not good enough, Liz.' His hectoring tone rang out across the table at me.

Julius left it at that and turned to the next item. But he would have noted that Bob had stuck up for me and he wouldn't have liked it. I felt grateful for the support because Julius had made me feel inadequate even though he was one hundred per cent right about Dianne Lucas. It is well known that she is strange. There are stories of her holding seances in her sitting room to get in touch with her dead first husband. I should have thought about her eccentricities and sent a crew to interview her about her book. But why did Julius always feel the need to belittle everyone all the time?

As we left the meeting I mouthed a thank you to Bob who gave me a small nod. Bloody Dianne Lucas and her stupid hair; she was going straight onto my blacklist. Oh yes, I keep my own secret blacklist of guests who I will never book again. They get on my list if they fail on camera, as Dianne did today, or if they act out of order. I have always found it significant how a celebrity treats junior members of staff, like our runners who get them a coffee and book them a cab. Many a celebrity will put on the most charming face when sitting on the sofa with the cameras running, but I've seen some of them behave horribly to the runners; sneering or snarling at them for no reason. They go straight onto my blacklist. I enjoy the fact that they don't realise they are reducing their time in the limelight because of their treatment of staff they think don't matter.

I sometimes wonder how I have survived in live television this long. It can be a bloody and brutal business. When I started working in television seventeen years ago I was idealistic and perhaps a bit foolish. I was working on a series called *Celebrating Our Unsung Heroes*. Julius Jones was then head of features and he tasked me with finding a coal miner who was on the point of retirement after a life spent underground. We planned to make a big fuss of the miner and his wife. We'd bring them up to London to sit on the sofa with our popular breakfast stars, screen a brief package about his life of hardship and then beam in a pre-recorded farewell from his workmates which was guaranteed to reduce his wife, if not the miner, to tears. Bingo. Real people, real feelings, real television, Julius said.

It wasn't easy finding a working miner, nearly all the mines had been shut down, but I did find Albert, a man who had gone down the mines at the age of fifteen. I liked him. He was a proud man. This was a big thing in his life and he had told his village he was going to be on the telly. A group of them had gone down to their social club that morning to watch the live transmission of his interview which was scheduled for eight-fifteen. Julius Jones was in charge of the show that day and he overran the running order by nine minutes, which is unheard of. He was in a rage and he told me he was going to pull the eight-fifteen story. I said you can't, his whole village are waiting to watch it. He shouted at me: 'If you can't fucking deal with this you shouldn't be on the team. Now get out there and sort it!'

I took Albert and his wife into our café. We made a point of giving our guests a good breakfast after the show, and I had to break the news to them. I was ashamed at how we had treated Albert, as if his life story did not matter. We ate bacon and eggs but I was finding it difficult to swallow the food. As I was escorting them to the taxi we crossed the atrium and the big boss, the MD of StoryWorld, was walking in. Albert stopped him.

'You let my village down today,' he said.

The MD looked over at me.

'Is this true?'

I nodded miserably. 'Albert's village had gathered to watch his interview. We had to cut it.'

An hour later Julius Jones hauled me into his office and he was incandescent.

'You naive little bitch! Landing me in it. I won't forget this.'

But I'm still working at StoryWorld. I was a researcher then and now I'm head of features and Julius Jones has worked his way up to become the director of programmes. He is my boss.

I called my team in and we went through the list of who we had booked for the rest of the week. I was under pressure to deliver a strong interview of the day tomorrow. Simon was keen that we go with a member of the public with a human interest story. A single-parent dad called John had written in to our agony aunt, Betty.

'John's wife upped and left him with their three young children. He's given up work and built his life around his kids, but he's worried now because his daughter is hitting teenage-hood. He feels she needs a woman around to talk about girl stuff and does Betty have any advice for him?' Simon said as he passed me the email.

I read what John had written and it was the most marvellous letter.

'It's wonderful, Simon, but he's an unknown.'

'I've spoken to him on the phone. He's a natural. He came out with all these brilliant funny stories about his kids. And look at him.'

Simon handed me a photo he'd printed of John seated on a sofa with his three children climbing over him, two boys and a girl. The sofa was worn, the room was shabby but the kids looked happy. He was a good-looking man with a friendly open face.

'He is rather attractive,' I said.

I handed the photo to Molly, my other researcher.

'I wonder why he hasn't got himself a girlfriend then,' she said.

Molly and Simon get on but there is an inevitable rivalry between them for stories. She was pushing her idea for Fizzy to interview a footballer who had brought out his memoir; actually it was more of a misery memoir than a sporting one.

'It's not only about football, it's also about his tough child-hood and it's surprisingly well written and revealing,' she said.

'Why does everyone think footballers are stupid?' Simon said.

I was reading the back of the book.

'And he wrote it himself? Not a ghostwriter?'

'All his own words...'

'Maybe next week, Moll; I'm not keen to do two book stories back to back.'

'I've got this feeling John from Sheffield will be great. I think Fizzy will love him. We get her to empathise with him and she can ask viewers to email or tweet us any suggestions about dealing with teenage girls,' Simon said.

'That's Betty's territory,' I said.

Betty is our formidable agony aunt and she covers these types of issues on her weekly slot, but she was away doing a lecture tour in Canada. It was high risk but in the end I decided we would invite John from Sheffield as our interview of the day. Some of our most successful items have involved ordinary people and Simon's instincts are sound.

Chalk Farm flat, 7.15 p.m.

I was home by seven-fifteen tonight which wasn't too bad. I pay Janis, a woman who lives locally, to be with my daughter Florence until I get back. Flo complains it's stupid because at fourteen years of age she is fine to be left on her own, but she gets on well with Janis who has been her childminder for years. Janis cooks her supper and they talk. I learn all kinds of useful stuff about Flo from Janis, which I'm grateful for but which also makes me sad because Flo stopped confiding in me a while ago. When she was younger we were incredibly close and she was my best cuddly little girl.

Janis left and I knocked gently and popped my head round Flo's bedroom door. One of the great fights between us has been about how I barge into her room unannounced. Now I try to remember to knock first. Flo's bedroom was in near darkness except for the glow of her tablet which lit up her face. I love that face more than any other face in the world. She did not smile when she saw me but she did not scowl either.

'Had a good day, sweetheart?'

'Yeah, OK. Dad called.'

'How's he doing?'

'He said Granddad will pick me up if I get the train on Friday.'

'Great.'

Every two or three weeks Flo spends the weekend with her dad Ben and his parents in Portsmouth. We have to be flexible about it because Ben works as an aerial photographer and sometimes a big job will come up at the weekend and he can't see her. Sometimes she will go down on a Friday night, which I prefer because it gives her longer with her dad.

'I'm making chilli. Do you fancy some?'

She shook her head.

'No, ta. I'm stuffed.'

She was keen to get back to her tablet so I closed her door. It was one of our better exchanges because recently we rarely talk without angry words passing between us.

As I chopped the onions I reflected that I would have a free weekend. Ben and I set up the weekend arrangements after we divorced and I try hard not to let it slip. Before our split I couldn't understand those women who try to stop contact and who bad-mouth their exes, especially when they do it in front of the children. But afterwards, when things got ugly, I would find myself biting back my anger and frustration in front of Flo. There was a lot of anger and disappointment to process after ten years of being together and I'm sure she must have overheard our heated words from time to time.

CHAPTER TWO

StoryWorld TV station, London Bridge

John, the single-parent dad from Sheffield, was terrific. Fizzy connected with him at once and she got him to talk openly about the struggles he'd had since his wife left him and their three kids one afternoon. It was out of the blue, he said. There had been no warning signs and no message left. His wife had asked a neighbour to keep an eye on the kids till he got back from work and then had driven away in the family car. When John got back he'd tried to call her, getting more and more anxious when he couldn't get through. But it was only after putting the kids to bed that he saw she had taken her clothes, her jewellery and one framed family photo. He has not heard a word from her since and he thinks she had some kind of breakdown. He has had to cope with the children's questions and their misery at this rejection by their mother. Children so often take the blame for these things onto themselves, he said. I thought of my Flo when he said that. Did she feel she was responsible for Ben and me breaking up? Fizzy asked him what was most difficult and he replied that with his daughter, the oldest of his three, reaching thirteen he was feeling out of his depth.

You can't fake authenticity and we've been flooded with emails and tweets from viewers with all kinds of advice as well as about thirty marriage proposals! I am planning to do a follow-up story with John in a month or so and I can see him becoming part of our StoryWorld family. Even Julius was pleased at the morning meeting.

'I don't know why that item worked so well but it did,' he said.

Julius shuffled his running order and script into a neat pile in front of him. We were waiting for the signal that the meeting was over because no one gets up to leave until he indicates that discussion has ended.

He said: 'I've been thinking about the overall look of the show and I've come to a decision. From now on I want our presenters to wear pastel colours. People wake up to us every day and it's our job to lift their spirits and to offer them a cheerful start. I don't want to see *any* black or dark blue or dark green on anyone on camera. Dark colours say misery, we associate black with death. From now on StoryWorld will be yellow, it will be pink, it will be pastel. Is that clear?'

'Sounds good to me,' Fizzy said.

Fizzy is close to Julius and I'm sure he had briefed her on this before the meeting. It was Julius who gave her that first break as our weather presenter and her rise since has been meteoric. A lot of us resent how well those two get on and we are careful around Fizzy for this reason. Some of the team even think that they are lovers. I don't think so; it looks more like a master and protégée relationship to me. After Fizzy's enthusiastic endorsement there was an awkward silence in the meeting room. I am the producer who deals with most of the presenters so I had to say something.

'Julius, I can see your point but how am I going to get Gerry and Ledley into pastels?'

Gerry is our astrologer and he favours a smart tailored look with a navy blazer or dark jumper. Ledley is our cook. He's tall and slim and he goes for a relaxed anti-fashion style. He'll come in wearing an orange shirt with dark red jeans or

14

a printed pattern shirt with worn black jeans and boots and he gets away with it. He has even been written up in a magazine as a good example of street style. I couldn't see Ledley agreeing to wear a pink shirt.

'You can put Ledley into chef's whites. And tell Gerry it's the brand, the StoryWorld brand. People don't want dark colours and misery in the morning. They want upbeat stories and light bright colours. I want this implemented straight away.'

Bob the news editor spoke up now.

'I assume we're talking the feature presenters here, Julius? News can hardly be pastel.'

Bob runs the team of news reporters and they are overwhelmingly male and macho. In every TV station there is a great divide between the features team and the news team which is why his support of me yesterday was unexpected. Julius gave Bob a hard look.

'I want to see the news reporters in pale blue shirts,' he said, standing up, 'from next Monday.'

The meeting was over and Julius walked out of the room. I was keen to talk to Bob about this latest development and followed him to his office. I could tell by the way he was walking that he was furious. He sees himself as a serious news man in competition with much larger outfits. He prides himself on getting exclusives and on selling these on to other TV stations. We reached his office and he slammed his door shut.

'Pastels! Such bullshit,' he said, throwing his papers onto his desk.

'You'd think we were a supermarket or an airline. Welcome to StoryWorld... fasten your seat belts,' I said.

'You know what gets me? It's a fucking great power trip,

that's what this is all about. It's about *him* getting *us* to do something and there's never any room for discussion.'

It was true and I wondered if Julius was punishing Bob for his intervention yesterday. He has pockmarked cheeks and dark angry eyes and he's weirdly attractive and magnetic. He's been at the station about two years. As a rule the news editors don't last long here. Sooner or later they clash with Julius and Julius always wins any power struggle.

'What are you going to do?' he asked.

'Carry it out, of course,' I said.

'You've worked with him a long time, haven't you?'

'I have and I've learned to pick my fights. I'm not going to fight over what colours people wear.'

He knelt down to pick up the papers that had slid off his desk onto the floor.

'Yeah, but just the once I'd like him to get what's coming to him,' he said.

I went downstairs to get myself a coffee from the staff café which is called the Hub. The management spent a shed-load of money on this café and got an architect in to design it. Julius has a theory that if you give the staff a good place to eat and drink they are more likely to put in the long hours. There is a central circular food and drink bar and spreading out from these like the spokes of a wheel are stylish lime-green and orange designer tables and chairs. The lighting is trendy and can be changed to create different moods – we use the Hub for presentations sometimes. The menu caters for all types and all allergies. Gerry Melrose, our astrologer, was sitting in there drinking a diet Coke. He told me recently that he's on a diet and is aiming to shed a stone. He's in his late-forties and his partner, Anwar, is younger than him and Gerry worries about his appearance. No time like the present, I thought, as I sat down opposite him. He was wearing a rather nice dark blue jumper over a crisp white shirt.

'How are things with you, darling?' he asked.

'OK,' I said, stirring half a spoon of sugar into my coffee. 'Julius has this new idea. He wants all the presenters to wear pastel colours; yellow, pink, pale blue. But not dark blue like your nice jumper, and definitely no black. He was adamant about it. Said it's the StoryWorld brand to be bright and cheerful and he wants us to implement this straight away.'

'Pastels can be fattening, you know?' Gerry said.

'I know they can.'

'What's he got against dark colours?'

'He says they stand for misery and death,' I said, trying to resist the impulse to roll my eyes.

'That's an Aquarius for you, free thinkers, mould breakers.'

'Julius is an Aquarius?'

'Oh yes. I did his chart a while back.'

I tried to imagine how Julius would have reacted to this. Julius is the most private of men and he would have had to give Gerry the exact time and location of his birth.

'I guess I'll have to buy myself a few new shirts then. I don't usually go in for pastels,' Gerry said.

'Thanks for taking it so well.'

Gerry sipped his diet Coke.

'Will we get a clothing allowance for the new shirts?'

I'm fond of Gerry, even though I think astrology is enjoyable nonsense, but he does like to drive a hard bargain on money matters.

'Not sure. Leave it with me.'

I went upstairs to congratulate Simon on his excellent choice of John from Sheffield as the interview of the day.

17

It was good to be home earlier tonight. Flo was in her room and as she was leaving Janis told me a new family has moved in across the road. There's a daughter, Paige, who is a bit older than Flo and they had been talking. Flo was dead chuffed to have made friends with a girl of sixteen, Janis said.

She left and I decided to make macaroni cheese. I don't eat much during the day and when I get home I like to make something from scratch. I'm an average cook but cooking helps me to decompress. Macaroni cheese is one of my favourite comfort foods and I made a creamy sauce with extra mature Cheddar and a bit of Gruyère I had left over. As I grated the Cheddar I was thinking about John from Sheffield and his story which had moved our audience today. It brought back the painful time after Ben and I split up. Flo had just had her seventh birthday and was a happy and settled child. Ben and I had been going through difficult times for a while but we had managed to protect her from the worst of it and our separation came as a complete shock. She was confused and upset and I noticed a definite change in her. She started to cry at minor things and would cling to me when I dropped her off at school, pleading with me not to leave her. It was tough having to pull her fingers off and walk away. She had seen one parent leave and was frightened the other one might be off too. She wanted to sleep in my bed every night. Poor little mite, it hit her hard.

I put a good pinch of nutmeg into my sauce and kept stirring. I took it hard too. Ben and I had been together for ten years. I met him shortly after I joined StoryWorld as a junior researcher and he was working as a cameraman and on a higher salary than me. I was vulnerable. My darling dad had died suddenly the year before and looking back I can see that there was always an imbalance in our relationship. I let Ben take the lead on most things, like where we would live and how much we would spend on things. I was a bit of a pushover really. So being on my own with Flo has stretched and challenged me. I have had my moments of blind panic but I know I have become stronger.

Flo came out of her room.

'How was your day, darling?'

'I hate today. I hate double maths,' she said.

Mr Crooks, our cat, was curled up on our squashy yellow sofa in his favourite spot with his nose resting in his fur, blissfully asleep. Flo picked him up with a deep sigh and took him back to her room. I sat down on the sofa. I love the colour yellow in a home. It's so cheerful and my sofa just asks to be stretched out on.

I cleared my emails, turned off my mobile and made myself a mug of tea. I value these quiet times. When I split up with Ben we sold our small house in East Finchley and I found this two-bedroomed garden flat in Chalk Farm. There's not much of a garden, it's more a patio with potted plants, but there's room enough for Flo and me to have two deckchairs out there in the summer and to pretend we have a garden. It's not a big flat inside either. Both our bedrooms are small doubles. It does have one beautiful large room, the living room, which is also our kitchen and dining room. There are doors at the far end which open onto the patio and I bought the flat because of this room. It's costing me more than I can comfortably afford and a great slab of my salary goes on my mortgage every month. But my flat is my haven. Often, late at night, when Flo is asleep, I'll sit here on my sofa with the doors open, listening to the thrum of the city and enjoying the feeling that this is my little corner of the world and no one can get me here.

CHAPTER THREE

StoryWorld TV station, London Bridge

Start of a new week and Harriet Dodd arrived today. I was walking out of the morning meeting with Julius when this young woman with light red shoulder-length hair approached us. She had hooded eyelids which gave her a sleepy look, though she sounded confident as she extended her hand towards me.

'I cannot thank you enough for this opportunity. I've always wanted to work in television.'

She had the well-bred voice and the poise of an expensively educated girl and she was dressed immaculately. I wondered what my team would make of her.

'You must be Harriet,' I said.

'Yes. Please call me Harry, everyone does.'

She smiled at me and then glanced over at Julius and smiled at him and I could see that his interest was aroused. He introduced himself and they shook hands.

'My father sends his best wishes to you,' she said.

'Please send mine back,' Julius replied.

That grated on me. She was already working her contacts. Harriet followed me to the quartet of desks outside my office that belong to my team and I presented her to Molly, Simon and Ziggy, my runner.

'Please show Harriet how to log on and we're meeting in my room in fifteen minutes,' I said.

They joined me and we spent the next hour discussing several ideas we were working on for the show and I could see that Molly and Simon were observing Harriet rather carefully. I was observing her too. Maybe because of her hooded eyelids she has a closed face that you can't read. She has beautiful shiny hair which is the colour of apricots and she was dressed in a cream silk blouse which had to be designer, tucked into a burgundy leather pencil skirt with kitten heel courts the exact same shade of dark red. Now, we television people earn good money and we can be a stylish crew but honest to God, Harriet's ensemble was in another league.

'There's a lot to learn about turning an idea into good TV,' I said to her. 'I'd like you to shadow Simon this week and he can teach you the basics.'

I saw an expression flit across Molly's face. Was she aggrieved that I hadn't asked her?

'And then next week I'd like you to shadow Molly. That way you'll get a good insight into how we work in this team.'

They got up and left my office. About ten minutes later Julius walked in without knocking, flicked my door shut and sat down opposite me.

'So that's Edward Dodd's daughter.'

'Yes, and she's twenty-six,' I replied crisply.

He laughed.

'Oh, Liz, you and your suspicious mind...'

'What can I do for you, Julius?'

'I'm planning an outside broadcast for October. I've secured a sponsor and they want something human interest and inspirational.'

He knows I love doing outside broadcasts and it is an aspect of my job that gives me huge satisfaction. They require a great deal of planning and longer hours than usual but when they work they can be special.

'Great. Shall I work up a few ideas?'

'Let's brainstorm now,' he said.

That is Julius for you. I had a week's worth of items to produce and he expected me to drop everything to discuss ideas.

'Not now. Can we do it over lunch?'

He stood up.

'OK. See you at The Brasserie at one.'

He left and I saw how he leaned into Harriet's desk and said a few words before he sauntered away. In all the years I've known him, Julius has held a more senior position than me at StoryWorld, and now he is Top Dog. Sometimes I look at him and think, I could do what you do, but I would do it differently. I would try to take the staff with me through praise and encouragement, not through fear. He is a bully, not always, but often enough to generate unease in all his senior managers. He has made me feel afraid in the past. He is also talented and very clever. He has a phenomenal memory and doesn't forget past conflicts, but then nor do I. How could I ever forget that night?

Our TV station is housed in a converted Victorian warehouse which is right on the river near London Bridge. I've worked here for years yet I still find that the building gives me a lift when I arrive in the mornings. The architect who converted it used its space to great effect and there's this dramatic light-filled atrium which you enter from the street. Off the atrium are the main studio, the small news studio, dressing rooms and the Hub, our staff café. There are two staircases, on either side of the atrium, which take you up to the executive offices above; features is on the left and news is on the right. It is a very showbiz building and I have some-times used the interior for my stories. One year I even staged a fashion show, using the staircases to great effect.

I walked down and out onto the riverside and headed towards The Brasserie which is near Tower Bridge. This is his favourite restaurant and they make a fuss of Julius when he goes there. It was a fine autumn day, bright and blowy, and I was feeling good about my life and my job. There are times when I feel so lucky to be working in television because no two days are alike. Julius was seated at a corner table and he'd ordered a bottle of Chablis.

'To go with the oysters,' he said.

'You're having oysters?'

'Join me. They're fantastic here.'

He ordered a dozen oysters and a side order of fries for us to share. We talked outside-broadcast ideas as we drank the wine, which was very fine and dry.

'What about a fire station? Everyone loves a fireman,' I said.

'Too risky; we would need a fire or an accident to happen that day and it might be a quiet one. Have you noticed how rarely we carry fire stories these days? Maybe the health and safety people have achieved something after all,' he said.

The platter of oysters arrived, already opened, and he put some on my plate. He reached for the black pepper.

'How about a hospital then? I know it's an obvious choice but there would be a lot of human interest stories on the wards,' I said.

'Might be a downer, don't you think? Death and disease... The sponsor wants something inspirational.'

'I'm sure we could find stories of courage in the face of adversity and I could see Fizzy being great with the patients. They'd love her and the staff would too. Let me do some research.'

We agreed I would work the idea up; find a suitable hospital and recce it.

I asked him if he would like my sixth oyster. Five had been enough for me. He shared the last of the wine and told me he had got his taste for oysters when he was a student and worked at an oyster bar at Mersea Island in Essex.

'What was that like?'

'Cold and smelly most of the time. We prepared the fish in this shack out the back and had to wear wellington boots and PVC aprons. But it was interesting too. They have big oyster beds there, you know?'

'I don't know the place. Did you say Mersea *Island*?'

'Yes, it's one of those places people don't know about; an estuary in Essex and a beautiful peaceful spot. You should take your daughter there.'

He rarely talks about his past, though I had heard he was from Essex. We walked back to the station along the riverside and stopped to look at a brightly painted barge which was making its way up the river. He pointed it out to me and I was thinking it made a pleasant change to be with him when he was in this more collaborative mood. I didn't let my guard down though. I know how quickly his mood can change.

Chalk Farm flat, 9 p.m.

Flo was feeling low tonight. She was lying on her bed stroking Mr Crooks. He's a large scruffy tortoiseshell with a black and orange striped face and golden eyes. He joined us when Flo was nine. She'd been nagging me for ages about having a cat and I kept resisting. In the end, thinking that she was an only child and probably felt lonely at times, I agreed and we went to a cat rescue centre. She fell in love with him at first sight

25

and was determined to call him Crookshanks after Hermione's cat in *Harry Potter*. Hermione was her heroine then. We brought him home and he soon became Mr Crooks and he's a fixture on her bed at night. She said she didn't want anything to eat and she hauled Mr Crooks onto her stomach and tickled him under his chin.

Later, I was sitting at the kitchen table cleaning my jewellery with a silver cloth. One of my weaknesses is earrings and I have a lot of silver pairs, some plain and some with semi-precious stones. I find the task of cleaning them a calming thing to do even though you end up with black fingers. I asked Flo if she wanted me to clean her necklace. She has this silver chain with charms which is special to her. I gave it to her on her thirteenth birthday and plan to buy a new charm for it every year. To my surprise she got her chain and joined me at the table, watching as I used the soft cloth to shine up the silver. I made us both a hot chocolate and we didn't talk at first, we sipped our chocolate and after a while she started to talk about her weekend and I found out what was making her feel low.

'Dad's got this new girlfriend,' she said, and her face was a picture of absolute disgust.

'Really?'

'Yeah; he met her in a casino.'

The minute she said the word 'casino' my heart started to beat fast but I tried not to show my unease.

'Does she work in a casino?' I asked.

'I think so. She was there *all* the time. Granny said she was all over him like a cheap suit.'

I smiled inwardly. It was such a Grace thing to say. Grace is Ben's mum and she has a way of taking the measure of people and putting them in their place with a few well-chosen words. We have stayed close in spite of the break-up and she once told me I am like the daughter she always wanted. That made me feel happy because I love her dearly, but it also made me feel a bit sad that my own mum is a distant figure.

'We didn't get a chance to talk alone, not even once,' Flo said.

'I'm sorry, darling, but you're still his number one girl; always will be. He's told me many times that you're the best thing in his life.'

As I got ready for bed I thought about it. Ben had to be gambling again. He has an addiction to poker and it is this which finally broke our marriage. We had two good TV salaries coming in to our joint account but I had noticed that Ben was running up big overdrafts most months. I would ask him where all the money was going and he could never give me a convincing explanation.

'Presents for you and Flo,' he would say.

It was true he often came home with these little loving gifts for one or other of us. Flo loved these surprise gifts but I was far more ambivalent about them. They were things we didn't need. I know it sounds churlish but I was already worrying about how money ran through Ben's fingers. I didn't make a firm enough stand when he was evasive about where all the money was going. One evening he brought back a beautiful art deco figure of a woman and handed it to me. She was about fourteen inches high and made of green metal and standing on a black base. She was naked with her head thrown back and was holding a ball aloft.

'She's *Luer* by Max Le Verrier. The base is marble and the ball is onyx. She's vintage art deco,' he said.

I could tell straight away that the figure must have cost a lot.

'She's beautiful, stunning in fact, but my birthday is months away...'

'I wanted you to have something beautiful,' he said.

What I didn't know then was that Ben had had a good win that day and on his way home, and in his euphoria, he had gone into an antiques shop and bought me the little figure. I thanked him as sincerely as I could though my insides were churning. Beautiful though she is, that little figure makes me feel sad because she represents the time when Ben was slipping ever deeper into his addiction to poker.

He left StoryWorld when we split up and he works now as an aerial photographer. The work is highly skilled and well paid, but if he's gambling again he will burn through his cash in no time. He pays a small amount of maintenance each month for Flo and it barely covers her childcare costs. I don't push for more because what matters to me is for her to see him regularly. I found myself getting worked up at the thought he hadn't spent any time alone with her all weekend. I picked up my mobile and punched in his number.

'Is something up?' he asked.

He sounded sleepy.

'I have a sad girl here,' I said.

'What do you mean?'

'Flo said she hardly had a moment alone with you this weekend.'

'That's not true.' I heard the defensive edge in his voice.

'She looks forward to her weekends with you. Please make her your priority when she comes down.'

'Fuck's sake, Liz, what is this?'

He was angry immediately and that made me angry too.

We always could fire each other up in an instant.

'And you're back in the casino?'

'Get off my back,' he said, and hung up.

Now I was furious and knew I wouldn't be able to sleep.

CHAPTER FOUR

StoryWorld TV station, London Bridge

I was standing in the atrium reading the links into the show when Gerry came out of make-up. He was wearing a jaunty primrose yellow shirt but his face was serious and he indicated we should find a quiet corner to talk. My heart sank. I knew he was being courted by the opposition. Were we about to lose him? He is a ratings puller and I was thinking fast about what I could say to persuade him to stay with us. We found two armchairs tucked behind a potted palm in the atrium.

'Liz, darling, I cast your chart last night.'

'Oh, thanks, that was so kind of you.'

'I'm actually quite concerned. There are some difficult transits in your chart. And you must beware Scorpio women for the next few months. Really. There could be trouble ahead!'

I thanked him for doing my chart and for the advice and hoped that I sounded as if I meant it, as Gerry gets riled when he thinks people dismiss astrology. It was gratifying to be given this bespoke reading by a celebrity astrologer, however nonsensical it was. I knew that people paid well to have dedicated chart readings from Gerry. I told him he was very important to our show; our viewers loved his broadcasts and I wanted to extend his contract for a further two years. He was thrilled at this and as I accompanied him to the studio door he gave me a big hug before he went in.

'Thanks for the vote of confidence,' he said.

I watched Gerry and Fizzy from the gallery and noticed how

the camera crew shoot Fizzy from her best angle. Fizzy has always had the sense to keep the camera crew and the floor manager onside. Her predecessor was a woman who treated the crew like an underclass well beneath her notice. They got their own back and would make a point of shooting her from the most unflattering of angles. Fizzy would never make that mistake and the technical team at StoryWorld like her.

After the morning meeting I called the team in to discuss the outside broadcast. Molly offered to do the location research and we discussed the kind of hospital that would work best.

'Human scale and community based is what we're looking for,' I said.

I made a point of explaining to Harriet how an outside broadcast works.

'We go out with the cameras and capture the action as it's happening so we'll be filming live on the wards. We make sure we line up good guests beforehand for Fizzy to talk to. But it needs to look spontaneous, as though she's popped in to see them for a chat. And we'll have some pre-recorded stories, too, which we play in throughout the show. It's high risk and high energy and you'll learn a lot from it.'

'Liz loves doing OBs,' Simon said.

'I do.'

I saw Fizzy standing at the threshold to my office and beckoned to her to come in.

'Sorry to interrupt but can we have a quick word later?' she said.

'It's fine. We're coming to an end. Come on in.'

Fizzy entered and I saw her dart a glance at Harriet.

'This is Harriet Dodd, our new researcher,' I said.

Harriet got up and shook Fizzy's hand. Today Harriet was

wearing a tailored white shirt and high-waisted grey trousers. A gold chain nestled at her throat. That girl can dress. As the two women surveyed each other I sensed a competitive charge between them.

'I met your father at the Children of Inspiration auction,' Fizzy said.

'Oh, I was there. It was a great evening, wasn't it?' Harriet said.

'It's a neat idea for sure; get the audience to cry and they're bound to dig deep in their pockets,' Fizzy said.

It was an aggressive comment to make and at best implied cynicism at how Harriet's father ran his Children of Inspiration nights, which are the flagship event of his newspaper.

'It raised a record amount of money this year so I guess Dad is getting it right,' Harriet said.

Fizzy's eyes flashed and Simon, intuitive as ever, stood up quickly and said: 'We'll leave you to it.'

Molly and Harriet followed him out of my room and closed the door behind them.

'How can I help, Fizz?'

Fizzy watched through my window as Harriet seated herself next to Simon and tossed her head, saying something to him we couldn't hear.

'I heard you'd taken her on,' she said.

'Yes. She's here on a trial for three months.'

Fizzy perched on the arm of my sofa.

'I've heard through the grapevine that she's trouble and I thought I'd better give you a heads-up.'

'Trouble?'

'She was given a job at her daddy's paper. Friend of mine works there. She got off with the married features editor. Went after him from day one and it caused a right old rumpus.'

'What happened?'

'Oh, you know, features editor loses the plot, distraught wife, weeping children, the usual.'

Fizzy was examining her fingernails as she said this. Her nails were immaculate with a French manicure.

'I'm not sure what to say,' I said.

'I thought you should know. Store it away and keep an eye on that one.'

'OK. Have you heard about the outside broadcast?'

'Yes, Julius told me.'

'I thought we could get Ledley involved. Maybe get him to cook for the patients.'

Fizzy laughed. 'You want to kill them off?'

'You two are great together and the patients would love it.'

She jumped up. 'You know best. I'm off for a fitting.'

After she had gone I thought about what Fizzy had said and wondered why she had made a point of telling me that story about Harriet. Fizzy has that syndrome, limelight syndrome; you know, the one Princess Diana had. She craves the limelight and wants to be the centre of attention all the time. She can tolerate male stars alongside her so she gets on fine with Gerry and Ledley. But try to promote any woman and she doesn't like it. She is such a driven person and I guess it's why she's so successful. She comes alive in front of the camera and her face is transformed and as long as I give her the big interviews she's as good as gold. But if I don't, or if she thinks any other woman is being promoted, she can be incredibly difficult. I've come to the conclusion that being on camera, being in the limelight all the time, is corrupting.

*

This afternoon I was walking across the atrium to the reception desk when a motorbike courier arrived. He handed over a small Jiffy bag to the receptionist and it was addressed to Julius.

'Thanks. We were expecting that,' the receptionist said.

Next minute, I saw Harriet approach reception. She must have overheard and she asked for the Jiffy bag. I followed behind her as she skipped up the stairs and carried the package over to Julius's office. I saw her tap on his door and go in, closing the door behind her. There's a rumour in the station that Julius gets his cocaine delivered by courier and I wondered why Harriet was running errands for him. It rang a slight alarm bell after what Fizzy had said. And it is not Harriet's but Ziggy's job to deliver packages.

Ziggy is my runner and she's nineteen years old. She was given her name by her spaced-out mother. She has been working at the station for two months, both as our runner and as general assistant to my team. I set up a scheme two years ago with Southwark Council. We offer a one-year paid internship to a young person who has been in care. To my surprise Julius was behind the scheme and backed me all the way when I presented the idea to the MD. The scheme was approved and now I meet every year with the child protection team at Southwark Council. They identify possible candidates for the internship. Then we spend a day interviewing the shortlisted youngsters. It is always tough having to choose a single candidate when I know that the scheme would help each one of them. I mentor the interns during their year and give them references when it ends. My last two interns were young men who have both gone on to get full-time jobs in the media and this has made me even more committed to the scheme.

Ziggy is the most vulnerable of the three so far. She had the most horrific childhood. Her mother was a heroin addict who died when Ziggy was nine years old. It was a social worker who found little Ziggy lying next to her mother's dead body. Her father died a year later, also of a heroin overdose, but he had played no part in her life. She was fostered at a number of homes since the age of nine. She's a thin little thing with a pale face and short dark hair that sticks up. She's bright and did well in her GCSEs, considering her troubled and unsettled upbringing. She had no desire to go to college and told her social worker that she was keen to get a job.

I saw Ziggy standing by our big printer and walked over. She was dressed in her usual outfit of baggy boyfriend jeans and a faded black T-shirt. She was hugging her thin arms over her chest and round her ribs as she watched the printer disgorging its copies. I've seen her do that hugging thing before and it reminds me that she is vulnerable and feels the need to protect herself from a hostile world. I suggested to her that we have a catch-up in the Hub later this week.

Chalk Farm flat, 8 p.m.

I was on my knees putting dirty clothes into the washing machine and thinking about how Julius had looked as I left the station tonight. I had walked past his room and he was sitting with his chair turned to face the wall where a framed certificate of one of his awards was hanging. I could see his profile. He was staring at the certificate but it was the expression on his face that struck me. He looked worried and sad. He must have caught my movement out of the corner of his eye because he turned his head and swung his chair round. I waved at him and he waved back, but he didn't smile.

After all this time working together you would think I would know Julius well, and at some level I do. He is intensely private but I have picked up a few scraps of knowledge over the years. I know he comes from a modest background and that his parents ran a post office in a small town in Essex. He moved into the democratic world of television and reinvented himself as Julius. Few people know that he was born Nigel Jones and I found out by accident. It's an interesting choice of name. He has worked hard to become a successful and award-winning programme maker and I respect him for that. Occasionally you get glimpses of a decent man struggling to get out.

I had reached Flo's favourite T-shirt at the bottom of the pile and I picked it up and sniffed it. Yes, it was unmistakable, the smell of cigarette smoke. I didn't stop to think or count to ten; I got up and went straight into Flo's room without knocking on her door.

'This smells of cigarettes,' I said, holding up the offending T-shirt.

An expression flitted across her face but I couldn't interpret it.

'You didn't knock,' she said sounding aggrieved.

'Are you smoking, Flo?'

'No!'

'So why does your T-shirt smell of smoke?'

Flo rolled her eyes in the infuriating way she often does these days.

'Paige smokes,' she said, as if she was stating the obvious.

'You're saying your clothes smell because your friend smokes?'

'Yes.'

'Please don't do this. Smoking's not clever or cool, you know.'

'So why did you and Dad do it then?'

'That was when we were students, years ago, and I gave up when I got pregnant.'

I still craved the occasional cigarette but I wasn't going to admit to that. It's a mistake to get into these arguments with Flo.

'And frankly it's irrelevant whether Dad and I smoked in our twenties. You're fourteen!'

She scowled at me and crossed her arms over her chest and I could see I wasn't going to get anything else out of her. I left her room and shut her door with a sharp click. I knew I had not handled the conversation well. A low-key approach works better with Flo and best of all is when I can defuse any potential conflict with humour. But I rarely manage to control my anxieties about her. I wish I could be more like I am with my team where I am able to keep a lid on my emotions. I put her T-shirt into the machine, added extra fabric softener and turned on the wash cycle. I would ask Janis if she thought Flo was smoking.

The changes in Flo's behaviour started around the time of her thirteenth birthday. Friends had warned me that this would happen and said don't get upset if she started to pull away from me. It was entirely normal and we would probably go through a rocky phase and then she would come back and our relationship would be stronger than ever. I dreaded it though because we had always been so close, and being a mum to Flo and working to give her a good home is one of the defining purposes of my life.

I remember that when she turned thirteen I took a photograph of her sitting out in our little garden. There was a warm light on the wall behind her and it is a lovely tender picture. Her hair is pulled over one shoulder and there is such a freshness and a ripeness about her face that it makes my heart ache to look at it. She has her dad's dark brown eyes. I printed three copies of this photo and put them into nice frames. One sits on my desk at work. One I sent to my mum who lives in Glasgow, and the third one I sent to Ben. He phoned me when it arrived and said how proud the picture made him and what a wonderful daughter we had. It was a special moment because it is rare for Ben and me to share kind words and to feel so united.

CHAPTER FIVE

StoryWorld TV station, London Bridge

Simon made me laugh this morning. I'd told the team last week about the Great Pastel Colour Edict. This was greeted with much derision from Simon and Molly as I'd expected. Now Simon was describing how there has been an outbreak of pink shirts at StoryWorld, not only among the presenters but also among the journalists.

'The *news* journalists,' he said, grinning widely.

We are all involved in the deep-seated rivalry at StoryWorld between the news and feature teams. The news boys look down on us because we deal with the softer side of life and they deal with death and disasters. But it is the feature content of our shows which pulls in the viewers.

'They want to suck up to Julius and they've found their inner pinkness,' he said.

We all laughed, except Harriet who was looking awkward as if she didn't get it. I think she's finding it tough to settle in. Her first attempt at an interview briefing note for Fizzy was poor. The guest was a woman who had scored a surprise hit TV show on the art of embroidery and needlework. Harriet's brief was not much more than a cut and paste job from the press release the publicist had sent us. When our meeting came to an end I asked her to stay behind. I sat down next to her on my sofa and picked up her notes.

'This needs a lot more work, Harriet,' I said.

I could feel her bristling next to me.

'In what way?'

'There's not enough here. It's very thin on any detail that Fizzy could use in an interview.'

'But I've included everything which the company sent me,' she said.

'We never just rely on their releases. They are simply promoting their show but as a researcher you have to find other angles and other talking points so that Fizzy can sustain a conversation.'

Harriet looked down at her notes.

'Where do I find those?'

'You research her life and look for interesting details about her. It's easy enough with Google and Wikipedia. And trawl through any news stories about her. Find out what she was doing before she had her hit show. Is she a city or a country person? Does she have pets? What does she love doing in her free time apart from sewing? You know: the stuff of life that reveals a person.'

Harriet nodded. 'OK.'

'And when it comes to layout what I do is divide it into bullet points on the point of the interview, then the key background and talking points and finally I list suggested questions. Try to keep it to two sides, though.'

'Suggested questions? Doesn't she think up her own questions?'

'No. We do that.'

'But surely that's the job of a presenter. It's what they do, isn't it? Ask the questions?'

She seemed genuinely affronted, as if Fizzy was being lazy.

'Look, Fizzy may be interviewing up to six different people in any one show. She can't be expected to know all the angles.

40

So we think about what she should ask them to get the best out of the guest. Do you see?'

I handed her back her piece of work and her cheeks were slightly flushed.

'Have another go at it. You'll soon get the hang of it. Ask to see a couple of Simon's briefs. He's got them down to a T.'

'I was wondering if there are any PR launches this week?' she said.

I knew it. She thinks working in TV is all glamour and glitz, whereas in fact there's a lot of routine and graft to being a researcher. I had to grit my teeth to stay civil. I did not want to piss off Saul Relph, our MD, but really she was irritating and vacuous and would never have made it here if we'd gone through a proper job interview process.

'We share out the launches and I update the team on them as they come in.'

'I'm particularly interested in fashion,' she said.

'Thanks for letting me know that,' I said drily.

She stood up and left my room. I watched her go out and sit next to Simon. He is cute-looking in a Harry Potterish way. As she slid into the seat next to him I saw him push his spectacles up his nose and look at her seriously. He took her notes from her and I saw him start to write all over them while she watched him. She was getting him to do her work for her and this made me even more cross.

This afternoon I had a difficult meeting with Betty, our agony aunt. She is back from Canada and had heard about the John from Sheffield item. She sees it as her territory and wants to take it over when we get John back into StoryWorld again. She said as much to Fizzy and sharp words were exchanged between the two women. Betty had come to me to adjudicate.

41

'I was away so I won't complain that you went ahead with this item but let us remember John wrote to *me* for advice, not to Fizzy,' Betty said.

It was typical of Betty to say she wouldn't complain when in fact that was exactly what she was doing.

'Had you been here we would have had you do it, of course. But now we've aired the first interview it's difficult to change horses midstream.'

'Change horses?' Betty said in a mildly outraged tone of voice.

When I recruited Betty she was working as a senior probation officer who was running an advice column in a publication aimed at prisoners' wives. I had seen her column and liked what I saw. She was in her mid-fifties, had encountered all sorts of dark stuff during her career and was down to earth and no-nonsense. She made the transition to TV agony aunt well but I've noticed that being on camera does something to people. It spoils them. Why else would she be making a fuss about this?

'Fizzy feels the way she dealt with the interview helped get the viewers onside and she's committed to continuing with it.'

I hadn't checked this with Fizzy but I knew that all hell would break out if I tried to take John of Sheffield away from her. And Betty needed reminding that I was the boss here.

'I'm not happy about this,' Betty said.

'I'm sorry you feel that way but let's move on,' I said.

There was more presenter angst this afternoon. Julius rang me at four and said could I come to his office straight away please. When he summons me like this it nearly always means trouble. I checked my hair in the mirror by the door and put on lipstick to bolster myself. He has the large corner office with the best views over the river and acres of polished oak floor. I tapped on his door.

'Come in,' he called.

I was hardly through the door when he was striding across his room. He came up close to me, so close that I could smell his aftershave and I thought he had a triumphant look on his face.

'Your precious Ledley's been a naughty boy,' he said.

I took a step away from him. I know he resents the fact it was me who spotted Ledley and signed him up. I first saw Ledley when I was having dinner at his Jamaican café in Balham. He was walking around the café talking to his customers and making them laugh and I knew immediately that he had star quality. I persuaded him to do a screen test and now he's one of our most popular presenters.

'What's he done?'

'Only the most blatant product placement.'

'What do you mean?'

'Haven't you noticed how he always uses a particular brand of cooking oil? It seems to turn up in most of his revolting recipes.'

'Well, yes, I had noticed that.'

'And you weren't suspicious?'

'No.'

'Turns out he's getting a nice little retainer to plug that product.'

'You've got proof of this?'

He smiled in a nasty way. 'Oh yes.'

'Damn,' I said wearily.

I sat down on his leather sofa.

'I know you think he can do no wrong,' he said.

'It's not that. He's so popular and so easy to work with and now I'm going to have to bawl him out.'

'Let's get him up now and we can do this together,' he said.

I could tell he was relishing the thought of hauling Ledley over the coals. He was almost rubbing his hands at the prospect. Julius likes nothing better than to exert his control.

'No, let me deal with it. Please.'

'If I see that brand of oil one more time...'

'You won't. Leave it with me.'

I headed out of his office. Sometimes I hate my job. I seem to lurch from one trivial crisis to another.

Chalk Farm flat, 10 p.m.

I phoned my best friend Fenton to have a good old moan about work and about having Harriet imposed on me. Fenton lives in Kent, in Folkestone, and I would be lost without her. Most of us have someone in our lives who acts as our moral compass; the person who we ask of ourselves how would they judge my behaviour in this situation? It's not my mum, even though she is a brave woman who does her best. No, that person, my moral compass, is Fenton. We met at the University of York where we were both studying history and we've been as close as sisters ever since.

'We have a new member of the team, Harriet Dodd, and she's a real little princess with a highly developed sense of entitlement.'

'Oh dear, one of those.'

'Her daddy is a newspaper editor and doesn't she know it.'

Fenton works for a charity based in Dover that supports refugees who have arrived at the port. She helps traumatised people build a new life in the UK and her colleagues and daily problems are very different from mine.

'How irritating.'

'She's in my team because Daddy pulled strings and got the MD to push her forward. There's something about highly entitled people that really riles me and you should have seen her face when I said she actually needed to do some research.'

'Well I think your MD is at fault here. He must know you'll be carrying her.'

'As if he cares about that! He's far more keen to keep in with his pal Edward Dodd. This will probably get him a seat at the Wimbledon final next summer.'

One of our pet beefs is the way that men, especially establishment men, do favours for each other and close ranks when challenged.

'Can she be trained up?'

'Yes, we can train her up, but in the meantime Simon and Molly will have more to do and they're already stretched. She was getting Simon to do her work for her today.'

'My advice is keep holding her feet to the fire. She'll either make the grade or bail out and that's a win-win either way,' Fenton said.

'I wish we could go on one of our nights out,' I said.

'Stay up all night and watch the sun rise,' she said.

Fenton and I were inseparable at university and became known as the terrible twins. We could be wild. Talking to her always makes me feel better.

I was twenty-seven when I had Flo. I was the first in my group of friends to become a mum and this created a distance between me and them. When you have a baby your life is changed fundamentally and you gravitate towards people going through the same overwhelming experience. I got to know the mums on my street and we would share our anxieties and also the deep pleasure of noting our baby's daily development – thrilling to us but dull to everyone else. My child-free friends were going off on city breaks to Barcelona and Bruges and trying out the latest restaurants. My spare cash was spent on baby equipment, baby clothes and toys. I did keep in touch with Fenton, of course, but during those early years of motherhood I saw less and less of my college friends.

This threw Ben and me together most of the time and far from cementing our marriage it opened up a rift. Being a parent to a young child is profoundly energy-sapping and frequently boring. Ben hated that we could never finish a meal without interruption or just go out for the evening with no planning. Ben is an adrenalin junkie and throughout our relationship we had done things on the spur of the moment. He would come home on a Friday night and suggest we drive to the Brecon Beacons to do a climb or go to Newquay to surf. We were both earning good money and before Flo we spent it on holidays and wetsuits and country house hotels. We had some great times, but you don't go climbing or surfing with a baby in tow.

Ben would get cabin fever after a few days holed up with Flo and me. He started to stay out late some nights and I think it was at this time that he got into poker and gambling large sums of money. He could get his adrenalin hit from risking his salary on the turn of a card.

I walked through the flat and turned off the lights. I stood at the window that opens onto our little garden and could see the moon rising over the roofs and chimneys of my street.

CHAPTER SIX

StoryWorld TV station, London Bridge

The only presenter who is being difficult about wearing pastels is Sal. Sal is a stand-up comedian who does a weekly slot for us; a wry look back at the news events of the week. She's funny, irreverent and spiky. When I raised the subject of the new pastel policy for presenters she got touchy with me and said there was nothing in her contract about the station dictating what colour she should wear. I agreed but said it was now station policy.

'Station policy,' she repeated, with an edge to her voice.

'Yes.'

We were talking on the phone and her attitude was grating on me.

'Julius policy, you mean,' she said.

'He's the director of programmes, Sal, so if he says it's policy then it's station policy.'

I hoped I had said enough for her to fall into line.

When she came in to do her slot today Sal was wearing a dark green top and a string of large brightly coloured beads. She arrived late and there was no time to talk to her before she went into the studio, which I am sure she did deliberately. I was watching from the gallery and as she sat down on the sofa I saw Fizzy's eyes flash with alarm. She knew at once that Sal was carrying out her own one-woman rebellion against Julius. The way it works is for Fizzy to feed a few scripted questions and this lets Sal launch into her script about the week's news and topical events. She was especially funny today and there's no question she's a talented woman who brings a fresh element to the show.

It was lucky that Julius was away this morning. The post-mortem meeting was chaired by Bob, the news editor. There's a more relaxed atmosphere when Julius is away. Bob lets us all pitch in and discuss the show freely. Fizzy was in a good mood and she was laughing at Bob's comments. Her wardrobe has undergone an overhaul since the Great Pastel Colour Edict. She was wearing a pretty pale green dress with white daisies on it. It was a young look for a woman of thirty-eight but it suited her. No doubt all these new clothes of hers are being paid for by the station. There was only a passing reference made to Sal's item and I thought we'd got away with it.

Around noon Julius came into the office. I saw him walk past my room and he looked irritable and his jaw was clenched. Twenty minutes later he called and said come to my office now. I knew from his voice that he was in a bad mood. Sometimes I play for time but today I walked straight over and I was hardly over the threshold before he barked at me: 'Sal, does she know the new rule?'

'Yes, I told her last week, but you know she's being awkward about it. And it's her thing isn't it, being anti-establishment? Surely it doesn't matter if a single presenter—'

He actually punched his desk with his fist.

'It does matter! Who the fuck does she think she is? Does she think she's bigger than the station?'

'No but—'

'Tell her to wear pastels next week or she's out! I mean it.'

His voice was venomous. I am sick of being Julius Jones's punchbag. He can be hateful. I turned on my heel and left his office before I said words I would regret about him being a bully; and over something so bloody stupid too. When I got to my room I shut the door, poured myself a glass of water and stood at my window looking at the activity in the street below. Everyone down there looked to be rushing to their destinations and their faces were strained and anxious. Most of the time I feel lucky to have my job but it is at moments like this when I think about leaving the station. I've been here a long time, almost as long as Julius, and he thinks I will never leave. I'm on a good salary and I need it to pay my huge mortgage. Golden handcuffs, it's called, being paid so much money that you feel you can't leave your job.

My fear of debt has got worse since Ben and I split up. Several times I've had the same dream about a starving naked woman standing outside a clothes shop as a woman in a fur coat walks past. I told Fenton about it and she said that maybe I was both the starving woman and the woman in the fur coat.

I sat down and called Sal. The phone rang and rang and I was about to hang up when she picked up.

'Sal, Julius is not happy. Take it from me, he's deadly serious about this colour thing. *Please* go along with it. After all, what does it matter? It's only your clothes. It doesn't affect what you say in any way.'

'Sorry, Liz. You know I've got a lot of time for you. But Julius Jones is such an arse.'

'He says you'll be out if you don't wear pastels next week,' I said.

I had put it as bluntly as I could. She needed to know the score. There was a pause on the other end of the line.

'That man must have a very small penis.'

49

It wasn't Sal at her wittiest but I laughed to ease the tension between us.

'Look, I don't want to lose you. I love your item.'

'Then let me go on being *me*,' she said.

'We all have to make compromises, you know.'

I left it there, hoping she would see sense. I had to make compromises every week. Honestly, there are times when I feel like slapping the presenters!

After lunch Julius sauntered into my office.

'Did you speak to Sal?'

'Yes. I made it clear.'

'Good. She's a stroppy cow. I need one of your researchers to come to a meeting with me now to take notes,' he said.

Julius has a PA, Martine. He's the only one of us who does these days and I didn't see why one of my team should do this for him.

'I thought Martine took notes for you?'

'She's on leave today.'

'We're very busy. Is it essential?'

'Yes it is; a potential new sponsor. Let Harriet take the notes.'

'I was going to suggest Ziggy. I'm trying to give her more to do,' I said.

'No way. She's far too scruffy.'

'She's very bright, Julius.'

'No. Let Harriet come, she's well turned out.'

I stood up and called Harriet into the office. I explained she was needed to take notes at a sponsor meeting. I saw her flush with pleasure as she followed Julius out of my room. I stood at the threshold and watched the two of them walking away. Molly stopped her typing.

'Where are they off to?'

'A meeting with a sponsor; Julius needs a note-taker.'

'Only we were right in the middle of doing work on the hospital shoot,' she said.

Molly can be abrasive at times but she has a good sense of humour when she relaxes. She has a broad flat face and dark blonde hair which she gets from her Dutch father. She wears jeans and Converse sneakers to the station most days, works hard and has a lot of integrity. I rarely put her on the celebrity interviews, though, as they don't interest her at all.

'How's Harriet getting on?' I asked.

'She's struggling. Did she have any experience of this work before?'

'She worked in papers but never in TV. I'd appreciate it if you'd give her your support. I can see she needs some hand-holding.'

'Sure. Is she going to be made permanent?'

'Too early to say. Where's Simon?'

'He's gone for a coffee with Betty. They're doing her mail.'

Betty adores Simon and always asks for him to go through her mail with her. She puts a lot of effort into her weekly advice slot and her stories come from viewers' letters and emails. I went in search of them as I needed to build bridges with Betty after our last tense conversation. They were sitting in the Hub with a sheaf of printed emails on the table between them.

'Can I get you guys anything?' I asked.

'I'd love another hot chocolate,' Betty said.

'Can I have a sparkling water please?' Simon said.

I queued for the drinks. Bob the news editor was sitting at a table by the window with Fizzy and she was laughing at something he was saying. I have my suspicions about those two. I think it more likely Fizzy is having a secret affair with Bob than with Julius. She claims they are good friends because they both come from Burnley. You would never guess that Fizzy was from Burnley, though she does mention it on air from time to time; talks about her love of the Football Club and how her dad took her to the games. Bob is married and has two teenage girls and you can tell straight away that he is from Burnley. He will make a point of showing he is a northern man in what he considers to be a southern softie set-up.

I know a lot of people have this idea that TV stations are cauldrons of lust and sex with the presenters and journalists and technicians always at it. There is a grain of truth to this idea. We all spend long hours at the station and there is often a febrile atmosphere around the place. I've known of several liaisons between colleagues in my years at StoryWorld, and of course I met Ben here. But it does grate on me when I come up against the assumption that I've held onto my job all this time because of some sexual shenanigans. Yet here I was thinking the same thing about Fizzy. I joined Betty and Simon at the table with their drinks.

'We have a few crackers this week,' Simon said.

'Tell me.'

'A woman who is pregnant by her married boss and can't decide whether to have the baby or a termination. Her biological clock is ticking and she's desperate to have a child, but she's afraid of doing it on her own. He's made it clear that if she goes ahead she'll get no support from him,' he said.

'That's tough,' I said.

'What would you do in that situation?' Betty asked as she sipped at her hot chocolate. She is a large woman and has a sweet tooth. Her being large seems to enhance her status as an agony aunt. There's comfort and reassurance in her bulk.

'Wanting a child is such a powerful thing and if I was in my mid-thirties I might go through with it and sod the man,' I said.

'This woman *is* in her mid-thirties,' Simon said.

'Yes, but the child won't get the best start in life if the mother has no partner and no financial security,' Betty said.

'Lots of women have done it on their own successfully,' I said.

'Long-term research shows a child does better if there are two parents,' Betty asserted.

I bristled at this.

'Not if the parents are warring all the time.'

Simon jumped in. 'We've also got a sixteen-year-old boy who wants to know how he should tell his parents that he's gay.'

Betty put her cup down.

'That was a heartfelt email. The poor troubled lad, his parents sound uptight and I'll need to go carefully with that one.'

'I look forward to hearing it tomorrow,' I said.

My one criticism of Betty is that she takes a conventional approach to most issues. I wish that sometimes she would be more subversive in her advice.

In the evening I was taking Gerry and his partner Anwar out to dinner to celebrate his new longer contract with Story-World. I had arranged for Janis to babysit. I must stop using that word babysit; Flo gets insulted when I do. I wanted Gerry to feel cherished and had asked him where he wanted to go. He said Anwar was raving about a place in Soho called the Social Eating House so I booked us into there. After the team had left for the night I changed into a dark red velvet shirt and put on my silver drop earrings with the ruby stones; not real rubies, of course, semi-precious stones, but I like the way they catch the light. I brushed my hair. My hair is black and I've worn it in a short bob, without a fringe, for years. A bob is nice and low maintenance and I pay Ellen in make-up a small fee to cut it for me every two months. I peered in the mirror and saw a few more grey hairs at the parting. I applied dark red lipstick and was squirting perfume onto my hair when Julius walked in unannounced again.

'Nice smell,' he said.

'Jo Malone. Wood Sage and Sea Salt.'

'Very you; nothing conventional for Liz Lyon.'

'How did your meeting with the sponsor go?'

'Pretty good; I think I've landed them.'

Julius is brilliant at getting sponsors on board and it is one of the reasons his position at StoryWorld is unassailable.

'And was Harriet helpful?'

'She was like a rabbit caught in headlights.'

'That's strange. I find her rather poised and confident,' I said.

'It must be the effect I have on her,' he said with an annoying smirk.

I turned to pick up my handbag.

'Where are you off to in your glad rags?'

'I'm taking Gerry and his partner out to dinner to celebrate the new contract.'

'Where are you taking them?'

'This place in Soho Gerry wanted to go to: the Social Eating House.'

'Mind if I join you?'

I was surprised at this.

'Really?'

'Yes. Gerry's a lot of fun and the food there is sensational.'

'I heard he did your chart for you,' I said, arching my eyebrows.

He gave me a surprisingly sweet smile. I reached for my phone and called the restaurant and changed the booking from three people to four. I knew Gerry would be flattered that Julius was joining our dinner.

'What's his partner called?' Julius asked as we drew up outside the restaurant in a taxi.

'Anwar, he's an actor.'

From the street the restaurant looked more like a commercial building and its name was a battered street sign. Inside it was all warm reds and browns with banquette seating and subdued lighting. There was a separate cocktail bar on the first floor, The Blind Pig, and Julius took over and insisted we have pre-dinner cocktails. I hadn't met Anwar before. He has beautiful dark eyes, is well-toned and expensively dressed and he must be at least twenty years younger than Gerry. He's not had much acting work from what I can tell. His last job was a walk-on in *Casualty* two seasons ago.

We went downstairs and Julius was charm itself as we ordered our dishes, and he couldn't have been more different from the man who had bawled me out about Sal earlier that day. He ordered an expensive red wine, more than I would have gone for. Julius signs off my expenses so I didn't worry about that. The food was outstanding. Gerry chose the five course sampler menu which had a procession of dishes: prawns, foie gras, hake, duck and chocolate. He must have decided to ditch his diet for one night and he can't have any scruples about eating foie gras either!

As the night wore on and we had started on our third bottle of wine it was clear to me how much more in love Gerry is with Anwar than vice versa. I'm sure Gerry bankrolls the relationship and the way he looked at Anwar all evening made me feel a bit sad. There is often this inequality in love relations. And then Gerry asked me about *my* love life. It was an awkward moment as I didn't want to talk about it in front of Julius.

'Forget love life, Flo is my priority,' I said.

Julius's interest was piqued and he pressed me.

'Oh, come on, Liz. You're an attractive woman. Who's the fella?'

I took a sip of the red wine.

'Why should there be a fella?'

'Stop holding out on us,' he said.

'Well, sometimes, when Flo is in Portsmouth with her dad, I see Todd. He's a director.'

'Todd Fisher?'

'Yes.'

'He works for us, doesn't he?' Julius said.

'Not on a regular basis; he's a freelancer.'

'But you met him at the station?' he persisted.

I was finding this more and more embarrassing.

'Yes.'

Julius was not going to let it go.

'And how does your daughter feel about him?'

'I don't invite him back to my flat when Florence is there.'

'Ahh, he's your fuck buddy, is he?' Julius had emphasised his words.

'I *hate* that phrase!'

'I think I know who you mean. He's the guy who did last

56

year's outside broadcast? He's Australian, isn't he?' Gerry asked.

'Yes, he's directed several OBs for us,' I said.

'He's quite a hunk,' Gerry said, grinning at me.

'Let's leave it please,' I snapped at Gerry.

There was a moment of strained silence.

'And what about you, Julius?' Gerry asked.

'I'm on my own; Amber and I parted company six months ago.'

Amber was a fashion stylist he had been dating for a few years. She was a high gloss, high fashion woman and I hadn't seen her smile once. Simon and I had nicknamed her The Pouter. So he was on his own again and this would explain his appearance at our dinner tonight. He is forty-five years old, has never married, has no children and StoryWorld is his life.

Chalk Farm flat, 11.15 p.m.

Flo was asleep when I came in and Mr Crooks was curled up at her feet. I paid Janis and saw her out. I should not have snapped at Gerry at his celebration dinner and I rang him.

'Sorry I was sharp with you, Gerry. I snapped at the wrong person.'

'It was a lovely evening and I was being nosy.'

'You're a mate and I don't mind you asking, but he's got no right to keep on probing.'

'He did seem awfully interested in who you were dating.'

Gerry was fishing again and for a second I wondered if there was any way he could know about what had happened between Julius and me. No, it wasn't possible, but I could feel embarrassment and irritation rising again.

'It's hard to have a private life at StoryWorld, isn't it?'

'Tell me about it, darling; it's impossible for any of us to keep secrets,' he said.

CHAPTER SEVEN

Betty's advice slot was a good one this morning. I was sitting in the gallery with the director as Fizzy and Betty discussed the two problems from our viewers. We always let members of the public know in advance if their letters are going to be discussed and we change their names and locations. Fizzy asked viewers to email and tweet in their thoughts on the topics of the day.

'And don't forget to use our hashtag StoryWorld.'

She read out the first problem from the woman who was pregnant by her married boss. What should she do? It was almost a reprise of the discussion we'd had the day before in the Hub. Fizzy was in favour of the woman proceeding with the pregnancy while Betty made the arguments against being a single mum. I liked the fact that Fizzy was sticking up for lone parents and she was less supportive of Betty's advice than usual. She didn't challenge her directly but she put the opposing point of view well. Fizzy summed up by reading first an email which said:

> You will bring nothing but misery if you go ahead with this selfish pregnancy. Think about the family of your boss. This will tear them apart.

She then read a tweet which said:

Follow your heart. If you want this baby it will
be blessed. What a child needs is lots of love
and you have that to give. #StoryWorld

'Two contrasting responses from our viewers there, Betty,'
she said.

They turned to the second email, from the sixteen-year-old
boy who was worried about telling his parents that he was
gay. This wasn't as successful a discussion. Fizzy was less
engaged with the topic and Betty did most of the talking. No
one else would have noticed it but I sensed a slight coolness
between them on the sofa today. I watch these two women all
the time so I can pick up the slightest nuance in their body
language and treatment of each other. I was obscurely pleased
to see this minor falling-out. I left the gallery as Fizzy started
the next interview.

I'd told Julius I would need to miss the morning meeting
because I had to recce a hospital we had identified as a
potential location for the outside broadcast. Our work on it
was gathering momentum, which is as well given how little
time we have been given to set it up. Molly and I went to
look at St Eanswythe's, a community hospital in Bermondsey,
down the river from StoryWorld. We had arranged to meet
Connie Mears, the senior manager who runs the hospital. St
Eanswythe's is a Victorian red-brick building with tall
chimneys and ornate tiles across its façade. As we got out of
the cab I wasn't sure whether it would fit the bill as it had
an institutional, almost forbidding look to it. But once inside
the building the atmosphere was different. It's clean and
cheerful and you get the sense this is a well-run place. There's
a children's ward, general wards and surgical wards. I liked
Connie Mears. She wanted to know what exactly the

broadcast would entail and I explained that with her permission we would pre-record a few patients so we could tell their stories in more detail. The actual live broadcast would last two hours, although we would need to start setting up from five in the morning. She has agreed to it.

Molly and I walked back to the station as it wasn't far and we were cock-a-hoop about securing the hospital. Many organisations are suspicious of TV crews and won't let you anywhere near them. They have a point: TV reporters are notorious for wanting to expose institutions rather than praise them. Molly and I discussed the kind of stories we wanted to build the broadcast around and we were both fired up about it. As I came up the stairs to my office I saw Simon sitting in a huddle with Harriet and she was crying.

'What on earth's happened?' I said.

Harriet leapt up and rushed to the ladies' toilet without a word. Simon indicated we should go into my room. I hurried in and he closed the door, leaving Molly standing outside looking irritated.

'Fizzy came down here ten minutes ago and tore Harry off a strip for her briefing. Said it was crap!'

'Damn.'

'Harry stood up to her and it got nasty.'

'If Fizzy's not happy she should talk to me, not to Harriet.'

'She came looking for you but you weren't here so she launched into her. She was in a foul mood.'

'Can I see the offending brief please?'

Simon came back into the room with the brief and I called Molly in too.

'Moll, will you go and check Harriet's OK? Fizzy gave her a tongue-lashing over this brief.'

I read the brief. The guest had been a top city trader. He had

had an epiphany and changed his life completely to work for a charity for the homeless. There was plenty of scope in the subject for an interesting interview but Harriet had produced a poor piece of work, thin on detail and with only four suggested questions which were banal. I could see why Fizzy had reacted against it. She would have had to improvise the interview.

'I'm going to see Fizzy,' I told Simon.

Fizzy was sitting in her dressing room and Ellen was touching up her make-up. When she saw me walk in carrying Harriet's notes her face took on a sulky look. I sat down and watched in silence as Ellen completed her work. When we were alone I said: 'I'm sorry this wasn't up to scratch but I wish you'd spoken to *me* about it.'

'How can I be expected to interview someone for six minutes with so little background?'

'It is thin on detail but—'

'Thin on detail? It's crap and you know it. You have no idea what it's like when I'm out there on my own and have to conjure up questions out of thin air with nothing to go on.'

'I'm sorry.'

'I was struggling out there and ended up asking him what bloody football team he supported! That's how desperate it got.'

'She's new to this work and—'

'She should never have been given the job in the first place,' Fizzy said in a hard voice.

'Maybe, but she's here now and you do know, don't you, that it's on the direct instruction of Saul Relph.'

Bloody presenter power! Fizzy needs reminding that the TV station doesn't work just because of her. She may be the face of StoryWorld but we are the ones who come up with the ideas that keep her on air.

'Look, I'm keen to make this work. She's crying in the Ladies at the moment,' I said.

'Don't be taken in by her tears. I'm suspicious of that one. Attention-seeker!'

There was something going on here I couldn't quite fathom. The briefing Harriet had written was poor but I wondered if Fizzy was getting worked up because Julius was showing an interest in Harriet.

'I'll check Harriet's briefs in future, but *please*, if you're not happy come to me.'

I got up and left Fizzy's dressing room. I went to the Hub and bought four coffees and a Coke for Ziggy. I took them upstairs to my office and called in Molly, Simon and Harriet. It's Ziggy's job to stay at the desks outside and monitor any calls when we are in meetings. Harriet's hooded eyelids were puffy and pink from crying and her cheeks were blotchy. She looked vulnerable for the first time since I'd met her, rather than the entitled rich kid she'd presented up till now. I handed each team member a coffee and opened a packet of ginger nuts I'd brought in to work.

'Try not to take it too much to heart. We've all been bawled out at various times, haven't we?' I said to the others.

Simon and Molly nodded.

'Oh yes. We have the scars,' Simon said.

'She was *so* nasty,' Harriet said.

'Live TV is a tough gig and tempers get frayed. You have to grow a thick skin if you want to work here. Now let's put it behind us because I want to tell you about the hospital Molly and I have chosen for the OB. It's called St Eanswythe's and it is human scale and friendly. Moll did well to find it. I have a feeling this OB is going to be a good one.'

When I got back to the flat I expected to find Flo there because on Friday nights, when Flo doesn't go to Portsmouth to see Ben, we have what we call our Friday night veg-out. I buy pizzas and nachos and ice cream and we get into our pyjamas, slump on the sofa, watch rubbish telly and eat fast food. I look forward to these evenings as a time when I can relax and forget about StoryWorld. But Janis told me that Flo was over the road at Paige's house. I was fed up that Flo had jettisoned our veg-out without asking me.

'You've seen a lot of her; what do you make of Paige?' I asked Janis.

'I'm not sure about her. I wonder why a sixteen-year-old is showing so much interest in a fourteen-year-old,' Janis said.

'Yes, I wondered about that. At their age two years is quite a gap.'

'I think she's quite knowing and she likes it that Flo looks up to her. It would be good if you met her. Flo is definitely falling under her spell. She couldn't wait to get over there this evening.'

I decided to do it there and then. I paid Janis for the week and crossed the road and walked up the tiled path. It was a large semi-detached Edwardian house and, unlike most on our road, it had not been converted into flats. I rang the doorbell and waited. Eventually a teenage girl with very blonde hair, almost white, and a stud in her nose opened the door a crack.

'Hello. Are you Paige?'

She opened the door a bit further.

'Yeah.'

Her voice was suspicious.

'Well I'm Florence's mum.'

64

They say you make up your mind about people in the first seven seconds and my first impression of Paige was not a positive one. She was dressed in what I would call wannabe rock chic: ripped black jeans and a black top which was slipping off one shoulder. She wore large hoop earrings and looked bored. Flo must have recognised my voice and she came walking towards the door slowly. She looked less than pleased to see me. In fact her face was tight, as it usually is now whenever I encounter her with any of her friends. Paige had not moved from her position on the threshold so I remained on the doorstep feeling distinctly unwelcome. My impulse was to offer an explanation for my appearance but I made myself stay quiet and see who would speak first.

'Hi, Mum,' Flo said eventually.

'Hello, darling.'

Paige moved from guarding the threshold and said: 'Do you wanna come in?'

She had the trace of an American accent.

'For a minute perhaps.'

Paige and Flo turned and I followed them into the kitchen at the end of the hall. This was a large kitchen, big enough to hold a table with six assorted chairs around it and a wide dresser against the wall. The room had a scruffy, unloved feel about it. There were wilting chrysanthemums in a vase on the window sill with a full ashtray next to it. A stained roasting tray was lying on the table with a few oven chips in it and two plates smeared with tomato ketchup. The smell in the kitchen was a mixture of fried food, patchouli from a candle that was burning on the dresser and cigarettes. There were also several bottles of spirits on the dresser, vodka, gin and whisky. I was doing that protective mum thing you do, instinctively carrying out an inventory of the room, assessing the risk factors. I looked at the ceiling to see if there was a smoke detector and couldn't see one.

'Are your parents in, Paige?' I asked.

'No, they're at work.'

'Ahh, I see. I wanted to introduce myself. Do you know what time they'll be back?'

Paige shrugged.

'Not sure. Think Mum said she was gonna be late tonight.'

I could see all too clearly the appeal of Paige's house. With absent parents the two girls could do their own thing, cook oven chips and smoke to their heart's delight. I wanted to get Flo back over the road into our flat.

'Why don't you come over to ours? I've got pizza and I'm making flapjacks tonight.'

I had made up the bit about the flapjacks on the spot. Flo loves my flapjacks and I hoped I had the ingredients in the cupboard. Paige looked over at Flo who shrugged and looked non-committal.

'We were going to watch *Vampire Diaries*,' Paige said.

I could see that Flo was waiting for Paige to decide what they should do. This made me feel even more irritated but I bit back my irritation.

'We have Netflix,' I said.

Another look passed between the girls. They liked being in that unsupervised house and they knew they would not be able to smoke under my roof. But I was offering nice food.

'OK,' Paige said finally.

Before we left the house I reminded Paige to blow out the candle on the dresser. She gave me a strange look but went over and did it.

'Should you leave a note for your mum saying where you are?'

'I'll text her later.'

As soon as we arrived at our flat the girls retreated to Flo's room and shut the door. Later Mr Crooks came in and yowled at the door until Flo let him in. I put on the oven to heat up and plugged in the earphones to my iPod as I made the flapjack mixture. James Blunt is my guilty pleasure. I love his strange voice and his heart-sick ballads but I know better than to play them out loud in the flat. I greased the baking tin then melted the butter, brown sugar and honey in a saucepan. I use honey rather than golden syrup. My favourite track came on, 'Same Mistake', and I sang along to the chorus about it being no good his being given a second chance because he'd just make the same mistake again.

These words resonate strongly with me. I am always attracted to the same type of man and it usually ends in tears. I am more careful these days and am keeping Todd at arm's length, but it is inescapable how much like Ben he is. Todd worked as a cameraman like Ben, although now he is a director. He is also a man who enjoys taking risks. I took the pan off the heat and stirred in the porridge oats.

The next track was 'Carry You Home'. I try to bury the memory but it will resurface. Seven years ago I had a frightening experience with Julius. It was the night of the staff Christmas party. StoryWorld make a point of throwing a good bash at the end of the year and the party was held in the atrium which had been transformed into a 1980s-style disco with loud music, flashing lights and lots of booze. I had recently split up with Ben after months of bitter fights. Flo was staying with my mum in Glasgow and I was going to join them in five days' time for the Christmas break. I had been holding difficult emotions down for months and I was like a pressure cooker ready to blow as I set off for the party.

I remember I was wearing a satin shift dress the colour of blackberries which I'd bought for Christmas. I was hyper all evening, drank too much and later I was dancing with wild abandon to 'Total Eclipse of the Heart' and 'I Will Survive', getting some of my misery out of my system. Julius was standing at the edge of the dance floor watching me. I saw him and at one point I even suggested he join me. He shook his head but still he watched me. Finally I'd had enough. It was late and I knew I was on the cusp of making a complete fool of myself. I grabbed a glass of water, glugged it down and headed up to my office to get my bag and coat. It was a smaller office in those days which I shared with an assistant producer. Suddenly Julius was standing there at the threshold. He walked in and kicked the door shut behind him.

'You're gorgeous,' he said. 'I've always fancied you.'

I remember feeling gratified at his words and I smiled drunkenly at him.

'Bet you say that to all the girls.'

'I mean it. But you've always been Miss Untouchable.'

He crossed the room to me fast, grabbed me and kissed me. It was a nice soft kiss at first, our lips making gentle contact and I kissed him back. He slid his tongue between my lips and the kiss became more intense as he moved his hands up to hold my head closer to his. I responded to this kiss too. It was strange and sexy and exciting. I hadn't kissed another man in a sexual way for over ten years. He ran his hands down from my head to my back and we rocked back and forth still kissing. His hand slid down and reached my bottom and he squeezed me hard, too hard. He started to pull my dress up. We were still kissing and he was breathing fast. I could feel his erection pressing against me. It was all getting too rough and my pleasure was turning to alarm. I tried to pull away from him but he rubbed himself up against me and was almost groaning. As I struggled more he suddenly slammed me against the wall.

'Come on, Liz. Let's fuck hard.'

He had got his hand inside my knickers now and he stuck his third finger right up me.

'You can now,' he breathed in my ear. 'You're a free woman.'

He was moving his finger inside me and then he put his second finger up me too and I was frightened by his roughness and his insistence. I didn't want to have sex with him. I pulled my face away from his and said as strongly as I could manage:

'No. No. NO! Get off me.'

He was inflamed. There was no other word for it and still he was fingering me roughly with one hand while with his other hand he was unzipping his trousers. I found the strength to push him away with all my force and his hand came out of me. By now I was half sobbing, I grabbed my bag, ran to the door, wrenched it open and fled to the ladies' toilet. As I locked the cubicle door I was trembling so hard. He wouldn't follow me in here, surely? After a while I wiped myself with toilet tissue and saw that there was a trace of blood on the paper. I sat on the toilet seat and wept. Two women came in and I held my breath and listened as they talked and giggled and applied lipstick. The party was still going strong downstairs and you could hear the bass thud of the disco.

I tried to get my breathing back under control and I waited until the toilet had emptied. I slipped out of the Ladies and left the station by the back exit. I saw no sign of Julius and I stumbled along by the riverside until I saw the orange beacon of a taxi. Once in the dark safety of the taxi I let the tears come again and I cried all the way back to Chalk Farm. When

I reached my flat I locked and bolted the door. We had just moved into the flat and it didn't feel like home yet. There were unpacked boxes everywhere and it was all strange and unfamiliar. I couldn't stop crying so I called Fenton. It was two in the morning but she answered on the fourth ring. She listened as I told her my story punctuated by sobs and gulps.

'Get the first train down to Folkestone tomorrow, sweetheart. I'll meet you at the station.'

'But I've got all these boxes to unpack.'

'The boxes can wait. You're not going to be on your own this weekend. We'll walk by the sea and I'll treat you to fish and chips.'

I did as she said because she was right, I could not face being on my own in the new flat without Flo. It was such a comfort to see her face as I got off the train at Folkestone Central. Fenton has red hair, hazel eyes and a wicked smile. I think of her as a Restoration woman, warm, passionate and brave. She hugged me and took my overnight bag. She lives in a fisherman's cottage down near the harbour. It's a two-up two-down and Fenton has made it into such a welcoming little house with its floorboards painted a different colour in every room. I sat in her kitchen as she made us a large pot of tea and slices of buttered toast and Marmite. Later, we walked along by the edge of the sea. Fenton is a great listener and her presence has a calming influence on me.

'I think you need to report him, love,' she said finally.

'I don't think I can. I must have been giving off mixed signals. I mean I asked him to dance with me!'

'You're allowed to ask a man for a dance.'

'And when we first started kissing I responded. I did. I was enjoying it, but then he got too rough, way too rough. It was horrible but he didn't rape me.'

'He didn't rape you because you pushed him away.'

'I feel so stupid and so ashamed.'

'Why are you taking all the guilt onto yourself?'

She had stopped walking to look at me.

'Come on, let's sit down,' she said.

We sat on the pebbles and watched the seagulls wheeling through the December sky. The sea was as grey as the sky and the foam was yellowish-white and scummy like dirty soapsuds as it smashed onto the pebbles. I shivered and Fenton put her arm around me.

'I don't know how I'm going to face him on Monday.'

'I wish you'd report him. But if you're not going to report him then you need to take the power back. Tell him he was way too rough and he frightened you.'

'The thought of saying that, of saying anything about it, makes me shrivel inside.'

'You know a lot of men go on being bullies because they get away with it,' she said.

She stood up and helped me to my feet.

'Come on, it's cold. Time for those fish and chips I promised you.'

They do the best fish and chips down there. We bought haddock and chips and a giant gherkin each, added lashings of salt and vinegar and walked back to the beach to eat them. You're not supposed to but Fenton throws her leftover chips to the seagulls and braves the disapproving glances from other people. She says seagulls are wild and beautiful and she doesn't understand why they get such a bad press.

When I returned to work on Monday I was a little stronger after my two days with Fenton. There was no sign of Julius and his PA told me he'd gone off early for the Christmas break. I had to get through three more days at work and I was so relieved he wasn't around. Then I too locked up my office and travelled on the train for five hours to Glasgow to join my mum and Flo. It was always going to be difficult, our first Christmas without Ben, but I was obsessing the whole time about what had happened between Julius and me. Should I report him? And if I didn't, how would I be able to behave normally around him? I couldn't afford to give up my job. My mum is a serious person and I hadn't been able to confide any of this to her. How could I tell her I'd had a near-rape experience with my boss at the staff Christmas party two months after separating from Ben?

Enough! I didn't want to think about that horrible time in my life any more. The flapjack mixture was ready and I spooned it into the baking tin and flattened it with a wooden spoon. I put the tin into the oven to bake.

I fed the girls pizza and warm flapjacks, as promised, and they took the plates from me without comment as if they couldn't drag their eyes from the vampire drama on Flo's tablet. Around eleven p.m. Paige decided to stay the night with us and she texted her mum to tell her this, so her mum and dad must still have been out and I wondered how often they left her alone in that big house.

Saturday

I indulged myself with a long lie-in and then carried a mug of tea back into my bedroom and sat up in bed. I had opened the blinds and watched as the autumn sun gilded our small garden. The flat was silent so the two girls were probably sleeping the sleep of the dead which adolescents seem able to do. Flo and I had made a plan for the day. We were going to get her a new jacket and some jeans from Top Shop. I had said

I'd go with her even though I hate the crowds and scrum of Oxford Street. I got up and ran a deep bubble bath. I shaved my legs and was having a nice soak when Flo came into the bathroom around noon and perched on the edge of the toilet seat. Her hair was all tousled and her face was puffy from sleep and she looked sweet.

'Hello, sweets,' I said.

Flo yawned and stretched her arms above her head.

'Hi.'

Her voice was croaky.

'Did you two sit up late?'

'We watched two films.'

'Were they good?'

'They were all right, seen them before.'

Flo doesn't do enthusiastic any more. She was excitable as a little girl and would shriek with enthusiasm at lots of things but now she thinks it's uncool to enthuse. She got up.

'We're going to Camden Market in a bit.'

Her look at me was challenging.

'But we were going clothes shopping,' I said.

'Yeah, but if you give me the money I'll get the jeans for myself.'

'Sorry, sweets, but I'm not going to do that.'

'Why not? You hate shopping!'

I don't trust Flo with money because she has inherited her father's spending gene and money burns a hole in her pocket. If I gave her the cash it was unlikely she'd come back with jeans and a jacket.

'I want to be there when you choose them, like we agreed.'

'You said you hated Oxford Street!'

Flo and I can go from civil to angry in ten seconds flat and her voice was aggressive.

'We made a plan,' I said firmly.

'You are SO controlling!'

She stormed out of the bathroom with the inevitable slamming of the door. I felt like shouting something after her but remembered that Paige would hear me if I did. I got out of the water, wrenched out the plug and pulled a towel around me. I locked the bathroom door and caught sight of my angry face in the cabinet mirror. I had planned to cook them a brunch of scrambled eggs and grilled bacon but sod it, they could fend for themselves.

In the end Flo went off to Camden Market with Paige but without my cash. As she was leaving the flat I asked her what time she'd be back and she shrugged and said with a curl of the lip that she didn't know, as if my even asking her was an affront. Paige did not thank me for letting her stay over. I felt both angry and sad as I watched them walk up the road chatting together. They had left the kitchen in a mess with toast crumbs everywhere and butter and jam smeared on the work surface. I took one look at it and called Fenton.

'Another bloody bust-up. You know I can't remember a weekend with Flo in the last year when we haven't had an argument.'

'Poor love. You could do without that,' Fenton said.

'I know I should be the grown-up and not rise to the bait but when she's rude it makes me wild.'

'Is there any way you can resist that?'

'I wish I could, but she presses all my buttons.'

'You handle conflict at work all the time,' Fenton said.

'It's different at work. I think I actually find it easier to mother my team than to mother Flo.'

'It's because you two are so close. '

'I feel I'm failing with her.'

'That's rubbish and stop beating yourself up. God, we're all expected to be perfect all the time. You have a lot on your plate and frankly I think you're amazing.'

'No, *you're* amazing,' I said and we ended the conversation with our game of trying to outdo each other in compliments. What would I do without Fenton?

Flo and I did not really make up and there was a tense atmosphere for the rest of the weekend. I got into bed on Sunday night thinking that I hadn't enjoyed my two days off and was almost looking forward to being back at work the next day.

CHAPTER EIGHT

StoryWorld TV station, London Bridge

I made my way down to the gallery and watched Ledley doing his cookery demonstration. He was wearing chef's whites and making crusted onion dumplings. There was no mention of the banned cooking oil. Fizzy relaxes with Ledley. She sits on a high stool by the kitchen area of the studio as Ledley demonstrates his dish of the day. She often teases him about the ingredients he uses and how high in calories his dishes are. He gets her to sample them and today he skewered a dumpling with a fork, wrapped the fork in a napkin and presented this morsel to Fizzy with a little bow. She laughed and nibbled at the edge of the dumpling.

'Delicious and wicked,' she said.

We do regular polls and Fizzy and Ledley come up as the viewers' favourite duo. I love Ledley too. I'd talked to him about the cooking oil issue and he had taken it well. He said he understood my concern and would be careful in future to use a range of products when he was in the studio. He was no trouble on the issue of clothing either and had moved into chef's whites straight away. How I wish the other presenters were as grown-up and laid-back as Ledley.

Mid-morning, Simon knocked and came into my room.

'Good weekend?' I asked.

'Yeah, pretty good, thanks. I meant to tell you, last week I saw Julius coming out of that private hospital on Great Portland Street and he looked pretty rough.'

'Really? When was this?'

'Thursday morning. I was wondering if he was ill?'

I thought back to Thursday. It was the day Julius missed the morning meeting and then bawled me out about Sal. Could he be ill? I found the idea disturbing. I think of Julius as invulnerable, indestructible, a force of nature.

'He *was* in a bad mood on Thursday. I'd be sorry if he was ill.'

'That's because you two are the mummy and daddy of this place,' Simon said.

'What a funny thought...'

'It's how we all think of you.'

'Do you? I can't think why... unless it's because we've both been here so long? We are the ancient ones...'

I had answered lightly but the thought of Julius and me being seen in this light, as the mummy and the daddy of the station, made me feel uncomfortable.

'It's because he's the one who shouts at people and you're the one who goes around soothing everyone afterwards.'

I smiled at that.

'He does have his moments. But I hope he's OK.'

'Anyway, thought I should tell you...'

'Yes, thanks. He's so private and if he is ill he won't let any of us in on it. It's probably best to keep this between us.'

'Sure.'

'Oh, and he split up with The Pouter; he told me that last week. Now, can you get the others in here?' I said.

This week I planned for the team to shoot the stories we would use during the outside broadcast at St Eanswythe's hospital. Simon and Molly had gone down there to identify possible interviewees. Simon had talked to a young man called Dirk who had wrecked his right leg in a motorcycle accident and had to have it amputated. He was starting his rehabilitation and was willing to talk about this, which was exactly the sort of dramatic story we were looking for. How does an active young man cope with amputation? Molly had found a woman who had breast cancer and who was a regular on the oncology ward. Molly said she was feisty and articulate on the subject of how she wouldn't give in to the cancer beast and would kick its ass. I'd asked them to check with Connie Mears, who ran the hospital, that we could proceed with these interviews. We had the full cooperation of both patients but I had promised to keep her fully informed. Connie Mears had called me on Friday. She hadn't said it in so many words, because of patient confidentiality, but she gave me a strong steer that the prognosis for Naomi Jessup, the woman with breast cancer, was poor. She suggested we might wish to reconsider her as an interviewee. This was a problem. Molly had stressed how keen Naomi was to talk about her illness and she was passionate about filming her.

My team came in and took their usual seats. It's funny the way people have their favourite places. Molly and Simon always sit in a specific chair and Harriet goes for the sofa.

'We've been allocated a crew for Wednesday,' I told them.

'Oh no! I'm away on Wednesday,' Simon said.

'Are you?'

'Yes, I *have* to go to St Albans. Some family stuff.'

'I'm sorry you'll miss it but I have to make use of that crew. You know what it's like here.'

I could see how fed up Simon was that he was going to miss the shoot. It is rare for us in the features team to get access to a camera crew. The news team have first call on the crews. Most of our pre-recorded feature stories are supplied by independent production companies. This means that my team get little chance to go out with crews and learn about that side of production.

'Molly and Harriet, you'll need to go with the crew. Please make sure Connie Mears is kept in the picture throughout and don't forget to get all the contributor release forms signed. It's very important with these stories.'

Harriet looked puzzled.

'We need permission to broadcast interviews and they're the forms we get people to sign. It's a legal requirement,' I said.

'We call them blood chits,' Molly said.

'Won't you be coming?' Harriet asked.

'No, we can't all be out of the office. Molly will show you what's needed.'

I got up and fetched the Tupperware box I had brought into work.

'Anyone like one of my home-made flapjacks?'

There were a lot of flapjacks left over and I felt a pang that Flo and Paige hadn't eaten many of them. Flo was growing up and leaving behind the favourite things of her childhood and sometimes it felt like my team were my new children.

I knew it! Fizzy and Bob must be having an affair. I was coming back from lunch with an agent and we had met at a restaurant tucked away near Russell Square. I'd had to go to her because she could dictate whether or not we get Ashley Gascoigne, a major A-lister, for interview next week and I want him on the show very much. Over lunch we'd agreed that I could have Ashley but I had had to promise airtime to two of her B-listers who are appearing in a Noel Coward revival on Shaftesbury Avenue. We parted outside the restaurant and I was walking up Gower Street. There are a number of discreet three star hotels along that road and I saw Bob and Fizzy walking into the entrance of one! Fizzy was wearing dark glasses and Bob held the door open for her. It was three in the afternoon and neither of them saw me as they entered the hotel. I think Fizzy may have a thing for married men. This is not the first time she's got involved with someone else's husband.

I had a meeting back at base at four with Julius and the sponsor to update them on how the outside broadcast is shaping up. I took an instant dislike to the sponsor, who represents one of those awful tax-evading companies who are doing this show to try to shine up their tarnished image. We call it polishing a turd. The man kept going on about the need for inspirational stories which would lift the spirits of the viewers. I played along and said that the hospital we had chosen was a community one which was well respected in the neighbourhood. We had selected moving stories to tell, including Dirk, the brave young man who had lost his leg and was determined to rebuild his life.

'And I'm going to put Ledley into the hospital kitchen to cook for the patients.'

'I like that idea,' the sponsor said.

'Ledley is very popular with our viewers and I'll get Fizzy to join him and she can help him deliver the food to the patients.'

Julius didn't say a lot. I was thinking about whether he could be ill and I kept scanning his face for any tell-tale signs. I know his face so well. I've had years of watching him at the morning meetings, trying to gauge his mood. I probably know the contours and the expressions of his face in the way that one gets to know a lover's face. I found that idea quite disturbing. The sponsor seemed content with my update and he stood up and shook hands with me. Julius walked him to the door and asked me to stay behind.

'You did well,' he said when he came back.

He sat down on his sofa, not behind his desk.

'Thanks. The team are working hard on it. He's a bit of a sleazeball, isn't he?'

'Dealing with sleazeballs is one of the delights of our business,' he said.

We exchanged a look of recognition, almost of warmth.

'Is everything OK with you?' I asked.

He looked down at his hands.

'My brother Steven is poorly.'

'I'm sorry to hear that. What's wrong?'

'Another chest infection. He gets them a lot, but this one is hanging around too long.'

'Is he, I mean, has he been hospitalised?'

'No, it hasn't come to that thankfully. He finds hospitals frightening places. He likes to be at home with his things around him. I've got a nurse coming in to be with him. I can't get in till lunchtime tomorrow so will you chair the morning meeting?'

'Of course.'

He stood up and I had the urge to comfort him so I touched his arm and gave it a gentle squeeze.

'And I wish Steven better soon,' I said.

I remembered that day I had seen Julius at the zoo. It was the week after Flo's tenth birthday and I had taken her to London Zoo in Regent's Park. Flo loves animals and when she was younger her walls were plastered with posters of kittens and rabbits and ponies. Now it is pictures of half-naked young men. We had had a brilliant time and particularly

81

liked Penguin Beach at feeding hour. You cannot help but smile when you watch penguins. We had headed over to the Reptile House where it was warm and dark. To my great surprise I saw Julius standing by one of the display cabinets with his arm around another man's shoulder; he was pointing at a giant lizard. Both men were smiling and there was a sweetness and a softness about Julius's face that I had not seen before. Then he saw me and his face closed down at once. I gave a tentative wave, not sure whether he wanted to talk to me. But I walked over with Flo anyway.

'Julius, you've met Florence before, I think?'

'Yes, hello, Florence. This is my brother Steven.'

Steven, who was in his thirties and had Down syndrome, smiled shyly at us. He was dressed in jeans and a leather jacket that looked expensive.

'Hello, Steven,' I said.

Flo squealed in excitement: 'Oh look at that!'

She was pointing at a bright green snake which was coiling itself with infinite grace down a twisted bare branch. Steven moved right up to the glass case.

'I like him. He's pretty.'

'He's a great colour, but I'm glad he's behind that thick glass,' I said.

'I like snakes. I'd like to hold him,' Steven said.

'Have you been to Penguin Beach yet?'

'We saw them feeding the penguins. They eat raw fish,' Flo said.

'Buckets of it,' I said.

Steven was clapping his hands in excitement and hopping from foot to foot.

'Oh, please can we go see the penguins, Nige?'

'Yes of course, that can be our next stop,' Julius said.

I had forgotten that Julius was born and raised as Nigel. We all shook hands quite formally and I watched them walk out of the Reptile House. Julius was holding Steven by the hand and I found the sight of their retreating figures moving.

Now, as I headed back towards my office, I spotted Flo sitting with my team. She and Harriet were flicking through a magazine and chatting. I'd forgotten that Flo was coming into StoryWorld. She had been on a school trip to Tate Modern up the river and we'd agreed she would come here afterwards. She and Harriet were poring over a fashion spread in which members of the public are photographed in the street and their outfits are ranked for style appeal. I saw another side of Harriet. She was being friendly to Flo and talking to her as an equal, not in any way as a schoolkid, and Flo was loving it.

'I need twenty minutes to clear my emails and then we're out of here,' I said.

I went into my room and Flo stayed outside with Harriet and the team.

Gourmet Pizza, Gabriel's Wharf, South Bank

I decided it would be nice for us to eat out for a change so when Flo and I left StoryWorld we walked along the river. There were blue and white lights strung in the trees. We reached Gabriel's Wharf and she spotted the red awning of Gourmet Pizza and wanted us to eat there. A patio heater was blazing over the outside tables so we sat down and watched the people strolling by the river. Flo was raving about Harriet.

'I love the way she does her hair. Did you see those tortoise-shell combs she was wearing?'

'She does have lovely hair,' I said.

'But it was the way she styled it, Mum, did you see?'

'Yes, it was very pretty. Let's order, shall we?'

I handed Flo one of the large menus and we read the pizza toppings out to each other.

'It has to be Quattro Formaggi for me,' I said.

'You always have that.'

'I can't resist all that melted cheese. There is nothing, and I mean nothing, more comforting than melted cheese. What about you?'

'I'd like the Pollo Cajun please.'

We made our order.

'I love the way she dresses too,' Flo said.

'She is very stylish, but maybe she dresses a bit old for her age?'

'No, Mum. Not at all. She's got the look.'

Our drinks arrived. I'd ordered a glass of red wine and Flo had diet Coke.

'She was telling me about this new music place in Camden, the Cat and Mouse. It gets the best bands and she goes there and there was a piece about it in the magazine.'

'I wouldn't have had Harriet down as a person who went to gigs.'

'Well she does. And she knows the best places to go.'

It seemed that Flo had a new role model and it made me think of Harriet in a slightly different light. She had taken the trouble to talk to Flo. Maybe she had a kinder side to her.

Chalk Farm Flat, 11 p.m.

After Flo was asleep I made myself a large mug of tea and sat looking out at our little garden. I bought outdoor lights for it last weekend and they're on a timer. They look so pretty twinkling along the walls. I had opened the French doors and I heard the cry of a fox in the garden next door. It is a strange, shrill, anguished sound, almost a shriek. And I could detect that unmistakable pungent smell on the air. I worry that the foxes might attack Mr Crooks, but he's a pretty belligerent beast and can probably look after himself.

I remembered our day at the zoo again. The first animals I had taken Flo to see were the wolves. I had made a point of this because when Flo was tiny she was terrified of wolves. She had seen the evil wolf Maugrim on a TV series of *The Lion, The Witch and the Wardrobe* and his long pointed nose and sharp teeth had horrified her. From that point on Maugrim had become Flo's bogeyman; the scary thing under the bed. It had taken years of me telling her that wolves were actually good animals to counter this fear. Even on our day at the zoo, the day we met Julius, she had held my hand tightly as we watched the wolves roaming their enclosure.

CHAPTER NINE

I chaired the morning meeting and I think Bob was put out that Julius had asked me to do it instead of him. The show had been a bit flat and Fizzy was complaining about the quality of guests she'd had to interview that morning.

'I can't spin gold from straw,' she said.

I book the interview of the day so I was being criticised here. I told Fizzy that I had secured Ashley Gascoigne for next week and this perked her up no end. His latest TV series is getting huge audiences and there is a Twitter storm about his appearance after every episode.

'Can we show the clip where he strips off and washes in the river?' Fizzy said.

This scene had gone viral on YouTube and had even ousted Mr Darcy's wet-shirt moment. I watched Bob for a reaction but he gave nothing away.

'It is one of those scenes you can watch again and again, isn't it, so yes, let's screen it,' I said.

Now Bob did react.

'You know if we were saying this about a scene involving a half-naked woman you'd both be up in arms in a shot.'

When Bob is irritated his Burnley accent becomes more pronounced. Unlike Fizzy he has clung to his northern identity. Fizzy and I laughed at him, united.

I went downstairs to meet Gerry in the staff café. He was clearly despondent and I bought him a cappuccino and a pain au raisin because he said he needed sugar and bugger the diet. He had printed off his predictions for the week ahead and he showed these to me. As well as the predictions he always has a topic of the week where he uses astrology to analyse a particular subject. This week his topic was financial compatibility in couples. There was a dark edge to every one of his forecasts and also to his topic.

'Oh dear, looks like we're all in for a bumpy week,' I said when I had read his script.

'It goes like that sometimes.'

He unrolled his pain au raisin and popped a large piece into his mouth.

'Is everything all right?' I asked.

He chewed on his pastry and said in a low voice, 'Trouble with Anwar.'

'I'm sorry to hear that.'

'His bloody family keep asking for money all the time and he's an actor, for chrissakes! You know how little they earn. I think the average salary for an actor is something like three thousand a year. But they think he's rich and they expect him to send money every month; a substantial amount of money.'

'He'll have to say no.'

'But he won't, Liz. It's what I've said again and again and we had another big row about it. I pay the mortgage, I buy the food, I pay for our holidays. I'm happy to do it, but why should I keep funding his whole bloody family?'

He tore off another piece of pastry and chewed furiously. Now I understood why Gerry drove a hard bargain over his fee and his expenses. Anwar must be a drain on his resources. Fizzy and Bob walked into the café and sat at their usual table by the window. Gerry noticed me noticing them.

'Are you thinking what I'm thinking?' he said.

'What are you thinking?'

He gave me a sad smile.

'It's always sex or money, isn't it? And when the planets are aligned the attraction is irresistible.'

I often forget that Gerry believes in astrology.

I had an ideas meeting with the team at noon and Simon was pushing to do a story on the sixtieth anniversary of the publication of *The Lord of the Rings*. Anniversaries are the staple of TV stations and we scan lists of them to see if there is anything we can turn into a TV story.

'It's the second biggest selling novel of all time. I thought we could screen clips from the films and I've found this academic who knows all there is to know about Tolkien and Middle-Earth,' he said.

'We've had some bad items with academics. They don't seem able to communicate their ideas within the time,' I said.

'We've had two awfully boring ones that I can remember,' Molly chipped in.

'But this guy is so good. He doesn't go in for jargon at all and he communicates really well,' Simon said, flashing an irritated look at Molly.

I wondered if Simon was a Tolkien fan as he was fired up about his idea.

'Check the film clip situation. If we can get the clips I could see it working,' I said.

Molly then told us, reluctantly, that Naomi Jessup, the cancer patient she wanted to interview for the outside broadcast, had taken a turn for the worse.

'She's really ill but she's still so keen to do the interview. I think she sees it as her last chance to say something meaningful. We've got the crew tomorrow and I'd like to go ahead.'

'This makes me uneasy, Moll. What will she say? I thought the point of her interview was she felt she could fight the cancer?' I said.

'I don't know exactly what she'll say, but I feel it could be an important interview. And I'd like to do it very much.'

'I don't want us to exploit her.'

'I wouldn't dream of exploiting her!'

'Not intentionally; but what if the interview doesn't work out and we don't transmit it? Isn't that even more unkind than standing it down now? It's bad enough when we let down members of the public who are fit and well but to let down a dying woman...'

'Trust me on this one; please,' Molly said.

When my researchers argue strongly for a story I feel I should trust them so I agreed she could proceed with the interview. Simon handed her a list of questions he had compiled for Dirk, the young man who had lost his leg. Molly read these through.

'I'll do my best,' she said.

'Is Molly going to do the interviews?' Harriet asked.

It was the first thing she had said at the meeting. She had not offered a single idea or even commented on the others' ideas.

'Yes. There's an art to it and I don't think you're ready to do interviews yet,' I said.

Harriet assessed Molly with sudden interest.

'You're on camera?'

'Doesn't work like that. I ask the questions off camera and then we piece it together,' Molly said.

'And I'll be doing the edit on the Dirk story,' Simon added.

Harriet lost interest once she realised that Molly would not be on camera. I had been thinking about how much Ziggy would learn if she could be present at the outside broadcast, but I needed one of my team to be the link person back at the office on the day.

'I'd like Ziggy to be part of the OB team, if possible. But this means I need one of you to volunteer to stay here in case of emergencies,' I said.

There was silence in the room. I waited.

'I don't mind staying here,' Harriet said.

'Are you sure? I'd appreciate it.'

'No problem.'

'Thank you.'

'And can I leave early on Friday? My granny is going into hospital for an op and I'd like to visit her afterwards,' Harriet said.

'How early are you thinking?'

'Around four, if that's all right.'

'OK, but you'll need to make up the hours next week,' I said.

They left my office. Harriet has been with us for a while now and yet she is still detached from the team and not very interested in our output. I have seen her walking around the building though. I saw her downstairs talking to the camera crew after the show and last week she was over in the newsroom talking to one of Bob's reporters. The news team sit on the opposite side of the building to us and they use the right branch of the staircase and we use the left. It is symbolic of the gulf between the two teams. I wondered at the time what she was doing over there as she does not strike me as a news person. The bottom line is that she's in a features team that is under constant pressure to produce items and I need my researchers to come up with ideas, but I was grateful that she'd volunteered to miss the action at the OB.

Julius arrived at the station around lunchtime and as he walked past my room I saw Harriet get up and hurry after him. Intrigued, I rose and moved to my door to watch them. I saw Harriet follow Julius to his office, talking to him as he walked. He nodded to Martine, his PA, and held his door open for Harriet. At almost the same moment Fizzy had come upstairs and was walking towards his office and she saw Harriet going in. Fizzy stopped in her tracks. She turned and said a few words to Martine who got up from her desk. They conferred for a couple of minutes and Fizzy walked away looking cross. I was unsettled by it too.

About fifteen minutes later Harriet returned to her desk, settled herself in front of her PC and said something to Simon. She looked pleased with herself and Molly, sitting opposite, gave her an odd look. I had an impulse to come out and ask Harriet what she had been talking to Julius about. It is unusual for any of my team to have direct contact with him. There's a hierarchy at StoryWorld and I am usually the conduit for messages from Julius. He knows her father, of course; both he and the MD do, and I know that they count Edward Dodd as an important contact. Also Harriet is one of those people who believe that every door is open to her. Her sense of entitlement is huge. But what did it matter, after all? I picked up my glass paperweight and stood at my window. I held the paperweight in the palm of my hand, then lifted it to eye level and moved it back and forth to catch the light so that the brilliant colours within the glass glowed. And then they blurred as I blinked my tears away.

I spent an hour this afternoon, longer than I intended, discussing with Ziggy how her placement is going. We found a table in the Hub. When I chose her for the internship Southwark Council supported my decision but said it was possible that she would not last the course. They told me she had struggled in care and had a record of running away from her foster homes. She had a tendency to sabotage good things which were offered to her, they said. In fact, Ziggy is settling in well and she told me she likes working at StoryWorld. I asked her what she had learned so far about making TV programmes and her observations were interesting and original.

'Is there any area of work you're most interested in, either on the editorial or the technical side?'

'I like watching the craft editors at work,' she said.

'Oh, me too. I love the editing process.'

'It's cool how they put the stories together.'

'If you're interested in editing I can look into some training opportunities. The first step would be to train up as a digital technician. Would you be OK with doing an evening course?'

'Oh yeah, defo, thanks.'

She gave me a crooked smile and it made me feel warm inside. I think the aspect about her which touches me the most is the sense I get that she doesn't feel she has a right to be loved. She expects to be rebuffed and when she is given any encouragement she is surprised and abashed by it. She's a clever girl and I'm going to help her get the training she needs.

Chalk Farm flat, 7.45 p.m.

I had been on the edge of sadness all day because today is the anniversary of when my darling dad died. Dad was a professor at the University of East Anglia and his subject was medieval history. When he got the job at UEA he and Mum moved from London to a village outside Norwich and they bought a house which had this large garden, the size of a meadow. They were both so happy with this move to the country and Dad had started to keep bees. His beehives became one of the great passions of his life. He was at the bottom of the garden checking his hives on that Sunday afternoon when he suffered a catastrophic heart attack and died on the path. He was fifty-three years old. His sudden death caused an earthquake in our small family. I don't think Mum and I have really ever got over it. It has made me more fearful and I know it affects the way I watch over Flo. I was twenty-three when Dad died and still studying for a masters. I was doing that to please him as he took great pride in my academic ability and it was he who had persuaded me to do a post-graduate degree. When Dad died there didn't seem any point any more and I gave it up. A year later I was working at StoryWorld as a junior researcher. I've often thought that if Dad hadn't died when he did I probably wouldn't have gone into telly and I wouldn't have got married so young.

My mum, who is a teacher, moved back to Scotland to live with her sister in Glasgow. She got herself a job in a large and demanding school and she thrives on it. She is due to retire soon. Mum has to have a purpose in life and she's planning to do volunteering overseas. She has never said it in so many words but I feel that she doesn't approve of my line of work. She thinks I'm capable of doing more serious work and I know she would prefer it if I was a teacher or a social worker.

There was such a heaviness inside me. I picked up my favourite photo of Dad, dusted the frame carefully, kissed his face and put it back by my bed. He had not lived to see Florence. She knows nothing about her granddad except the stories I tell her. There are so few people we truly love in our lives. I would call Mum to see how she was doing on this saddest of days.

CHAPTER TEN

StoryWorld TV station, London Bridge

Julius was back chairing the morning meeting. I was still thinking about what Simon told me about seeing him come out of that hospital. If it wasn't Steven he was visiting then what was he doing there? The meeting was an ordeal because Julius and Bob both said that they thought the feature content of the show had been weak and they discussed their criticisms at some length. I was seething and kept waiting for Fizzy to say a few words in support of me but she stayed out of the discussion while the men held forth as they love to do. I felt then what I have often felt during my years at StoryWorld; an assertion of male power and a closing of male ranks.

There's a place in every organisation where key decisions are made and it's a place I cannot go. I've been in many a manager's meeting and sometimes I've even chaired these discussions. And then, when it comes to the moment of decision, I am left out in an obscure way as if that moment has already taken place somewhere else. And that somewhere else is the gents' toilet or, more precisely, the executive gents' toilet.

One night I gained entry. I had been working late and the building was empty. I walked past Julius's corner office and saw the locked door of the executive gents' toilet with its security button pad on the wall. I knew the code and on impulse I tapped in the four numbers and opened the door. An overhead light came on as I walked in. It was large and bright with an abundance of white tiles striding up the walls and there was the gurgling of water. I looked around. There were three pristine urinals in a row and three cubicles and three washbasins. On the wall were three Dyson hand dryers. Three! No one had to wait here to dry their hands. I used one of the cubicles, flushed it, washed my hands and used one of the dryers. I looked into the mirror. I was the image of a successful executive woman but oh, my fearful eyes.

With Simon away and Molly and Harriet over at St Eanswythe's hospital with the crew, it fell to me to go through the viewers' emails with Betty to select the ones for discussion. We did this in my room and I sent Ziggy to get Betty her usual hot chocolate. Just as Gerry had done, Betty was also angling for the station to buy her some pastel-coloured outfits.

'I found these on the Jaeger site. They'd fit the bill nicely, wouldn't they?' she said.

She had printed off images of two blouses, one in an apple green and one in a shade of peach. To my eyes they looked matronly and they cost a hundred and twenty pounds each.

'Don't you have any light-coloured tops at home?' I asked.

'Not that would be smart enough to work on camera.'

'I'll see what I can do.'

Julius's Great Pastel Colour Edict was costing the station dear. Betty said she had come up with the idea of running a themed discussion for the next few weeks which she wanted to call Focus on Life Crises.

'Life Crises? That sounds a bit ominous,' I said.

'Hear me out. Good things as well as bad things can throw people into crisis. Getting married, having a baby, moving into your first house. These are all nice events but they stress people out.'

'That's true,' I said, thinking about the move to our flat in Chalk Farm. I recalled feeling empowered that Flo and I would have our own place but also fearful at the huge mortgage I was taking on.

'And then there are the difficult life events which most of us will go through at some point in our lives. I'm thinking here of divorce, of facing redundancy or retirement and of bereavement.'

I nodded. Losing my dad had been my first and my worst life crisis, far worse than my divorce from Ben.

'I get letters on these topics all the time and I feel I don't do them justice. So my idea is to run with this as a theme for several weeks, with letters on a single topic each week.'

She sat back in her chair and looked at me.

'Will it work with you doing a whole session on a single topic? We usually cover at least two topics a week to try to appeal to as wide an audience as possible,' I said.

'But that's the whole point. There's a lot to say on each of these areas.'

I couldn't pinpoint why the idea was making me feel uncomfortable or why I was resisting her. We were going through a bad patch, ever since the John of Sheffield incident. These were all important areas to discuss. Betty gave me a steely look, the kind of look I imagined she would once have given a prisoner who was misbehaving.

'I want to go deeper this time,' she said.

Simon is better at managing Betty than I am.

'OK, let's give it a go,' I said.

We turned to the mound of emails on my desk which Ziggy had printed for us and divided them into subject piles.

Todd called at lunchtime. I haven't seen him for several weeks. We arranged to spend Saturday night together as Flo would be in Portsmouth with her dad. We agreed to meet at his flat in Balham. It was on one of our first dates in Balham that I had talent-spotted Ledley. We had gone to his Jamaican restaurant, the Caribbean Shack, for dinner, had drunk rum punch and eaten his celebrated Brown Stew Fish. I had watched how Ledley moved around his small cheerful eaterie and made his customers laugh.

'He's a legend in Balham,' Todd said.

I got Ledley's details as we were paying the bill and told him I'd be in touch. Todd and I walked back to his flat arm in arm. He told me something then which made me want to go on seeing him. He said at night when he walks home, if it's late and dark and he sees a lone woman approaching him on the street, he makes a point of crossing the road so that she has the pavement to herself.

'I'm a big fella and I think I can look intimidating, so I get out of the way.'

'That's such a good thing to do.'

I squeezed his arm and I knew I was going to sleep with him. His flat is above a greengrocer's and there's a smell of cabbage as you walk up the narrow staircase to his door. Inside it's rather basic because Todd doesn't care about home comforts; he's the kind of man for whom home is where he hangs his hat, though he does possess a huge state-of-the-art TV for watching sport with one big easy chair positioned in front of it.

That first date was over two years ago. As I put down the phone I realised that our relationship has hardly evolved at all since then.

I spent the afternoon clearing my backlog of admin, checking expenses and assessing proposals from independent production companies. I researched possible courses for Ziggy which would start her on the path to becoming a digital technician. It was strange not having any of my team sitting outside my office. I was locking up when Molly came back from the day's shoot. She dumped her rucksack on her desk.

'You've had a long day. Where are the others?'

'Zig is helping out in reception and Harry had to get away early.'

'How did it go with Naomi?'

Molly turned a glowing face to me.

'It was amazing. She's so brave and so inspirational. I think you're going to love it. Do you want to see the rushes now?'

'I need to get home. We'll watch them tomorrow. And Dirk, how was he?'

'He was excellent too; showed us his prosthetic leg and it's kind of high-tech and made specially for him. He said he's determined not to go into a wheelchair. I made sure we got lots of cutaways as he strapped on the leg. I think Simon will like what I got.'

'And the ICU nurse?'

We had got permission from Connie Mears to interview an intensive care nurse who worked in the unit at St Eanswythe's as there was no way we would be allowed to film in there on the day of the broadcast.

'Another winner, I think. I don't envy her that job. Every case in that unit is life and death.'

'Well done, Moll.'

Chalk Farm flat, 7.45 p.m.

The Paige influence continues. Janis told me tonight that Flo has asked her to get in some oven chips. I have always had a down on oven chips. I tapped and popped my head round the door and Flo was talking to one of her friends on her mobile so we just waved at each other and I backed out of her room.

As I was seeing Todd on Saturday night I hand-washed my best red satin bra and knickers. I bought this expensive set a few weeks into my relationship with Todd and when I brought them back to the flat I sneaked them into my bedroom as if I had done something a bit illicit. They were in a fancy bag with ribbon handles and wrapped in swathes of tissue paper and I pushed the bag under my bed. Later that evening, when Flo was asleep, I had stripped off, unwrapped them from their tissue paper and put them on. I stood and looked at myself in the long mirror. The bra pushed my breasts up nicely. Just wearing them made me feel sexy and made me want to have sex. The door opened and Flo walked in.

'Mum!'

I was instantly embarrassed and grabbed my dressing gown and pulled it on.

'Why did you buy those?'

I was actually blushing.

'Even mums need a treat sometimes.'

She sat down on my bed and pushed the tissue paper onto the floor.

'I had a nightmare,' she said.

Ben called at nine and said Flo can come down on Friday night. We had a civil conversation with no reference to our last row. One of my lasting regrets is how I behaved towards him when he started to struggle against his addiction to poker. He tried to talk to me about it early on. He came back late one night looking awful. He must have had a big loss. He slumped at the kitchen table and I asked him what was wrong, where had he been?

'I played a game of poker and I lost a bit of money; a lot of money.'

'How much money?'

'Too much,' he said.

I felt frightened then.

'Why are you doing this?'

'I don't know.'

He looked so lost and I had no idea how to help him. But the time I feel most ashamed about was months later when his addiction was escalating. He came home ashen-faced and by then I knew what that meant. I had seen our latest bank statement and the amounts of money he was withdrawing were excessive. I was out of my depth. How could you get a grown man to change his behaviour? I recall that I didn't feel a shred of sympathy that time, just anger.

'You're jeopardising our entire future with this crazy, stupid game!'

I pulled the bank statement out of my bag and held it up to him. He wouldn't look at it; he turned his face away.

'Look at these sums.' I was jabbing my finger at the withdrawals listed on the statement.

'You've changed, Liz. You've changed so much since we got together.'

'Of course I've changed. I'm a mother now.'

'We used to have fun. You used to have time to do things with me.'

I could not believe that he was shunting the blame onto me. We hissed horrible, bitter, damaging things at each other because Flo was asleep down the hall. That was the time I should have sat down with him and said he needed help and that I would support him through it.

The last thing he said that night was that I had always held something back from him and that stung because I knew it was true. I did hold a bit of myself back from Ben. We are never so vulnerable as when we love. I felt I could never love a man totally, unconditionally and without holding something back after my dad died, because losing him had been so terrible. The only person I give unconditional love to is Flo.

I woke at two a.m. with a pounding heart. I sat up in bed in the darkness as the symptoms of panic built inside me. What had I been thinking of, letting Molly film Naomi Jessup? The sponsor had stressed he wanted inspiring upbeat stories. And Julius would never agree to us transmitting an interview with a dying woman. I recalled he'd had reservations about us broadcasting from a hospital, saying won't it be all disease and death. I had reassured him it would not be depressing. Molly had been on a high about her interview with Naomi but StoryWorld was the home of cheerful stories. I could foresee a difficult conversation with Molly and cursed myself for letting my heart rule my head.

CHAPTER ELEVEN

StoryWorld TV station, London Bridge

Sal came in to do her look back at the week's news events and she was wearing a black top. She had draped a yellow and green scarf around her neck, as a concession, I suppose, to jazz it up. I was watching from the gallery and I saw Fizzy's eyes get very round. The director, sitting next to me at the controls, said: 'She's definitely pushing it.'

We all know you don't openly defy Julius. Sal launched into her script, which was as funny and irreverent as usual, but there was a manic quality to her delivery. One of her subjects was the furore which had been raging all week about women breastfeeding too publicly in cafés and restaurants. Sal was on the side of the breastfeeders and she poked fun at a commentator who had labelled these women 'breastfeeding militants'. She did a funny riff on people who make unlikely militants: bird-feeders, pond-cleaners; watercress eaters. We went to the ad break and the floor manager walked over and unclipped Sal's mic.

'Bye, Fizz,' Sal said with a wry smile at her.

Fizzy was shuffling on the sofa as Sal walked out of the studio waving to the camera crew as she went. I rushed out of the gallery and as I got to the studio door Julius was standing there. He would have been watching the programme from his office and had come straight downstairs to confront Sal. He didn't look angry though, he looked calm. Sal emerged from the studio.

'I'd like you both to come to my office,' he said.

I think Sal had been expecting this. We walked behind him up the stairs and along to his room in silence. He opened the door for us and said to Martine: 'No calls.'

He closed the door and strode behind his desk.

'Please sit down.'

I sat down but Sal stayed standing next to me and Julius looked at her for a long moment. I would have quailed under that gaze.

'It is clear that you are not happy appearing on our show,' he said.

'I'm not happy being told what colours I can wear. There was no mention of colours in my contract.'

He turned to me.

'How long does Sal's contract have left to run?'

'Julius, can I say Sal brings something to the show that we don't get from anyone else—'

'How long does her contract have left to run?'

He had not raised his voice at all and his quietness was more menacing.

'Five months. But can we take some time out here and not rush into any decision?'

Julius stood up and flashed me a look that was both icy and contemptuous. He hates to be challenged at any time and he had decided to sack Sal.

'The station will pay you the five months you are owed. Now pack your things and go because you will never sit on the StoryWorld sofa again.'

Sal actually laughed at this.

'The hallowed StoryWorld sofa; how will I live without it? Thanks for the great material, Julius. Sacking me because of the colour I wear. I can do a lot with that. Bye, Liz.' And she turned and left his room.

I stood up to leave.

'Don't you dare go after her,' he said quietly.

I watched Sal retreat from our view as Martine turned a worried glance in our direction.

'Think about it. She may go to the papers and how does it make us look? Sacking her on these grounds?' I said.

'She's a stroppy cow and I'm glad to see the back of her. And if the papers cover it, that's fine by me.'

'For the record, I think you're making a mistake. She brought a unique voice to the show.'

'Most weeks it was a feminist rant. I doubt she's as popular with our viewers as she thinks she is,' he said.

'Her viewer ratings are good.'

'You know, you're a talented woman, Liz, but you'll never get to the top if you're not prepared to stand up to egos like her.'

'After all these years of working here I'm world class at dealing with egos,' I said, and I left his office.

Back in my room I was shaking with a mixture of nerves and pride that I'd stood up to him. I was craving a cigarette, which happens when I'm very wound up. I wondered about calling Henry, the floor manager, who is one of the few people left in the station who still smokes. I walked downstairs to find him and I knew that it wouldn't take long for this story to get out. Sal was our first casualty to the Great Pastel Colour Edict. How ridiculous it all was and no wonder people despised television.

Henry joined me in a cigarette break at the back of the station. He lit my cigarette and I inhaled deeply.

'Why did Sal do that?' he asked.

I felt the smoke going down into my lungs and calming my head.

'She thinks he's an arse and wanted to stand up to him.'

'We've all wanted to do that at times.'

'But why couldn't she see the whole stupid thing is about his need to be in control? It's actually quite childish,' I said.

'It's a shame. I like Sal and I'm sorry to see her go.'

'Me too. Thanks for the cig.'

The cigarette had soothed me. I walked back upstairs thinking that the way Julius had sacked Sal, almost Nero-like in his sense of absolute power, reminded me yet again of the need to be vigilant. Childish it may be on one level but I have seen a lot of sackings at StoryWorld over the years and often for standing up to Julius. It is why few of us feel safe working here. I saw Molly at her desk and asked her to join me in my room.

'Do you want to look at the rushes now? I've started a rough edit,' she said.

'This afternoon would be better, but I have to tell you there may be a problem.'

'A problem – what do you mean?'

'It came to me last night that Julius will object to this interview.'

'But you haven't even seen it yet!' Molly said, her flat cheeks flushing a deep red.

'I'm at fault here, Moll. I got a clear steer from Julius and the sponsor that they want upbeat stories. Julius said no disease and death. I'm *so* sorry. I should have thought this through more. I don't know why I didn't.'

'No disease and death, but we're filming in a hospital!'

'I know. They want manageable disease, picturesque disease, pastel disease,' I said, my voice rising in my distress. I put my hands to my head. 'You know what a plastic world we create here.'

'Please watch it. Please. I think it's a special interview.'

'I will, this afternoon, but I had to be straight with you about this. It's unlikely we can transmit it.'

The phone rang on my desk. I picked up and it was Fizzy.

'Can we have a private word, Liz?'

'Give me ten minutes. Do you want to come here?'

'Will you come to my dressing room? I'm resting up.'

'Of course. Can I get you a coffee?'

'No thanks. I'm off coffee.'

'I'll be down in ten.'

'I'll book us a viewing room,' Molly said.

She left my room and I felt ashamed of myself. I walked downstairs to the café, bought myself a coffee and wondered what Fizzy wanted to talk to me about. I reached her dressing room, by far the nicest one in the suite of rooms. It had just been redecorated and Fizzy had chosen fiendishly expensive wallpaper with sepia flowers all over it which is too chintzy for my taste, but what Fizzy wants, Fizzy gets. I tapped and went in. I was thinking about my conversation with Molly and how I had let her down. Fizzy was stretched out on her chaise longue; yes, she does have this rather beautiful antique chaise longue upholstered in rose-coloured taffeta. She was wearing a cream silk kimono and sipping at a glass of water with a slice of lemon floating in it.

'Are you OK?' I asked.

'I was tired after the show.'

I pulled up a seat and sat at her feet. She was paler than usual.

'Is something wrong?'

Fizzy put her glass down, wriggled into a more upright position and shot me an irritated look.

'I told you to watch that girl.'

'Harriet?'

'Martine tells me she's in hot pursuit of Julius. She skips down to his office all the time and she's invited him to a film premiere tonight.'

'Tonight? Are you sure?'

Harriet had told me she had to leave early, at four o'clock, to visit her grandmother in hospital.

'Yes, at Leicester Square. Her father got her the tickets and an invite to the champagne reception beforehand. Martine thinks she's angling to get a screen test!'

Martine would know. She is Julius's gatekeeper. She and Fizzy are close because Fizzy started work at StoryWorld as a PA and all credit to her that she didn't drop Martine when she became famous. Martine is older than her, has no desire to be a TV star and idolises Fizzy. My relationship with Martine is, unfortunately, more fraught. She is such a Julius loyalist and from time to time, after I've stood up to him, she will give me the cold shoulder, sometimes for months at a time.

'I wouldn't worry about that. Julius will see right through it and anyway, Harriet hasn't got what it takes,' I said.

Fizzy's insecurities get on my nerves. She is self-obsessed and we all pander to her all the time. But had Harriet lied to me? Had she asked to leave early so she could get to the premiere?

'What time is this premiere?'

'The reception starts at five. Why?'

'And is Julius going?'

'Martine said it's unlikely. The point is she's hanging around him at every opportunity and making a nuisance of herself. She's young and she's very ambitious,' Fizzy said.

'But with little personality, or if she has she's shown little evidence of it so far.'

'What makes you say that?'

'She doesn't come up with any ideas and she seems a bit bored by it all,' I said.

'She's not interested in being a researcher. Her sight is set on being in front of the camera. Surely you can see that?'

I sighed. It had already been a difficult morning and it wasn't even eleven.

'I think you're right about her being interested in Julius,' I said.

'It's what she did at her father's paper; went after the features editor; had an affair with him.'

'We can't stop people having affairs, Fizzy.'

I wondered why I had said those words and suddenly was embarrassed. I stood up and put my coffee cup down by her washbasin. There was an awkward silence as I rinsed the cup and saucer under the tap, then dried my hands.

'Did you hear that Sal was sacked this morning?' I said.

Fizzy drew her kimono more closely around her.

'She had it coming; thought she was more important than the station.'

'That's what Julius thinks, but I'm sorry she's gone. Look, don't worry about Harriet. She's a silly star-struck girl who is batting her eyelashes and behaving in a foolish way. She's no threat to anyone.'

'I don't think she's a threat for a moment,' Fizzy said crossly with a toss of her head.

'Well then.'

'But I want her out of here.'

I had almost decided that once the three months were up I would ask Harriet to leave. She did not deserve to be made a permanent member of my team. But Fizzy demanding it like that annoyed me.

'That's above my pay grade. As I told you before she's here because the MD wants it. By all means have a word with Saul.'

'Maybe I will,' she said.

The current MD, Saul Relph, is a remote figure, unlike the man who was in charge when I arrived at StoryWorld. Saul Relph has been here for five years but he has always kept his distance from the staff. He looks after the shareholders and lets Julius run the station. Which is why it was unusual for him to intervene as he did to get Harriet placed in my team.

Harriet left at four sharp. I thought about challenging her about where she was going, but in the end I left it. I went down to the viewing room and Molly played me the rough edit of her interview with Naomi Jessup. It ran nine minutes, far longer than would ever be transmitted; our stories run three to four minutes long. Naomi Jessup looked older than her thirty-three years and she was so thin. She was sitting in a chair by a window in the hospital room and the light from behind her lit up the papery almost translucent skin of her face. She had no hair or eyebrows and had tied a jaunty scarf around her head. She said in a surprisingly strong voice that she knew she was dying and it was almost a relief because she had battled for so long. 'You battle because you have hope,' she said, 'but hope is an extension of suffering. Hope puts you on the rack.' She knew she was beaten now and it was less frightening than she thought it would be. We all have to die sometime. She talked about the wonderful people she had met on the oncology ward, other patients who were facing death like her. It helped to talk to them. She talked about her family briefly. Her reticence here spoke volumes. She said every day mattered now. We sat in silence at the end of the item.

'That's a special piece of work,' I said.

'Thank you.'

'Her point about hope was so moving. I'll show it to Julius. You'll need to cut it down to four minutes first.'

But not today, I thought. I won't show it to him today after the sacking of Sal this morning.

'Do you think he'll let us transmit it?'

'Probably not; but I'm going to try to persuade him. I'd like to see this go out.'

Chalk Farm flat, 9 p.m.

I had a horrible headache tonight. I had taken Flo to Waterloo station and she gave me a big hug before she went through the barrier. I needed that hug. It was lovely because often when we are out together now she won't show me any signs of affection. I had watched her retreating figure as she swung along the platform. She's getting tall and she had her overnight bag slung over her shoulder and could have passed for older than fourteen. As she opened the carriage door I waved and blew a kiss. She waved back and disappeared into the train.

Flo stays at Ben's parents', Peter and Grace, in Portsmouth and she adores them both. They have lived in that house for years and it's a comforting place to stay. Before the divorce Ben and I would go down there about every six weeks so they could see Flo, and we would sleep in what had been Ben's childhood room. Peter and Grace are far more active and involved grandparents than my mum is because she lives so far away in Glasgow. I remember one weekend we went with them to their local pub to have a Sunday roast. This pub had a big garden with those wooden tables with benches on either side and at the bottom there was a slide for children. Peter,

111

Ben's dad, had taken Flo down to the slide and had stood there patiently as she climbed up and slid down again and again. She was about four years old at the time. They came back up the garden and he seated her next to him. Grandpa Peter always talked to her in a grown-up way even when she was little. He now asked her what she wanted to be when she grew up. Flo did not even think about this for a moment but replied at once:

'I want to be a bride.'

Ben and I burst out laughing and Flo looked put out.

'Oh, darling, it's just that being a bride only lasts for one day,' I said.

How I loved it when Flo was little. I bought myself a large packet of honey-roasted cashew nuts from a kiosk and ripped the bag open and was stuffing them into my mouth as I went down the escalator. Sitting on the Tube as it rumbled along to Chalk Farm I folded down the top of the packet and put them in my bag, only to retrieve them a minute later and scoop another handful of cashews into my mouth. When I came out of the station I had eaten two thirds of the packet. Disgusted at my greediness I left the nearly empty bag on a wall.

When I reached my flat the quietness and the emptiness made me want to cry. This was the second time this week I have been tearful and it's not like me – I pride myself on being stoical. I spend so much time at work holding down anger or frustration so now I told myself to feel the pain, don't run away from it. I stood in my living room and let myself become overwhelmed by a sense of loss and sadness. My tears were a release from the tension of the week. Mr Crooks came in and stood mewing piteously by his food bowl. It was empty with dry food crusted round the edges. His water bowl had a film of dust floating on the top.

'Poor boy, she didn't feed you.'

It was Flo's job to feed Mr Crooks. I picked up his bowl and scrubbed it clean, feeling irritated with her for doing that adolescent thing of only ever thinking about herself. It was hardly an onerous task to feed her cat. I gave him a pouch of food and refreshed his water bowl.

I took two paracetamol for my aching head and ran a bath, pouring my favourite rose oil under the tap. The oil turns milky as it hits the water and it has the most divine smell. I lit a candle, turned off the bathroom light and stepped into the fragrant water.

Chalk Farm flat, Saturday morning

It had turned cold and I switched the heating on. I was tidying the flat and had ventured into Flo's room to look for mould-encrusted plates which she will often stash under her bed. It was then that I felt a draught in her room. There are shutters at the bedroom windows but there was a definite chill coming from outside. I unlocked and folded the shutters back and saw at once that the bottom left windowpane was broken. My first reaction was terror. Someone had tried to break into our flat last night! I thought back. I'd been in the bath and then had an early night. I hadn't heard a thing. I had taken two paracetamol and these make me sleep more deeply than usual. I examined the broken pane more carefully. The glass had been knocked outwards; shards were lying in the window well below. Surely the glass would have fallen into the room as the pane was smashed? Down among the fragments of glass on the ground was a pile of cigarette butts. Understanding dawned. This was no attack from outside the flat. Flo, and probably Paige, had broken

113

the window and not thought to tell me. They must have thought the wooden shutters gave protection enough.

I got a brush and pan, opened the window to its full extent and lowered myself into the window well. This is part of my property and in front there's a small raised garden which belongs to the flat above. The window well is not an easy space to get into and I had to squat to sweep up the glass fragments and the cigarette butts. There was a pungent smell, a mixture of damp and of foxes. Strong weeds were growing out of the brickwork at the bottom. I would need to get those pulled out before they damaged the fabric of the building; another task to add to my to-do list. It never stops.

Balham, Sunday morning

I woke in Todd's large and lumpy bed. He had rolled onto his side taking most of the duvet with him. I slid out and went to his bathroom. It was clean enough in there and I wondered if he had cleaned it for me. Over the bath he had hung a large wooden sign which was yellow and had words painted on it in bright blue letters:

HOORAY, HOORAY THE FIRST OF MAY
OUTDOOR FUCKING STARTS TODAY.

The paint was peeling. He had bought it in a street market and thought it dated from the seventies. He's such a lad. I got back into bed and stroked his naked back before heaving some of the duvet over me. He turned and grabbed me and we lay fitted together in the warm nest of his bedding.

We had gone to a music pub the night before. I had expected Todd to favour rock music but this pub did indie

114

folk. There was a singer-songwriter with an acoustic guitar and Todd loved it. We were drinking pints of Guinness and in the break between sets I told him about the broken glass and the cigarette butts in the window well. I rarely talk to Todd about Flo.

'I'm not sure what I should do.'

'Think back to you at fourteen. Were you a model kid?'

I reached over and wiped the Guinness foam off his top lip with my thumb.

'Course not. I used to clash with my mum all the time, mainly over clothes and make-up, skirt too short, eyes too black.'

'Exactly; she's a teenager and they're built to break rules.'

'I'm not worried about the breakage, though she should have told me. But the smoking? She's only fourteen.'

'Is it so terrible? I bet she's a good kid.'

'She *is* a good kid. But I hate the idea of her smoking. I think it's a girl thing, you know, more than boys. I've often seen young girls coming out of the school gate and lighting up.'

'I thought it was all e-cigs these days?'

'Not my Flo. She's fallen under the spell of an older girl, Paige, and she comes from a smokers' house. Their kitchen reeked.'

'If you come over heavy and do the banning thing it will make smoking even more desirable.'

It was helpful talking to Todd about Flo. It made me feel less alone and I wondered why I hadn't done it before. Apart from Fenton I rarely tell anyone what is going on in my head.

We got up an hour later and Todd cooked us a brunch of scrambled eggs and pork sausages.

'I do love a man who cooks a good breakfast and these sausages are sensational,' I said.

'They're Gloucester Old Spot, the best sausages I've found over here.'

'And not burned to a cinder either. I'm impressed.'

'You implying we Aussies only know how to barbecue our meat to a crisp?'

I grinned at him and pushed down the plunger in the cafetière. I had heated milk to go with our coffee and I poured us each a mug. He was watching me and I noticed a tiny shift in his face as I pushed the mug over to him.

'Thanks. I didn't say anything last night because I didn't want to spoil our evening...'

'What is it?'

'I have to go back to Australia for a few months. My dad is ill.'

'Your dad?'

'He's got cancer.'

'Oh no. Todd, I'm so sorry.'

'Mum says there are things they can do but... she asked me to come home.'

'Of course, you must go at once.'

'I'm flying out next week. It won't be for ever but...'

He didn't finish his sentence. He didn't want to say he wouldn't be back until his father had died. I put my hand over his and stroked his knuckles. He didn't say anything and I felt my response was inadequate. I got up and hugged him and my eyes filled with tears. My emotions are all over the place at the moment.

'Why the tears, Liz? You always seem so strong, so untouchable.'

I blew my nose and tried to smile.

'Untouchable? After last night?'

'You know what I mean. At work. You come over as the consummate professional, calm and in charge and a little bit haughty.'

He was not the first person to have said that about me. I am able to be calm and professional at work, most of the time. I wondered if my team thought of me like that too. It's a front. And I can't seem to be calm at home; I'm an emotional mess at home.

'It's not what it feels like inside, believe me.'

'It's a turn-on for us fellas,' he said.

'I was thinking about my dad,' I said.

When we parted in the late afternoon we hugged each other tight and there was such a closeness between us, the warmest feelings I have experienced for ages. It's the first time I have let Todd see me feeling vulnerable, and now he is going away.

CHAPTER TWELVE

StoryWorld TV station, London Bridge

Great excitement at the station this morning as Ashley Gascoigne, the A-lister, arrived to be interviewed by Fizzy. She had made a special effort and was looking more glamorous than usual with her strawberry-blonde hair piled up on top and wearing a dress of palest pink which suited her colouring. A crowd of fans had gathered outside the station and they were thrilled when Ashley stopped to sign autographs. They were all taking selfies with him which would be shared on Twitter and Instagram at the earliest opportunity.

Celebrities are often disappointing when you meet them face to face. They are usually smaller and less striking than they look on screen, as if the camera has made them more heroic. But Ashley Gascoigne was extremely good-looking and charismatic in the flesh. He has curly dark hair and intense brown eyes and I found myself feeling flustered as I took him to the green room. He had three people with him: his assistant, his publicist and his stylist. I welcomed them and offered them refreshments. Ziggy was in the green room serving the coffees and teas and I loved that she was unfazed by the proximity of Ashley Gascoigne. I thought Julius might come down to say hello but he stayed away. He watches the show from his office. He says you get a false sense of things if you watch it from the gallery. It is true that when mistakes happen on air they look more catastrophic from the gallery. Ashley's publicist asked for a green tea and drew me aside.

118

She wanted to know if the station had a back exit.

'Yes, there is. Don't you want to leave by the front though? I'm sure there'll be some press there,' I said.

'We don't need it and he's already done the autograph thing. Get our cars to meet us at the back. I want a quick getaway.'

I didn't like her. She hadn't said please and she gave the impression that she was a woman used to giving orders and to people jumping to attention. But all her power came from the reflected glory of Ashley Gascoigne. I asked Ziggy to make sure the taxis were at the back of the studio at the end of the interview.

I accompanied Ashley to the studio door and the floor manager took him in. I sat in the gallery next to the director and we had scheduled fifteen minutes for this interview, far longer than our usual slot, as I wanted to make the most of having such a big name on the sofa. Fizzy was enjoying it and was on great form. We rolled in three clips during the interview, including the famous one of Ashley stripping and washing in a river, which had had the womanhood of Britain swooning. Fizzy said after the clip that this trumped Mr Darcy swimming in the lake and Ashley took this with good grace. We went to the ad break and I came out of the gallery and saw his publicist shouting at Ziggy. I hurried over.

'What's going on?'

'This idiot girl hasn't got the cars where I asked!' the publicist said.

'But I told them to go out the back,' Ziggy said, hugging her arms around her ribs tightly.

'Where the fuck are they then?' she hissed.

'No need to talk to her like that!' I said.

The publicist turned to me. 'What?'

'Don't speak to my runner like that.'

She narrowed her eyes. 'Oh, I get it. Now you've had your interview you don't care. Last time I'll let him be booked onto this crap show.'

Ashley was coming out of the studio door with his assistant at his side and the publicist shut up. I wondered if he knew what a bitch she was. I went over to him and thanked him warmly for coming to StoryWorld.

'My pleasure, I enjoyed it,' he said.

'We've booked your cars for the back exit as requested and they should be there any minute.'

I walked with him to the exit and when we got outside the two cars were waiting for them. There was also a handful of fans who had gathered there. Ashley stopped to chat to them briefly and to sign more autographs. I shot a glance at the mean-spirited publicist and gave a small smile. Ashley and his assistant got into the front car and she stepped into the second car with the stylist and they drove off. I've made an enemy there. I walked back in and Ziggy was hovering in the reception area as if she was waiting for me.

'No one's ever done that before,' she said.

'Done what?'

'Stood up for me. Thanks.'

At the morning meeting Julius let Fizzy rave on about Ashley Gascoigne and what a difference it made to get a true A-lister on the show.

'I loved every minute of it,' she said.

We all congratulated Fizzy on her interview and I was feeling good about my job. As the meeting came to an end I asked Julius if we could have a quick word. The outside broadcast was the next day and I had decided this would be the moment to show him the Naomi Jessup interview in the afterglow of the Ashley Gascoigne success.

'Sure.'

I followed him to his office.

'I have an interview I want to show you. Molly filmed one of the patients at St Eanswythe's. She is dying of cancer and—'

'Dying...'

'Hear me out. The way she talks about it is so moving and inspirational and I'd like your view on it.'

'OK,' he said.

'Give me ten minutes and I'll get it set up downstairs.'

When Julius joined me in the edit suite it was just the two of us as I knew Molly would get too passionate and might argue with him if he was critical of her work. She had cut the interview back to four and a half minutes and it was even more powerful at this length.

'It's good work,' he said when it was finished.

'I thought so too.'

'But we can't transmit it as part of the OB.'

'The sponsor asked for inspirational and this *is* inspirational.'

He swung his swivel chair round to face me.

'Liz, thanks for showing it to me but you know the sponsor will not want this in the show. We pitched it as a community hospital with good team spirit and patients on the mend.'

'I sometimes think we underestimate our audience,' I said.

'Maybe we do.'

'Seriously, some of the best reactions we've got have been to difficult stories, stories we've taken a risk on.'

'I'm sorry to disappoint you and your team member but this is not going out as part of the OB.'

He is the director of programmes and he gets the last say. We both stood up. He hesitated at the door of the edit suite.

'Don't think I don't appreciate the extra hours you've been putting in to make this OB work,' he said.

I flushed at his praise; it was a rare enough occurrence. He opened the door for me and we parted at the top of the stairs. Molly was watching me intently as I walked towards my office and I made a slight shake of my head.

'Come into my room.'

'He's said no, hasn't he?'

'Yes, I'm afraid he has, but he thought it was excellent work, and it *is* excellent work.'

'What's the good of that if it doesn't get shown?'

'I argued for it and I know how disappointed you must feel.'

She was looking down at the floor as she said: 'We get so little time with a camera crew here and I think I need to develop that part of my work. It's what I want to do long-term.'

Molly is an honest person. There is no side to her and she was telling me that she wanted to leave the station. I can't afford to lose her. There is already too much for the three of us to do as we are still carrying Harriet.

'You must know how much I value your work Moll.'

In the afternoon I completed the running order for the outside broadcast. I included the Naomi Jessup interview as the standby tape. We almost never use the standby tape. In fact it has never happened at any of the OBs I have produced. But there has to be at least one available for the director to screen should the live link go down. Molly had been looking upset all day. I went out to the team and over her shoulder I saw that she had the *Guardian* jobs page up on her screen. She closed her screen down quickly but she must have known I had seen she was job hunting.

For Simon and Ziggy a sense of anticipation was building about the outside broadcast. We had to be at the hospital by five-thirty a.m. and I'd told Molly, Simon and Ziggy that they could book taxis to get them there. I reminded Harriet to be at her desk by six thirty in case we needed anything at the last minute and she could have a taxi too. The team were packing up to go when I did a last check on the paperwork.

'Stop a minute, guys; not so fast, I can't find Dirk's release form.'

'They're all in the folder,' Harriet said.

'His isn't. I've checked twice.'

Harriet looked sheepish and I remembered that she had snuck off early on the day of the hospital shoots and Molly had returned to the station on her own.

'You were in charge of this. Did you get the form from Dirk?'

'I thought I had,' she said.

I was furious in a flash. It was her passive response as much as her error that angered me.

'*I told you* how important those forms were. We can't transmit without it. Is he still at the hospital?'

'No,' Simon said. 'He's gone home. Look, I'll track him down tonight and I'll get the form signed. It's my story and—'

'No! Thanks for the offer, Simon, but this is for Harriet to sort out. You three get off now and I'll see you first thing tomorrow.'

They picked up their rucksacks. Simon was looking worried as he left with Molly and Ziggy. I turned to Harriet.

'You've got time to put this right. Here is Connie Mears's number.' I wrote it down on a post-it note. 'That's my home number too. Connie is the senior manager. Call her now and get Dirk's address and then go over to his place and get the form signed.'

'Will you call Connie Mears?' she said in a helpless voice which made me even more enraged.

'No. You've got to do this. If you want to become a researcher you have to take responsibility and see things through.'

She sighed and looked down at the post-it note.

'I know, I'll ask Dad to send his driver round to pick up the form.'

'You will not. You will go and see Dirk personally and get that form signed. I need to know by ten at the latest that it's sorted. Call me at home once you've got it.'

I picked up my bag and as I left she was sitting at her desk using the phone. All the way home in the Tube my anger against Harriet raged. Dirk's interview is the best of the stories we've got now that we're not transmitting Naomi Jessup. Harriet would have let Simon do the graft for her, or her dad's driver, if I hadn't intervened. She is such a little princess. Occasionally I've allowed a story to go out without a contributor release form, but it's a risky thing to do and it leaves the station vulnerable. This was a sensitive story about a young man's amputation and I couldn't risk it.

Chalk Farm flat, 7.15 p.m.

I gave Flo a photo-card signed by Ashley Gascoigne. I'd asked him to put her name on it and to my surprise she was pleased with it. She sat with me at the kitchen table. I was chopping an onion to make a cheese and onion frittata and my eyes were watering.

'Guess what? Paige's dad says he can get our names on the door for the Cat and Mouse on Friday night. Can I go?'

She sounded excited.

'What's the place called?'

'The Cat and Mouse. You know, the one I told you about.'

'Did you?'

'Yes. The club Harriet goes to. In Camden Town. Everyone at school wants to go there.'

'Don't you need ID cards for those kind of places?'

'Not if our names are on the door.'

My first instinct was to say no but I played for time. I got up and rinsed my fingers under the cold water tap.

'These onions are very strong.' I blinked away the tears. 'Let me think about it, sweets.'

'What's the problem? Her dad's going to be there.'

'Those places have an age bar for a reason, you know.'

'I'm not going to drink alcohol or anything. I just want to see the band and we've got free tickets.'

'Let me check out the venue and—'

'It's not like you'll be at home to hang out with,' she said.

'Flo, I said I'll look into it. I'm not going to say yes tonight.'

I said it as calmly as I could but she got up from the table with a jerk.

'Why d'you have to be so uptight about it?'

'I'm not being uptight about it.'

'Yes you are!' she shouted.

'You think you'll get what you want by shouting?' But I had raised my voice too. All my buttons were pressed.

'You are the most horrible controlling mother in the world!'

This was followed by a great slamming of her bedroom door. I stood outside her door and shouted through it.

'And you're behaving like a spoiled brat. One day that door will come off its hinges!'

'Leave me alone!' she shrieked from her bedroom.

I was shaking with anger and I left the cooking and went into my bedroom. Why did my rows with Flo escalate so fast? I thought back. She had been pleased with the Ashley Gascoigne card but in minutes she was shouting at me and I was shouting back. Why was I able to control my anger at work but not at home? I felt a failure as a parent and I wanted to call Ben and tell him that he didn't know what he was missing.

When Janis first came to work for me she told me a story that has stayed with me. It was a hot afternoon and after she had picked Flo up from school she took her to Primrose Hill to find a breeze and to eat sandwiches on the grass. They had walked to the top of the hill where there is this panoramic view of London spread out below with all its buildings, cranes and spires. Flo pointed to the view and said: 'That's London and my mummy works there.'

It makes me sad when I think of Flo saying that. She was missing me and she probably wished she had a stay-at-home mum who would pick her up from school every day. Her comment tonight that I wouldn't be around for her to hang out with had stung because it was true. I spent so much time at work, not at home. I wrote down the name of the venue, the Cat and Mouse. I haven't met Paige's mum or dad yet but the father works in the music industry which is presumably why he can get them the tickets. Would it be OK to let her go? She was so keen on the idea. But I don't like the way Paige is left alone in their house so often and I doubt that the father would make the best of chaperones. Flo said Harriet goes to the Cat and Mouse and I can check it with her tomorrow.

Ten past ten and Harriet called. She had tracked Dirk down and had the contributor release form duly signed. She sounded positively resentful and was talking as if she had done me a favour. I had to bite back the harsh words I wanted to say to her, that it was her sloppiness that had caused her the late night. Instead I thanked her for calling me and reminded her that she needed to be in the office by six-thirty a.m. to monitor calls for the team. As I went to bed I thought that I was being too easy on Harriet and maybe that was because of who her father is and the MD connection. I had been harsher with Amanda. She had been in my team three years ago and, like Harriet, she was passive and one of life's whiners. I have a low tolerance for whingeing as we work in an industry that most people would love to join. When Amanda complained about the long hours I would snap that we weren't working in the Siberian salt mines, for God's sake! She brought out my nasty side and she didn't last long in my team.

As I turned out the light in my bedroom I reflected that maybe I was being over-protective with Flo and that I needed to cut her some slack.

CHAPTER THIRTEEN

St Eanswythe's Hospital, Bermondsey, 6 a.m.

The outside broadcast truck was parked in the hospital car park. It took the technical guys a while to find the right position to get an uninterrupted uplink path to the satellite but finally we were getting a good signal. We have four cameras: three will be set up in the wards with the fourth one in the hospital kitchen in the basement. Ledley was already down there preparing the ingredients for his cooking demonstration. He was going to make Jamaican patties and a cake for the patients. Fizzy arrived ten minutes ago and we go to air at eight a.m.

There is such a heightened atmosphere to an outside broadcast. It's unlike any other kind of programme-making and what makes it work is when the whole team pull together as one. Simon and Molly arrived and I put them in charge of lining up the patients for Fizzy to talk to as we move through the wards. Ziggy arrived ten minutes later and she would be the on-site runner and would do the fetching and carrying. All three had taken my advice and were wearing trainers as they will have to move fast around the hospital which has miles of corridors; we have all been issued with a map of the hospital layout.

Once we go on air I will be sitting in the mobile control room with the director and the PA. It's a tight squeeze in there with a production gallery including a bank of monitors showing the output from the four cameras. We will be in voice contact with Fizzy, Ledley and the floor manager throughout. It was at an OB that I first met Todd two years ago. Our show was coming from the Natural History Museum and it had been a six-camera operation. I was sitting close to him in the truck as he directed the cameras. It was an ambitious shoot but it had gone brilliantly and when the credits rolled Todd and I were euphoric. Our first date followed soon after. And now he is on the other side of the world.

I walked around the hospital making last minute checks that everything was in place. Connie Mears arrived just after seven and I thought she looked nervous. She has something to lose if it goes wrong today and if the hospital is shown in a poor light. She was amazed at the length of cabling we had laid down for the lights and the sound feeds. The cameras are on radio links to allow the crew to get in close to any interaction Fizzy has with the patients. Connie and I wished each other luck and I went to find Henry. I was glad it was Henry, our most experienced floor manager, who was on duty. During an outside broadcast the floor manager is the key member of the team because he creates order among all the strangeness and unfamiliarity of the location. He was drinking a coffee and eating a bacon roll by the catering van. We discussed the trickiest part of the show, which was when we had to get two cameras down from the wards to the kitchen in the basement. We would be doing this during an ad break and the turnaround time was going to be short. He threw his paper cup in the bin.

'Time to get Fizzy into position,' he said.

Henry took Fizzy along to the children's ward which we had selected as the ideal place to open the show. It was a cheerful ward with nursery rhyme figures painted on the

129

walls. Little Miss Muffet sat next to Humpty Dumpty on his wall while Jack and Jill were climbing a hill with their pail between them. There was a play area at the end of the ward with lots of small red and green chairs set in a circle. Fizzy was seated on one of these mini-chairs with the children grouped around her. She had brought along a stack of her photo-cards and the children were asking her to sign them and she was adding smiley faces and kisses to her signature. It was a good icebreaker in the build-up to going on air. Fizzy explained to the children that once the red light on the top of the cameras came on they would be recording and they would be on television. The children were wriggling with excitement and the nurses in attendance looked almost as excited. I wondered if the children would go quiet and shy when we started rolling, because cameras can have that effect.

I hurried back to the truck and five minutes later the PA was counting us down to go on air. The opening shot looked good with Fizzy sitting in the midst of the children. She stood up and welcomed viewers to St Eanswythe's hospital. She gave a few facts and figures about the community it served and how many patients the hospital had treated last year. Then she sat down with the children and chatted to them. Most of them had at least one cuddly toy with them and Fizzy wanted to know the name of each toy. She told them she still had her blue bunny which had been her favourite toy when she was little. One little boy wanted to know the name of the blue bunny and Fizzy replied Smelly Bun. I don't know if she made this up on the spot but the children thought it was very funny.

'Time to move,' the director said into Fizzy's earpiece.

She stood up and all the children waved to her as she walked with a ward sister showing her the way to an adult ward. When she got there she sat on the beds and talked to two adult patients who had been vetted in advance and who had interesting stories to tell. More to the point, they were comfortable talking to her. They looked thrilled to have her there so close to them, the famous Fizzy Wentworth. It was time for Fizzy to link to our first ad break.

'There's lots more to come from this wonderful hospital serving its community. Be sure to stay with us,' she said.

'So far so good,' the director said.

We were coming off this ad break to the kitchens in the basement and we had four minutes to get the second and third cameras down there to do the Ledley and Fizzy item about hospital food. It was tight but the cameras were handheld and we'd had a rehearsal. The crew got the cameras set up in time. Three members of the hospital cooking team had been selected to talk to Ledley and Fizzy about the challenge of producing food for the patients. It was hot and airless in the basement kitchen. It would have been hot in there anyway but the lights we had rigged up had increased the temperature even more. There were pungent cooking smells too. We came out of the ad break and Fizzy did the opening link on autopilot. She had turned waxy pale as if she might faint.

'Fizzy's ill!' I said.

'Move the camera onto Ledley,' the director said.

I spoke urgently to Henry via his earpiece.

'Get Fizz out of the kitchen now. She's not well.'

The cameras were now on Ledley who had realised what was happening and he took over without a moment's hesitation. He ad-libbed with the hospital cooking team and drew them round him to look at his ingredients. Later, Henry told me that Ziggy stepped in and off camera she had got Fizzy onto a chair and some water to her white lips.

Fizzy sat forward and put her head between her knees for several minutes. Then Ziggy helped her out of the hot kitchen and into a room with a window, opened it wide and sat with her.

Ledley was superb. He kept the banter and the laughs going with the hospital cooks for far longer than was intended. He revealed the special ingredient that he always used in his Jamaican patties.

'I add turmeric to the flour, which gives the pastry that nice yellow colour,' he said. He took a tray of yellow-gold patties out of the oven and laid them on the surface. 'I made these with ground beef and scallions. Come and try them.'

The cooking team each took a patty and bit into them as Ledley watched with a smile. As they gave the thumbs up he looked into camera: 'And for pudding I'm making pineapple upside down cake.'

When I saw that Ledley would be able to keep this going till we reached the next ad break, I ran out of the truck and found Fizzy. She was sitting on a chair by an open window. I had five minutes to decide what to do.

'I had a terrible wave of nausea,' she said.

'I thought you were going to faint.'

'My legs were going. It was so hot and it stank in there.'

She looked less white but there was sweat on her upper lip.

'You're not well and you don't have to keep going, Fizz. Let me get a car for you. Ledley can do the rest of the show. You know how good he is with people.'

She lifted a determined chin.

'I'll be OK in a minute. I want to keep going.'

I made a snap decision.

'OK, but I'm going to run the standby tape to give you longer to recover. And get make-up here now,' I shouted.

I spoke to the director via my mouthpiece.

'Run the standby tape of Naomi Jessup off the ad break. Ledley will have to link into it and we'll get him up to the oncology ward now.'

'OK. I'll get camera four there now,' the director said.

I turned to Ziggy.

'Get Henry and Ledley to the oncology ward now. I need to brief Ledley urgently.'

Ziggy raced off. I looked at my map of the hospital and ran to the ward. Ledley would have to ad-lib the link into the Naomi Jessup interview. There was no time to prepare autocue. But I could at least write Naomi's name in large letters on a card so he got that right.

I saw Henry, Ledley and Ziggy hurrying towards me and camera four was setting up. It was going to be a complete change of mood for Ledley who had been laughing and joking in the kitchen minutes before. I told him that this was a very moving tape of a young woman who was dying of cancer and he must link to it carefully and sensitively. Ledley nodded as I wrote Naomi's name on a large piece of card which Ziggy had fetched for me. Henry put Ledley into position. He had taken off his chef's whites and was wearing a dark patterned shirt underneath which looked all right. Make-up powdered his forehead and cheeks to get rid of his shine as I listened to the PA in the truck counting down to his link. The director had run a thirty second StoryWorld promo straight after the ads and that extra thirty seconds saved us from crashing the link. My heart was hammering because by doing this I was defying Julius. The camera moved in on Ledley's face as he started to speak.

Ledley's intro was sensitive and heartfelt. He got it exactly right. We had four minutes while the tape ran to get Fizzy into position outside the operating theatre for the next interview. She was due to speak to the hospital's head of surgery. We had asked if we could shoot inside the theatre but Connie had drawn the line at that. You could see parts of the surgical machinery through the window. Fizzy looked almost back to her usual self because make-up had put some blusher on her cheeks. The consultant was everyone's idea of such a figure, a distinguished-looking man in his fifties with hair greying at the temples and Fizzy was faintly coquettish as she asked him about his work. This interview led in beautifully to our next pre-recorded package which was the story of Dirk and his amputation. I headed back to the truck and watched as the director played in the Dirk tape. He glanced over at me.

'That was a close-run thing.'

'Yes,' I said.

'But it was worth it. The standby tape was very good.'

'Thanks.'

We made it to the end of the broadcast with Fizzy doing the rest of the links, though we let Ledley distribute his patties and cake to the patients without her involvement as she was still feeling queasy. As the final credits rolled the director and I exhaled with relief; it had been a tense last forty minutes.

'Is she OK?'

'I'm sending her home now,' I said.

I got out of the truck and told Ziggy to get a taxi for Fizzy. Fizzy was sitting by the catering van sipping a bottle of water. Ledley was still in the hospital signing autographs.

'Straight home to bed for you,' I said.

'I think I've got a stomach bug.'

She sounded subdued.

'You were a true pro, as ever, Fizz. Thank you.'

She got to her feet slowly and I wondered if I should send Ziggy in the taxi with her.

'Will Loida be there when you get home?'

She has a cook-cum-housekeeper called Loida who works at her house most days, does all the cleaning and shopping and is protective of Fizzy.

'Yes, she'll be there.'

I saw her into the taxi. Then I walked around and thanked every member of the team for their fantastic efforts. Molly was so happy that her story had been transmitted.

'The director thought it was brilliant,' I said.

'I hope Naomi was watching,' she said.

'How is Naomi?'

'She hasn't got long.' Molly blinked several times to stop the tears that were pooling in her eyes.

I was especially pleased with Ziggy. She blushed when I told her that Henry had said she had acted fast and helped save the day. I then went to find Connie Mears. She was delighted with how well the hospital had come out of the broadcast. We said warm words to each other. I asked Simon to stay behind to help Henry who was overseeing the de-rig of the OB equipment.

I sat down by the catering van with a cup of tea for a few minutes. I had had such an adrenalin surge at the point of crisis that now I felt completely wrung out and I still had the rest of the working day to get through. I knew we had delivered an excellent OB but I had yet to face Julius who had scheduled a meeting to discuss the broadcast back at StoryWorld. Julius hates being defied and I dreaded what awaited me.

As I had expected Julius called me into his office before the meeting on the OB. He launched straight in.

'Why did you go against my express instructions?'

'Before you say anything else you need to know that the Naomi tape was our standby tape. When Fizzy got sick I had to make some extra time for her to recover and that's why we screened it.'

'You chose a tape I had said not to transmit as your standby?'

'Yes, but obviously I didn't think we'd use it. I mean it's the first time I've ever had to use a standby and—'

He cut right across me.

'I'll say it again; I tell you *not* to transmit a tape and yet you make it your standby.'

He was working up to sack me as he had sacked Sal. And there had been an element of defiance in my choice of that as the standby tape. My mind was racing. If he sacked me I would employ a lawyer and fight it every step of the way.

'But it worked fine in context,' I said.

The phone rang on his desk and he snatched it up in a fury. 'I said no calls!'

I heard Martine's voice saying something and Julius said: 'Put him through.'

It was the sponsor. A fairly long conversation ensued in which the sponsor appeared to be heaping praise on the OB and the very moving stories we had produced. Now I felt my legs begin to tremble because if the sponsor was happy I would be spared. Finally Julius put the phone down.

'We have a satisfied sponsor,' he said in a neutral voice.

He stood up.

'The rest of the team are waiting.'

I followed him into the meeting room.

The director of the OB was in there with Henry, the PA and the senior cameraman as well as Bob. The director gave his report. The links had worked well throughout, he said, but if we had had five cameras in operation it would have eased the pressure on the team. He heaped praise on Ledley for his masterly change of mood and said he thought the Naomi Jessup tape was outstanding. I winced when he said that because it was like pouring petrol on the flames of Julius's anger. I was glad Fizzy was not present. She would not have liked how much praise Ledley's performance was getting, his humour in the kitchen and his sensitivity when linking to Naomi's interview. In fact, he had been the star of the OB.

'Well done, Liz,' Bob said.

I felt it was important to act low-key as I did not want to provoke Julius further.

'Thank you, it was great teamwork. Did the sponsor spot Fizzy's wobble?' I asked Julius.

'No, he didn't mention it. What was it?'

'She thinks she's got a stomach bug. She was great to keep going and I'd like to send her a big bunch of flowers.'

Bob looked concerned as Julius nodded.

'Of course; send her all our love.' He stood up. 'My thanks to Liz and the team for their work on the OB; it delivered on its objectives.'

He swept out of the room and Bob glanced at me quickly. He could see that Julius was not happy with me. I headed out of the room and Martine got up from her desk.

'Can we have a quick word?' she said.

'Sure.'

She looked irritated and I wondered what was coming

now. I could feel the vein in my temple throbbing which meant a stress headache was on its way.

'Will you have a word with your new researcher, please?'

'Harriet?'

'Yes. While you were at the OB she was hanging around here, again. It's not the first time she's sought Julius out and she needs telling it's not appropriate.'

'The thing is, she knows him through her father.'

'Maybe, but it's not how we do things here,' Martine said.

'I'll have a word with her.'

'I'd appreciate that.'

Chalk Farm flat, 11 p.m.

Earlier in the evening Flo had asked me again if she could go to the Cat and Mouse with Paige on Friday. She hadn't been rude this time but she was impatient when I wouldn't agree.

'I've had the most full-on day ever, Flo, and I'm knackered.'

I had forgotten to check out the venue or to ask Harriet about it.

'I'll let you know tomorrow for sure,' I said.

This drew a disgusted sigh from her.

'I need to let Paige know,' she said.

'Tomorrow, I promise.'

I must remember to do this tomorrow.

Sitting up in bed, I was exhausted but my mind was active and I wasn't ready to sleep. It was likely that Julius was still furious with me for defying him but the sponsor had loved the OB. When it works, an outside broadcast is live TV at its best and I loved the camaraderie it had created among those of us who had been there. Ziggy had risen to the occasion and showed initiative and I hoped this would build

138

her confidence. I switched my bedside lamp off and stretched out. Simon and Molly had both been commended for their stories and now Molly would stay on at StoryWorld.

CHAPTER FOURTEEN

StoryWorld TV station, London Bridge

Our flagship interview this morning was with a former Labour cabinet member, an eminent man who had come in to promote his memoirs. Fizzy had recovered from her stomach bug and was back on the sofa. She went in hard almost from the top.

'We've heard from an impeccable source that your wife recently had private health care?'

'I'm not here to talk about my wife's health,' he said, glaring at her.

'We heard it was a knee replacement operation,' Fizzy persisted.

'She was in a lot of pain,' he said through gritted teeth.

'But private health care? Doesn't your party argue that that is paying to jump the queue?'

'I'm not here to talk about this.'

He held up his book in front of him as if it was a shield which could protect him from her line of questioning.

'Your constituents have to wait, no matter how much pain...' Fizzy was saying as he stood up, tore the mic from his jacket and walked out of the studio without another word. I raced out of the gallery and saw him as he emerged from the studio red-faced and in a fury. I tried to speak to him but his minder was at his side and she hissed at me: 'What a set-up! You'll be hearing from us.'

I trailed behind them as they headed for the exit but neither of them would accept my apologies or even speak to me. I knew this would cause a media feeding frenzy. The moment the show was over I followed Fizzy to her dressing room. I rarely challenge her straight after a show but today was different.

'Why on earth did you go in so hard on him?'

Fizzy looked startled but Julius strode in at that exact moment and said: 'Brilliant, Fizzy. Great job. We'll be all over the tabloids.'

'It's *not* brilliant at all!' I said.

He had briefed her to do it, of course. She would never have gone in so hard without encouragement from Julius. No doubt he had got the story from some pinstripe-suited friend of his. But I would be the one who would have to stay late to deal with the fallout. The clip of the politician pulling off the mic and marching out of our studio had gone viral. Social media and the tabloids love nothing better than a good old-fashioned spat. I called the publisher to apologise and they were icy cold with me because the memoir had barely been mentioned. As for Twitter, the station was being castigated for showing political bias or praised for showing balls, depending on the political persuasion of the tweeter. I was still taking calls about it at nine p.m.

Earlier I had called Flo at home and explained I was going to be late. Janis had to leave at seven and Flo would be on her own.

'I'm going to order a taxi for you, darling, and you can do your homework here.'

Usually she likes coming to the station and getting a snack from the Hub.

'No need, Mum. I can go over to Paige's.'

'Are you sure?'

I wasn't keen on her doing that but I was under too much pressure to argue. It was nearly ten when I decided I could leave the station. My shoulders and neck were rigid with the tension I'd been holding in all day. I stood in front of my mirror and shrugged my shoulders up and down several times to release the tightness. I headed for the ladies' toilet and as I walked in I heard a woman sobbing behind a locked cubicle door. Nearly everyone had gone for the night and I wondered if it was one of the cleaners. I wanted to be out of there so much but there was something about the quality of the crying that disturbed me. I tapped on the door and asked if I could help. The person stopped mid-sob. Slowly the door opened and Harriet came out of the cubicle. She was a mess, with mascara smudged under her eyes and her lips had that swollen quality you get after a long bout of crying.

'Harriet! What's wrong?'

She went over to the handbasin and splashed cold water on her face. There were no paper towels left and she looked around and went to get a piece of toilet paper to wipe her face.

'Harriet?'

Finally, she looked at me.

'What's happened?'

'Julius Jones assaulted me. Sexually assaulted me.'

I was stunned. We both stood there in shocked silence looking at each other for a long moment. Then I took her to my office and got her to sit down. She slumped onto the sofa and was trembling violently. I poured her a glass of water and sat down next to her and my hands were shaking too. She sipped at the water and hiccoughed a couple of times.

'This happened tonight?'

She put her glass down on the floor and a ragged sigh escaped from deep within her.

'Yes.'

'Here in this building?'

'Yes.'

'Where did this happen?'

'In one of the edit suites,' she said in a tiny voice. She wasn't looking at me.

I felt sick even thinking about it. We don't have a dedicated human resources person at StoryWorld. Any problems on staff welfare fall to our operations director Tim Cooper.

'I better call our operations director,' I said gently.

'No!' Harriet leapt to her feet, kicking over the glass in the process, and water leaked onto the floor.

'You're terribly upset. But we must do this right and I must report it.'

'You're not to tell him!'

She didn't look upset now, she looked furious, and the rapid change in her demeanour was unnerving.

'But this is so serious and—'

'I won't have them talking about me. *I won't!* I told you but if you tell anyone else I'll kill myself.'

She said those exact words. Then she ran out of my office, hurled herself down the stairs and sprinted out of the station. I gave chase but by the time I got outside there was no sign of her in any direction. I went back inside and the security guard looked at me curiously. He had seen Harriet fly out of the building.

'Staff troubles?' he asked.

'Can you call me a cab straight away, please?' I said.

I sensed his eyes following me as I walked up the stairs to get my stuff. I looked down towards Julius's office and it was in darkness. Apart from the security guard the building was empty.

I have never had to deal with anything like this before and sitting in the back of the cab I realised I had mishandled it. Aren't you supposed to get a victim of sexual assault checked by a doctor? And wasn't it my duty to report an accusation like this immediately? But Harriet said I must say nothing. I was so anxious about her. She had looked almost deranged when I said I needed to report it. I rang her mobile twice but it went to voicemail. I was also worrying about what Florence might be up to at Paige's house at this late hour. I felt I would explode if anything else stressful happened to me.

Chalk Farm flat, 11.15 p.m.

The moment I got in I checked on Flo's room and she was lying in bed asleep. I stood looking down at her face, my sweet innocent girl, then crept out of the room closing the door softly behind me. There was no way I was going to be able to sleep. I made a pot of tea and sat at my kitchen table and called Fenton, always my port in a storm.

She listened and understood the significance of it at once, remembering another call I'd made to her seven years before.

'It brought back memories of that night, you know...'

'Of course it would,' Fenton said.

'I felt sickened but you know the first thought I had? That maybe I had led him on and maybe she had too because she's been hovering around him all the time and that thought makes me feel so bad.'

'You did not lead him on and even if she did that is no justification for an assault.'

'I know it isn't. I feel a total cow. I've never liked Harriet but I need to remember she's a young girl and I have a duty of care to her and...'

I had started to cry and couldn't say any more.

'Let those tears out,' Fenton said in her lovely warm voice, which made me cry even harder.

'I think of Flo and of all the predatory men out there and how am I ever going to protect her?' I gulped.

'You're doing a very good job.'

'But what do I do about Harriet? She's forbidden me to say anything.'

'You need to take legal advice. I know a good woman who specialises in cases like this. Take this number down and call her first thing.'

'I will. I keep trying Harriet on her mobile but she's not picking up.'

'Then there's nothing you can do till tomorrow, is there, sweetheart?'

'But she won't do anything silly, will she? She went from tears to rage in an instant and she looked so strange. I'm worried she might do something, you know... dangerous.'

'Kill herself?'

'I know it sounds melodramatic but she said she'd kill herself if I said anything about it to anyone.'

'Leave it for tonight, love. You're feeling anxious but I'm sure she won't do anything.'

I walked around the flat straightening things. I emptied the dishwasher and dried the bottom of the cups before putting them away in the cupboard. I watered the plants on the window sill. It was nearly one but I knew I would not be able to sleep because the incident with Julius seven years ago kept flashing into my mind as a series of vivid images. The moment he had slammed me against the wall was the most vivid of all. I checked on Flo once more and she slept on peacefully. I bent down and kissed her downy cheek and made myself go to bed. I knew tomorrow was going to be a very difficult day.

CHAPTER FIFTEEN

StoryWorld TV station, London Bridge

I was in early and feeling wrung out. I had left the flat before Flo was up. Her school is fifteen minutes away and she leaves it late to fling on her clothes and walk to school with Rosie, her classmate. If only she would spend more time with Rosie, who has two younger brothers, a sensible mum and the added attraction of a dog. Flo used to hang out at their house all the time but she's seen less of Rosie recently. It's the superior attraction of Paige at work. I gave a sharp knock on her door before I left and popped my head round the door.

'I'm getting up,' she said in a drowsy voice.

'I've got to get in early. Your lunch money's on the table. See you later, sweets.'

As soon as I was behind my desk with the door closed I rang the lawyer whose number Fenton had given me. Her phone went to answer-machine and stated that her hours were from eight a.m. so I walked downstairs and spotted Julius entering the building. I rushed into the Hub to get away from him. Ten minutes later I slipped into the gallery to watch Fizzy opening the show. I told the director I was handing over to him. It was rare for me to miss the live transmission.

'Everything OK?' he asked.

'I've got to make a phone call that can't wait,' I said.

'Don't worry, I'll cover for you.'

When I got through to the lawyer she said it would be better for us to have a face to face meeting but I pressed her to give me advice over the phone, said I was happy to pay for her time but I needed guidance at once. I repeated what Harriet had said to me last night but gave no names.

'What alarmed me the most was her saying she'd kill herself if I reported the incident.'

'And have you said anything to anyone?'

'No I haven't,' I said, thinking that Fenton didn't count. She was the most honourable person in the world.

'Good, because you have a duty of confidentiality here. Under no circumstances must you confront the accused man. That would be a breach of confidentiality and would muddy the waters of any future action.'

'I have no intention of confronting him! I want to know what I should do, what's the right thing to do.'

'You must reassure your employee this is entirely confidential until she makes a formal complaint. Sexual assault is a criminal act and you should encourage her to report it to the police. The Metropolitan Police has a specialist unit called Sapphire that deals with rape and sexual assault. It would be worth you looking it up. There's a lot of guidance on their site.'

I wrote down the details she gave me.

'I'll do that.'

'Tell your employee nothing can happen until she makes that formal complaint to the police.'

'OK.'

'It's also a good idea to note down what she said last night, as precisely as you can, as an aide-memoire for your eyes only. Do this straight away. It's so easy to forget exactly what is said in these situations.'

'And what should I do about her today? She's not answering her phone. Should I go round to her house?'

'I would advise against you doing that. I suggest you tell her to take the day off but that you will need to speak to her soon.'

I thanked her and she said she was available for further advice and would invoice me. As I put the phone down I realised I would have to pay for this legal advice personally. I couldn't claim it as a work expense.

I started an email to my home address on everything that had happened last night. Outside the office I saw Simon arrive at his desk and pull his rucksack off. He looked over at me as if to come in but I shook my head. I noted down the words Harriet had used. She had given me few details of what had happened but she had said that the assault took place in an edit suite downstairs. I noted down the time I found her in the Ladies' cubicle and how she had clearly been crying for a long time. I wrote that I hadn't seen Julius in the building after about seven-thirty that evening, but I was stuck in my office fielding calls from the media and he could have been in the building. I described how Harriet had reacted so dramatically when I said I should report the assault to our operations director and how she had run out. I dated the document, sent it to my home email and deleted it off the StoryWorld system at once. Then I called Harriet again. Her phone went straight to voicemail so I left a message saying she should take the day off and I reassured her I had spoken to no one about what she had told me. I ended by saying please call me as soon as she felt strong enough to do so.

I found the link to Sapphire, the specialist unit run by the Met. I wondered if this was set up in the wake of all the complaints about how the police treat rape victims. There was a list of frequently asked questions and definitions of assault. Sexual assault was defined as if someone intentionally touches another person, the touching is sexual and the person does not consent. Serious sexual assault entailed penetration so what Julius did to me with his fingers that night would count as that.

There was also an interactive graphic called My Decision. This was a step-by-step guide to what you should do if you had, or knew a person who had been sexually assaulted. I clicked on the button: *I know someone who has been assaulted*. This took me through to questions like: *How can we preserve evidence?* Too late for that, I thought. There was a button on *Information about the Havens* and I clicked on this. The Havens turned out to be three sexual assault referral centres in London. They were open twenty-four hours a day, seven days a week and were managed by King's College Hospital. They were independent of the Met and it said that they would not share information with the police unless the victim wanted them to. I took down the details.

It was time for the morning meeting and I was dreading walking into that room with Julius at the head of the table. Harriet's allegation and my memories were scouring my mind. I was going to find it a huge challenge even to look at him. I reached the meeting room and slid into my seat, busying myself with the running order of the day's show. I'd called down to the gallery when the credits were rolling and the director told me that the show had gone according to plan. Tim Cooper was there today. He rarely attends these meetings as he's not a programme maker. He is the person who will have to deal with this when Harriet reports her allegation. He is a company man through and through and not big on sensitivity.

Julius, who never misses a thing, asked me why I had missed the show and I mumbled that a pressing staff issue had arisen. Then I raised my eyes to his face and held my look, even though my heart was swooping and dipping. He didn't react in any unusual way at all.

'As I predicted, StoryWorld is all over the papers,' he said with satisfaction.

He had spread a pile of newspapers on the meeting table. Fizzy and Bob were turning the pages and she was elated at the number of them which featured her looking pert and the former Labour cabinet member looking murderous. How could Julius be acting so normally when he had assaulted a young girl? He pushed *The Times* over to Fizzy.

'That's a good shot,' he said.

Thoughts were knocking around my head like a ball in a squash court. Perhaps he didn't do it? It was only an allegation. Perhaps Harriet had lied?

'I like this one best,' Fizzy said, holding up the *Daily Mail*.

But why would she make up something like that? And she had been dreadfully upset, almost deranged. The headlines above the pictures of Fizzy were all anti-Labour except for the *Daily Mirror* which was more critical of Fizzy's line of questioning. I was expected to coo at all this coverage but could not say a word. Harriet had already lied to me, hadn't she? She said she was going to visit her granny in hospital when she was actually going to a film premiere. But this was a lie of a different order. Surely Harriet wouldn't, couldn't, lie about something as serious as this. It could be career-ending for Julius if it was true. It could mean prison!

'All good PR for the station,' Julius said. I remembered how he wouldn't take no for an answer when he had come on to me. That was seven years ago. Now he was an even more powerful man and Harriet was twenty years his junior. If I had found it difficult to push him off me how much more intimidated would she be? I recalled the sound of her sobbing. Something very bad had happened.

Now Julius was saying he had asked Tim to join us because we needed to start a process of cutting the budget for the next six months. Bob and I exchanged glances at this; it was so like Julius to spring this on us.

'Ad revenues are down again this quarter,' he said.

'I thought you'd made some good deals on sponsorship,' Bob said.

'I have but I can't work miracles. Over to you, Tim.'

Tim said cuts had to be made across the board and he had come along to update us on the process of identifying what those cuts should be. I have a decent amount of money to hire in freelancers and without it I couldn't produce the amount of TV we do with my tiny in-house team. Every year I have to fight to retain this particular pot of money. Tim had opened a folder of spreadsheets and he pulled out my features budget and laid it in front of me.

'The features freelance budget will have to be cut, Liz,' he said.

'No!' I said.

I'd said it loudly and Tim looked pained.

'I beg your pardon?'

'I can't accept *any* cut if you expect me to produce the same amount of output. I need every penny I've got to keep us on air.'

Tim shot a look at Julius.

'The news budget is getting cut too,' Julius said.

'Oh, is it?' Bob said.

'Bob's team is three times the size of my team. I *have* to be able to hire in freelancers.'

'And you think I don't?' Bob growled.

Julius put up his hand.

'I'm not going to continue with this now. We wanted to give you a heads up that a cut in budget is required from *all* teams. I will have one-to-one meetings with you this week and we can go through the figures in detail then.'

'Good plan,' Tim said.

'Fine by me,' Bob said.

My face was hot and I did not trust myself to say anything. The men were closing ranks as they always did. I remembered their smart executive toilet with the three hand dryers and the ladies' toilet last night with Harriet searching for a paper towel to dry her face. Julius picked up his papers; his signal to us that the meeting was over. I rushed from the room. I could hear Bob and Tim talking about last night's football. I was not ready to face my team so I walked downstairs and out of the building.

I strode along by the river away from StoryWorld, sat down on a bench and thought about Julius and Harriet and Julius and me. Seven years ago I had not reported him. The only action I had taken was to write him a letter. It was Christmas and I was in Glasgow with Mum and Flo and I had spent the days agonising over what words to use. In the end I wrote as truthfully as I could about how his actions on the night of the party had made me feel. I acknowledged that I had responded to his kisses at first but then he had tried to push things too far, too fast and he should have stopped at my first 'No'. His roughness and his insistence had frightened and upset me. I read the draft over the phone to Fenton. She said I was taking on too much responsibility for what had happened but I had been as direct as I could and it was how I felt. I put the much amended letter into an envelope, wrote *Private and Confidential* on the front and sellotaped it shut. Then I slid it under the door to his office on the morning I knew he was returning to work. My Christmas had been ruined.

The first time we saw each other was excruciating. I did not know how to respond to his laconic greeting as a group of us were sitting down for an ideas meeting on our second day back. The other people around the table were sharing tales of their Christmases, of family rows and food catastrophes and there was lots of laughter and I couldn't join in. All day long I was on tenterhooks that he would be aggressive or embarrassed towards me or something, but he never made any reference to my letter or to the night of the party. Slowly, gradually, it became easier to be in a room with him and after about a year I no longer felt awkward. I never forgot the incident, how could I, but I stopped thinking about it all the time. We went on working side by side as colleagues. I pulled out my mobile and texted Harriet:

I hope you got my message this morning. Look after yourself and please text me you are OK. Liz

Back at base I called the team in for our regular meeting. Ziggy had joined us, which she does once a week. She had shaved her hair very close that weekend and Simon had been teasing her about it, calling her a suede-head. It made her look more vulnerable, almost ill, and she was looking strained and anxious, I thought. I told them that Harriet was poorly and wouldn't be in.

'But she is coming back?' Ziggy said.

'Yes,' I said, although I didn't know if that was true. Would Harriet come back to StoryWorld?

I kept the meeting short. They got up to leave and Simon hovered by the door, holding it open for Molly and Ziggy to go out.

'You OK, Liz?' he asked.

Simon picks up when I'm not all right and there was no point in pretending everything was fine.

'I had a bad night last night and I'm feeling shaky today.'

'You were here late, weren't you?'

'Very late.'

'Anything I can do to help?'

My mobile pinged and it was a text from Harriet. I clicked on it at once. All it said was: *Got yr msg. I'm OK. H*

I stared at the screen for a moment. Then I became aware that Simon was waiting for me to say something.

'Will you do the recipes with Ledley? I don't feel up to it. I think he said he wanted to do a spicy soup.'

'Sure thing.'

I reached for a post-it note and wrote down the name of the oil which Julius had banned.

'And check he doesn't use this brand of cooking oil. Do it discreetly but he mustn't use it.'

'No problem. You should try to get away early. You look knackered,' he said.

Chalk Farm flat, 11 p.m.

I feel so low tonight. I had a horrible row with Flo. She asked again about going to the Cat and Mouse with Paige and I said no way was she going. I said it far too emphatically. I should have been more diplomatic and given my reasons. The truth was that I hadn't even checked the venue out; I just had the strongest feeling that I did not want her to go there with Paige. She is fourteen and has no idea how predatory some men can be.

I listened at her door and all was quiet within. We hadn't spoken since she'd screamed at me. I went into my bedroom

155

and called Fenton and it all came tumbling out.

'Horrible, horrible day. I'm feeling paralysed by guilt and shame and unable to focus on anything. I have a fourteen-year-old daughter. What if a man had sexually assaulted her? I would do something then, wouldn't I? But Harriet has made this accusation and I've done nothing.'

'But there's nothing you can do until Harriet makes a complaint,' Fenton said.

'I know, and I must speak to her, explain that to her.'

'Did you see Julius today?'

'He seemed completely normal this morning. I told him I was dealing with a staff issue and there wasn't a flicker on his face; not a flicker.'

'You've often said he's a complete chameleon.'

'But would he honestly assault the daughter of Edward Dodd? He's such an operator. He knows how power works. Wouldn't his instinct for self-preservation kick in?'

'He nearly raped you.'

'I was a woman without power,' I said.

'Oh, darling, you sound so low.'

'I am low. I feel like I want to run away from this, from everything, really.'

'Is everything else OK?'

'Flo and I had a screaming match. She called me a hideous hag!'

Fenton laughed. 'Sorry, love, but that girl of yours does have a way with words.'

I smiled in spite of myself.

'What was the row about?'

'I won't let her go to a music club with this sixteen-year-old who lives over the road. I'm not keen on this girl but I didn't handle it well.'

156

'Why aren't you keen on her?'

'She's very knowing and she treats Flo like she's her little follower. And Flo is so grateful if Paige pays her any attention. Her parents are out all the time and I get the impression that she's allowed to do pretty much what she wants.'

'Difficult; the glamorous older girl...'

'I wish Flo had never met her. And this thing at work, I don't know, I just didn't want Flo going out with her.'

'Your Flo loves you to bits no matter what she says when she's angry.'

'She loves you, her aunty Fenton. Will you come and stay soon? I'm in serious need of your good sense.'

'I can come this weekend if that suits?'

'I'd love that.'

We agreed she would come on Friday night. I know I am leaning on Fenton too much, calling her all the time about my problems and not asking her about hers. I'm not sure I have the capacity at the moment to be needed back if she did confide her troubles. Some friend that makes me. I heard a noise coming from the garden and Mr Crooks darted through the cat flap with a clatter. It was the foxes again; they were having a fight in the garden next door and one was trying to scrabble up onto my wall. I saw the fox's pointed face as it reached the top looking for a route to escape. It ran along the wall and disappeared into darkness. Mr Crooks wound himself around my legs and I stroked his head.

CHAPTER SIXTEEN

StoryWorld TV station, London Bridge

I have rarely felt so little like coming into work. There was a feeble part of me that wanted to call in sick and lie in bed under the duvet with a good novel and read myself out of this feeling of horrible anxiety. But home is not an easy place either as there is near silence from Flo. The Cat and Mouse gig is happening tonight and she feels deeply aggrieved that Paige will be going along without her and that she will be missing the event of the year! I told Flo that Fenton was coming for the weekend. Flo loves Fenton but I got no reaction from her this morning. When Fenton comes to stay I put her in my room and I get in with Flo. When she was little she loved to share a bed with me but this time I thought I should make up a bed for myself in the sitting room.

I put in a call to Harriet first thing and there was still no pick-up from her. I asked her to call me mid-morning when I would be out of the meeting and we could talk confidentially. There was guidance I needed to share with her, I said. As I put the phone down I reminded myself that it is my duty to encourage her to go to the police and when she does all the bricks will come tumbling down. I dread what lies ahead. If Julius is accused he will lash out at me just as much as at Harriet. The phone rang and I picked it up fast thinking it would be Harriet. It was Henry, our floor manager.

'Gerry won't come out of his dressing room. Says he can't go on air!'

'What?'

'He's locked the door and I think he means it.'

'I'm on my way.'

I rushed down the stairs and along the corridor and stood outside the dressing room that Gerry uses. I tapped on the door.

'Let me in, Gerry; it's Liz.'

There was no answer but I could hear movement from within.

'Come on, love, let me in.'

I heard him moving behind the door, a pause, and then he unlocked the door and stood there facing me. He was crying hopelessly.

'Anwar's left me.'

I took him into my arms and hugged him.

'I can't go in front of the camera. I can't do it.'

He had been crying for a while. His eyes were bloodshot and his nose and lips were red and swollen. I gave him another squeeze and stood back.

'It will all be over in fifteen minutes and then you and I are going to go out for a walk and get a coffee and you can tell me all about it.'

'I can't, Liz. I hoped I could, but not today. I just can't.'

'Yes you can because you know how much your audience loves you.'

I rubbed my hands up and down his arms and nodded encouragingly. He gulped and twisted his hands together.

'But I look a fright.'

'We'll get Ellen in here super quick and say you have a bad cold, OK?'

Ellen had patched him up as best she could with concealer but Gerry still looked puffy around the face as he sat down on the sofa next to Fizzy. The showman in him kicked in as soon as they came out of the ad break.

'Got the most frightful cold, darling, but didn't want our viewers to miss my predictions for next week,' he said.

'You're a star, Gerry. Over to you,' Fizzy said.

Gerry launched into his forecast. I watched him for three minutes then slipped out of the gallery and hurried upstairs to Julius's office. He was sitting on his sofa watching the show on the large TV mounted on the wall. Most of his office is high-tech with its ergonomic desk and designer German desk lamp but his chair is an aged leather Baedekar which he's had for years. None of our offices come anywhere near to Julius's. He was scribbling notes on his pad as I walked in and I steeled myself to speak to him.

'I'm going to have to miss the morning meeting. Do you want me to send Simon along to cover?'

'Why?'

'Gerry's had some bad news and I've promised to spend time with him, as soon as the show is over.'

'What bad news?'

'Personal stuff. I need to get back to the gallery now. OK?'

He was looking at me curiously and I was finding it hard to return his gaze. I looked at my fingernails instead.

'You know it's my job to look after the presenters, to make them feel cherished,' I said.

'And what about you?'

'What about me?'

'Are you OK?'

'Yes. Why do you ask?'

'You've seemed on edge all week,' he said.

'It's been one hell of a week.'

'OK. Get Simon to cover the meeting.'

Gerry and I walked along by the river. He had put on a pair of sunglasses and as he talked tears continued to slip down his cheeks.

'We've been fighting for months, over the money thing, you know. But this time it's different. I'm sure he's met another man.'

He stopped walking and his shoulders shuddered as he was gripped by a deeper bout of crying.

'Poor love. It's so painful.'

'Don't know how I'm going to go on without him.'

He blew his nose on a large cotton handkerchief. We walked on. This whole area of the riverside has been transformed over the years I've been working at StoryWorld. There used to be stretches that were near derelict. Now trendy cafés and galleries and gift shops compete for attention. I suggested a coffee shop I knew that was tucked away from the riverfront and we settled ourselves into a corner.

'And my finances are blown, you know. He cost me *so* much.'

'That couldn't go on, could it?' I said.

'No, it could not. He's a taker, through and through.'

His despair was turning to anger which I thought was probably a good thing. He picked up his large cup of cappuccino and took a gulp.

'He was totally self-obsessed, like all actors are. Never asked me about how I was feeling,' he said.

'Do you have any family close by? Somewhere you can go this weekend?'

'My friend Dennis is in town. We were going to a musical with him tonight.'

'That's good. How do you know Dennis?'

'We were at school together; he's my oldest friend. He lives in Bath and comes up several times a year.'

The first few days after a split are the worst, but I remembered how weekends go on being difficult when you are newly on your own.

'Is he staying at yours?'

'He was going back on a late train but I could ask him to stay, I suppose. He doesn't know about Anwar yet.'

His voice wobbled.

'Do that. When I split up with Ben I found having a close friend around helped so much,' I said, thinking of Fenton.

When I got back to the station Ziggy was sitting on her own. I asked her if there had been any calls for me and she said Betty had called. She was looking pinched and worried, as she has for the last couple of days, and I asked her if everything was all right. She said it was but her face and her body language said the opposite. Something is troubling her and I sat down in Harriet's seat.

'You know I haven't forgotten about finding you a course to go on. I've sent for details for one that looks good.'

'Thanks.'

'And we will pay the course fees, you know.'

'That's cool. Thank you.'

She didn't look much happier.

'Is Harry any better?' she asked.

'She's still poorly,' I said.

'But she is coming back?'

'Oh yes.'

I went into my room. I wish she would confide in me what it is that is troubling her. It may have nothing to do with work, of course, but she has asked about Harriet twice.

It was about an hour later when Fizzy appeared at my office holding a posy of pale pink roses which she handed to me. We have fresh flowers in the studio every day. It is one of the things that Fizzy insists on. Some studios opt for fake flowers which can look OK on camera but Fizzy always says they look cheap and nasty. A fresh posy is delivered to the station every morning at six-thirty and is placed in a vase on the table in front of the studio sofa. Most days Fizzy takes the posy home with her, though sometimes she gives it to Ellen or Martine. Today I was the recipient.

'They're lovely. Thanks.'

Fizzy was wearing a sky blue wrap-over dress that fitted snugly over her breasts and hips and she perched herself as she always did on the arm of my sofa. It's as if she doesn't have the time to sit down. She often has this weirdly manic quality to her; either that or the times when she does a languorous slump. There is no in-between state with Fizzy.

'Is Gerry OK?' she asked.

'He's in a state. He split up with his partner last night.'

'I thought it might be something like that. He did look awful this morning, poor old thing.'

'Less of the poor old thing, if you don't mind, he's not much older than me.'

She smiled at that.

'We all need to rally round and support him through this break-up,' I said.

'Of course. You know I'm awfully fond of him.'

'Will you suggest going for lunch or dinner next week? I know that would mean a lot to him.'

'Yes, ma'am.'

She did a mock salute.

'And where's Harriet? I haven't seen her around for a

couple of days.'

I wondered if that was the reason she had come to see me.

'She's poorly and I told her to stay home till she feels better.'

Fizzy stood up and smoothed her dress over her stomach and hips. I sensed she wanted to say more to me so I smiled at her and said: 'What have you got planned this weekend?'

'Oh, nothing special.'

There was a droop to her lips as she said this. Of course Bob would not be available to play at the weekends.

'Shall *we* do a lunch next week?' she said.

'I'd like that.'

'Friday?'

'Perfect.'

'I'll take you to my club,' she said.

It was late afternoon when Harriet finally called me. She spoke quietly and she sounded subdued.

'I'm so glad you called. How are you?'

'I've been sleeping a lot since, you know...'

I went through the details I had learned over the last two days; that she needed to report the assault to the police, to the specialist unit at the Met. I told her about the Havens too; how she would get confidential support from them.

'Until you make a formal complaint to the police I can do nothing here,' I said.

She made no comment or even a sound as I talked and at one point I asked her if she was still there.

'Yes, I'm listening,' she said.

There was still that strange detached tone of voice from her. I had expected tears or anger, not this quietness which unnerved me.

'I hope that's all clear, Harriet.'

'Yes, very clear, thank you.'

'You'll think about this.'

'I'm not going to report him to the police.'

She had said it quietly but firmly.

'Why do you say that?'

'He's such a liar and the woman always gets the blame in these cases. I can't face it.'

'Please think about this. There's a dedicated team at the Met now. Take down the website and check it out.'

I spelled out the links to Sapphire and the Havens but I sensed Harriet was only noting them down because I had asked her to.

'I can't talk any more. My father is due home any minute.'

'Have you told your parents?'

'No way. I have to go now.'

'OK. Take care of yourself and please keep in touch. Feel free to call me at any time at work or at home.'

I gave her my home number again and I could hear a man speaking to her. I assumed it was her father. She clicked off the connection without saying goodbye. The whole conversation had been out of kilter and I wondered if she had taken a tranquilliser or a sleeping tablet.

It was nearly four when Julius called me.

'Let's do the budget meeting now. Can you bring me a printout of your annual spend?'

I couldn't face being in close proximity to him for an hour or more. It was bound to be a long drawn-out meeting, with Julius haggling over every line.

'I can't at such short notice. I have to get away sharpish tonight.'

To my surprise he didn't argue.

'Monday afternoon then; have a good weekend,' he said.

He sounded so normal and so reasonable. Could this be a man who had sexually assaulted a young woman in an edit suite?

Chalk Farm flat, 8 p.m.

Fenton arrived at eight. I had prepared the ingredients for a pasta carbonara because we all love that and I could throw it together in twenty minutes once we were ready to eat. Flo was standing at my side slicing the tomatoes for a salad. She was still barely talking to me. I watched her fierce concentration as she sliced the tomatoes into perfect rings and was filled with a rush of tenderness towards her. Fenton arrived in a flurry of bags and hugs. She pulled out two bottles of Malbec wine for me, my favourite, and a present for Flo wrapped in pink tissue paper. It was an upright black velveteen hand that you could stand on a table and use the outstretched fingers to hang rings and earrings on.

'I love it' she said and hugged Fenton.

Fenton is so good with Flo. She would have made a great mum and it is one of the great sadnesses of her life that she can't have children.

Chalk Farm flat, Saturday

I wanted us to have lunch out as my treat. I'm conscious that Fenton has less money than me because she works for a charity. She would feel awkward if we went somewhere pricey so I suggested we went to a noodle place in Camden Town.

166

'Why don't you ask Rosie along?' I said to Flo.

We picked Rosie up on the way and sat on the benches and ate our bowls of fragrant noodles with chopsticks. Flo had painted her nails dark blue and Rosie took a picture of them for her Instagram account. Fenton pulled a gift card out of her wallet.

'I'm in desperate need of a pair of boots. There's nowhere to buy good boots in Folkestone and Mum gave me this gift card. Is there one of these near here?'

Flo looked at the card. 'They've got a shop in Hampstead.'

'It's up the hill, we can go there,' I said. 'And what about you two? Do you want to come?'

Rosie had been scrolling through her smart phone and showed it to Flo.

'I want to see that,' Flo said.

It was the latest in a dystopian trilogy and was showing at the Odeon in Camden. I gave Flo the money so that she and Rosie could see the film and I could be alone with Fenton. I was rewarded with a peck on the check and the girls hurried out of the noodle bar talking non-stop once out of our earshot.

'She's a great kid. No problems there,' Fenton said.

'She appears to have forgiven me. It must be your benign influence. Come on, let's go boot hunting.'

We walked to Hampstead up the long hill. It was an invigorating walk with clouds scudding across the sky and red and amber leaves tumbling from the trees.

'I had this strange stilted conversation with Harriet. She says she won't report Julius because she'll be the one who'll be humiliated if she goes through with it.'

'She has a point. That happens way too often,' Fenton said.

'I know it does but I can't do anything if she stays silent. It was like she wanted to get off the phone as quickly as she could. She said very little and I didn't even get to ask her if she was coming back to work.'

'Poor kid.'

'The thing I'm still struggling with is that Julius would know that Harriet, as the daughter of Edward Dodd, has the protection of her class.'

'And you think that would deter him?'

'I'm sure it would. It's horrible to think that he'd have less restraint if it was a woman with no connections, but I think that's how it is with him.'

'How truly vile.'

'You know he comes from a modest background and he's worked hard to reach the top. Why would he jeopardise everything he's worked for?'

'Maybe he's become so used to wielding power that he feels nothing can touch him,' Fenton said.

'I guess so. And of course I didn't report him. I'm feeling shitty about that.'

'You're too quick to take responsibility when things go wrong.'

'But if I had reported him...'

'You think this wouldn't have happened?'

'Yes.'

'There you go again; shouldering the blame. You've done nothing wrong.'

Flo approved of Fenton's choice of boots. They were knee-high burgundy leather, a close fit and less practical than the style Fenton usually buys.

'Mum, I need a pair of boots too,' Flo said.

'Do you?'

'I'd really like a pair of Doc Martens.'

Doc Martens were a change in style for Flo. She has always been a girlie girl. The image of Paige flashed into my mind. I had seen her last week when I came out of Chalk Farm Tube. It was her shock of white hair that caught my eye. She was standing outside the Roundhouse with two men; one of them could have been her father. She was wearing a short tartan skirt and black Doc Marten boots.

'That will have to be a Christmas present. They cost over a hundred quid,' I said.

Chalk Farm flat, Sunday

I roasted a chicken with all the trimmings: carrots, parsnips, runner beans, stuffing balls and roast potatoes. I opened one of the bottles of Malbec Fenton had brought. I love to cook a roast and lay the table to look nice. It makes me feel like I'm being a good mother. I refused to let Fenton help so she sat and watched me and told me about a case she had recently resolved successfully. Her work entails getting legal assistance for refugees and helping them to settle here. I poured Malbec into her glass.

'You love your work.'

'I do,' she said.

'I envy you that.'

'You like yours too, most of the time. It's just tough at the moment.'

'What do I do? Fill the morning hours with chatter for tired mums and shift workers.'

'It's more than that.'

'Is it? It's a case of bread and circuses, isn't it? Distract people from their problems,' I said.

'Come on. You've run health campaigns...'

'That's one of the few things I'm proud of.'

'This is you feeling low, darling.'

'Maybe; but I still think Mum despises what I do.'

'You don't know that for certain.'

We had talked about this before, how my mum would have preferred me to be a teacher or a social worker.

'I'm not sure I'm fit for any other kind of work now,' I said.

'You stay there to give Flo a good home. That's heroic in my book.'

'Thank you.'

I don't think Fenton realised how much it meant to me her saying I was heroic. It felt like a vote of confidence and I needed that very badly with everything that was going on.

The meal wasn't ready until two-thirty and Fenton said she would need to leave by five to get back to Folkestone. She had spent the whole two days shoring me up and it was only in the last hour she was there, when Flo had retreated to her room, that she started to tell me about a man she has fallen for. Fenton sees at first-hand the terrible conditions of people arriving at Dover, often in container trucks, and this is how she met Bill. He's a detective in a unit that investigates the trafficking of people and crimes associated with illegal migrants.

'The real stumbling block is that we've got such different views on refugees. He thinks they're on the make and that I'm a soft touch,' she said.

'Is he a hard man?'

'He makes out he is but I've seen him with his son and there's a tender side.'

She ran her finger round the top of her glass.

'I don't see how it could work really, but I am so attracted to him.'

'And...?'

'I think the feeling's mutual.'

'I love the early stages; when you feel terribly attracted to a man but you don't know if anything is going to happen.'

We clinked our glasses.

'Go for it and be happy, darling. You deserve it,' I said.

It had been such a tonic having Fenton to stay and I didn't want her to go. I walked with her to Chalk Farm Tube and we hugged each other and agreed we would do a short holiday together straight after Christmas while Flo was staying with Ben. As I walked back I thought about Fenton in love; ahh, that explained the sexy boots.

Later that evening Flo joined me in the kitchen and sat at the table to work on a school assignment on endangered species, a subject close to her heart. I pulled the remains of the chicken from the carcass and decanted the leftover vegetables into a big bowl. I would make bubble and squeak on Monday night. Maybe put a poached egg on top. I recalled how I once roasted a chicken for Ben in the early days of our relationship. I hadn't realised the giblets were in a plastic bag deep inside the cavity of the chicken and had put it in the oven without taking them out. Once it was roasted Ben had started to carve the chicken, complimenting me on how good it looked. And then he discovered the giblet bag and fished it out on the carving fork. I was mortified and told him not to eat it; I'd poisoned it with cooked plastic! But Ben said the meat would be fine and he teased me about it for years.

I was thinking about what Fenton had said; that I didn't have to feel so terrible about what had happened. As long as

I did right by Harriet and impressed upon her the need to report the assault there was little more I could do. The doorbell rang and my heart sank.

'Are you expecting someone, sweetheart?' I said, praying that Paige hadn't decided to drop by to shatter our Sunday evening cosiness, which was a rare enough event these days.

'No, nobody.'

I went to the door and Harriet was standing there, several steps back from my entrance, outlined by the light thrown from the street lamp. I was shocked to see her. She was all buttoned up and belted in a trench coat with the collar up and she was shivering.

'I hope you don't mind me coming here.'

'Of course not. Come in, come in.'

She followed me into our hall.

'I best take my boots off; I've been walking on the Heath.'

'It's good to see you.'

She unzipped her boots and I couldn't help noticing they were made of the most glorious soft black leather. She followed me into the living room. It could have been an awkward moment but Flo was pleased to see her and Harriet was friendly back. I took her coat. Underneath she was wearing a black polo neck and skinny black jeans and she stood in her stockinged feet looking around.

'What a lovely room.'

Flo got up and showed her our little garden through the doors at the end. The outside lights were twinkling along the walls.

'That's so pretty.'

'Can I get you a hot drink, or a glass of wine if you prefer?'

'A small glass of wine would be nice, thanks.'

'Is red OK?'

'Thank you.'

She sat at our table and I poured us both a small glass of the remaining Malbec. We wouldn't be able to talk in front of Flo but her turning up was highly significant. No member of my team has ever been to my flat. I wondered how she had found my address. That didn't matter. What mattered was that she had sought me out and I hoped it meant that she trusted me. She asked Flo what she was working on. I watched Harriet's face as Flo explained her assignment. She was writing up the case of the northern white rhino, she said. Flo pulled up photos on her tablet to show her. I have always found Harriet uncommunicative and as I am a person who is drawn to talkative outgoing people I think this makes me underestimate quieter more reserved people. She was listening to Flo and her face was calm and I couldn't work out what she was thinking.

'There's only one male left in the whole world, in Kenya. He's being guarded against poachers. So sad, isn't it?' Flo said.

'Awful. There are some evil men in the world.'

Harriet flashed me a look as she said this and I made a small nod. She asked me how Simon, Molly and Ziggy were and we had a superficial conversation about work which skirted around the thing we needed to talk about. It started to rain and we heard the drops against the windows.

'I better go. I'll get a taxi home,' Harriet said.

'Where do you live?'

'Islington, I'm still at home with the parents.'

That surprised me; at twenty-six, I assumed she would have her own place. She took out her phone.

'Do you need a local number?' I said.

'No thanks, I've got an account.'

'I'm glad you came round.'

It wasn't until the two of us were standing on the pavement waiting for her taxi under my large StoryWorld umbrella that she told me what she had come to say.

'I've been in therapy for a while, and my therapist told me I must stop running away from things.'

'You told your therapist what happened?'

'I tell her everything. I saw her on Friday.'

'How are you feeling?'

'A bit stronger.'

The taxi drew up at the pavement. It was a glossy black Mercedes, no Uber cars for Harriet, I thought. She moved to go but I put my hand on her arm.

'Does this mean you're going to report Julius?'

'No, I can't go through with that. But, I've thought about it and I'd like to come back to work tomorrow.'

CHAPTER SEVENTEEN

StoryWorld TV station, London Bridge

Julius wasn't in this morning and Bob chaired our post-mortem meeting. As we came out of the room I saw how he watched Fizzy walking away down the stairs. She swings her hips as she walks and I often feel that although she is thirty-eight she has the demeanour and body language of a much younger woman. He is clearly smitten.

'You had your budget meeting yet?' he asked me, dragging his eyes away from Fizzy.

'No, I've got that pleasure this afternoon.'

'Be prepared. He's determined to cut.'

'By a lot?'

'Five to ten per cent.'

'Sod that!'

'He said it's time to thin out the teams.'

'If my team got any thinner it would disappear. Where is he this morning anyway?'

'Don't know. He called last night and said he couldn't get in till later.'

Bob's intelligence was useful but it made me feel anxious. I would need to be ready to argue at my meeting with Julius. I was glad he wasn't in as it gave me time to assess how Harriet would cope with being back at work. I was determined to watch him like a hawk at their first encounter. As I walked back to my team I saw Harriet standing by her desk. I raised my hand to wave at her and then thought that might be too revealing. From the team's point of view she had been away because she was ill and now she was back, no great cause for a fuss. She was dressed in a navy blue dress with long sleeves with white cuffs and a white Peter Pan collar. She had put her hair up into a bun. Looking at her it occurred to me that Harriet expresses how she feels in the way she dresses. It may not be conscious but last night it was the belted trench coat with the collar up for our impromptu meeting and today it was this outfit. There was something self-dramatising about her demure mode of dress.

'Good to see you back,' I said.

Ziggy was being solicitous, offering to get her a drink from the Hub. Harriet smiled her thanks but said she was fine. I wondered why Ziggy was fluttering around Harriet in this way. Surely Harriet would not have confided in Ziggy? That didn't make any sense. I asked the researchers to come into my office for a quick meeting as I had to do work on the budget. As soon as they were seated Simon said an idea had occurred to him that morning after seeing a poster at the Tube station.

'I thought we could do a StoryWorld panto,' he said.

There was a puzzled silence.

'Not a real panto, of course, but in December we could construct a whole show around a panto theme. The presenters could act out certain roles. Fizzy could be Cinderella in her rags and Ledley could be Prince Charming and Betty the Fairy Godmother. They'd all be in costume and we could dress the set. I think it could be a lot of fun.'

We spent the next ten minutes throwing in ideas about how this could work. I said we'd have to think up a good role for Gerry because he was a born performer; he could be Buttons perhaps. Molly wondered if we should go so far as to write the script in rhyming couplets? I was pleased when

Harriet made a suggestion saying Ledley could cook a dish that reflected the theme, pumpkin pie, for example. I was grateful to Simon for suggesting the panto idea. It had generated a cheerful discussion and had helped Harriet ease herself back in after her absence.

'What a lovely creative lot you are. Here are your research briefs for the week. Off you go. I've got to do detailed budget work now.'

I pulled the figures up on my screen and scanned each budget line. No way was I going to agree to a 5 per cent cut or any reduction in my permanent team. I would have to agree to a smaller cut. I had not yet replaced Sal's comedy slot. Buying in talent like Sal was expensive as she wrote original material for us each week. I could live without it and replace her with a sofa expert who would cost less. I wondered about returning to the idea of employing a fashion journalist. About three years ago there had been talk of employing Amber, who was then dating Julius, to present a segment on fashion. I had had one meeting with her and we had discussed some ideas, including how she could analyse trends and offer advice on creating designer looks for less. It was cheap-to-make TV as we could use promo stills for celebrity-style tips. I was keen on the idea although I had not warmed to Amber. Then, when I discussed it with Fizzy, she had resisted any notion of employing Amber as a presenter. Julius hadn't been keen either. Maybe he thought it was too close to home. If I was to get the idea through now I would need to find a male fashion expert. I was sure Fizzy would have no objection to that.

Mid-morning, the phone rang. It was Connie Mears from St Eanswythe's.

'I'm sorry to have to tell you that Naomi Jessup died in the early hours of this morning.'

'Oh no.'

'It was peaceful. I wanted to ask you to thank your employee Molly Dorff. It was clear to us all that they had connected and Molly's visits gave her comfort.'

Visits? I hadn't realised that Molly had been visiting Naomi since the outside broadcast.

'I'll pass that on.'

I planned to tell Molly in the privacy of my room, but as I looked over to the team I could see that she already knew. She had gone white. I came out and took her by the hand and led her into my room, closing the door. She sank onto the sofa and covered her face with her hands and wept. I sat next to her and stroked her back gently.

'Connie Mears said that your visits were a comfort to Naomi,' I said after a while.

Molly sat up straighter.

'She saw her interview,' she said.

'She saw it go out?'

'No, she was having treatment that morning. The next evening I took my laptop in and showed it to her. She liked it a lot.'

'That was a kind thing to do and I'm glad she saw it.'

'Me too.' Molly's voice wobbled.

After she had gone I thought how that put our problems into perspective; that poor young woman, dead at thirty-three, a life completed too soon.

At lunchtime Simon, Harriet and Ziggy went out to lunch together. Simon had suggested they go to a café nearby to work more on his panto idea but Molly had chosen to stay behind. She was writing, typing fast and with a don't-come-near-me concentration.

It was about half an hour before I was due to meet with

Julius when I got a call from Martine.

'We're going to have to move your budget meeting to tomorrow. He's not coming in today, after all,' she said.

I knew it wasn't worth asking if anything was up. Martine guards Julius's privacy as if she is dealing with state secrets. It has been one of the sources of conflict between us. She gave me a new slot for the next day.

At the end of the afternoon I asked Harriet to pop into my office.

'How's it been for you today?'

'It was good to see Si and Moll and Zig,' she said.

'It was good to have you back.'

She pulled at the cuffs of her dress.

'Where is he?'

'He hasn't been in today. But he'll be back tomorrow and you need to prepare yourself for that.'

Her face is not an open book like Molly's. It is partly her hooded eyelids that give her face a closed look and I couldn't tell if she was upset.

'And you still don't want to take this any further?'

'I don't. I can't,' she said.

'It's not a question of can't. I hope you know I'll support you. I won't let him bully you.'

'I just want to go on working here.'

Did she think that if she reported Julius she would get the sack? This made me feel uncomfortable as she is only here on a three month trial and she has few enough employment rights.

'If you change your mind you must let me know. You don't have to suffer this in silence.'

We had got through the day but Julius would be back tomorrow and sooner or later she would encounter him. I looked through my door to the desks outside. Simon and Molly had gone for the day but Ziggy was still sitting there. She was doing that hugging thing she does which makes me feel uneasy, wrapping her arms around her thin frame and rocking back and forth in her chair. Something is troubling her.

'I'll see you tomorrow,' Harriet said.

'Yes, see you tomorrow,' I said, feeling I had failed her somehow.

Chalk Farm flat, 8 p.m.

I made the bubble and squeak, my own version of it using the leftover roast potatoes and vegetables from Sunday. My mum would always make it the traditional way, using cabbage and mashed potato and lots of pepper. She would shape the mixture into round cakes, dust them with flour and fry them until they were crisp and golden brown. I remembered how much Dad loved that dish.

As I cooked I was thinking about the first year after Ben and I split up. Flo and I were getting used to living in this flat without her dad and she kept getting ill. They were minor ailments, but the sort that meant I couldn't send her to school or leave her with a childminder. I had to take days off work to look after her, often at short notice. I remember feeling terror that StoryWorld would use my absences to get rid of me. Over the years I had seen other team members despatched on flimsy grounds. I had taken on a huge mortgage and hanging on to my job had never been more important. I was sleeping badly and had started to do obsessive–compulsive things like checking three or four times every night that I had locked the front door or turned off the gas hob. I would be lying in bed and had to get up to check on these things even though I *knew* I had locked the door and turned off the gas. I had an overwhelming feeling of being on my own and of carrying too heavy a load.

Flo got ill again for the fifth time in as many weeks. It was a sore throat and temperature and once we were through that I booked an appointment with my GP while Flo was at school.

'I want to talk to you about Florence. I'm wondering why she's getting ill all the time. Can it be because of the separation?'

I listed her various illnesses.

'These are normal childhood ailments. She'll have picked these up at school.'

'She never used to get ill all the time.'

'She's building up her immune system and she'll be fine. I'm more worried about you.'

'Why me?'

'You appear to be under a lot of stress.'

I could feel tears pushing up but I held them in and swallowed hard.

'I do feel horrible a lot of the time,' I said at last.

'Are you experiencing any kind of symptoms?'

Gradually she coaxed them out of me. I shared my feelings of anxiety, my shortness of breath and my obsessive–compulsive actions.

'These are all symptoms of general anxiety disorder. I'm not going to prescribe you antidepressants though. I'm prescribing a holiday instead. It's clear you need a break.'

'I can't possibly go away. I've been missing too many days as it is.'

'That's the anxiety speaking. The roof won't fall in if you take a week off work. Book a package holiday, somewhere

181

where you can spend time with your little girl and do the simple things, plus get lots of rest. If you're calm she'll be calm.'

'I wish I could.'

'Please take a break, soon. Stress is a killer. It can take years off your life. If you can't get away I can recommend a course of meditation which may help.'

She's a brilliant doctor who refuses to reach for the prescription pad. I thought about what she said but I did not take her advice. I soldiered on for the next few weeks feeling shaky and out of control until one morning my anxiety reached such a pitch that I couldn't leave the flat or walk Flo to school. I was dizzy, as if I was standing on a tall building and might throw myself off. This scared me and I called my doctor.

'You sound short of breath,' she said.

I was trying to gulp in great mouthfuls of air and my heart was beating too fast.

'I can't breathe properly,' I said.

'I think you're hyperventilating.'

She talked me through how to deal with it and I went to see her again. That afternoon I called work and said I had to take one week's leave of absence, unpaid if necessary. I said an urgent family matter had cropped up. It had got to the stage where I was beyond caring what they thought any more.

I found one of those last-minute holiday sites and booked a budget hotel in Brittany. Flo was excited by the large Brittany Ferries ship we travelled on and the fact that the ship had its own shop. We spent a week sitting on a beach and I threw myself into building elaborate sandcastles, complete with a moat. One afternoon Flo and I got so absorbed in the task that we accumulated a small group of French children who helped us in the construction. They ran to get seawater in their buckets and as fast as they poured the water into the moat it sank into the sand and yet still they ran to get more water.

In the evenings I would find a harbourside café and Flo and I ate moules and frites most nights. I got into bed early and Flo snuggled up against me as I read to her. While she slept next to me I read my way through two novels and that was a treat. It was our first holiday without Ben and it was all right. When we got back to Chalk Farm I put an ad in the local paper and that was how I found Janis.

What I realised tonight is that one of the subterranean causes of that horrible period of anxiety must have been what happened between Julius and me. I had pushed it down and refused to think about it. But that doesn't work, does it?

CHAPTER EIGHTEEN

StoryWorld TV station, London Bridge

Julius was back this morning; he did not look well at the meeting and was clearly feeling irritable. There were dark shadows under his eyes and his jaw was clenched. At one point when Bob was holding forth he started to drum his fingers on the table. Martine had told me that our budget meeting would be straight afterwards so we left the meeting together and walked in silence to his office. He opened the door for me and motioned me to sit in front of his desk.

As I sat down I said: 'That young woman with cancer, Naomi Jessup, died yesterday.'

He gave a slight flinch at this and seated himself with a sigh.

'That's tough.'

I wondered why I had told him that. It could have reactivated his hostility towards me but I wanted him to know that our screening of her story had been timely and a good thing to do.

Martine had given him a copy of my budget. He stared down at it for a minute or two and I could feel tension building in me. Since Harriet's allegation, being alone with him makes me feel hugely uncomfortable.

'I'm not going to waste time. Our revenue is down the last two quarters. You will have identified the cuts you can make so I suggest you share them with me.'

'Is it a blip?'

'What?'

'The problem with the revenue; or are we talking something more permanent?'

'I doubt advertising will ever get back to former levels. Come on. What have you got?'

I offered up half the cuts I had identified the day before. These amounted to 1.5 per cent of my annual budget. A cold smile flickered on his lips as he scanned my list of cuts and I experienced a wave of revulsion against him as I imagined him with Harriet in the edit suite. I wondered if he knew that she had confided in me and if he felt any guilt at all. The atmosphere between us was crackling with tension.

'You know you can cut more. Bob's budget has taken a five per cent hit and he's had to let go of people.'

'He started from a better place than me.'

'That's arguable. News is more expensive than features.'

We both wanted the meeting to be over. He was distracted and had glanced at his watch twice. It is one of those absurdly expensive watches that you see in glossy magazines, often modelled by Hollywood A-listers.

'Do you want to hear my arguments?' I said.

'No I do not. Get the cuts up to three per cent and I'll sign off on it.'

I offered the further cuts that I could live with. Julius reached for his pen and initialled the lines that would be cut. He signed the bottom of my budget and pushed it across the desk towards me.

'You've been let off lightly,' he said.

I felt a small bloom of satisfaction that I had been cut less than Bob – if Julius was telling me the truth, of course. I stood up.

'Oh, and Liz?'

'Yes?'

He pulled my latest expenses sheet from a drawer and tapped at it.

'This has got to stop.'

He was pointing at the clothing expenses I had signed off for Gerry and Betty to buy pastel-coloured shirts and tops.

'But we asked them to change their wardrobe.'

'Tough. They want to be on the sofa they can bloody well supply their own clothes.'

We paid for Fizzy's on-screen clothes, so she was in that special category of indispensable. He cared less about the other presenters. Martine must have seen that I was about to leave because she came to the door.

'Julius, it's the hospital on the line.'

His face changed and the budgets were forgotten.

'Put them through,' he said.

I left his room and stood at Martine's desk. I recalled that his brother Steven had been ill.

'How is Steven doing?'

'He's worse. He's had to go into hospital.'

'I'm sorry to hear that,' I said.

'Julius needs our support' she said.

Back in my room I stood at my window and stared at the streets below. Julius was under pressure. Bob has to get rid of some members of his team and that meant times were hard indeed and it would lead to gossip in the Hub and a tremor throughout the station. I doubted any of my team felt truly secure in their jobs. I asked Molly to join me.

'Moll, I wanted to tell you that I've been thinking about your Naomi interview. It's a brilliant piece of work and I'm going to enter it for an award.'

She flushed with pleasure because more than anything Molly wants to be a film-maker.

'Thank you. I hope it helped other people, you know, who are facing stuff.'

'I'm sure it did.'

'I'm off to see that non-fiction publisher. I should be back by three,' she said.

We get a lot of our story ideas and our interview guests from non-fiction books; memoirs, of course, but also books on history and sport and science. Molly likes doing these and she has built up a solid group of contacts with publishers.

'Stay off politicians for now, please,' I said.

'Point taken.'

We smiled ruefully at each other.

At lunchtime an email from Todd appeared in my inbox. It was after ten p.m. in Sydney and he told me that he'd spent the day at hospital with his dad. His father was having chemotherapy and it was unnerving to see his once strong father looking so frail. His father was not going to get better. He wanted to tell his dad he loved him but the words had got stuck in his throat and they'd spent his whole visit talking about sport. He needed to find freelance work soon or he would go nuts. His mum was in pieces, and sitting around in his parents' house all day was doing his head in. He ended his message with *I miss you*. X. It was a more emotionally revealing email than any talk we had ever had. I was missing him too, even though we had not seen each other that often. Fenton thinks that I held back from getting too deeply involved with Todd because my relationship with Flo has to be the primary one.

I came out of my office and Simon was sitting on his own with a pile of printed-out emails on his desk.

'How are you getting on?'

'OK, but I wanted to ask your advice on which letters we should go with.'

Betty was launching her Focus on Life Crises series with an item on coping with a new baby.

'It's not my greatest area of expertise,' he said.

He pushed three letters over to me.

'I've got it down to these three. They're interesting in different ways but we can't do them together. You'll see when you read them.'

I sat down next to him in Harriet's chair and read the letters. The first two dealt with straightforward new baby problems. The mums who had written to Betty described the challenges of feeding and sleeping routines, sore nipples, exhaustion, a reluctance to have sex, a tendency to weepiness as well as fierce joy. They were vividly expressed and reminded me of my first weeks with Flo. In the third email a young mum had written about her post-natal depression and it was on a different level altogether. She wrote how she had no feelings for her baby whatsoever and she asked Betty if she was a monster to feel like this. It amazes me how candid some of our viewers are with their problems and it is a big responsibility for us.

'We *have* to do this one, don't we?' I said, handing him back the post-natal depression email. He read it again.

'She'll have to take up the whole slot if we go with this one,' Simon said.

'You're right. We couldn't put a happy mum and baby letter next to it.'

'That's what I thought.'

'If she thinks it's too dark she can go with the other two, which are good letters. It's her series, after all. Where are the others?'

'They're downstairs in the guest dressing room. Harry brought in a bag of clothes for Zig, stuff she doesn't wear anymore, and Zig wanted to try them on.'

'That was nice of her. She dresses beautifully, so lucky Ziggy.'

Ziggy was the last person in the team that I had expected Harriet to make friends with because they come from such different worlds and have such different expectations of what they are entitled to. There was something going on between those two that I couldn't quite fathom. Had Harriet confided in her? Later, when they came back to their desks, I could see that Ziggy was wearing one of her new acquisitions, a pale grey jumper with a boat neck that looked big on her with her thin little neck and shaved head. Simon must have made a comment because I saw her smile shyly.

Ledley has asked to see me tomorrow, said he'd give me lunch at his café and that there was an issue he needed to discuss with me. He wouldn't be drawn on what it was but said it was something good.

There was no sign of Julius this afternoon so Harriet has been spared an encounter with him. I feel the trouble of it bubbling under the surface all the time.

Chalk Farm flat, 8 p.m.

Flo had period pains this evening and she was grumpy. I filled her Peter Rabbit hot water bottle and took it through to her.

'Put this on your tum, it might help.'

She lifted a tragic face towards me.

'Thanks, these are the worst cramps I've ever had.'

'Poor baby.'

I sat down on the edge of her bed.

'Things aren't so hot at work at the moment,' I said.

'Why, what's happened?'

'They're cutting all the budgets and some of the reporters will have to leave.'

She looked alarmed.

'You're not going to get the sack, are you?'

I had forgotten how much of a catastrophist a fourteen-year-old can be.

'No, not me; but it shook me up all the same. It's a difficult time to be made redundant; two months before Christmas. And there aren't the jobs in TV out there.'

'Is Harriet staying?'

'For the time being she is. She's on a three month trial.'

'I like Harriet.'

Flo wriggled down under the duvet clutching her hot water bottle.

'I *wish* I could have my Doc Martens before Christmas.'

'Honestly, Flo, I just told you people are losing their jobs and you want a pair of hundred quid boots early!'

She looked aggrieved.

'I want to go to sleep now.'

I hurried out of her room and closed her door too sharply.

'Now who's slamming doors?' she shouted from her bed.

My feelings for her are often this weird mix of irritation and love.

I got the ironing board out and started to press Flo's school shirts. Ironing calms me. When hers were done I started on my tops. Red is my colour, usually the darker shades: burgundy, aubergine and crimson. I occasionally splash out on something scarlet; usually when I'm feeling excited or happy. When I started going out with Ben I was on a high and I bought myself a bright red leather biker jacket. God, I loved that jacket. It was the most I had ever spent on an item of clothing and now it's tucked away at the back of my cupboard. I'm not light-hearted enough to wear it at the moment.

I sat in bed later and wrote a long email to Todd which was mainly about what was going on at work. I made no reference to Harriet's allegations though it was the thing that was worrying me the most. Nor did I mention the death of Naomi Jessup from cancer. I told him I was missing him too and I was. Having him in the background of my life during the last two years had brought me more comfort than I had realised. I have all these people relying on me who I have to guide and comfort but no one other than Fenton who I can turn to. But that's just the way it is. My mum would say that I made my bed and I have to lie on it.

CHAPTER NINETEEN

StoryWorld TV station, London Bridge

Betty had decided to discuss the two happier mum and baby letters which surprised me. Baby talk is not Fizzy's thing but this morning she made an effort to engage with the advice Betty was giving.

'A new baby can feel like a thunderbolt in your life, a complete transformation of what went before,' Betty said.

'A nice thunderbolt though?' Fizzy asked.

'It's like a watershed; life before baby arrives and life after. It changes you.'

I wondered for a moment if Fizzy was getting broody and I felt vaguely sad for her because at thirty-eight and without a settled relationship I doubted if she would be a mother now. The item finished and I went out to thank Betty. She told me she had written back to the depressed mum saying she most definitely was not a monster and enclosing a list of forums that offered support to mothers with post-natal depression. She is good like that.

I caught the Tube from London Bridge and arrived at Ledley's café in Balham around one. He was in a buoyant mood and took me upstairs to his flat. He had prepared us a large platter of jerk chicken with rice and peas on the side. Ledley doesn't drink but he wanted me to have a glass of rum punch. Slices of orange and a large cherry floated on the top of my drink.

'This is gorgeous. So what did you want to discuss?'

He smiled broadly.

'I've been offered a deal by a food manufacturer. They want to use my name on a marinade. They're gonna call it "Go Luscious with Ledley"!'

'That's terrific news.'

It was a long name for a product but maybe long names were in vogue.

'You can use it with meat and with fish. They told me it's gonna be stocked in supermarkets and they want me to front up their ad campaign.'

'That's great, Ledley.'

'Yeah, and they've asked me to come up with ideas for giveaway menu cards and I thought I should clear it with you.'

There had been that trouble with the cooking oil product placement and it hovered in the air between us.

'Sounds brilliant and the more coverage you get the better. But we will need to be careful that we don't use your marinade on the show.'

Ledley looked disappointed.

'What, never?'

'We have to keep a clear line between editorial and advertising,' I said.

He picked at the chicken on his plate.

'Are you having a launch?' I asked.

'Oh yeah, they've got big plans for a launch.'

'Fantastic. We'll get Fizzy and Gerry along to that and there's no harm in you mentioning the launch on air, only the once, mind,' I said.

When I got back to StoryWorld I put in a call to Julius to tell him about the Ledley deal. In the past I would have walked down to his office and told him face to face, but not now. He said fair play to Ledley and our conversation was over quickly. Outside my room I saw that Harriet was typing on her laptop. She peered at her screen and chewed on her nails and her whole demeanour was troubled. I came out of my office.

'Is everything OK?' I asked.

She turned a strained face to me and immediately I thought about Julius. Had they had an encounter while I was out?

'I'm struggling with this brief,' she said.

'What's it about?'

'Brad Robinson, Friday's guest. I don't know why we're interviewing him.'

Harriet had a point. Brad Robinson is an actor in a long-running soap but there was no real reason to be interviewing him this week, except for the fact that his wife left him recently in the most public way to go off with a younger man on a rival soap. The tabloids had been running the story all week, as they do when they scent pain and humiliation in a celebrity life. I had been approached by his agent to have him on the show. I'd asked if we could talk about the marriage breakdown and she'd said approach it discreetly and don't make it the first question. Harriet said she didn't know how to phrase a question that would allow Fizzy to do this.

'You start off with a question about his soap role and how it has developed over the years; maybe even run a clip of his finest hour when he won an award,' I said.

'I saw he'd won an award. It was ages ago though.'

'Doesn't matter. It was a storyline about his character fighting alcoholism and it was powerful stuff. Then you put in a question like: You've had years of being in the spotlight,

Brad, but have the last few weeks been especially difficult? That gives him an opening if he wants to talk about it.'

'But what if he doesn't?'

'I think he's coming on our show precisely to get sympathy from the viewers but he doesn't want to look too overt about it,' I said.

Harriet nodded slowly.

'So it's a kind of game?'

'Sort of...'

I had a guilty pang as I recalled that last week Gerry had analysed the breakdown of Brad Robinson's marriage from an astrological point of view.

'He's the wronged party here. I don't think he'll dish the dirt on his wife but I'm sure he'll reveal his torment,' I said.

'I see. OK.'

I didn't want Fizzy bawling her out over her brief again.

'And make sure you list the more lurid claims from the tabloids about the break-up, for background. Fizzy under stands the rules of the game.'

'I will. Thanks for the help.'

There has been a significant change in Harriet's behaviour. I've noticed that she stays physically close to the team these days. She lunches with Ziggy or Simon most days and there is no more of her roaming around the building which she did when she first came here. I hope I've done the right thing by staying quiet about her allegation. Yet again Julius is getting away with his vile behaviour. Molly looked up at me.

'Liz, Naomi's funeral is next Tuesday. I'd like to go and her mum said they'd be happy for me to be there. Can I take a half day's leave?'

'I wouldn't hear of you taking leave and it's a credit to you that they want you there.'

It was around four when I got a call from Gerry. He has got into the habit of checking in with me regularly since he broke up with Anwar.

'Liz, did you get my script?'

I could tell from his voice that he was feeling low.

'Yes thanks; it's a good topic.'

His topic of the week was about how resilient different star signs are when confronted with emotional difficulties.

'Glad you liked it. You know we Pisces are the most sensitive in the Zodiac,' he said.

'How *are* you doing?'

'I can get through the weeks OK, work and stuff you know, but the weekends are absolute torture. Everywhere I go I see couples doing stuff together; being happy together.'

I recognised that feeling, the conviction that other people had made a better job of relationships than I had and the sense of failure.

'You're bound to feel like that for a while but it won't last.'

'Doesn't feel like that.'

'I've been there. I promise you there comes a point when you start to feel good about being on your own rather than trying to make a relationship work that just couldn't.'

'I'm so sad. We did have our good times, you know.'

His loneliness was thrumming down the line at me and I wondered if I should offer to see him on Saturday as Flo was due to be in Portsmouth with her dad. He's a friend as well as a colleague and the split was recent. But I didn't suggest it. My reserves of compassion had run dry and I needed a weekend on my own with no demands from anyone.

Two hours later I locked my office and saw Harriet in front of me heading home. She reached the top of the stairs and was walking down to the exit as Julius was starting to walk up. They saw each other and she stopped in her tracks. Then she continued down the stairs with her face turned conspicuously away from him. This was the woman who when she arrived had been skipping down to his office at every opportunity and who showed boundless confidence. Now she looked positively cowed by his proximity. They passed each other without a word and he continued up the stairs, though more slowly. He saw me standing at the top and our eyes met and held. He knew I had seen their encounter on the stairs and I was at a loss at what to say.

'Good night' was all I could manage to gasp out.

Something has happened between them. There can be no doubt about that.

Chalk Farm flat, 7.30 p.m.

When I came out of Chalk Farm Tube the wind was up but at least the rain had stopped. There's a red-brick Victorian church at the bottom of our road which has stood empty for years. As I walked past tonight I saw a sign saying that the church was going to be developed into flats. I gazed up at the building which has always dominated this area. It has arched windows running down both sides and a huge wooden door covered with graffiti. I wondered if the developers were going to pull the church down or transform it internally and leave the exterior intact. I didn't like the idea of the church being demolished.

Flo was on the phone and went into her room as I came in. I put three sweet potatoes in the oven to bake and phoned Fenton for an update on her relationship with the sexy detective. Things have progressed and they are going away this weekend for three nights in Amsterdam. She sounded happy and excited.

'We're getting the Eurostar and Bill has found us a hotel right on the canal.'

'Sounds romantic,' I said.

Fenton spends all her time looking after others and she deserves more than anyone to have some happiness. But as I put the phone down I felt a bit bleak. It had highlighted my sense of being on my own. I tapped on Flo's door.

'Do you fancy a baked sweet potato?'

'Mmm, yes please.'

She joined me in the kitchen. She had eaten at five with Janis but Flo is tall and able to eat what she wants without putting on an ounce. She was in a good mood.

'I got an A for my project on the northern white rhino.'

'That's fantastic. Can I see it?'

She went into her room and returned with her folder. She opened it at the last page.

'Look what the teacher said.'

Her teacher had written at the bottom of the project: *This places the plight of the northern white rhino in context and highlights the implications for species survival. Excellent work.*

'Well done, darling. You've made me feel very proud.'

The sweet potatoes were perfect, with lashings of butter melting into their orange flesh. I served them with goat's cheese and broccoli but left the broccoli. It was the warm earthiness of the potatoes I had craved. Fenton once said I cook more comfort food than anyone she knows.

It was around nine when Grace called me.

'Have you heard from Ben this week?'

'Not yet.'

'Only he was supposed to come over to eat with us last night and he didn't show.'

'He hasn't told me whether he wants Flo to come down this weekend. Has he got a big job on?' I asked.

'I don't know. Let her come down on Friday night anyway. Pete and I will meet her at the station. And if he rings you'll ask him to call me, won't you?'

Grace sounded worried. After Flo's casino comment I wondered what was going on in his life. For some reason a memory came to mind of an autumn day when Flo was five and Ben and I had taken her to fly a kite on Parliament Hill Fields. The kite had been my birthday gift to Ben and I'd bought it at a specialist shop. It was a rectangular box kite with one end green and the other end bright red. Ben was determined to get his new kite flying even though there wasn't much wind that day. To begin with he had held Flo by the hand and they had run down the hill with Ben holding the kite aloft. They couldn't get up enough speed to launch it even with her little legs pounding down the hill. So I sat on a bench at the top with my arms clasped around her as he laboured up and down that hill until he finally got the kite up into the sky and I cheered and Flo clapped. It's important to remember the happy times we shared.

CHAPTER TWENTY

StoryWorld TV station, London Bridge

We got through to Friday without further drama. Gerry was in and I went down to make-up to see how he was doing. Ellen was plucking his eyebrows and she rubbed in a little bit of cream to make them lie smooth.

'Thanks, darling,' he said.

He swivelled round on his chair.

'I've been telling Ellen I'm going to a luxury spa this weekend. I'll be off straight after my slot and blow the expense.'

'Good for you,' I said.

'I have more spending money these days, for obvious reasons.'

'Every cloud,' Ellen said.

She was in on the drama of Gerry's life too. There are few presenters who can resist sharing their woes while their make-up is being applied and their outfits titivated.

For our lunch Fizzy had booked us into a small private dining room at a club where she is a member. It was in Soho and you would have walked by without knowing it was a club, so unobtrusive was its brown front door. Inside it was all narrow twisty staircases and dark wood-panelled rooms that could have graced a novel by Dickens. It was just the two of us in a room at the top. The waiter was wearing one of those long white aprons and I asked for a red wine and Fizzy ordered a

Virgin Mary. He left the room briefly. When he returned he opened a wooden hatch in the room and our drinks were pulled up by pulley and presented to us on a silver tray.

'So good,' Fizzy said, sucking deeply on her straw. 'Thanks for inviting me here. It's nice that it's so private.'

We consulted the menu which was self-consciously retro with dishes like shepherd's pie with braised turnips and semolina with raspberry jam for pudding. I chose the fish pie and Fizzy asked for an omelette with herbs.

'We've known each other a long time, haven't we?' she said.

When Fizzy joined the station as a PA I had been a junior researcher.

'And I've always admired how you cope with everything, Liz, especially after you and Ben split up.'

This turn in the conversation was so unlike Fizzy.

'That's kind of you to say so.'

'How do you do it?'

'Oh, I have my wobbly days, believe me.'

'You never seem to show it.'

My fish pie was good, creamy with chunks of salmon and cod and the occasional prawn. Fizzy was toying with her omelette. She took one more mouthful and then pushed the plate away from her.

'You haven't eaten much. Was it dry?'

'It was fine. I want to ask your advice but this has to be *totally confidential*.'

'Of course.'

She wiped her mouth on her napkin and folded it twice neatly along its original seams then folded it again. I sensed her trepidation and I stopped eating.

'I'm pregnant.'

'Wow! I wasn't expecting that.'

'Nor was I.'

She gave me a rueful smile. The thought hurtled into my head that it had to be Bob's child. I reached for her hand.

'How many weeks are you?'

'I'm not entirely sure: seven or eight, I think.'

She touched her left breast and then her right one.

'But these boys are getting bigger.'

'Was that why you were sick at the OB?'

'It must have been. I did the test straight after.'

I squeezed her hand.

'Are you happy about this?'

'I'm very conflicted about it.'

'Tell me.'

'Part of me wants this baby. But I'm not married and, well, I can't go public about the father.'

'OK.'

'I'm scared I'll lose the support of viewers and if that happens I know what Julius will do. Goodbye my slot on StoryWorld.'

'Does he know?'

'I told him yesterday and he advised me to have a termination.'

'As if it's as easy as that!' I said.

'I know.'

'Did you have a scan?'

'I haven't done any of that stuff yet.'

'And Bob, what does he say?'

She gasped and her eyes widened in alarm.

'You know about Bob?'

'Yes.'

'Oh my God, is it that obvious?'

'I saw you two going into a hotel one afternoon.'

'We were spotted. Christ!'

She was agitated and turned in her chair to face me full on.

'You mustn't tell anyone, Liz. Really. We *can't* have Bob's name getting out. Julius thinks the father is Geoff.'

'I won't say a word.'

'Promise me.'

'I promise.'

'I let him think it was Geoff's,' she said.

Fizzy had been involved with Geoff for several years which was why Julius had made that assumption. Geoff was also married.

'But what did Bob say?'

She picked up the folded napkin and slapped it against the edge of the table.

'He said he's crazy about me but his kids are still at home and he has to see them through till they go to college. He's got two girls in their teens.'

'He needs to think about you too, Fizz.'

'He's in a bad place at the moment. He's heard a rumour that Julius is going to cut the news operation even more, turn the bulletins into three-minute celebrity news round-ups and do a deal with a newspaper for the headlines.'

'I can't see that happening. I think he's being a bit paranoid there.'

'Maybe, but what it comes down to is he doesn't want this kid. He wants to stay married and if I go ahead I'm on my own.'

'Do you want this baby?'

'It's my last chance pregnancy, isn't it?' She rested her hands on her stomach. 'Yes, I think I do.'

'OK.'

'But I don't want to be shunted off to a mother and baby slot in the afternoons. I love my job. I can't bear the thought of losing it.'

I am cursed with this need to fix things.

'You know, I think the thing to do is to front it up. Speak directly to the viewers. Say you made a mistake and got pregnant by a married man. You deeply regret that and will never reveal his identity, but you want this baby very much. We can get our viewers onside.'

'You think so?'

'I'm sure of it,' I said.

'I'm not sure.'

'Give yourself time to think about this, Fizz, please.'

Her face was sad as she asked me if I wanted a coffee. I sensed she wanted me to stay longer with her.

'That would be nice.'

She yanked on a rope pull by the wall, another affectation of the club. The waiter reappeared and she ordered a coffee for me and a peppermint tea for herself.

'They have lovely glass teapots here,' she said.

The waiter left the room.

'If I do go public I can see Betty giving me the third degree. You know her view on unmarried mothers.'

'Bugger Betty!' I said.

She looked at me, surprised, and then she started to giggle and that set me off and we laughed and laughed and I felt closer to her than I had ever felt before.

CHAPTER TWENTY-ONE

Chalk Farm flat, Saturday

Ben had been in touch finally and we arranged for Pete to pick Flo up from the station on Friday night. Grace rang to say she had arrived safely. That was the cue for a major slump on my part. I was worn out by the events of the last few weeks and I lay in bed until mid-morning. I thought about Harriet who had left the station on Friday night looking cowed as she passed Julius. And then I thought about Fizzy and the decision facing her. She has two powerful men trying to influence her, playing on her fears about what will happen to her career if she goes ahead with the pregnancy. There are few enough mothers who are senior women working in television. It's been written about: how it's less than the national average. It's partly the long hours and the assumption that you don't leave work until the programme is ready. But you also get sucked into thinking that working in television is a privilege; it puts you at the centre of things and that is a difficult thing to give up. Ranged against these forces was the tiny life fluttering inside her.

This afternoon I took a walk along the canal towpath from Camden to Islington. I like this walk, though you have to be aware of a few psycho-cyclists zooming up behind you. The narrowboats along this stretch are well-kept and jaunty. Most of them are painted dark green or blue with decorative name signs picked out in scarlet and yellow lettering. A few of the decks had piles of logs neatly stacked for the wood-burning stoves within. You can peer through the windows and get a glimpse of the lives lived there. Part of me thinks it would be delightful to live in such an unusual space. Then I think about what it would feel like coming home on a dark night and walking along the towpath. It feels a sinister place here at night.

I have been caught out many times in my life by taking action when I'm in emotional turmoil. I needed to weigh up the evidence of Harriet's allegation of sexual assault as objectively as I could. There was that encounter on the stairs between Harriet and Julius, the way she turned her face away as if she couldn't bear to look at him. And she has changed since that night I found her sobbing in the Ladies. She is less confident than when she arrived at StoryWorld. She sticks closer to the team, which has actually meant her becoming more of a team member and more likeable. It is this change in her behaviour which reinforces my belief that something bad has happened to her, an experience that has fundamentally shaken her sense of herself.

Ziggy has changed too. She got a lot of praise for showing initiative at the OB and she was starting to come out of her shell. But she has looked pinched and anxious the last few days. She was supportive to Harriet when she came back to work and they have become unlikely friends. Either Harriet has confided in her about Julius and the assault or, possibly, Ziggy overheard a conversation. She gets around the building in her role as our runner. Something is definitely up with Ziggy.

I had reached Islington and I walked up the metal stairs and onto the high street. I stopped to get a tea and a rose-flavoured macaroon and sat at a table in the window looking out at the shoppers on Upper Street. Harriet told me she lives in Islington, with her parents. It's probably one of those grand Georgian houses down by Highbury Fields which cost millions. I don't think she'll go to the police now. If she doesn't report Julius he'll get away with it. Again. I bit into the macaroon and my mouth was filled with an intense perfumed sweetness. Another thought occurred to me: Julius does not come down to my office any more, not since the night of the incident. We are on the same side of the building and he used to saunter down a lot. Not any more. He's avoiding Harriet. We think we can read people but can we really? I had read that an accomplished liar can look you in the eyes and lie and lie. Julius tells lies. Even his name is a lie; he was plain Nigel Jones until he reinvented himself.

I caught a bus back to Chalk Farm and went upstairs. I was turning it all over as we chugged down the hill towards King's Cross. Two children were running shrieking up and down the aisle of the bus while their mother made feeble attempts to stop them. There was what he did to me at the Christmas party seven years ago. I don't like to think about it but I have to. Our kisses had turned too quickly to him pushing his fingers up me. He was rough and insistent and had made me bleed and he wouldn't take no for an answer. Fenton thought I should have reported him then. How I wish I could discuss this with her again but she's in Amsterdam with her sexy detective.

I reached my flat and unlocked the door. I hate the way Julius made me feel seven years ago and I hate the way he often makes me feel now, that I'm a pushover and powerless. He'll never admit when he is wrong about anything. Nothing ever seems to dent his power and his mantle of untouchability. Julius did it. I'm sure he did it.

I woke up and I knew what I had to do. I had Saul Relph, our MD's home email address. It was Saul Relph who had asked me to take Harriet into my team as a favour to his friend Edward Dodd and I had a duty of care to her. I cannot report Harriet's allegation because I don't have her permission to do that but I can tell him what Julius did to me.

I opened my laptop and typed in his address. I wrote CONFIDENTIAL FOR YOUR EYES ONLY in the subject line. In our business there's a mantra: never put anything in writing that can be used against you in the future. But what was the alternative? Saul Relph is a remote figure and I could never talk to him about this. It would be excruciating to say it to his face. Writing it down would give me some control. My skin prickled as I started to write the details of what had happened between Julius and me. I struggled with how much detail I should include. He is the overall boss of StoryWorld and whatever I wrote would be out there in the world in black and white for ever. But he needed enough detail to know how serious the incident had been. I said I had been at the Christmas party and described how Julius had followed me upstairs and had slammed me against the wall; how he had said 'Come on, Liz. Let's fuck hard'; how he wouldn't take no for an answer and had been rough with me. How I'd had to push him off me to stop intercourse taking place. I read through my draft several times. It was strangely cathartic to see it written down. I deleted the reference to 'Let's fuck hard'; that was a detail too far.

My finger hovered over the send button. If I sent it the MD would know my shaming secret. If I didn't send it Julius would be off the hook, again. He has been allowed to bully us all for years. I brought to mind the way he had sacked Sal and the last time he had snarled at me. I was steeling myself to press the send button. If I didn't send it I would have given up on the values I once held and absorbed the corrupt values of the TV station. No, I would wait. I needed to be sure before I lobbed this hand grenade.

Chalk Farm flat, Sunday evening

When Flo got back from Portsmouth the first thing she said was: 'Granny was crying.'

'Grace? What was that about?'

'I don't know and she tried to hide it when I came into the kitchen but she'd been crying for sure.'

'That's not like her at all. I hope she's OK. I'll ring her in a bit.'

'And Dad was in a weird mood all weekend. He looked awful, Mum, he hadn't shaved and he didn't want to go out.'

'Oh, darling, was it a difficult weekend?'

'I'm glad to be home.'

I hugged her.

'I'm glad to have you back.'

I put my nose against hers.

'Grasshopper kiss.'

Then I kissed each of her eyelids.

'Butterfly kiss.'

She smiled. It was a thing we used to do when she was little, though we hadn't done it for ages.

When she was tucked up in bed with her tablet I went into my bedroom and called Grace. She said she would call me back soon; she couldn't talk at the moment. Something is wrong and it has to be that Ben is gambling again. I opened my laptop and reread my confidential memo to Saul. I jumped as the phone rang and it was Grace.

'Honestly, I'm in despair. Everything is falling apart for him. He spent forty-eight hours last week gambling non-stop. Forty-eight hours without sleep. It's an addiction.'

'Yes, it is.'

'He's in no shape to work and he's got all these debts. He asked tonight if he can move in with us. He and Pete have gone to collect his things.'

'I'm so sorry.'

'You knew about the gambling, didn't you? Is that why you left him, Liz?'

'Yes, it was.'

'I wish you'd told me about it.'

'I couldn't, Grace, I couldn't do that.'

'You just said you had different attitudes to money and that his spending was making you unhappy.'

I could tell that Grace was feeling resentful that I hadn't been more open with her.

'It was for him to tell you. I'm sorry.'

'He says he's tried to fight it and I believe him. But then it gets hold of him again and it controls him. I feel so helpless,' she said.

I was too sad to send the memo to Saul Relph. I couldn't sleep as thoughts of Ben kept me awake. He's forty-four and he's going back to live with his parents and he isn't working. I could say goodbye to any monthly maintenance payments from him. They weren't much but they did help with Flo's costs. Strongest of all though was my feeling of sadness that clever, talented Ben has lost his way so profoundly. You make a decision about your life, as I made the decision to leave Ben, and the implications of that decision go on working themselves out for years to come. I have never been able to grasp the significance of what I am doing while I am caught up in the doing of it. My understanding of its meaning can take months or even years to become clear to me.

CHAPTER TWENTY-TWO

NOVEMBER
StoryWorld TV station, London Bridge

It was a cold drizzly morning and the leaves on the pavements were slick and slippery as I walked to the Tube. I'd had to coax Flo out of bed and was running late. I joined the director in the gallery but had missed the first item of the show. He said Fizzy was low-key this morning and I watched her carefully. She was doing a professional enough job but was not as spirited as she usually is, but then she had had a weekend on her own to consider her huge decision. I wondered if she would go through with the pregnancy. If she did there would be a major fallout with Bob and he would be a formidable opponent if you went against his wishes.

At the end of the morning meeting I waited for her and we walked down to her dressing room.

'I've realised that what I represent for Bob is pleasure, an escape for him from domesticity and routine. We create our own pleasure bubble, our lovely afternoons in bed after a gorgeous meal. No mention of work ever. We banished it. But a baby isn't part of all that, is it?'

I recalled the months following Flo's birth; the feeling of profound exhaustion as if I hadn't slept for days and the being tuned in to my tiny baby's every whimper.

'No, it's something primeval. It's one of the few times in your life when you give yourself over completely to another person.'

'That sounds scary.'

'It's life-changing for sure, but my life never felt more right than when I first held Flo and looked at her little face.'

'But you are naturally maternal, Liz.'

'I don't think so. I struggled at the beginning. I still do.'

I thought about my fights with Flo over her smoking and over the Cat and Mouse.

'Oh, you are. You're like a mother to your team. I'm not like you. I like to look nice. I like male attention. One of my biggest thrills is when I know a man is falling for me.'

'That is a great feeling,' I said.

'But it doesn't last. I've never been so torn about anything in my life.'

'That means you need to give yourself more time.'

I went upstairs. Outside my window I could see the rain was still falling and the team were subdued as they trooped into my room at noon. Ziggy was wearing another of Harriet's tops this morning; at least I assumed it was one of hers as it was a soft-looking oatmeal jumper, probably cashmere. Ziggy had pulled the arms down so that they covered most of her hands. You could just see her bitten fingernails peeping out. I watched Harriet settle herself on the sofa and tried to assess what she was feeling. She appeared to be OK, but you couldn't tell what was going on beneath that calm exterior. Simon rather half-heartedly suggested bringing John of Sheffield back onto the show to get an update on how he'd been getting on.

'There have been developments. He's started dating and he sent me a funny email about the perils of dating when you have children in the house and you don't want them to know. Lots of creeping down the stairs at sunrise to unlock the back door,' Simon said.

'I doubt that will work. Teenagers seem to hear everything

and especially the things you don't want them to hear. Well, mine does,' I said.

Molly leaned forward in her chair.

'But if he's dating now won't he lose his sympathy appeal with our viewers? It was the lone dad thing that was appealing.'

'Who is John of Sheffield? He sounds like a saint,' Harriet asked.

Simon smiled briefly.

'He's this good-looking man we had on the show, a single dad, in need of female support.'

The room fell quiet.

'Can you give us an update on the budget situation, only we've heard that they're cutting the news team,' Molly said.

So that was it. Molly is straight as a die and asks outright what the others must have been talking about. Bob had acted fast. Tim Cooper had insisted that as members of staff were being made redundant we had to be vigilant in following company procedures. I thought Bob was going to wait till the end of the week to reveal the cuts to his team.

'I've had to make cuts too but none of you are going anywhere,' I said.

Their relief was palpable and the mood in the room changed at once. Molly talked through the list of ideas she'd developed since her meeting with the non-fiction publishers.

'Next week we should do Jan Clayton. Her book is going to be huge. They're calling it *The Female Eunuch* of today. It's feminist and funny.'

Simon, who is growing a beard at the moment which makes him look older, was sceptical.

'Fizzy's not great on the feminist stuff,' he said.

'She was OK with Sal,' Molly fired back.

'Could we get a counter view in? Maybe generate a debate,' I said.

'I don't see why we need to do that with Jan Clayton. She's big enough news on her own.'

Harriet suggested we cover the latest work from Central Saint Martin's fashion course. She had been to an exhibition at the college.

'They've got an amazing record for turning out young British designers. I was thinking maybe we can bring in some of the outfits and put them on mannequins. We can interview their star pupil or teacher, or both.'

'I like that idea,' I said.

After they had left I realised that I had implied by my words *none of you are going anywhere* that Harriet would be staying on long term too. But she hasn't proved herself yet.

Gerry called me at lunchtime.

'How was the spa?'

'Fabulous and it did me a power of good. You'll never guess who I bumped into there?'

'Tell me.'

'Amber, you know, Julius's ex.'

I just stopped myself from saying 'The Pouter'.

'How is she?'

'Oh, she's in good form. She was there all weekend and we kind of palled up. She recommended I go for an Ayurvedic consultation and I'm so glad I did. Turns out I've been eating the wrong kind of food for years.'

He explained that he had filled in the Ayurvedic questionnaire and he was Kapha dominant. This meant he needed hot spicy foods to ginger up his constitution.

'That's why I put on weight. My system is very sluggish.'

He sounded far more cheerful.

'And I know why she and Julius split up,' he said.

'Really?'

'He was on the point of asking her to move in with him. You know he's got that gorgeous penthouse in Limehouse? Right on the river.'

'Yes. I've been there once,' I said.

I remembered his flat. It was huge and light-filled and the epitome of minimalist taste. I could see no evidence of anything personal on show and I guessed that Julius had hired an interior designer to style it for him. He had a roof terrace with stunning views of the river. That's what money can buy you, lots of space and an unimpeded view.

'Amber had all kinds of plans for that flat but then he moves his brother in with him.'

'Steven?'

'Yes. Steven was living with their parents but apparently Julius said they were getting frail, so he moved Steven in with him for the foreseeable.'

'Whatever you think about Julius his feelings for his brother are genuine,' I said and it was true. Julius is kind to his brother. He loves his brother.

'Amber thought it was unreasonable. She said it was a ploy to stop him committing to her.'

Amber had struck me as a vain, self-obsessed woman I thought, as I put down the phone.

It was probably the imminent departure of some of the news reporters but I felt low all afternoon. The rain had finally stopped. It was dark by four and I wanted to get home and turn the heating up and make comfort food. Martine rang me at five.

'Julius would like a word,' she said.

It was ridiculous how her saying such innocuous words should make my stomach clench as it did.

'Did he say what it's about?'

'No, but can you come down now, please?'

I checked myself in my mirror by the door and brushed my hair. Julius was on the phone and he motioned me to come in and I stood there for an age while he finished his call. Whoever he was talking to was making him irritated and his voice was getting snappier by the minute. I did not want to sit down and prolong things so I stood and looked at the framed award certificates from the Royal Television Society on his wall. I felt foolish standing there but couldn't bring myself to sit down either. I won an award once. Four years ago I ran a health campaign to raise awareness of prostate cancer and the need to have regular check-ups. I got celebrities to endorse the message and produced an online fact sheet. I even secured sponsorship to get the fact sheet translated into Urdu and Hindi. The majority of our viewers are female but every woman will have a father, a brother, a husband or a son and the idea was to get the women to encourage their men to get checked up. It was a big deal for me, winning that award. The ceremony was black tie at the Grosvenor House Hotel. I asked Mum if she would come to the ceremony as my date. I wanted her to see that television can achieve good things. Mum had said congratulations and that she was proud of me but she couldn't get away from her job for a mid-week event in London. I still feel a pang of hurt about that.

Julius hung up.

'Sit down.'

He was terse and I did not sit down.

'I'm up to my eyeballs, Julius. What is it?'

'Tell Ledley we want his food producers to put their ad campaign on our station.'

'I don't think we can insist on that.'

'Of course we can. Ledley would be nothing without his slot on our show. He was a nobody until we gave him airtime.'

'Hardly a nobody. And I made a big thing to him about no product placement in his slot.'

'I'm not talking about product placement. I'm talking about advertising. Tell him we'll offer them a good rate.'

'I'll mention it.'

His face darkened. 'I obviously didn't make things clear enough at our budget meeting. We're hanging by a thread. Don't *mention* it; *tell him* that's how it's going to be.'

'I'll do my best.'

He thumped the desk with his fist.

'I'm sick of the way you always treat Ledley with kid gloves. You should bloody well know where your loyalties lie.'

'That's rubbish.'

'Why are you resisting my perfectly reasonable request?'

He had raised his voice and I raised mine.

'All I'm saying is I can't guarantee—'

'Just bloody do it!'

Now he was shouting and I'd had enough of his aggression.

'Stop bullying me and stop bullying my team!'

'What do you mean by that?'

'I know you assaulted Harriet. How could you do that?'

He stood up at my words and now he looked menacing.

'She told you that?'

'Keep away from my team.'

'When am I meant to have done this?'

'Wednesday before last, I found Harriet sobbing in the Ladies' late that evening.'

'And where precisely did I assault her?'

'In one of the edit suites.'

'Crap! I'll tell you what happened. She wants to be on TV, thinks she can be the next Fizzy. So I gave her a screen test and she was fucking awful.'

Now he was talking too fast and I knew he was lying.

'A screen test?'

'Yes, she was crap. I showed it to her that night and told her it didn't work out.'

My mind was leaping. But Harriet would have told me if there was a screen test. He had made this up to explain his being in the edit suite with her.

'So show me this screen test,' I said.

'It was so bad I junked it. She didn't get what she wanted so she's making up stories, evil little stories.'

'There must be a copy somewhere.'

'I told you I junked it.'

I didn't believe him. If there had been a screen test he would have shown it to me to prove his story. That would have cleared him.

'I don't believe you. There is no screen test.'

'You are so damned naive. I'd have thought you knew how this business works by now!'

His voice was full of contempt.

'You're hateful.'

'She's a typical spoiled rich kid. Thinks it's enough to know the right people. She's never done a real day's work in her life.'

'Stay away from her or I'll... I'll report you.'

'You're being hysterical, again.'

He shouted this after me as I stormed out of his room. Martine heard that and she gave me a curious and cold look.

Her loyalty to Julius is total and anyone who crosses him makes an enemy of her.

I was seething all the way home on the Tube. He is a bully and a liar.

Chalk Farm flat, 7.30 p.m.

As soon as I got home I booted up my laptop. I read through my memo to the MD one last time. Julius had had this coming for years. I pressed send.

I put on the kettle and made myself tea and my hands were trembling as I reached for my favourite mug. There was no going back now. I saw that Mr Crooks's bowl was empty as Flo came out of her room.

'You haven't fed Mr Crooks,' I said.

'Sorry.'

She got out the bag of his dry food and filled his bowl. Then she ran fresh water and filled that bowl. I was surprised that she hadn't snapped back at me as she usually does when I ask her to do something. We stood and watched Mr Crooks eating.

'Do you remember the day we got him?' I said.

'I loved him the moment I saw him, it's his stripy face that did it.'

Mr Crooks's face is orange on one side and black on the other and it does give him a rakish air.

'He's a character,' I said.

It was nice feeling united with Flo like this.

'Is it OK if I do a sleepover at Rosie's on Friday night?'

'Has her mum said that's OK?'

'Yes, and I can go straight to hers from school so Janis needn't come.'

This gave me enough time to stand Janis down and save some money.

'That's fine, darling.'

'Thanks, Mum.'

Rosie was on the scene again and that was good news as far as I was concerned. She is a friendly wholesome girl and I hoped that the sullen Paige's influence was on the wane.

CHAPTER TWENTY-THREE

StoryWorld TV station, London Bridge

My sleep was fitful and I woke with a sick feeling in my stomach at the thought that I had lobbed the hand grenade. In an hour or two I would have to sit across the table from Julius after our furious row last night. I wished I hadn't shown my hand, I wished I hadn't said I'd report him. That was a bad move on my part. But surely Saul Relph wouldn't send my email on to him when I'd marked it as strictly confidential? But what if he does; what if he closes ranks with Julius who is his right-hand man? I would know soon enough.

I walked slowly from London Bridge towards StoryWorld, not wanting to reach the building or face what might be awaiting me. I spotted Molly walking in front of me and she looked the most formal I had ever seen her in a black coat rather than her usual parka. I caught up with her.

'Hi, I need to leave by eleven-thirty today. Is that all right?' she said.

'Naomi's funeral?'

'Yes. Do I look OK? I borrowed this coat from a friend.'

'You look most suitable. Now, I don't want you coming back here afterwards, Moll.'

Molly is so scrupulous it would be like her to come back to the station for the last few hours of the day.

When we assembled in the meeting room after the show I sat on the same side as Julius so that I would not have to look at his face. There was a brief discussion of that day's show but it was clear to us all that Bob wanted to say something. He got his moment and he told us that the reporters who were leaving his team had been told by him personally yesterday.

'It was tough but it had to be done. Two of the journos are likely to appeal their redundancy. They may make waves. I wanted you all to know what's going on,' he said, pulling back his shoulders and looking pleased with himself.

'Good work, Bob. You need to play hardball with the two who are kicking up,' Julius said.

'I intend to.'

Bob is the kind of man who likes to get difficult actions dealt with as fast as possible but it would have been far better if he'd thought to warn us about this yesterday. A TV station is a highly volatile environment and trouble in one quarter reverberates across the whole building. Already a tense atmosphere could be felt from the Hub to the studio and the offices.

I got out of the room without having to speak to Julius. The one look he had given me was cold. We had screamed abuse at each other yesterday and I had to assume that Saul Relph had not sent him my email. I was weak with relief. I should not have sent that email, it was too much of a hand grenade.

Molly had already left for Naomi Jessup's funeral when I joined the team outside my room. I told Ziggy that I had managed to get her onto a course to train as a digital technician. She flushed with pleasure.

'Thanks for that.'

'Go, Ziggy,' Simon said, standing up and doing a high five across the desks which Harriet then did too. It made me feel good to see them being so supportive to her.

'Monday night sessions starting in two weeks,' I said.

Harriet was working on her Central Saint Martins' fashion idea.

'How's it going?' I asked.

'I've found the right tutor to interview and she's going to select the student.'

Harriet was dressed in the same demure mode which she has favoured since she came back to work. Her cream Fair Isle cardigan was buttoned to the neck and she had plaited her hair away from her face. I preferred this Harriet, the team-player.

'Good work,' I said.

Yes, I thought as I went into my office, I had done the right thing. My team need me to be strong and to protect them no matter how fearful and wobbly I feel inside.

All day long I kept checking my home email as I was sure Saul Relph would send his response there. It was hard to settle to anything but I told myself I had to stay calm. I had every right to report the incident between Julius and me. I looked at my to-do list. At the top I had written *Speak to Ledley about getting the food company to advertise on StoryWorld*. It's the kind of call I hate to make. Pulling rank and saying that because we had made him a household name he owed us. And then an idea occurred to me. Ledley had said they planned to hold a big launch for their product and we had our atrium. We've often used it for publicity events. It's a large space with a touch of theatre about it with the two staircases sweeping up on either side. I could get their team in to discuss this and introduce them to our sales team and let them do the hard sell. I called Ledley at once.

'What a great idea. You're brilliant, Liz.'

'I'll need to speak to their PR team and get them in to take a look.'

He gave me the number of the PR agency. I have arranged for the senior publicist to come in on Friday and I'll get Ledley along for that too.

It was after six and I checked my home account for the umpteenth time before shutting down my PC. Nothing had come in from Saul Relph. I cleared my desk and locked my room. Simon and Harriet were still working on their research briefs as I said goodnight. As I came out of the main entrance I saw Bob standing in the paved area that fronts our building. It was not the kind of night to be hanging around. A cold wind from the river was whistling around the open space of the forecourt and whipping up grit. Commuters were streaming by on the way to the Tube, their faces a picture of weary endurance. Bob stepped out right in front of me.

'We need a word,' he said.

I realised it was me he had been waiting for.

'Can it wait till tomorrow?'

'No, it can't.'

His whole demeanour made me know what was coming.

'You can butt out of Fizzy's pregnancy,' he said.

Over his shoulder I could see Tim Cooper coming out of the building, striding towards us.

'You want to say that a bit louder?' I said.

He clamped his lips together but continued to stare at me with furious eyes. I wanted to get away from him and tried to think what I could talk to Tim about so I could walk to the Tube with him. Tim always leaves work promptly and the talk in the station is that he has a difficult and demanding wife waiting for him at home. But he was upon us in a flash and as he walked past we both said goodnight.

'What are you thinking of, feeding her all that crap about the joys of motherhood?'

'You've got a nerve!'

'She's not the maternal type. Anyone with half a brain cell can see that.'

'I've known Fizzy a lot longer than you and—'

'You're telling her to do something that will ruin her career.'

'I'm not *telling* her to do anything. I said she should give herself time to think about what is a huge decision for any woman.'

'Like I said, butt out.' His voice was very aggressive.

'And you have her best interests at heart, I suppose? This is you trying to cover your arse. Do you have any idea how a woman feels after an abortion?'

I walked away from him as fast as I could. I had not experienced such pure clean anger for a long time.

Chalk Farm flat, 7.15 p.m.

All the way home in the Tube my anger was bouncing back and forth between Bob and Julius. Two bullies who think they can order the world in their image. And Julius is a liar as well as a bully. I was itching to check my home email again. It was twenty-four hours since I'd written to Saul Relph. Surely he should have responded by now?

I arrived home and followed Janis onto the pavement as she was leaving as I did not want Flo to overhear me.

'Flo's doing a sleepover at Rosie's on Friday and she'll go straight to hers from school,' I said.

'So you don't need me?'

'Is that all right?'

'Not a problem.'

'I wanted to ask you about Paige. Do you think Flo is getting less besotted with her?'

'I don't think so. She goes onto WhatsApp or Snapchat or whatever they use now with her as soon as she gets home,' Janis said.

'Still?'

'Every night.'

'I hoped she was pulling away. Nothing we can do about it I guess.'

'Don't worry, as soon as Paige gets herself a boyfriend she'll drop Flo,' Janis said.

We said goodbye and I went inside. I took my laptop into my bedroom and turned it on. Saul Relph had just sent his response. My fingers were trembling as I clicked his message open.

Dear Liz,

I read your email with concern and I have been considering the best course of action.

The incident you refer to took place seven years ago, before my tenure as MD, as you know. You have waited a very long time to report this. You say the event took place at the Christmas party and I am assuming that alcohol had been consumed.

You appear to have a professional working relationship with Julius. Are you sure you want to proceed with a formal complaint? Please

think about this carefully and let me know if
you wish me to take this matter further.

Yours as ever

Saul Relph OBE

I was devastated by his response. It was so cold, so
dismissive. Yes, it had happened seven years ago but it was a
near-rape experience and he should be alarmed that his
director of programmes, his precious lieutenant, was capable
of doing that. And what the hell did he mean by that reference
to alcohol being consumed? Does he think I led Julius on by
drinking? It was not my fault Julius wouldn't take no for an
answer. Now he knows my shaming secret and he doesn't
want to take any action. He has left the decision to me. I had
an insight into why so many rape victims stay silent. I used to
think it was men who created the moral order. I don't think
that any more. I think most men are content with the status
quo, like a quiet life and don't want to shake things up. I read
it again. His 'are you sure' and his 'think about this carefully'
make it clear that he wants me to drop it.

I didn't know what to do with myself. I needed to talk to
Fenton but she would be just back from her long weekend
with Bill and would be keen to tell me all about it and I didn't
want to rain on her parade. Every time we had talked recently
it had been her role to comfort me and that wasn't fair. I made
myself sort the laundry instead. Flo has this habit of flinging
her clean clothes along with her dirty clothes into the wash
basket. She does this when there are piles of clothes on her
floor, things she has tried on and discarded, and it's her way
of clearing up her bedroom. There were three clean T-shirts

in the basket and it always riles me. I separated the clean from the dirty and sniffed the dirty tops. There was the smell of cigarette smoke but also a sweet, herby, aromatic smell that I recognised from my student days. Flo, no doubt egged on by Paige, had been smoking weed. I sat back on my heels. I couldn't face a confrontation with her tonight. Saul Relph's response had made me feel humiliated. Either I carry on and insist he follows it up and all that that entails or I let it go. If I let it go it makes me feel rotten, like the classroom sneak.

CHAPTER TWENTY-FOUR

StoryWorld TV station, London Bridge

There was a poisonous atmosphere between Bob and me at the morning meeting. Anyone with an atom of awareness would have noticed how we were being icily polite to each other as we discussed the crew allocation for the rest of the month. He and I had been tentative allies up till now and having him against me was going to make life more difficult. Fizzy, my occasional ally, was seated opposite me but she did not look in my direction once. She must have shared our conversation with Bob, otherwise how could he have known I'd spoken to her about the 'joys of motherhood', as he put it? And I couldn't bring myself to look at Julius. If the MD had shared my email with him I would have known, wouldn't I? I couldn't be sure. I had little idea of what the men at the top shared. For all I knew they were sniggering over it in their executive toilet. My sense of isolation and dread was growing. The others left the room as Julius asked me to stay behind and my stomach plummeted three floors.

'Where are you with Ledley's advertisers?'

His voice was calmer than on Monday but it was icy.

'I've got a meeting with their PR team on Friday. I've suggested they use our atrium for the launch and they're coming here to recce it. I will then get the sales team to follow up.'

He nodded curtly and said nothing further and I left the meeting room. My palms were sweating. I wanted to talk to

Fizzy so I dumped my papers with Ziggy and went down to her dressing room. Ellen was in there doing a clear-out of her wardrobe and told me Fizzy had gone out with Martine.

'Did they say where they were going?'

Ellen shook her head.

'I got the impression Martine wanted to share some gossip with Fizzy. You know how close those two are.'

I sat and watched as Ellen went through the hangers. Fizzy's outfits were jostling for space on the long chrome rail that extended the length of one wall.

'She's asked me to weed out her older outfits,' Ellen said. She held out a floaty chiffon dress on a padded silk hanger. 'Isn't this gorgeous?'

It was a full-length evening dress of dusty pink chiffon with brown swirls on it and far too frilly for my taste.

'I remember that dress. She wore it to the RTS awards,' I said.

Ellen was looking at it with hungry eyes, even though it was at least two sizes too small for her. A dress like that would cost more than her month's salary. I remembered she had a daughter, Tara, in her mid-twenties.

'Take it for Tara,' I said.

'Haven't you heard? Julius says we have to sell off wardrobe items now. No more giving to family members.'

'Things must be bad if it's come to that.'

I climbed the stairs and Molly, Simon and Ziggy were at their desks. Harriet was away from the office for two days because I had sent her on a training course on the laws relating to broadcasting. It's information which every researcher needs to do their job. I put her up for the course because recently she has earned the right to go on it. When I told her she said that it was her birthday the next day and she was pleased to be doing something interesting on her birthday. She will be twenty-seven and I've worked out that makes her a Scorpio.

I did the same legal course myself years ago and it made a big impression on me. They highlighted our key role in guaranteeing the health and safety of participants. We discussed a notorious case where a member of the public had died during the making of an entertainment stunt show. A man had actually died on camera when the stunt went wrong. I had left that course feeling chastened and filled with a powerful sense of responsibility about what we were doing. Blood chits indeed.

Later, Simon popped his head round the door.

'Shall we do lunch together? It's been a while,' he said.

Simon is such an intuitive man and he had probably picked up on my unease of the last few days.

'I'd like that. Give me fifteen minutes.'

I was leaving my office when my phone rang. It was Fizzy and she sounded downright panicky and breathless. She asked me to come to her dressing room straight away.

'I'm sorry, Simon, but I'm going to have to pass on our lunch; maybe later this week?'

Fizzy almost pulled me into her dressing room, closed the door behind us and stood with her back against the door.

'Martine just told me that Julius did a screen test with Harriet!'

'What?'

'A screen test! I knew she was angling for one. Did you know anything about this?'

'No. No, I didn't. Are you sure about this, Fizz?'

My mind was racing at a hundred miles an hour.

'Of course I am. Martine just told me. He came in on a Sunday and used the small studio to do it.'

Alongside our main studio we have a small studio with a single robotic camera which we use for news interviews when we need to do a quick turnaround. It can be operated by a sole technician so it was possible.

'Martine is one hundred per cent sure about this?' I asked.

'Why are you doubting Martine all of a sudden? She knows what he gets up to.'

But if he had recorded a screen test on the Sunday he could have been showing it to her that Wednesday evening in the edit suite, like he said. He could have rubbished it and that was why she was sobbing in the Ladies. I was winded by Fizzy's words as she paced up and down in front of me. I sank down on one of her chairs. Harriet had never mentioned a screen test. He must have been telling the truth after all. And I had sent that email to Saul Relph for nothing. Fizzy stopped her pacing and burst into tears.

'He's so disloyal. I know he'll shunt me off if I go through with the baby. He's already thinking about my replacement.'

Her sobs got more insistent.

'I'll have to have the termination now, won't I? I can't leave it any longer.'

I hugged her and she wept on my shoulder. I had never seen her cry in all the years I had known her. I could feel my fury against Harriet building. She had been lying to me all this time. If she'd made the allegation to get back at Julius over a negative screen test then she really must be deranged. I had to park my fury and think how to comfort Fizzy but I was hollowed out and didn't know what to say. Fizzy pulled away from me at last.

'What should I do?' she wailed.

'He told me there was a screen test and he told me it was crap.'

She was wiping her tears away with the back of her hands and looked terribly anxious.

'He said it was crap?'

'Yes. He said it was awful, only I didn't believe him.'

'What do you mean?'

'I didn't believe him about any screen test! Harriet hadn't said a word about it.'

I was feeling more appalled by the second. She had duped and manipulated me completely.

'I told you she's an operator. And he definitely didn't like it?'

'He said it was crap and he's junked it. There is no way Harriet is going to replace you.'

She did not look reassured at all.

'She may not have worked out but he'll find someone else.'

'Do you think you're so expendable, Fizz?'

More tears rolled down her cheeks as she nodded. She moved her hand down and stroked her stomach and for the first time I thought I could detect a slight swelling.

'Our viewers love you. They have a relationship with you. That can't be wiped away by a new person.'

'But if I'm not on screen? They'll forget all about me.'

'You'll come into the station with the baby. And I'll make sure we keep programming in stories about how you're getting on at home. Maybe we can run with a photo of the week.'

'I don't want to be typecast as a mother and baby presenter!'

'OK, OK, but there are other things we can do. They'll be dying for you to come back.'

She wiped her tears with a tissue and looked at herself in the mirror.

'I guess I could be off screen for a short time,' she said.

I thought this was a bad idea but I wasn't going to challenge her when she was feeling so fragile.

'But he's such a shit and I don't trust him.'

I assumed she was talking about Julius, not about Bob. She sat down in front of her mirror and started to apply cleansing lotion to the streaks of black on her face.

'I looked at my contract,' she said.

'And?'

'I'm seeing my lawyer this afternoon. I want to make sure it's watertight.'

'You need to keep calm,' I said; for the baby, I thought.

I walked upstairs on autopilot and headed straight for Julius's office. I had to speak to him, had to apologise that I hadn't believed him about the screen test. Harriet had lied and lied to me. I reached his room and the door was locked. Martine was approaching from the Ladies.

'Where is he?'

'Are you OK? You look pale,' she said.

'I need to talk to him, urgently.'

'He and the MD have gone to meet with their man at Ofcom.'

Ofcom is the regulator for TV and I cringed at the thought that Julius would be spending the whole afternoon with Saul Relph.

'What's that about?'

'It's their usual quarterly meeting,' she said.

'Is he coming back?'

'Not this afternoon.'

Chalk Farm, 7 p.m.

As I walked home from the Tube I had the dizzy feeling in my head which I get when I am deeply anxious. All afternoon I had been replaying everything Harriet had said and done since the alleged assault and also how Julius had behaved. The evidence looked different now I knew that there actually had been a screen test. He had seemed relatively unchanged. He had looked drawn and weary on a couple of days but his brother was in hospital which could explain that, whereas she had been cagey when I finally got through to her after the allegation. She had refused point-blank to go to the police. And she had never once mentioned the existence of a screen test. My years of experience and judgement counted for nothing. I had made a terrible mistake and had exposed myself to the MD. I stopped at the top of our road and held onto the church railings, taking deep breaths and holding the air in my lungs for a count of seven beats before exhaling fully as I'd been shown to do. There was a builder standing in the grounds of the church and he was watching me.

'You OK, love?' he called out.

'I feel dizzy.'

He walked up to the railing.

'Do you need to sit down?'

He pointed to a paint-spattered chair by the door of the church.

'I can't. I need to get home.'

'You look done in.'

He opened the church gate and helped me to the chair. I sat there for ten minutes and he left me alone. He went back inside the church while I sat on that chair and tried to get my breathing under control. There was masses of very old and dusty ivy clambering over the walls with tentacles embedded deep in the mortar between the bricks. On the lintel carved in huge letters was the message THE NIGHT COMETH WHEN NO MAN CAN WORK.

As soon as I got home I turned on my laptop and read through the notes I had made the morning after Harriet's allegation, the notes the lawyer had recommended I keep. They were so thin. Harriet had been crying a lot and her face was a mess but I hadn't noted anything about her clothes and I couldn't remember them looking dishevelled. She had said the assault took place in an edit suite. So Julius could have showed her the screen test in an edit suite and told her it was no good. So far, so plausible. Julius can be cruel and dismissive when he gives feedback. I could think of numerous times he had criticised my stories and he had never sugared the pill. I could imagine Harriet being outraged and possibly even incredulous at his rejection. After all, she had sailed through life with few enough obstacles up till now. Her sense of entitlement when she arrived at the station had been huge. I recalled her earlier lie about going to visit her sick granny so she could swan off to a premiere. I should have remembered that when I swallowed her story hook, line and sinker. I shut down my laptop. It is twisted to lie about something so serious that it could end a man's career.

At nine the phone rang and it was Grace.

'I'm sorry, Liz, but we think it's best if Flo doesn't come down for a few weeks. Ben's in no shape to see her at the moment.'

'But it's important he's in her life.'

'Let's leave it for a few weeks. He's trying to sort himself out. He's started going to these Gamblers Anonymous meetings.'

'That's good, I guess.'

'We think so. He's going twice a week, sitting in some draughty community hall with a bunch of strangers. We think he's being very brave,' Grace said.

'Don't you think seeing Flo might strengthen his resolve?'

'Not at the moment. He's reached rock bottom and needs to focus on himself. We all need to give him time to do that.'

'Is the new girlfriend still on the scene?'

I shouldn't have asked but I was curious.

'Oh no, she's disappeared,' Grace said.

This call added to my feelings of lowness and isolation. It was rare for me to feel at odds with Grace but surely when you are a parent you lose the right to focus exclusively on yourself. What could I say to Flo about her not being able to see her dad?

As I lay in bed I was still wrestling with what Harriet had done. I thought she had turned a corner. She had started being kind to Ziggy and was more of a team player. Yet all along she was manipulating everyone. How could I have been so blind?

CHAPTER TWENTY-FIVE

Chalk Farm flat, morning

I was awake before six. I can't go into work today. I'm in pieces. I called Simon early and asked him to deputise for me, told him I was sick and throwing up. I read through my notes on Harriet's allegation again and I cannot understand how I ever believed her. I do feel like throwing up.

Later Flo came out of her room and was surprised to see me sitting at the kitchen table in my pyjamas.

'Are you all right, Mum?'

'Not really. I'm staying home today.'

This was a rare event and she looked worried. I stood up and put the kettle on and stared at it, waiting for it to boil. I do not want Harriet in my team. I will get rid of her the moment her three month trial is over. I wish I could get rid of her sooner. I wish I could get rid of her today. She can go but I can never erase that email. The MD will always know what happened between Julius and me.

'I'll wait for Rosie outside. I can still go to hers tomorrow, can't I?' Flo said.

'Yes, darling.'

I kissed her on the cheek and waved her off though I wanted to hug her tightly and ask her to stay with me.

I lost Flo in Selfridges once. She was five years old and we were going to a Christmas party and Ben was away on a shoot. I had stopped in the food hall to buy a panettone to take to the host. There was a whole shelf of them to choose from, some were wrapped in pink and gold cellophane, others were in cardboard boxes tied with festive red ribbons. I picked up the box with the ribbons and handed it to the shop assistant. The confectionery department was a few steps beyond the cake section. It was an Aladdin's cave to a five-year-old, with its displays of handmade chocolates and jelly beans all the colours of a rainbow. Flo had set off towards it joyfully and when I turned round a minute later she was gone. I will never forget the terror that hit me at that moment. It was all-encompassing and stretched out in time. The shop assistant was ringing up my purchase but I turned and started to run down the aisles, calling Flo's name frantically. There were crowds of people doing their Christmas shopping and I elbowed my way through them getting angry looks along the way. Her little frame was hidden by the crowds as she walked wide-eyed among the mounds of brilliantly coloured sweets. She headed for a display that had helium balloons flying from the centre. By now I had reached the confectionery department and the smell of sugar and chocolate made me want to heave. A shop assistant told me later that she had seen Flo get up on her tiptoes and reach out to touch a foil-covered teddy bear. The bear wobbled and fell on the floor and broke into two pieces. Flo started to wail. It was her cry that I heard above the babble of shoppers and I lunged towards the sound to find a shop assistant comforting her as she stood there, looking so tiny, and pointing at the broken chocolate bear in the shop assistant's hands. I had a crushing realisation at that moment that this little person was dependent on me for her protection. I had to be ever vigilant so that she would not come to any harm or ever be broken like the chocolate teddy bear.

I lay on my bed and looked at the ceiling. It was the lowest I had been for years; lower even than in the build-up to my divorce. My feelings of failure about the breakdown of my marriage then was compounded now by my failure to read a situation properly and the fact that I had exposed myself. The one thing I had hung onto all these years was that I was good at my job and in control at StoryWorld. I had prided myself on my ability to lead a team and to manage the dynamic at work. People think I'm strong but I'm not; I'm weak and afraid. I wondered if I could even go on working at StoryWorld.

I didn't know it would be so hard to be a lone parent and the main earner or that I would feel so alone. Once I had been a promising and light-hearted student with Fenton and we had a world of infinite possibilities in front of us. Where had it gone? Then the tears came and I curled up in a ball, sobbing with a frightening intensity as if some inner restraining wall had finally been breached. I was swept up in absolute misery at the loss of my hopeful younger self, the death of my father, the end of my marriage and my failure at work. I cried and cried until my throat was sore and my eyes burned and finally I fell asleep out of sheer exhaustion.

I woke around two to the insistent ringing of the landline in the living room. I stumbled out of my room to get it and it was Gerry.

'Are you all right, darling? Simon said you're ill.'

'I've been sick.'

My voice came out thin and croaky.

'Did I wake you up, sweetheart?'

'I was sleeping, but don't worry.'

I sat down on a kitchen chair. I was still feeling befuddled from sleep.

'Will you be in tomorrow?'

'I think so.'

'Sounds like you need cheering up. Let's go out tomorrow night.'

'I'm not sure.'

'Come on, it will do you good. I'll find us a classic film to watch, maybe at the National Film Theatre. We can go for dinner afterwards.'

'Maybe that would be nice.'

'Course it would, darling.'

'Thanks for calling, Gerry.'

I put the phone down and went back to lying on my bed. I was still in my pyjamas and I hadn't opened my laptop or looked at a single work email. The crying had worn me out and I lay in a daze. Around three-thirty I heard a key in the lock. It was Janis and I had completely forgotten to tell her I was at home. She was surprised to see me emerge from my bedroom.

'Are you OK?'

'I've been sick. I'm sorry I didn't call you, you must let me pay you for today.'

I went to get my wallet.

'And you remember that Flo is staying with Rosie tomorrow?' I said.

'I hadn't forgotten. See you on Monday and take care of yourself, you look peaky.'

My puffy face and red eyelids could not be ignored. Flo came home shortly afterwards and I tried to behave normally as I made us supper. I will go into work tomorrow and somehow I've got to hold it together.

CHAPTER TWENTY-SIX

Chalk Farm flat, 6.45 a.m.

I had a hideous day yesterday but this morning I got up early, determined to pull myself together and put on my work face. I remembered that I was meeting the PR company from Ledley's food manufacturer. I looked at the outfits hanging in my wardrobe. I was going out with Gerry after work too. I chose a black trouser suit and a bright red shirt to wear under it. I applied my make-up carefully. My eyelids were still slightly swollen. As I took out my lipstick I remembered an article I had once read titled 'The Healing Power of Lipstick'. I thought it was an inflated claim at the time but actually wearing lipstick does give me a lift.

I tapped on Flo's door. She was already up and had piled some of her clothes on the bed.

'I'm off, darling. What time will you be back tomorrow?'

'Some time in the afternoon, I guess.'

I walked in and kissed her on the cheek.

'Well, text me when you're heading back and say hi to Rosie's mum from me.'

StoryWorld TV station, London Bridge

As we were going into the morning meeting I overheard Martine saying to Julius that the hospital had called and confirmed that Steven would be coming home that evening. Julius's face was transformed and he looked happy. I said little at the meeting but as I had been off sick the day before this went unnoticed. I have to find the right moment to make my peace with Julius. And I have to confront Harriet with her lies. But not today; I don't feel strong enough for either task today.

When I came out Ledley was standing in a huddle with my team watching an angry cat video on Simon's screen and laughing uproariously. Harriet was there too, back from her course. Ledley had come in to join me for the meeting with the PR team. I stood and waited until the video came to an end. I observed Harriet's dark knitted dress and her perfectly styled hair. Ever the actor playing a part, I thought; why hadn't I seen through her before? She turned to me.

'The law course was good and I learned a lot. Thanks for that,' she said.

I could barely bring myself to look at her. I gave her a brief nod and spoke to Ziggy.

'Have our visitors arrived?'

'Yeah, they're in reception. Shall I bring them up?'

'No thanks, we'll see them downstairs.'

I knew that Harriet was looking at me as we walked away.

'Are you going to charge them if they want to use the atrium?' Ledley asked as we walked downstairs.

'You know I'd love to offer it to them gratis but to be able to do that we need to get something out of it.'

'Get them to advertise with us,' he said matter-of-factly.

The two publicists hailed Ledley as a long-lost friend and much air kissing went on between them. He introduced me and then spread his arms wide.

'It's a great space, isn't it?' he said.

It *is* impressive when you see the atrium for the first time because of its high glass ceiling and the sweeping staircases on either side. The younger of the two women was like a puppy, immensely enthusiastic and taking lots of photos on her smart phone. The older woman was silver haired but her vocabulary was still rich in superlatives.

'Oh yes, it's beyond perfect. I can just see us dressing this as the coolest street party ever. We can have a mega-barbecue along one side.'

She pointed.

'Awesome idea,' puppy woman said.

I wondered about the wisdom of creating a summer street party in the middle of winter. But I had been to many a Christmas promotion in July and we could make it work.

'And the menu ideas from you, of course, Ledley,' silver woman said.

'That's easy. We'll do chicken legs and wings, barbecue ribs and corn on the cob.'

'All steeped in Ledley's marvellous marinade.'

'And a side dish of my curry potato and some plantain crisps,' he said.

'Dude food,' puppy woman added happily.

'Let's have a steel band. They would sound great in here,' Ledley said.

'Oh yes, that's inspired,' silver woman said.

'I know a great one; with nine musicians. And Liz says you can have the space for free if you put your ads on StoryWorld.'

'I'm sure we can look at that,' silver woman said, looking over at me.

I hadn't had to say a word.

I went upstairs to my office and it had given me a small lift knowing that I could still get things done because using the atrium had been my idea. I opened my account and there was a pile of emails to work through. I shut the door and got stuck in. All day I toyed with the idea of calling Harriet into my room and confronting her about the screen test. What stopped me was that my rage had not abated in the slightest. I need to detach myself from my emotions in order to talk to her calmly, as a manager should. It would be best to wait till Monday. I kept my door shut all day and the team picked up the message that I did not want to be disturbed. Not even Simon braved my fortress. He waved to me through the door as he left for the weekend.

I closed my PC down and walked over to my mirror. I was glad now that I had agreed to go out with Gerry and I combed my hair and reapplied lipstick. I was pleased too that Flo was with Rosie.

National Film Theatre, South Bank, 7.15 p.m.

It was a cold raw night but Gerry suggested we walk along the riverside from StoryWorld to the National Film Theatre and I welcomed the chance to be on the move.

'First things first, how are you feeling?'

'Better, thanks, and I'm glad to be out. It was a good idea.'

'Maybe you should look at what you're eating? You know I've lost weight over the last few weeks. I'm sticking to one main meal a day and exercising more.'

'You look good on it,' I said, and he did.

We strode along by the river and there was that Friday night feeling in the air. We were glad to get into the warmth of the foyer to queue for our tickets for the screening of Alfred Hitchcock's *Marnie*.

'It was made in 1964, so not quite Golden Age but it's a cracker,' he said.

'I've never seen it.'

'Tippi Hedren is perfect as the icy blonde.'

It was a popular choice and the queue was long. As we waited Gerry told me he had gone to a private show at the White Cube gallery with Amber on Wednesday night. He's meeting her for a roast on Sunday. She appears to be his new best female friend and that thought made me feel a bit forlorn, as if my role had been usurped.

'You're getting out a lot and that's great,' I said.

'I have to get out. I brood when I'm on my own.'

The film was a revelation to me. It opens with Marnie coolly stealing ten thousand dollars from the safe at her workplace. She then changes her identity with ruthless efficiency. You see her in a hotel bedroom packing a complete new wardrobe and washing dark dye out of her hair. She smiles at her reflection in the mirror as her blonde hair is restored. She comes over as super-efficient and super in control with no shade of guilt at what she has done. Here is a woman who has broken all the rules and is prospering in spite of it. Then enter the hero, Mark Rutland, who is attracted to her even though he knows she is a serial thief. There is a lot of talk about him being a hunter who likes to tame wild beasts. He is determined to tame Marnie and he blackmails her into marrying him. Later there's a tense sex scene where Marnie lies back and endures sex with Mark Rutland and she looks completely blank and cut off.

After the film Gerry asked if I'd be OK with Indian food as he's now convinced that hot and spicy dishes are what his sluggish constitution needs.

"They do mild dishes but are you sure your poor tum is up to it?' he asked.

'I'll be fine.'

We found an Indian restaurant near Waterloo station with

red and gold decor and linen-covered tables. We ordered gin and tonics from the waiter.

'How hot is your vindaloo?' Gerry asked him.

'You like hot food?'

'Oh yes!'

'You have to work up to a vindaloo. Maybe a bhuna or a jalfrezi?'

'How hot is the jalfrezi?'

'You'll find it hot, it has chillies in it.'

'OK, I'll have the chicken jalfrezi, thank you.'

We ordered a plate of starters to share and I selected two vegetarian dishes as my main.

'Do you mind if we swerve the poppadums and naans, Liz? If they're on the table I know I'll eat them.'

'Fine by me.'

The starters arrived and we both reached for the onion bhajis.

'I loved the film but I found the rape scene difficult to watch. I mean, I know sexual dynamics were different then but even so,' I said.

'It was controversial even then and Hitchcock was urged to drop it, but he was determined to keep it in.'

'I suppose a strong authoritative man who rescued a woman from her demons was seen as thrilling?' I said.

'He always called the film a Sex Mystery. I read a review written at the time and it described that scene as him "asserting his conjugal rights".'

'What a dreadful concept,' I said.

I've sometimes wondered if we could do a film slot with Gerry. He knows so much about cinema and I for one would find it far more interesting than his astrology. I think we watch Gerry more for his attractive personality and his funny asides with Fizzy than for what he says in his forecasts. The waiter brought our main courses. Gerry's jalfrezi was a hot shade of terracotta red. He looked at it with satisfaction as he tucked a napkin under his chin and asked for a second gin and tonic for us both.

'Strange thing Amber said to me on Wednesday,' he said.

I was spooning mattar paneer onto my plate.

'She hinted that Julius was having difficulty getting it up.'

'What?'

'She said there were definite problems in that area, not at the beginning but towards the end of their relationship.'

'Don't you think that's disloyal of her to tell you? Even if it's true...'

'But the poor love feels she's been abandoned by him. She says she wasted three good years on him.'

'I don't buy in to that.'

'Into what?'

'The idea that you waste time on a relationship,' I said.

Gerry's face was starting to glisten with sweat from the hot food. He dabbed at his cheeks and forehead with his napkin.

'I think I agree with you. However painful it was I wouldn't wish away my time with Anwar.'

'Is that good?'

I pointed at his plate.

'Fiendishly hot and wonderful,' he said.

It was late when we parted and I got the Tube home. It had been a good evening and I was tempted to get a taxi but there was a direct line from Waterloo to Chalk Farm and I couldn't justify the expense. The woman sitting opposite me looked grey and exhausted, bundled up in a Puffa coat and wearing stained trainers. I wondered if she was a shift worker on her way home from her labours. Her lids closed and she fell asleep, her head hunched into her coat. I watched her uneasy sleep and it reminded me how privileged I was to have a prestigious well-paid job. We rattled along. Julius would hate that Amber had confided in Gerry, and even more that I had heard the gossip. It had been disloyal of her to share that but now it was colouring my thinking about him, Julius having sexual difficulties. I had assumed he was highly sexed, all part of his lust for power. At Leicester Square a group of young men crowded into the central section of our carriage. They were drunk and shouting some kind of anthem. The weary woman woke up with a start and looked over at the young men with hatred. They were oblivious to her glare. She was invisible to them.

Chalk Farm flat, 1.30 a.m.

I was deeply asleep and my landline had been ringing for a while before I surfaced. I staggered out of bed and grabbed the phone in the living room. It was Flo and she was crying.

'Mum...'

Her frightened voice jolted me awake.

'Darling, what is it?'

'I'm at University College Hospital...'

'Hospital? Oh my God, you're hurt!' Terror surged through me and it felt as if my heart was going to burst. 'Oh Christ, what happened to you?'

'Not me. I'm OK, Mum.'

'You're OK, what's happened?'

'Harriet's hurt.'

'Harriet? I don't understand.'

'Please don't be angry.'

'I won't be angry. Tell me, darling.'

'I was at the Cat and Mouse with Paige and this horrible man was leching at me and Harriet came up and...' She started to cry harder. 'He punched her, Mum.'

'What!'

'He punched her in the face and she fell and she banged her head and it's all my fault.' She was crying so hard now that she couldn't speak.

I was trying to understand what she was telling me but it was so confusing, so unreal.

'Is Harriet OK?'

'The ambulance came. I went in the ambulance with her.'

'Is she OK?'

'I don't know. We're in A & E. Mum, please come!'

'I'm coming, darling, I'm coming now.'

I called a taxi, flung on my clothes and was waiting on the pavement as it drew up. Time stretches out when you need to get somewhere and I was willing the driver to go faster, go faster, to run the lights. There was less traffic on the roads at that time and it's not far from Chalk Farm to the hospital on Euston Road but that journey was an agony of time to endure. I ran through the doors into A & E and saw Flo sitting hunched on a chair watching the entrance doors, her little face a picture of dread. She flew into my arms. She finally surfaced from the longest hug.

'Sorry I lied.'

'Shhh now. You're sure you're not hurt?'

'I'm fine, now you're here.'

I hugged her close again.

'Where's Harriet?'

'They took her to the cubicles. Her mum arrived right after I called you.'

'Is she conscious?'

'I think so.'

It came out piece by piece. She hadn't been with Rosie. She'd gone to the Cat and Mouse with Paige. They hadn't arrived till ten p.m. and their names were on the door. They'd watched the band and it was crowded, hot and noisy. Paige had been dancing with a boy and Flo went to the bar to get water for them both. A drunk sleazeball old enough to be her father had homed in on her. Harriet had suddenly appeared and stood between Flo and the man. She'd said something to the man and he'd told her to get out of his way and when she answered back he had swung at her and hit her face. Harriet banged her head on a table as she went down. Then drinks had gone flying and tables had been overturned. Flo was kneeling by Harriet and she was out cold. Paige had disappeared when the trouble broke out. An ambulance had come to the venue. Flo had sat in the back of the ambulance with Harriet. The paramedics had been kind to her.

Flo's face was smeared and her clothes smelled of beer and cigarette smoke. She was wearing her black miniskirt but I didn't recognise the top which was made of shiny black material with a skull on the front. She had no jacket with her.

'I'm sorry, Mum.'

I felt no anger at all. I was filled with an overwhelming need to protect my girl and the deepest gratitude towards Harriet.

'Come on. We'll go and see what's going on,' I said.

Harriet was in one of the A & E cubicles and a woman was sitting on the side of her bed talking to a nurse. It had to be her mother – I heard her say: 'We'd like to get her moved into a private room as soon as possible.'

Harriet's eyes were closed. She opened them and she saw us. I had my arm around Flo's shoulders as I needed to keep her close to my body.

'Hello,' she whispered.

I was scanning her face and could see a large bruise forming on her right cheek. She closed her eyes again but she was conscious, thank God she was conscious. I leaned over her bed.

'Thank you, Harriet,' I said.

Her eyelids flickered.

'I'm Sophie Dodd, Harriet's mother.'

I pulled my eyes away from Harriet's face. I was looking at an older, more sophisticated version of Harriet, a woman with the same hooded eyelids as her daughter, but hers made her look patrician rather than sleepy.

'Liz Lyon. Flo told me what happened. I'm so shocked, so grateful to Harriet.' I was finding it hard to control my voice.

'The doctor said she's going to be OK. We've asked them to keep her in for a couple of nights to check for concussion or any after-effects,' her mother said.

'She was trying to help Flo. She did help Flo. She's so brave and I... I can't thank her enough.'

We said goodbye to Harriet who was drifting in and out of sleep and barely aware we were there. As we left, Sophie Dodd followed us out into the waiting area.

'I wanted to thank *you*. Harriet's had a tough time settling into work. She's trying to make something of her job now and she said you've been very supportive.'

There was little she could have said to make me feel worse.

Chalk Farm flat, 3.15 a.m.

Finally we were back in the flat.

'Can I sleep in your bed tonight, Mum?' Flo said.

'Course you can.'

253

She used to sleep in my bed all the time when she was little and scared of the dark. As she was getting undressed I noticed that she was wearing my best red satin bra under her top. She slipped it off and pulled on the T-shirt I handed her with a wary glance at me. Under normal circumstances this would have angered me, the idea that nothing I owned was off limits and that she felt she could help herself. I said nothing, it could not have mattered less. We got into bed and I held her close to me and her hair was sticky.

Chalk Farm flat, Saturday

We slept till lunchtime. I ran a bath for Flo with my best bath oil, she slid into the water and I left her to have a good soak. I wondered if I should call mum but she made a comment last year which still rankles with me. She had stayed with us for the weekend to prepare me for her plan to volunteer with the Voluntary Service Overseas once she retired. She had been to a workshop at VSO and they welcomed volunteers in their sixties she said. There was much work to be done in Africa and the projects that interested her ran for two years. She was sorry this meant she would see less of me and Flo if she did sign up but VSO paid for one visit back home a year. I knew she would go and I was fed up. I pointed out how little time she currently spent with Flo.

And that was when she said: 'This isn't about me, or *me* finding more time for Flo. You're a good mother to your team at work but you need to put Flo first. Before you know it she'll be all grown up and you'll regret the lost years.'

I'd argued with her saying how else could I give Flo a good home if I didn't work full time? But Mum was right. The hours at StoryWorld were so long and the demands so insistent.

I made us eggy bread with maple syrup. Afterwards we sat on the sofa and Flo put her feet on my lap. She plugged her earphones into her tablet and settled down to watch her favourite series. I stroked her feet. Last night had thrown things into sharp relief for me. Creating a good home for Flo and keeping her safe is what gives a purpose to my life. When I was her age there had been one girl at my school who had anorexia. She would bring a single orange in to school to eat at lunchtime and we watched as her head got larger in relation to her shrinking frame. Then she left the school and we never saw her again. But she was the exception. I had seen recent reports in the news that there was now an epidemic of eating disorders and self-harming among girls of Flo's age. How much did I know about what my daughter was thinking and feeling? Flo has long thin feet like her dad. Should I ring Ben and tell him what had happened? She took her earphones out.

'Paige ran away and she hasn't even texted to see if I'm OK.'

'True friends don't do that,' I said.

She chewed on her thumbnail.

'Darling, I'd prefer it if in future you invite Paige here if you want to see her. I'd rather you didn't go over to her house.'

'You don't like her, do you?'

When I thought about Paige I could feel my face hardening and my bile rising.

'I hate it that she ran away when you were in trouble. Thank goodness Harriet was there to help you.'

'Please don't tell Dad.'

I gave her feet a squeeze.

'Or Janis,' she said.

'I think you should tell Janis but I won't tell Dad.'

'Why do I need to tell Janis?'

'Because it's her job to be here when I can't be and I think she needs to know what's going on.'

We visited Harriet that evening. She had been moved to a private room on a different wing. She was sitting up in bed and the bruise on her cheek was darker. She was pleased to see us and pushed her hair away from her face and winced as she touched her cheek.

'Does your cheek hurt a lot?'

'It is sore.'

Flo had noticed the big TV on the wall.

'Does it have Netflix?'

'Yes, but I can't stay awake long enough to watch anything. I wish I could come back to work on Monday but Mum is insisting we go to the country for a couple of days. I'll take it as leave.'

'You don't have to do that,' I said.

'I want to. I don't want to keep being off sick.'

She turned to Flo. 'I'm dying for something to read. Does the shop downstairs have any magazines?'

'Yes, lots.'

'Can you get me a *Grazia* and a *Hello!*?'

She fumbled for her bag in the drawer by the bed.

'This is my treat,' I said, handing Flo a tenner.

We watched Flo walk out of the room.

'I hope the police find the thug who came on to Flo and did that to you,' I said.

'I won't hold my breath.'

'How old was he?'

'In his forties, maybe, and he was a fucking pleb!'

I had never heard Harriet swear before.

'Thank you so much for helping Flo.'

'I saw her by the bar and I could see she was in trouble. She couldn't handle him.'

I shuddered at the thought of what might have happened if Harriet hadn't intervened.

'I had no idea she was there.'

'You were angry with me on Friday,' Harriet said.

'Yes I was, and I'm sorry.'

'Did Julius say something?'

I did not want us to have this conversation. My feelings for Harriet were warm and grateful. My fury at her lying had dissipated and the last thing I wanted was to start accusing her of anything.

'It doesn't matter now,' I said.

'It does matter. Did he say something to you?'

'You sure you're up for this?'

'Yes.'

'I know about the screen test.'

Her expression was scared and ashamed at the same time.

'Have you seen it?'

'No, he said he's junked it.'

'He won't have. He'll keep it for sure.'

She was emphatic on that point.

'What makes you say that?'

'It gives him power, doesn't it?' she said.

I knew she had sent Flo to get the magazines so we could have this talk and I inched towards the question I *had* to ask her.

'Did he show it to you that night, the night I found you crying?'

'It was horrible. He said I would never make it on TV and

he was so cruel. I don't care about that any more, but I can't bear him to have it. Can you get hold of it and delete it?'

'Why does the screen test worry you so much?'

She shook her head. 'Please don't ask. It's too awful.'

I had to be explicit. 'But he didn't sexually assault you?'

'*It was as if he had.* It was totally humiliating and shaming.'

As she said this she looked guilty. She had lied and had caused me a world of trouble.

'I know I shouldn't have lied but he was vile about it, truly vile.'

I didn't feel any anger at that moment but I did wish that I had questioned her more rigorously that night and got to the truth that it was his rejection of the screen test that had caused her meltdown.

'He can be very cruel,' I said.

'Please can you get hold of it?'

'I don't think—'

'It was on a purple memory stick. I remember that. He'll use it to shame me and Ziggy.'

'Ziggy?'

'Yes.'

'Ziggy's in the screen test too?'

'Yes. She says she's not bothered about it but I know she is. I know she's terribly stressed out. We both are. He could show it to anyone.'

We heard Florence opening the door.

'Please get the test, *please*,' Harriet said.

Chalk Farm flat, Sunday night

I had forgotten how resilient a fourteen-year-old can be. By the evening Flo was already pulling away from our lovely

258

mother and daughter closeness and had retreated to her room to Snapchat with friends.

I was still deeply shaken as I sat on the sofa with Mr Crooks on my lap. So much had happened because I had believed Harriet's lie. If she hadn't lied I would never have revealed my shaming secret to Saul Relph or fallen out so badly with Julius. I recalled his words to me: *She didn't get what she wanted so she's making up stories, evil little stories.*

Ziggy was in the screen test too. What about Ziggy? She was no spoiled rich kid. She was an orphan, a vulnerable intern and the youngest member of my team. It was especially my duty to protect her. Julius did not want me to see that screen test. There had to be a reason for that. As I went to bed I made a resolve: I was going to get hold of that memory stick.

CHAPTER TWENTY-SEVEN

StoryWorld TV station, London Bridge

Monday morning dawned and I had waited for Rosie to arrive at our flat to walk to school with Flo so I was late into the station. I was still feeling reluctant to let Flo out of my sight. She, however, had bounced back and was irritated with me for fussing. On the way to Chalk Farm Tube I called Simon and asked him to watch the top of the show from the gallery. I had a plan. I was going to plant myself near Martine's desk and take note of her morning routine.

I hovered, flicking through the morning papers which are spread on a table outside the meeting room close to Martine's desk. She arrived ten minutes later looking grim.

'Good weekend?' I called over.

'Awful. Milo was sick on Saturday. And got the trots on Sunday.'

Milo was her beloved Jack Russell. I walked over as she hung up her coat and saw her take a bunch of keys out of her bag.

'Is he OK now?'

'A bit better. I've asked the vet's nurse to look in on him at lunchtime. That dog costs me a fortune.'

Her voice was fond. Julius had not arrived yet which was unusual. She found the key and unlocked the door to his office. I was making sympathetic noises as I watched her slip his key into her top desk drawer. Knowing Martine she would lock that drawer when she went out at lunchtime, but I would try later nonetheless. In order to search his office I'd have to choose a time when he was out and she was away from her desk. It wasn't going to be easy.

At the morning meeting Julius said he had been watching Fizzy's interview with the head of the Football Association from his dentist's reception and it was a cracker. The FA was embroiled in a major row about racism in the sport. A manager had been caught after an interview making racist comments to a pundit who joined in the banter, adding his own noxious views. The microphone had been on and though their comments hadn't gone to air a member of staff had leaked the recording to the press. Now both manager and pundit were suspended and the FA was investigating the incident. My team usually book the interview of the day but Bob's team had set this one up on Sunday. It was the talking point of the day and radio shows were running their phone-ins on kicking racism out of football.

'We were lucky to get him this morning, all the news outlets wanted him,' Bob said.

'It's good having a hard news interview from time to time, don't you think, Liz?' Julius said.

I had got down to the gallery in time to watch it and Fizzy had done a hard-hitting interview. Inwardly, I was seething at Bob's coup.

'I agree. Fizzy did a terrific job,' I said.

'I couldn't have done it without the extra briefing,' she said.

It emerged that she and Bob had come into the station on Sunday evening and he had coached her on the subject. I tried to catch her eye but she was resolutely ignoring me, addressing all her remarks to Bob or Julius.

Simon, Molly and Ziggy were seated at their desks and I

261

told them that Harriet had taken two days' leave and would be back on Wednesday. This meant extra work for Molly and Simon and I saw them exchange looks. I rarely allowed them to take leave at such short notice.

'Last minute trip, was it?' Molly asked.

There are times when I don't feel like justifying every last thing to my team and this was one of those moments. I nearly snapped at Molly but said yes and closed my door. I was consumed with how I could get into Julius's office and search for that memory stick. The screen test was the key to everything that had been happening. It had caused Harriet to accuse him of assault; it had sent Fizzy into a meltdown and Ziggy was also implicated. I had to get hold of it.

All morning I kept getting up and looking out of my window towards his office. Martine didn't budge from her position on guard outside his room. Around one I saw Julius leave for lunch. Ten minutes later Martine left her post. I had often seen her in the Hub and she would buy a sandwich and take it back to her desk. I came out of my room and Molly and Simon had gone for lunch but Ziggy was sitting there. She looked up at me, her face pinched.

'Is Harry OK?'

'She's fine,' I said and hurried on.

I had cut her short but I did not have long. I tried his door but it was locked. I stood by her desk and pulled at the desk drawer where she kept the keys. As I'd expected it was locked. I walked back and Ziggy was hunched over a Coke and a bag of crisps which appeared to be her lunch. I sat down opposite her.

'Harriet is fine. Her parents wanted to take her to the country for a couple of days,' I said.

Ziggy gave me such an anxious look then. I wondered if I

should ask her about the screen test but there was something in that look of hers that made me keep quiet.

The afternoon dragged on. I walked down to Fizzy's dressing room but she had left for the day. She was avoiding me and there was nothing I could do about it. Simon caught me on my way back and gave me the brief he had prepared for the return of John of Sheffield tomorrow. Fizzy will be interviewing him about how he's getting on being a sole parent to a teenage girl and two boys. He has started dating again, after years of celibacy. His appearance on our show in September had been the catalyst for this. The angle tomorrow will be how hard it is for lone parents to have a sex life. I could relate to that. It's Betty's territory and usually I would have told her that it was happening, but I was worn out with taking everyone's feelings into account and I didn't ring her. If she sees the interview and complains I'll deal with it then. I hope he'll be as good as he was the first time. I need a good 'real life' interview after Bob's success this morning.

Gerry called me at four and he was enthusing about his Sunday roast with Amber.

'We drove out to this pub on the river, near Henley. Divinely picturesque, Liz. She knows all the best places to go.'

I was only half listening. My hunch was that Martine would leave promptly as her sick dog Milo would be on her mind. Julius would have his own key but I hoped he was not as assiduous as she was about locking up. I would wait and try his office this evening.

'And she thinks she may be getting back with Julius,' Gerry said.

That made me pay attention.

'Really?'

'He has to go to a big do on Friday, some award ceremony, and he's asked her to be his date for the night.'

Martine left at five-thirty sharp. I waited as each of my team members packed their things and left for the night. They waved at me but did not come into my room. This was the first work day after Flo's horrible experience and here I was loitering at the station when I should have been at home with her; putting her first. I tried to clear my admin but I couldn't settle to anything. I kept getting up and looking down in the direction of his office. Julius often worked late. There is a long hours' culture at TV stations and when I first started I had noticed how the ambitious staff members would not leave their desks until the boss had gone. I'd stopped doing that years ago but tonight I had my reasons for staying. I decided I would give it ten more minutes and that was it. Flo needed me. I was locking my room when I saw Julius heading towards the stairs. I watched as he walked down and across to the exit. I waited until he was out of the building and then I hurried over to his office and tried his door. It was locked. I had not heard Bob coming up behind me.

'Trying to get into his office?'

I swung round. He was standing a few feet away but must have been deliberately stealthy to catch me like that and he had seen me trying the door. We had barely exchanged a word since our confrontation outside the station.

'I left something in there.'

'Oh yes?'

His expression and tone of voice were hostile. I made a move to push past him.

'It's none of your business,' I said.

'But you poke your nose into other people's business, don't you?'

I'd been feeling tense all day and I'd had enough of his aggression.

'You leave me alone or you'll regret it.'

'I know what you're looking for,' he said.

On the Tube going home I put it together. Fizzy must have told him about the screen test. She had been with him last night at the TV station, getting her briefing on the racism row. I wondered if they had had sex in her dressing room. Today, at the morning meeting, they had appeared close and united again.

Chalk Farm flat, 8 p.m.

Janis and I were standing on the pavement and I told her I didn't want Flo going over to Paige's house any more.

'The parents are never there. If they want to meet then Paige has to come here.'

'Nasty little bitch, isn't she?' Janis said.

'I'd like to throttle her with my bare hands.'

I've been worrying about how much longer I can go on paying Janis to come to the flat. Money is going to get tighter without any contribution from Ben. I know I am being overprotective but I hate the idea of Flo being on her own every evening till I get back.

I decided to make my carrot, onion and pearl barley soup. It's calming to make and comforting to eat. Flo joined me in the kitchen and sat down at the table.

'I told Janis what happened,' she said.

'I'm glad you did that, sweetheart.'

I thought her face looked peaky as it does when she is sad.

'Paige has unfriended me.'

I cheered inside but this had hurt her a lot.

'Well, that's her loss.'

The soup was simmering on a low flame and I sat down at the table opposite her.

'Peanut person,' I said.

She smiled wanly. It was not the first time I had made reference to this. It is one of my fond memories of her. We were at a party when she was four years old and there were these bowls of peanuts lying around. I'd told Flo many times that she should not eat peanuts. We'd done a story at work about the things children choke on and it had made me anxious, as so many things did in the early years of being a mum. She had pointed to the bowl of nuts.

'Can I try a peanut today, Mum?'

I said she could but she must chew it. She took one large peanut from the bowl, bit into it and swallowed it. Then she looked up at me and said with great pride: 'I'm a peanut person now.'

Later, I put on my laptop. My heart lurched when I saw that there was a new email from Saul Relph in my inbox. He was short and to the point.

Dear Liz,

It has been a week since you sent me your confidential email about the event at the Christmas party seven years ago.

Have you come to a decision about whether or not you wish to take this matter further?

Please advise.

Yours as ever,

Saul Relph OBE

Flo's disastrous night had pushed my email to him right out of my thoughts. His wording was cold again and the last thing he wanted was for me to make a formal complaint against his precious Julius. I kept my response short.

Dear Saul,

I too have been giving this much thought. It was a frightening experience but on reflection I have decided not to pursue this matter any further.

I would be grateful if this remains entirely confidential between you and me for the sake of future working relationships.

All best,

Liz

CHAPTER TWENTY-EIGHT

StoryWorld TV station, London Bridge

He did it again. John from Sheffield charmed Fizzy and charmed our viewers with his tale of life at the single-parent frontline. I think his appeal is that he talks so authentically and it is such a change from the celebrities and politicians who say what they think our viewers want to hear. We've been getting loads of tweets and emails and Julius opened the meeting by saying that was what StoryWorld was all about, airing real-life stories that other stations might overlook but which gave our viewers an insight into the things that mattered to people. He was briefly eloquent on the subject and I saw Bob's face darken. But that is the game Julius always plays. He builds one of us up one day and moves his favour to someone else the next day to keep us all feeling insecure.

He stood up and gestured to Martine and she walked into the meeting room carrying her laptop. She is a trained first-aider and Julius had invited her to talk to us about our responsibilities. I'm sure he had done that to make her feel important and we were all expected to go along with it. She had prepared a PowerPoint and started to talk through the slides and it was dull.

'Now it's important that each one of you nominate a team member to be a first-aider. I will train them up over the next three months,' she said.

I knew it would look rude to walk out on her presentation

but this had to be the moment to get into his office. I stood up, clutching my stomach.

'Terribly sorry, Martine, but I have to leave for a few minutes.'

She looked daggers at me.

'Bad stomach,' I gasped, hurrying out of the room.

I had perhaps ten minutes at most. Julius would not tolerate longer than ten minutes on first aid. The meeting room has windows on all sides so I had to make a detour as if I was walking to the Ladies and then I walked through the newsroom, down their stairs, back up the stairs on our side to reach his office from the other side. Three minutes gone already. His door was unlocked and I was in. It was weird how transgressive it felt to be in there on my own. I scanned his desk and there were orderly piles of running orders and sales figures and no memory sticks. His desk had six drawers; three on each side. The top one on the right had pens, paperclips, a stapler and a man's fancy manicure set. The second one down had a pad and a sheaf of expense forms. The third one down had a pair of cufflinks, a few name badges and at the back a stash of memory sticks. I scooped them up. They were all silver and black, standard StoryWorld issue. I was starting to sweat as I put them back. The top drawer on the left had a wedge of index cards with what looked like a speech handwritten on them. The middle left drawer contained a pile of StoryWorld photos and some foreign coins. The bottom left-hand drawer wouldn't open. I got down on my knees and tugged at it. It was locked. He hadn't locked any of the other drawers and I was sure the purple memory stick was in there.

'What are you doing?'

Martine was standing in the doorway and I was on my knees by his desk.

'Looking for my earring,' I said.

Thank God I'd had the sense to prepare a story.

'Your earring?'

My face must have been bright red as I stood up and hers was a picture of suspicion. I tried to sound normal.

'When I saw him on Friday; I was wearing my favourite turquoise—'

'You didn't see him on Friday.'

Her voice was cold.

'For Christ's sake, Martine, don't give me third degree. I love those earrings and—'

'I thought you had a bad stomach.'

'I do, but then I remembered my earring and—'

'And it was more important than listening to me. You're expected back in the meeting,' she said and her voice was icy.

We had never got on that well but I knew that today, by missing her talk and being caught under his desk, I had burned my bridges with her.

Mid-morning, Fizzy came to my office and closed the door firmly behind her. I was glad she had sought me out but could tell by the determined set to her face that she was not happy.

'I've come to a decision,' she said.

She probably did not even realise it but she brushed her right hand across her stomach as she said: 'I've booked myself into a clinic for a termination.'

I nodded.

'Don't try to dissuade me, Liz.'

'I won't.'

'Thank you.'

We looked at each other and I wanted to hug her but the team were sitting outside and would have seen it and thought it was odd. And, though she was holding herself together, a hug might make her start to cry.

'Can I do anything to help?'

'You're the only woman I've told and I was wondering if you'd come to the clinic with me?'

I reached over and squeezed her hand. 'Of course I will.'

'You'll need to be away from here at least half a day. I'm going to drive there and I'll need you to drive me home after, you know, afterwards.'

Now she did look as if she might cry.

'Wouldn't it be easier if we used taxis?'

'God no! I'm not going to let any taxi driver take me there and sell the story to the tabloids.'

'I hadn't thought of that.'

After she left I wondered why she hadn't told Martine. And then I realised it was because what Martine knows she relays straight back to Julius.

In the afternoon I took the Tube to Tottenham Court Road and walked to the Soho offices of a major talent agency. It had taken me weeks to get a meeting with their top booker, who is known in the business as the Tarantula. She has a roster of film and TV A-listers and my task was to persuade her that StoryWorld was the place to promote her people. She kept me waiting outside her office for thirty-seven minutes. I hate it when people do that; they are saying that their time is more important than your time. I was feeling disproportionally sad that Fizzy had decided to have an abortion. When I was a student, in my second year, I got pregnant by a fellow student at my college. We'd had this immature on and off relationship and the pregnancy was an accident. We were twenty years old and we weren't committed enough to each other or ready to go through with having a child together. We had both panicked and agreed it would mess up our degrees and our futures so I booked in for an NHS termination at the earliest opportunity. We split up for good about four months later and I thought I was OK about it. The strange thing is, I'm not even over it now, twenty years later. It has left me with an ineradicable sadness. Occasionally I have a sense of my unborn daughter – it is always a daughter in my mind – looking over my shoulder at Flo. I realised how invested I was in the idea of Fizzy going through with her pregnancy and with us taking on her critics together. But Bob had prevailed, her fears had prevailed. People say it is the woman's choice but is it really? It's hard to proceed if the father is against the pregnancy. Now she needed me to be supportive of her decision.

As I walked back into the station Simon was on his way out.

'I'm off to see Dirk. I thought maybe we could do a follow-up story on him. Get him in with Fizzy. See how he's coping with his prosthetic leg. He told me he's in the gym most days building his upper body strength and he sounded positive.'

'Good idea. Maybe he's another John. He's a brave man. Most of us would crumble after what he's gone through.'

'Are you OK?'

'I had a meeting with the Tarantula. She's very good at making you feel like you're a bit of shit on her shoe.'

'Did you get any guests from her?'

'Not a single A-lister. She offered me a couple of faders who need exposure.'

'She's evil,' he said.

Ziggy was sitting on her own at the team desks. She told me Molly had gone to a book launch in Piccadilly. It was the moment for me to talk to her about the screen test.

'Can you pop into my room?'

She looked alarmed as I closed the door and she hovered in front of my desk.

'Sit down, Ziggy.'

She perched on the edge of the sofa and I leaned against my desk towards her.

'Now I don't want you to get upset. Harriet told me about the screen test.'

Her head drooped and her cheeks flamed. After a long pause she whispered: 'I'm sorry.'

'*I'm* sorry because I know you're both worried about it.'

She was looking down on the carpet.

'Is that why she's away?'

'She'll be back tomorrow,' I said.

'It doesn't bother me as much as it bothers her. I thought she might leave, you know, because of it.'

'She is very upset about it.'

'He lied,' she said.

'Julius?'

'Yeah; he told me I would get a chance to use the equipment, help with the sound recording, you know.'

'But that didn't happen?'

'No.'

'So you took part in it?'

She looked up at me, stricken, and I wanted to know what was on that screen test so much.

'Won't you tell me what's on it?'

'I can't. I swore to Harry I wouldn't say a word.'

She was wringing her hands in her agitation. I couldn't push her; I knew what it felt like to have a shaming secret.

'Please don't get upset. I promised Harriet I would get hold of the screen test and destroy it.'

'Did you get it?'

'I've tried and it's impossible to get into his office. Martine is a Rottweiler. She caught me this morning under his desk!'

'I'll get it for you,' Ziggy said.

'No! I can't let you do that.'

'Why not?'

'You could get into big trouble.'

'No one notices me. I don't count.'

'Oh, Ziggy, of course you count.'

'I'm invisible to people like Martine.'

She was saying she was at the bottom of the food chain at StoryWorld and that was true.

'And I want to help Harry.'

'I'm sure you do but if you get caught... No, Ziggy, I can't let you do this.'

'But you tried to get it.'

'I can bluff my way out. I have reasons to go into his office. You get caught and they'll have you marched out of here and I won't be able to do anything about it.'

'I'm a runner. It's my job to go in and out of offices with packages. I do it all the time.'

I sat down on the sofa next to her. 'This feels all wrong,' I said.

'Please. You said we were a team. You said we had to support each other.'

I was touched that she had remembered my words.

'You know it's on a purple memory stick?'

She nodded.

'I think he's locked it away in the left-hand bottom drawer of his desk. That was the only one that was locked. He's hiding something in there.'

'So I'll have to pick the lock,' she said.

I was on the Tube going home and it was a second late night at the station; I have got to start putting Flo first. I was consumed with curiosity about what was on the screen test. Harriet and Ziggy will not talk about it and Julius is keeping it under lock and key. I realised I had recruited Ziggy, the most vulnerable member of my team, to do a job of breaking and entering.

During my walk home I wondered if I was doing a wrong thing for the right reasons. We were planning to steal something from his office. Sure, I wanted to help Harriet and Ziggy, but I also wanted to have something on Julius after all these years. Was that my true motivation?

CHAPTER TWENTY-NINE

StoryWorld TV station, London Bridge

At the morning meeting I had good news to report. Ledley's food advertisers are on board and StoryWorld will get a nice chunk of ad money from them in January. Julius thanked me formally.

'We need more of these kinds of tie-ups,' he said.

'And we're holding the launch of Ledley's marinade in our atrium in December. I'd appreciate it if senior managers would attend and show their support for him,' I said.

Bob looked stony-faced as Fizzy exclaimed: 'Go, Ledley.'

'Thanks, Fizzy, I'm asking Gerry and Betty along too.'

Harriet was back with the team today. She had applied make-up to her bruise and although I could detect a trace of purple beneath the concealer I doubted if anyone else could. She popped her head round the door.

'Hello.'

'Come on in,' I said.

She closed the door and I felt an impulse of warmth towards her.

'How are you feeling?'

'Oh, I'm fine physically, thanks. But I can't stop thinking about the screen test. Did you manage to get it?'

'Not yet, but we're going to.'

She looked doubtful at that.

'Won't you tell me why it worries you so much?'

'Please don't ask,' she said.

I didn't press her because I still felt indebted to her. I asked her about the Cat and Mouse instead. I wanted to know what kind of place it was.

'It's kind of a dive from the outside but they get the hot bands there.'

'Not a place for fourteen-year-olds though?'

'Definitely not.'

'Thank heavens you were there and you intervened. I can't thank you enough, Harriet.'

'How is Florence?'

'She's OK but that girl she was with has dropped her.'

'Teenage girls can be very cruel.'

'It's good to have you back and I'd like you to research a fashion expert for the show.'

I had decided it was time to give her some real responsibility, and fashion was her thing. She looked incredulous and then delighted.

'I'd love to do that, thank you so much.'

'Oh, but he needs to be male,' I said quickly.

'Why?'

I didn't want to be disloyal and share Fizzy's insecurities about female presenters.

'I think it will be interesting to have a male view on fashion. Think of a Gok Wan or a Brad Goreski.'

Fizzy and I left the station at twelve noon. I had instructed Simon to deputise for me for the rest of the day and Ziggy had cancelled my one afternoon meeting. Fizzy's car was parked at the back of StoryWorld. It was a Nissan Figaro convertible in pale blue and hardly anonymous. The seats were leather and the dashboard was retro style.

'Cute car,' I said as I clicked in my seatbelt.

The clinic she had booked into was on the border of Berkshire and an eighty-minute drive from London Bridge. Fizzy's face was set throughout the drive and she had put a CD into the player so that we didn't need to talk. I was feeling churned up and upset for her as we covered the miles. As we approached the gates she made an involuntary whimper. She drove slowly up the long drive that swept up to the clinic. It was a white 1920s building that looked more like a country house hotel and spa than a medical centre. She parked the car badly, screeching on the circle of gravel that fronted the building, and then negotiated her way into the car park. She turned off the engine.

'We're early,' she said.

'Let's go for a walk then,' I said.

We got our coats from the back seat. Hers was a beautiful champagne-coloured suede coat with a fur collar. We locked our bags in the boot and wandered through the grounds that surrounded the clinic. There was a November bite to the wind but we were both wrapped up warmly. Vistas of ancient evergreens opened up in front of us as we walked along and I spotted what looked like a walled kitchen garden at the end of one path. We sat on a bench under a spreading cedar of Lebanon.

'It's a beautiful park. Hard to believe what this place is used for, isn't it?' she said.

'It's so peaceful.'

'They do cosmetic surgery here too, you know,' she said.

That figured. I could see the lighted windows of the clinic through the trees. It would cost a lot to be treated here. We sat side by side and listened to the wind in the branches above our heads.

'You're not saying much, Liz.'

278

'I'm sorry.'

'You don't think I should have the termination, do you?'

'It's your decision, Fizz, it has to be. You're the one who has to live with the consequences.'

'Better get it over with,' she said.

We walked back towards the building and picked up her bag from the boot of the car.

'I feel scared,' she said in a small voice as I pushed open the clinic door.

Inside it was all white and bright and efficient. I was finding it hard to stop myself from saying you don't have to do this.

'I'll be here when you wake up,' I said.

The receptionist was discreetly solicitous. She would be used to dealing with well-known people, I thought. She directed us to a consulting room. Fizzy tapped on the door and a tall balding man in a white coat opened it, greeted us solemnly and indicated the two chairs we should sit on. He offered us each a glass of iced water.

'You have been fasting, Miss Wentworth?'

She nodded. His manner was soothing. He handed her a consent form which Fizzy had to sign and the doctor went through it with her. Fizzy got out her pen and signed the form without reading it further. We were then directed to another room where Fizzy was to undress and put on a green surgical gown.

'Don't go,' she said to me.

I helped her out of her dress, folded it and put it into her overnight bag. When she was down to her bra and knickers I could see the slight swelling of her stomach. I helped her into the green gown and her knees were trembling. A nurse entered the room and told Fizzy to follow her.

'Can my friend come with me?'

'It's best if she stays in the guest room,' the nurse said.

'I want her to come with me,' Fizzy said.

'I'm sorry; we're going to the operating room now. We can't let guests go there.'

Fizzy threw me a frightened look and started to follow the nurse down the corridor. I was fighting back tears as I watched their retreating figures. I said 'Don't' under my breath but she was near the end of the corridor and couldn't have heard me. Fizzy suddenly stopped. The nurse said a few words to her and she took several more steps. She stopped again. I was still standing at the threshold of the room she had left. She turned and was walking back towards me.

'I can't do this. Take me home, Liz.'

And then I hugged her and we were both crying.

The drive back with Fizzy was an altogether different affair from our unhappy journey there. She decided she was up to driving and I was looking out of the window and spotted a teashop near the clinic. I suggested we stop and get something to eat before we drove back to London because she had been fasting for hours. It was called The Crumpetty Tree and was one of those chintzy places with pretty china teacups and home-made cakes under glass domes. We ordered a pot of breakfast tea and debated the merits of chocolate Guinness cake with mascarpone topping or the lemon drizzle. I could tell that the woman who ran the teashop recognised Fizzy but she behaved as if she hadn't. Fizzy chose the lemon drizzle and the owner cut her a generous slice of it.

'I never eat cake,' Fizzy said.

She dug her fork in and chewed on the soft sponge.

'This is fantastic.'

It was only when we were paying that the owner asked if Fizzy would mind signing a menu.

'Of course, happy to, what's your name?'

'Genevieve.'

The owner spelled it out rather breathlessly as Fizzy wrote: *Wonderful cake, Genevieve, thank you* and signed her name with a flourish.

Fizzy was revived as she drove us back towards London.

'As I was walking towards the operating room I thought if I do this I will be unhappy about it for the rest of my life.'

'It is a huge thing,' I said.

'Huge and irrevocable. There are few things in life that are irrevocable, aren't there? I mean you can split up with a man and get back with him. Or leave a company and go back later. But a termination, that *is* irrevocable.'

As she pulled up where I planned to get out she said: 'He'll give me hell, you know, but he's got two children already.'

She drove off and I was happy that she hadn't taken that irrevocable step.

Chalk Farm flat, 6 p.m.

Janis and Flo were surprised to see me back so early. I slumped down on the sofa, completely drained by the emotion of the afternoon.

'There's some quiche left if you fancy it,' Janis said as she put on her coat.

It was about an hour later when I got a call from Ziggy. She sounded elated and for a moment I thought she had got hold of the memory stick.

'I got into his office. He was out and she was away from her desk. I'd hung onto this package I had to deliver so I had an excuse for being in there. But then I couldn't pick the stupid lock.'

I imagined her in his office trying to pick the lock on his drawer while Martine could have come back at any moment.

'I feel sick with nerves about you doing this,' I said.

'It's cool. I'll get a better tool next time.'

She sounded confident.

'And Martine didn't see anything?'

'Not a thing. I gave myself five minutes and when it wouldn't budge I got out and put the package on her desk before she came back.'

She's a smart girl with a cool head and if anyone can pull this off it is Ziggy. I found myself speculating again about what was on the screen test that was causing them both so much angst.

CHAPTER THIRTY

As I left the meeting this morning Ziggy followed me down to the Hub and I could see that she wanted to talk to me confidentially. I bought her a drink and we sat at the table the furthest from the food counter like a couple of co-conspirators. I noticed she was wearing a nice suede jacket which I assumed had once belonged to Harriet.

'I've got myself the perfect tool and I'm going to get that drawer open next time,' she said with satisfaction.

She seemed to be relishing the task ahead and I looked around the café nervously. Martine had come in and was queueing at the counter. Ziggy followed the direction of my eyes.

'You'll have to outwit her,' I said.

Ziggy was looking at Martine thoughtfully.

'Don't worry, I'll choose my moment.'

I went to find Fizzy in her dressing room. She was looking at herself in the mirror.

'My face is getting fatter,' she said.

'You look lovely. Ledley called and he's planning to cook Brown Stew Chicken tomorrow.'

'Yuk. Don't you think that sounds unpleasant?'

'Not the best name, perhaps, but it tastes great. It's a traditional Jamaican dish.'

'Just don't ask me to eat it. I'm feeling queasy every morning. Will you tell Ledley my stomach is upset and not to press me to sample it?'

'Sure. How are you, apart from the queasiness?'

'I'm good.'

Time is passing and her pregnancy is advancing and she's going to have to say something pretty soon.

'Have you thought more about sharing your condition with the viewers?'

'I think about it all the time, but it's so high risk, isn't it?'

'I could help you draft your words,' I said.

She peered into the mirror again and turned her head sideways and looked at her profile.

'Someone *is* going to notice my face is getting fatter. I simply don't have the energy to write anything at the moment. I've started having a sleep most afternoons.'

'Good for you. I'll do a first draft for you and you can tweak it.'

'Would you? Thank you, Liz.'

An hour later Harriet came into my office and she was the most animated I had seen her since she arrived at Story-World.

'I think I've found the perfect man for the fashion slot. He's called Guy Browne and he's fashion director at *The Gloss*.'

'*The Gloss*?'

'It's a high street fashion and celeb weekly. He's done some TV and writes a style blog with a decent following. He's on YouTube too.'

'Show me.'

Harriet got the link up on my screen and we watched a couple of clips: one of Guy being interviewed at London Fashion Week and another presenting a segment on denim for different body shapes. He's a nice-looking man in his early thirties and he has a good voice. The one thing we have to avoid is a voice that will grate with viewers.

'Yes, he looks good; fluent and he comes over kind of likeable,' I said.

'I'm glad you like him.'

'We still need to do a screen test, to be sure. Can you get him in, as soon as possible?'

'I could ask him to come in tomorrow?'

'That would be great.'

'And you'll be using the big studio?'

'No, we'll have to use the small studio. It's way too expensive to fire up the large one for a screen test,' I said.

She grimaced. She'd had experience of the small studio, of course, that Sunday with Julius and Ziggy. We exchanged a long look.

'Zig told me she's trying to get hold of the memory stick,' she said.

Every time I think about that I get a sick feeling because I know that I'm exploiting Ziggy and my fears on that score won't be stilled.

'You realise what a risk Ziggy is taking? If she gets caught I won't be able to keep her on.'

'But she wants to do this. She's all fired up about it,' Harriet said.

That was true and I could see there was no going back now but it occurred to me that Harriet could say that from a position of safety. She wouldn't lose her job if Ziggy was caught. And yet it was Ziggy who really needed her position at StoryWorld.

As I was leaving work Ziggy was still stationed at her desk. The others had gone for the night.

'You're working late,' I said.

She glanced up at me.

'Just biding my time, you know...'

We both looked in the direction of Julius's office. His light was on and he was still working.

'Please, please be careful,' I said.

Chalk Farm flat, 7.30 p.m.

Almost as soon as I got in Flo asked if she could go on a school skiing trip in January. She had all the papers with her. It looked expensive and then there would be all the clothes we'd need to buy for it. I thought it best to say no straight away rather than let her think it might be possible.

'I don't have the extra cash at the moment, sweets. Sorry, but no can do.' She pulled a sulky face.

'I really want to go. I'll ask Dad,' she said.

'Dad's going through a tough time financially at the moment.'

'He earns loads.'

'Not at the moment he doesn't.'

She was walking back towards her room. This was the time to tell her what was going on.

'There's something I need to tell you.'

She stopped and turned, looked at me warily.

'What is it?'

'Dad isn't working at the moment.'

'He's not working?'

'He's going through a bad patch and... well... Granny and Granddad are having to support him.'

'I knew he wasn't OK last time, I knew something was wrong,' she said.

'You were right, sweetheart. He's moved back in with them.'

'Poor Dad.'

She didn't say anything else but I could tell she was upset because she picked Mr Crooks up from the sofa and carried him into her bedroom with her. She cuddles him when she is sad. I stood at her threshold and watched her get onto her bed and start to stroke him. At times like this I'm a great believer in the healing power of comforting food and drinks.

'Would you like a hot chocolate and some toast?'

'Yes please.'

I made us both a drink and toast for her, spreading the butter thickly and slicing it into fingers the way she likes it. I took it into her and sat on the end of her bed.

'Thanks. What room is Dad in?'

'Oh, I don't know. Grace didn't say. Probably his old room…'

'But that's the room I always sleep in.'

I wondered if now was the time to tell her that she wouldn't be going down to Portsmouth for a while. I left it. She needs to absorb the bad news a bit at a time.

Sitting up in bed later I opened an email from Todd. He wrote that his father had arrived home from hospital that day and the consultant had told them all they can do for him now is palliative care. His father was calm about his approaching death but his mother was distraught. She was leaning on him more and more. He suggested that perhaps we could Skype each other and have a talk. The time difference makes it difficult. The best time to Skype Sydney would be around ten in the morning here and I'm always tied up at work at that time. I wrote back that maybe we could Skype at the weekend. I went on to describe Flo's disastrous night at the Cat and

Mouse and how much it had shaken me. I wished that he was back in the UK and that I could have talked to him about that awful evening. It was clear that Todd would not be coming back to London any time soon.

CHAPTER THIRTY-ONE

Harriet and I met with Guy, the fashion expert, in the Hub and it turned out that he knew Amber and was also acquainted with Julius.

'Amber assists with the styling on our shoots sometimes. And I've met Julius a couple of times at her place,' he said.

'He's our director of programmes,' I said.

'Yes, Amber told me that. So what do you want me to do this morning?'

'You'll be in our small studio. Speak directly into the camera for ten minutes about any fashion topic you want.'

'I brought along some photos of this year's Oscars' outfits. I thought I could talk about best and worst dressed,' he said.

We took him through to the small studio. Henry had arranged for a digital technician to fire it up and I sat next to him with Harriet on my left. We watched Guy through the gallery window as he was miked up and told to look into the camera and start talking after the countdown. The light came on and Guy launched into his commentary on the Oscars' outfits. He held up the first photo to the camera.

'This is how to do understated elegance in a custom off-the-shoulder Tom Ford gown. Her timeless Hollywood waves and red lips bring some much needed old-school glamour to the awards season. A lot of the stars at this year's ceremony would have done well to follow her lead. She is showing that less is most definitely more.'

Next he showed us a photo of a younger actor in a dress of bright metallic green with a huge fishtail fanning out at the bottom.

'The fishtail cut is clearly here to stay and while I can get on board with the Armani version, this is how *not* to do it. The metallic green of the dress is way too mermaid for this shape and the poker-straight slick hair does nothing to save the comparison. Fish out of water comes to mind here.'

And so it went on. He mixed up his good reviews with his bad. He knows his stuff but he made it accessible and made us laugh. I'm sure Fizzy will connect with him and he will be an excellent replacement for Sal. It was the first time in weeks that I felt good about my job. When the screen test was over I told Guy that the slot was his and we wanted him on air at the earliest opportunity. He is raring to go and we walked him to the exit. Harriet was doing fashion speak with him as she saw him to the taxi.

'Thank you for finding him. He's perfect because he'll bring some wit into the show and we've been lacking that since Sal went.'

'I'm so pleased,' she said.

'Come in for a minute.'

She followed me into my room.

'Your trial period is coming to an end and if you want the permanent job of researcher it's yours.'

She looked the happiest I'd seen her.

'I'm thrilled, I really am. Thank you so much.'

'I like your fashion ideas and I also thought you could take over more of the celebrity briefs,' I said.

The job of writing the celebrity briefs was always an issue in the team. Molly hated doing them so Simon tended to get overloaded. I could see Harriet making that area her own.

'Yes please, I'd love to. Does Julius know you're making me permanent?'

'I haven't told him yet. I don't have to clear it with him.'

'And there's no way he can block it?'

'Absolutely not.'

'Can we tell the others?'

'Yes, of course.'

I followed her out.

'I'm happy to tell you that Harriet will be joining us on a permanent basis.'

Ziggy and Simon looked pleased, Molly less so. Harriet suggested that after work they all go to Hays Galleria up the river and celebrate.

'Drinks are on me,' she said. 'Will you come?' she asked me.

'I can't tonight, sorry. Friday night is Flo's night, but have a great time.'

I went back into my office. I know why I made Harriet permanent and I'm not proud of it. She doesn't work as hard as Molly and Simon and she's thin on ideas, though recently her fashion ideas have been good. But she went to help Flo when she was in danger and that counts for so much.

Around six Harriet, Molly and Simon set off for the pub. I heard Ziggy say she'd join them in a while; she had something she had to do first. Thirty minutes later I was shutting my PC down when Ziggy appeared at my threshold. She came in, closed my door and, grinning widely, she held up a small purple memory stick. I leapt to my feet.

'Oh my God you're brilliant.'

She burst out laughing.

'It took me two minutes to pick the lock and it was lying there in the drawer,' she said.

We were both euphoric and I hugged her. She had timed it to perfection, slipping into his office when Julius had gone downstairs to change his clothes.

'I knew he'd be doing that because Martine had sent me to fetch his dinner suit from the cleaners. So I kept watching his office until I saw him coming out carrying the suit.'

'Brilliant.'

'Martine had gone so I whipped in there.'

'Genius. And Harriet will be overjoyed,' I said.

Ziggy nodded happily. She turned the memory stick over in her hand and then put it into the back pocket of her jeans.

'And now I'm going to get rid of it,' she said.

'Get rid of it?'

'Yeah; I'm going to throw it in the river.'

I shook my head at that.

'Let me have it, Ziggy.'

'No, I don't want you to have it.'

'Why not?'

'I don't want you to see it. It's going in the river.'

'Please don't do that.'

'I don't want anyone to see it ever again,' she said.

I could see that she had gained strength from outwitting Martine and cracking the lock on the desk of Julius Jones, the boss of StoryWorld. But I too wanted some of the power that having the memory stick would give me. At last I would have something over Julius.

'I can understand your feelings but I can do far more for you both if I have it.'

She looked down at the floor and kept her hands in her back pockets. I wanted to plead with her to give me the memory stick but I remembered that if I went on too much about something with Flo she resisted me all the more strongly. And Ziggy was not much older than Flo.

'I'm going to the pub to see Harry and the others now,' she said.

'I'll walk out with you.'

I grabbed my coat and locked my room. We walked down the stairs to the exit and I saw Julius and Amber standing in the reception area. He was dressed in black tie and looked good in his formal suit; striking and handsome. Amber was wearing a full-length dove-grey evening dress with delicate spaghetti straps and she was fiddling with her beaded clutch bag. They were on their way to that award ceremony Gerry had mentioned. Julius gave me a small nod but Amber ignored me and I felt frumpy as I walked past them. Ziggy and I parted company outside the building.

'Please don't throw it away,' I said.

Chalk Farm flat, Friday evening

I had a disconsolate Friday night veg-out with Flo. I was worried that Ziggy would throw the screen test into the river; that seemed in character. She has been screwed over all her life, why should she trust me? The sight of Julius going off to that award ceremony with Amber all dressed up to the nines had got to me too. He behaves like a total shit but still manages to continue with his privileged life.

I laid out our usual Friday night feast of pizza and nachos and dips. Flo wanted to watch back-to-back episodes of *Gossip Girl* on Netflix. She has a crush on the lead 'bad boy' character Chuck Bass. I sat next to her on the sofa but I wasn't taking it in.

Ben called me at eight-thirty this morning, which was early for a Sunday. I pulled myself up into a sitting position as he said he was getting the next train to London and wanted to take us out to lunch. I was surprised and when I told Flo later she said in a suspicious voice:

'Did you tell him about the other night?'

'No, I did not. This is his idea to go out for lunch.'

I did wonder why he was doing this. He was broke, apparently. Maybe he was trying to make amends to Flo for her not going down to Portsmouth.

Ben arrived several hours later. Flo ran to answer the door and he hugged her for a long moment and kissed the top of her head.

'Beautiful sproglet,' he said.

It's been ages since he's been here and about a year since I last saw him. His hair has receded and if anything this makes his large brown eyes, the eyes I fell for, even more striking. We gave each other an awkward hug.

'Good to see you,' I said.

'Come see my room, Dad.' Flo grabbed his arm.

'I'm making coffee,' I said.

When they emerged we sat at the kitchen table and I poured from the cafetière. He was looking around our room and he got up and walked over to my bookshelf. My little art deco figure *Luer* was in pride of place on the top shelf, holding her onyx ball aloft.

'I'm glad you've still got her,' he said.

'She's beautiful,' I said.

He nodded and I thought he looked apprehensive as he

said: 'Lunch is on me. Any suggestions?'

'There's a good food pub near here, The Wounded Hart, and we can walk there.'

Ben and Flo walked in front of me. She was chatting to him all the way and every now and then he put his arm around her, pulled her towards him and kissed the top of her head. The Wounded Hart is an old coaching inn on the junction of two roads and inside it has red stained glass at the top of its windows and scrubbed wooden tables throughout. Flo and I ordered the roast chicken with all the trimmings and Ben chose the roast beef. He asked for a bottle of red wine.

'Do we need a bottle?' I asked.

'I think so,' he said.

We must have looked like a typical happy family enjoying a Sunday roast together but Ben was keyed up. He downed his first glass of wine fast.

'How are Grace and Pete?' I asked.

'They're good. The best mum and dad you could ask for.'

He said that with feeling. When we had finished our meal he topped up my glass again and sat back.

'I need to tell you both some news.'

We looked at him expectantly.

'I'm going away for a bit. I've got myself a job overseas.'

'Overseas?' I said.

'Yes, an amazing job in Dubai. They want me to oversee all the aerial photography for a major land development out there.'

I was stunned at this news and Flo looked confused as Ben went on talking and explaining how great it was going to be.

'It's such an exciting project. They're creating land from the sea and building on it and your old dad is going to earn a mint.'

'This is definite?' I asked.

'My appointment was confirmed on Friday.'

Flo leaned into him.

'When are you going, Dad?'

'In a week, darling sproglet.'

She flinched at that and I gave Ben a cold look.

'I'll be back several times a year and you can come visit me.'

'It's a long way,' I said, and my voice was tight.

'Seven hours, not too bad,' he said.

'But I won't see you very often,' Flo said.

'Darling girl, it's not for ever. Only for a couple of years.'

'I guess we can WhatsApp and Skype,' she said.

'That's my best girl.'

He put his arm around her shoulders and avoided returning my look while she sipped at her diet Coke.

Chalk Farm flat, Sunday night

I called Ben after ten and said all the things that I couldn't say at our lunch.

'You'll never see Flo and these years are critical.'

'It's the only way and it's not for ever. I can't get work here. I've got to get out of the UK for a year or two and start again.'

'Flo needs you in her life now.'

'She needs a father who can provide for her. This way I earn a lot of money. Think how much that will help when she goes to college. And I could pay for skiing trips too.'

'That's a cheap shot. Skiing trips don't matter. Having a father in her life does.'

'I knew you'd give me a hard time. I knew it. We're not

talking about a bit of Brie this time. We're talking about how I can rebuild my life.'

He was referring to a ridiculous row we'd had years ago. We were recently installed in our small house in East Finchley and I'd invited the neighbours around for drinks and had prepared some nibbles. The centrepiece of the spread was a large triangle of Brie which I'd kept out of the fridge and it was oozing onto the plate to perfection. Ben came in just before the guests arrived. He poured himself a drink, cut off the top of the triangle of Brie and popped it into his mouth. I had gone into a meltdown about how he'd ruined my spread and he'd said it was an example of my obsession with appearances.

'Will you ever let that go!' I said.

'I was hoping that for once you would give me your support. But no chance of that!'

We hung up on each other and I realised that I was furious, that the emotion I've been holding down for years is anger. I felt like screaming. I felt like hurling the little figure he had given me across the room. I grabbed my coat and told Flo through her door that I was popping out to the off-licence. I had to get out of the flat and walk some of my anger off or I would break something. I am so angry about everything: about all the compromises I have to make at work; about trying to keep all the balls in the air; about the financial pressures and about how little Ben does for Florence.

It was very cold on the street as I charged to the bottom of our road and turned left towards the parade of shops. They were all closed and boarded up except for a pub I never went into and two doors down a doner kebab kiosk with its sodium yellow light and smell of cheap meat. I kept walking fast until I reached a small play park where I had sometimes taken Flo.

The gates to the park were locked and I peered through the bars. I could see the hunched body of a man in a sleeping bag lying right up against the small brick building that housed the toilets. The poor devil must have been frozen on that raw night. I turned and hurried back to the warmth of my flat.

CHAPTER THIRTY-TWO

StoryWorld TV station, London Bridge

All weekend I'd been wondering what Ziggy had done to the memory stick after she left me. She had gone off to meet Harriet and the others at the pub. Would she and Harriet have had a ritual flinging of the memory stick into the water of the Thames? I could imagine them doing that after a few drinks and cursing Julius as they did it.

When I got into the office I forced myself not to approach Ziggy. I must let her come to me even though I burned to know what was on that stick. I tried to focus on my tasks for the day. After the morning meeting I started to draft the words that Fizzy could use for her piece to camera about her pregnancy. I had been thinking about how she should do this. It was important to get the tone of voice right. There is that saying 'never complain and never explain' but on this occasion I thought it would be good for Fizzy to do some explaining. It might disarm our viewers if she admitted to having made a bad mistake in getting involved with a married man. She could say how truly sorry she was. Better she come clean now than if the dirt was dug up by others later. She could make clear that she would never reveal the man's identity and that that part of her life was over for ever. I included the phrase she had used at our lunch that this was 'her last chance pregnancy' and that she had thought long and hard about her decision. She had shed many tears but she wanted this baby and had so much love to give. She should end on a humble note and appeal to our viewers to forgive her transgression and support her decision to be a lone mother. I thought my draft read rather well and I printed out a copy to take down to Fizzy.

There are times when Fizzy strikes me as plain ungrateful and ungracious. She had shut the door to her dressing room and taken the draft from me without any thank you. She sat down and read through it quickly.

'Yes, it's fine but I don't like that reference to my last chance pregnancy. God, that makes me sound ancient!' she said.

'Those were the words you used, at our lunch,' I reminded her.

'Maybe, but I've known women get pregnant in their forties.'

'Well take that bit out then.'

'I will,' she said.

She found her pen and crossed out the offending line and read the draft through again. She chewed the end of her pen and changed a couple of words.

'Does Bob know what's happening?' I asked.

She looked up at me and I could see that she was under strain but I still felt irritated with her.

'He knows I didn't go through with the termination. He was a complete prick about it.'

I wondered if this meant that the affair was now well and truly over. Last year I had met Bob's wife, Pat, and his two daughters at the StoryWorld Christmas lunch for managers and their families. Flo had come with me and she chatted to his daughters who are a bit older than her. I sat next to Pat, his wife. She told me she had met Bob in Burnley when he was working as a reporter on the local newspaper. She had won some stupid beauty pageant, as she called it, and he had covered it for the paper. She had been seventeen, she said, and we had a laugh about how we'd ban our daughters now from entering anything so ridiculous and anachronistic. I warmed to her. She struck me as a strong woman and someone you should not underestimate.

It was mid-afternoon when Ziggy tapped and came into my office. I tried to prepare myself for her telling me that she had thrown the memory stick away.

'I talked to Harry about it and...'

She pulled the purple memory stick from the back pocket of her jeans and I felt a surge of elation.

'Harry says we can trust you.'

She handled it carefully, as if it might burn her fingers and mine. I looked at it lying in the palm of my hand; such a small object but with such explosive power.

'Thank you, Ziggy. And you're both OK with my watching it?'

'I guess, as long as it's only you.'

'I'll keep it under lock and key at home.'

Chalk Farm Flat, 10.15 p.m.

I closed my bedroom door, turned on my laptop and plugged the memory stick into the side. I had been itching to watch the screen test all night but I needed to make sure that Flo was settled first. I did not want to be disturbed. Julius had arranged the test for a Sunday; it's the one day we shut the station down. There would have been no one around to see him, except for the security guard. He had fired up the small studio and turned on the single robotic camera and the lights. He would have

301

been sitting in the mini-gallery that controlled lights, sound and camera. He had voice contact with Harriet and Ziggy throughout and I could hear his voice on the tape as he gave them instructions. He had somehow persuaded them that the only way he could gauge whether either of them had any screen appeal was for them to stage a seduction scene for the camera. Harriet was to be the seducer and Ziggy the reluctant lover.

The two women were sitting next to each on the sofa, both looking awkward. Ziggy was dressed in her usual jeans and a grey T-shirt. Harriet had dressed for the screen test and was wearing a cream wrap-over dress and boots. Julius told Harriet to start kissing Ziggy. Harriet made a move and kissed Ziggy on the mouth but Ziggy pulled away from her embrace. I heard Julius saying: 'Come on, girls, that wouldn't convince anyone. This is a dramatic scene. Make me believe it.'

That was when Harriet went for it. She held Ziggy's face in her hands and pushed her tongue between her lips.

'Much better,' he said.

He told Harriet to take off Ziggy's top which she did. Underneath Ziggy was wearing a scrubby little cotton bra that had been washed too often.

'Now take off your dress too, Harriet,' he said.

She stood up and undid the ties that held her dress around her and let it fall to the ground. Underneath she was wearing a pink lace bra with matching knickers. She kept her boots on.

'Very nice,' he said.

'Now undo Ziggy's bra, and do it slowly, as if you are loving every moment of this.'

Ziggy looked frightened at this point but still Julius's voice was telling them what to do and that they should think of it as a play, they were only acting. Harriet fumbled with the back of Ziggy's bra and dropped it on to the studio floor. Ziggy is such a thin little thing that she had no breasts to speak of. Julius told Harriet to lick Ziggy's nipples and Harriet leaned forward and started to do this.

'Take your bra off too and go skin to skin,' he said.

She slipped off her bra and tossed it onto the floor.

'That's good. Now I want you to push Ziggy onto the sofa as if you can't wait and pull her jeans off.'

Harriet and Ziggy exchanged glances at this and Ziggy gave a little shake of her head as if to say no, don't do that.

'Come on, girls. Don't go all shy on me. It's only a play. Convince me you're having a good time.'

Harriet pushed Ziggy down onto the sofa, undid the zip of her jeans and pulled them off. Ziggy was lying on the sofa with just her knickers on looking up at Harriet who was leaning over her.

'Now run your hands up and down Ziggy's body as if you're in the grip of a mad passion,' he said.

It was painful, horrible to watch. The two of them were doing everything he asked them to do. Ziggy had closed her eyes as Harriet touched her and he kept saying: 'That's great, keep it going, keep it going.'

I turned the laptop off. I was amazed at how upset I was at Julius. I thought he could be horrible but not this, not this. I remembered all the times he had bullied me and my colleagues and made us feel small. But I had not had him down as a voyeur.

I went into the bathroom and cleaned my teeth and washed my hands thoroughly as if I was the dirty one. I recalled the gossip Gerry had told me. Maybe Julius is impotent and this is how he gets turned on. How hateful to trick the girls into

303

doing this. To exploit Ziggy who has so little self-esteem. And to exploit Harriet too who must have thought that if she went along with it she would get an on-screen job. In spite of everything he has done over the years I would not have expected this. I had thought there was a decent man in there struggling to get out.

I went into Flo's room and she was asleep. She'd left her tablet and her phone charging. Both were fully charged and I took the plugs out of the wall. I looked down at her face and wondered how I could protect her from all the predatory men out there. It was an impossible task. Ziggy's face came to mind then, that expression as Harriet knelt over her and Julius was coaxing them to act out a sex scene. Ziggy has no living parents to protect her.

I put the purple memory stick into a wooden box which has a lock and key and locked it away. Julius had done it because he could; because he has power and he likes to exercise that power. But I have the screen test now; at last I have something on him. I could feel my anger and upset changing into something more like elation.

I slept fitfully and woke up twice through the night. I felt a wave of revulsion each time I recalled how Julius had found it a turn-on to watch two young girls undress and perform for him. Gradually I formulated what I was going to say to him the next day.

CHAPTER THIRTY-THREE

StoryWorld TV station, London Bridge

The show had started and after the first ten minutes had aired I could not wait a moment longer and told the director I'd be back before the end. I left the gallery and walked upstairs. I was filled with fear but also resolve. Martine wasn't sitting outside his room so I walked straight in and shut the door. He was sitting on the sofa with his pad and he looked startled at my entry. I went and stood directly in front of his TV and launched straight in.

'I've seen the screen test. It's vile what you did.'

His face changed at once and he stood up and went to his desk. He pulled at the bottom left-hand drawer and it opened because Ziggy had broken the lock. He looked inside.

'You stole it!'

'How could you do that to them?'

'You sneak into my office and you steal from my desk?' His voice was incredulous rather than angry.

'Two young vulnerable women; it's sickening.'

'Harriet, vulnerable? I don't think so.'

'And Ziggy? She's had it easy, has she?'

'It was a bit of fun.'

'You can't see how disgusting it was?'

'I don't suppose it would occur to you that one of them was a willing participant.'

'Not for a moment.'

'Harriet suggested they do the role play.'

'I don't believe you.'

There was a pause as he looked me up and down; his eyes travelled from my face to my feet and back to my face and it was unnerving.

'You're so naive, Liz, always have been. She's a screwed up little rich kid who gets off on sexual games.'

'No.'

'Yes, and I've got that on good authority.'

'She told me it was like being sexually assaulted.'

'Bollocks! She's play-acting.'

Martine had come back and she could see that there was a major confrontation going on between us and she knocked on the door. Her instinct was to support Julius and get me out of there but he waved her away.

'I could have you fired for stealing,' he said.

'Oh yes? And I could show the screen test to Edward Dodd. I'm sure he would be *very* interested.'

That stopped him in his tracks.

'You wouldn't do that.'

'Just watch me. If Harriet's so happy about the screen test then it won't be a problem, will it? But I know she feels violated by it.'

'Crap.'

But I had got to him.

'You know if I go down the station goes down,' he said.

'So you keep telling us. But there's more to life than StoryWorld. I'm telling you how things are going to be. Simon will be promoted to assistant producer and becomes my deputy. I get a dedicated features crew one day a week. Ziggy is training to be a digital technician. The next job that comes up in that area goes to her.'

He stared at me and I knew that he was calculating how

he could thwart me.

'Impossible. I give you what you want and it screws the news budget,' he said.

'Tough. There are cheaper ways to deliver news. It's non-negotiable.'

It was strange but I thought I detected a gleam of admiration in his eyes.

I walked downstairs back towards the gallery. I was shaking and sat in the atrium for five minutes to compose myself. For too many years I have placated and flattered and negotiated my way through conflict at StoryWorld. He had abused his power and had to be challenged, but I hadn't played by my rules. I had blackmailed him. Earlier I'd tried to play it straight when I sent my email to Saul Relph and that had backfired. No, I had played by different rules this time, men's rules. The feeling of power it gave me felt heady and alarming. I entered the gallery and watched the rest of the show as my heart settled into a normal rhythm.

I chose my moment to talk to Harriet and Ziggy. Simon and Molly had left for lunch when I asked them to join me in my room. As they walked in I saw them exchange nervous glances.

'I watched it last night. It's vile what he made you do and I told him this morning that I'm onto him and his sick little tricks.'

Harriet looked relieved and Ziggy giggled nervously.

'I wish I could have been there when you told him that,' Harriet said.

'If he *ever* makes any approach to either of you again you come and tell me at once. OK?'

They both nodded.

'He will never know how we got hold of it or that you are the hero, Ziggy,' I said.

307

'Yes, you are,' Harriet agreed.

'But not a word to anyone, ever, and we're going to put it behind us.'

It was mid-afternoon when Fizzy called me. She was nearly sobbing as she said: 'I've started to bleed.'

This time we got a taxi. There was no time to do anything else. She told the driver to take us to a private clinic on Harley Street. While we were sitting in the back of the cab she was whispering that she'd felt wetness between her legs and had checked. The blood was bright red and sort of clotty.

'Am I having a miscarriage?'

She was almost whimpering in her distress and glancing anxiously through the glass at the cab driver. It sounded bad.

'We'll be there soon,' I said.

The clinic leapt into action as soon as we arrived and Fizzy was taken away to have an ultrasound scan. I was shown into a discreet softly furnished waiting room with copies of *Country Life*, *The Lady* and the *Financial Times* on the table. I called Simon and told him I wouldn't be back for the rest of the day and he needed to deputise for me. I wondered what was happening with Fizzy. Was there anything the doctors can do once a woman has started bleeding? Her terror means that she wants this baby and she might be losing it.

It was ages later when the receptionist told me I could join Miss Wentworth in her private room. Fizzy was lying flat in the bed with her feet raised and her face was white.

'They gave me a scan and baby is still moving. The consultant asked me if I had any pain in my shoulders.'

'And do you?'

'No. What was that about?'

308

'I don't know. Did you ask him?'

Fizzy shook her head.

'I'm so frightened. I think it's touch and go. Will you stay with me?'

'Of course I will.'

It was going to be another late night away from home. Eventually Fizzy dozed off and when the nurse came in to check on her I asked her about the pain in the shoulders question.

'It's a symptom of ectopic pregnancy and your friend is all clear on that front,' the nurse said.

'And the baby will be OK?'

The nurse would not be drawn. I think they are told that you mustn't commit yourself one way or the other.

Around seven I put in a call to Janis and Fizzy must have woken up and heard me telling Janis to put Flo into a taxi to Harley Street. She was shaking her head as I was speaking into the phone.

'Why are you doing that? It's our secret, Liz.'

'I can't leave Flo alone for another evening. I can't. I won't tell her what's wrong with you. Please be calm, Fizz.'

'How can I be calm?'

'Shhh now…'

'What will you tell her?'

'I'll think of something.'

I poured her a class of water and stroked her arm as she took the glass.

'I'll say you're having your tonsils out. I'm going downstairs now to wait for Flo, OK.'

It was dark outside and the street lamps were glowing yellow. I saw people walking by with what looked like Christmas shopping. I had seen the Christmas lights blazing from shop windows as we had driven towards the clinic and in one window I had spotted a nativity scene. It felt an age ago that I had left home to travel to work and had had that showdown with Julius. I had hardly eaten anything all day and could feel the vein in my right temple throbbing which told me a headache was coming. When Flo arrived I would send her out to get us some sandwiches from the café around the corner. It was going to be a late night.

CHAPTER THIRTY-FOUR

DECEMBER
StoryWorld TV station, London Bridge

As I was about to go into the gallery to watch the show I got a call from Fizzy from her room in the clinic.

'The bleeding stopped completely around midnight.'

'Thank God for that.'

Flo and I had left at eleven when Fizzy was sleeping. The bleeding had slowed down and the nurse had said it was safe for us to go and she would ring me if Fizzy's condition worsened.

'He said baby's OK. But I've got to rest up till the weekend. I'm going to stay here for a couple more days. Will you tell Julius I'll be back on Monday?' Fizzy said.

'Course I will. Now you take it easy and I'll come and see you after work,' I said.

Fizzy rarely misses a show and I was glad that at last she was putting the baby first.

Ledley sat in for Fizzy and presented the show. He did a brilliant interview with Dirk about what life was like post-amputation. He was able to ask quite intimate questions without appearing to be intrusive. Next up it was Betty who was discussing divorce as her Life Crisis topic of the day. Again Ledley performed well and his discussion with her was thoughtful.

As the credits were rolling I asked the director: 'What did you think of Ledley?'

'Terrific. He's got the range, hasn't he?'

'That's what I thought.'

And then it came to me that Ledley can stand in for Fizzy while she is on maternity leave. She would find it a lot easier to accept a man doing her role temporarily than another woman. It would be great to have Ledley as the main anchor for a few months. He is such an easy man to work with.

At the morning meeting I told Julius that Fizzy would be away till the end of the week. Bob's behaviour was weird. He completely lost it over a news story that had been pulled at short notice by Julius. The story was about a company that had been named and shamed for its refusal to pay the minimum wage and for its record on tax evasion. It was hard-hitting and there followed a tense exchange between Bob and Julius about who should have the final editorial say over news stories.

'As news editor I know what's making the day's agenda. There's a report out at noon today on this company and it will be everywhere. We got it early.'

'And as director of programmes I can pull a story if I think it will damage the station's profitability,' Julius said.

'You're saying they're planning to advertise with us?' Bob asked.

'There's a good chance they will, yes.'

Julius gets to have the last word, of course, and Bob looked disgusted but he shut up at that. I recalled Fizzy telling me he had been incandescent when he found out that she hadn't had the termination. The strain is getting to him and this is the first time I have seen him confront Julius so directly. Julius asked to see me straight after the meeting. We walked in silence to his office and once in there we were exceedingly formal with each other.

'I would be grateful if you would enlighten me on the full story about Fizzy's condition,' he said.

In the past Julius would have contacted her himself so I think there must be a rift between them at the moment. He had advised Fizzy to have an abortion so maybe that was the cause of their current coolness.

'The doctor said she'll be all right in a few days but we need to give her time to fully recover.'

'You knew about the pregnancy, of course,' he said.

'Yes.'

His use of the past tense made me realise that he thinks Fizzy is away having her termination and this is why she isn't on air. She's keeping her cards very close to her chest.

'And has she told you who the father was?'

'No, and it's not my business to enquire.'

'Oh, but it is if it's going to affect her future performance,' he said.

'Fizzy is a professional to the tips of her toes and will be back on Monday,' I said.

'OK.'

'Have you signed the paperwork about the feature crew and Simon's promotion?'

'I'll do it today,' he said.

You'd better, I thought, because I have that purple memory stick at home.

I went for lunch with Betty and Simon. We had arranged it last week and I was pleased to get out of the station. I had booked us into an Italian restaurant near Tower Bridge. I ordered the rigatoni puttanesca, my all-time favourite sauce as I love the combination of tomato, anchovies, black olives and capers. Betty had selected cannelloni with a side order of courgettes in batter.

'We've been getting a good reaction to your series,' I said.

She had asked for garlic bread too and now lifted the plate and offered me a slice.

'Thanks. I was worried that the title might put people off but your instinct was spot on.' I added.

'Thank you, I'm pleased with how it's going and Simon has been such a help throughout.'

I looked over at Simon as he tucked into his pizza with extra pepperoni. I was looking forward to telling him that he would be promoted to my deputy. I plan to give him the title of assistant producer and it will mean a pay rise for him and he deserves it. It will be a less easy task telling Molly about the changes to the team structure as there has always been a healthy competition between the two of them. But I did have the fact of a weekly features crew which she can use for her stories and I hoped this would sweeten the message. I felt cheerful. It had been a horrible couple of months but we were coming out of it with my position strengthened and my team intact.

Simon had to leave before us and Betty and I stayed on to have coffee.

'Is Fizzy all right?' she asked me.

'She's poorly and won't be in for a couple of days.'

'I know she's poorly at the moment, but I was wondering if there was something else going on?' Betty said.

'Something else?'

'I've noticed a change in her recently. She's unsettled, almost feverish at times.'

Betty had worked as a probation officer and was good at observing changes in people's behaviour.

'She has been going through some personal stuff recently; a break-up that upset her,' I said.

It was sort of the truth because she had broken up with

Bob, but it was also a bit of a lie and I wished I couldn't lie so easily.

'I thought so. She snapped at me last week over something trivial.'

'She'll get through it. Now, are you planning to come to Ledley's launch next week? He'd love to have you there.'

I left the station at five to visit Fizzy at the Harley Street clinic. She was sitting up in bed and I think she had been crying because her eyelids were pink. I leaned over and kissed her on the cheek. There was a huge bouquet of flowers standing in a vase on the window sill and I could smell the lilies that were in the mix. She saw me glance at the flowers.

'From Saul Relph,' she said.

'How are you?'

'Doctor said baby's going to be OK.'

'Thank goodness.'

I sat down on the chair by her bed.

'But I've got to take it easy. I can go on working, he said, but no more parties or rushing around after the show.' She looked thoughtful. 'I thought I'd lose baby. My mum had a miscarriage, you know.'

'Before or after you?'

'Long before me. It was her first pregnancy.'

'What happened?'

'She was nineteen and engaged to my dad and her mum, my grandma, was organising the church wedding for them. My grandma is religious and when she found out that Mum was pregnant she made her dye her wedding dress a pale shade of pink.'

'No!'

'Oh yes, and Mum had to wear it. Grandma said she

couldn't wear white because she wasn't a virgin any more. It wasn't as if Mum was even showing.'

'And she made your mum broadcast her condition?'

'Yes she did, and believe me Burnley in those days was a very judgemental place.'

'That's horrible.'

'And then Mum lost the baby at four months and she was distraught. She didn't conceive again for years and Grandma said it was God's punishment on her.'

'Bloody hell, your grandma sounds terrifying,' I said.

Fizzy nodded.

'Is she still alive?'

'Yes, she is.'

'Are you worried about her finding out about your pregnancy?' I asked.

'No, because she's got dementia now and she won't understand what's happening.'

'But your mum will be pleased.'

'Yes, I think so. I haven't told her yet.'

I thought it strange that Fizzy hadn't told her mother the news. When I got pregnant with Flo I told my mum immediately and she was overjoyed, though we both cried when we talked about how Dad would never know he had a grandchild.

'Fizz, when are you going to tell Julius about the baby?'

Her face changed and she looked furtive.

'I don't know.'

'He thinks you're away because you're having a termination.'

'Oh well, sooner or later he's going to notice.'

She tried to say it breezily but there was an edge to her voice.

'You'd be better off telling him. You know what a control freak he is. He'll hate it if you don't tell him.'

Fizzy sighed and reached for a bowl of purple grapes by her bed. She offered them to me and I pulled off a small branch.

'Thanks.'

'Harriet seems to have faded into the background,' she said.

'She's trying harder to be a team player and I've decided to keep her on.'

'Did you have to do that? I still don't trust her,' Fizzy said, putting the bowl back on the bedside table.

'Stop worrying about Harriet. She's not going to make it onto the screen. Ever.'

'I hate grapes,' she said.

I wondered who had given them to her. Would Bob have taken a risk and come to the clinic? This was a place that looked after the rich and the famous and it wasn't unusual for paparazzi to be stationed on the pavement opposite. I wondered what the status of their relationship was now. I didn't tell her how Bob had lost his cool so dramatically this morning. The priority was to make Fizzy's pregnancy as stress-free as possible. I explained my idea of getting Ledley to stand in for her when she was on leave and she liked the suggestion.

'That could work. He won't try to stich me up,' she said.

As I left I reflected on Fizzy and her jealousies. She is always on the lookout for anyone who might upstage or replace her and it must be so wearing. Then I remembered how Bob and I compete. I wasn't immune from petty rivalries either.

CHAPTER THIRTY-FIVE

Ledley has done so well fronting the show these last three days and at the morning meeting Julius commented on this.

'I take it you are tracking the viewers' response to Ledley?'

'Yes I am, and we're getting excellent feedback.'

'I'd like to see it.'

'I'll get it over to you. It's good to know we can use him as a back-up presenter,' I said.

'And Fizzy is definitely back on Monday?'

'She is,' I said.

I looked over at Bob who was watching me. All week he has had a face on him, like he's suffering from a bad attack of neuralgia. He must be terrified about the great secret getting out one day and causing an earthquake in his family. Once Fizzy's baby is born there will be huge speculation about who the father is.

I was on tenterhooks waiting for Julius to mention my dedicated features crew. The paperwork was all completed and today he planned to announce it. I was feeling both excited and apprehensive because I would have to tell my team about the changes straight after the meeting. But first we had to sit through a report from Tim Cooper on how the budget cuts were being implemented. He can be long-winded and he went on at length about the two journalists who are fighting their redundancy and have taken StoryWorld to an employment tribunal for constructive dismissal. This would incur legal costs, he said.

'Annoying but necessary. Make sure we win,' Julius said.

Tim was done with his report and I gave Julius a meaningful look.

'One more thing before we go. I have decided we need more feature stories in the show to get the balance right. From next week Liz will be getting a dedicated crew one day a week to deliver more feature content,' he said.

Bob's face was a picture of incomprehension followed by fury. Julius stood up and he and Tim left the room together. I gathered my papers and was hurrying out of the room but Bob came up and stood right in front of me so I couldn't escape. He nodded his head in the direction of Julius's retreating figure.

'I *knew* there was something between you two,' he said bitterly.

I felt like slapping his face. He's the kind of man who thinks there is only one way a woman can make a man do something for her.

'We're not all cheaters like you,' I said.

Bob went white and I saw he was clenching his fists. I walked away from him with my head held high. We are enemies now and I can see no way back.

It was time to tell the team about the new structure and I planned to tell each team member individually. First up, I got Simon into my office.

'I've got some good news,' I said.

He was so happy about his promotion but of course telling Simon was the easy bit. I asked him to stay shtum until all the team had been told. Next it was Molly – she knew something was up because I was calling in each team member one by one.

'Is everything OK?' she asked before I had a chance to say anything.

'Yes it is. Do sit down, Moll. Against the odds I have managed to get more resources for the features team.'

She raised her eyebrows in surprise and I plunged on.

'I've got enough to pay Simon to be my deputy and I've also secured us a weekly features crew so that you can film more feature stories for the show.'

There was a long pause as Molly took this in.

'Simon is going to be your deputy?' she said at last.

'He is, with immediate effect. I need a deputy badly. And I want to change your role too. I'd like you to lead on the pre-recorded stories. It's your strength and I hope you can see that this is a vote of confidence in your film-making abilities.'

What I have always liked about Molly is her honesty and her directness.

'But it's not a promotion?'

'I'm afraid not. I couldn't get anything more this time.'

'I'm pleased about the crew, of course, but I'm disappointed that you have chosen Simon as your deputy,' she said.

She had been honest with me and she deserved me to be honest back to her.

'You are both very talented and hard-working researchers and critical to the success of the team. Simon has certain organisational skills which gave him the edge,' I said.

After Molly had gone I decided to get Harriet and Ziggy in together as the news would not have a specific impact on either of their roles. I told them the news and it was an easy sell because they both get on well with Simon. I realised that I hadn't been thinking about them much over the last few days. Fizzy's drama had pushed everything else out of my mind.

'How are things with you both?'

Harriet answered first. 'I'm getting lots of fashion houses on board. I sent them Guy's promo and they're already offering stills and footage for him to use.'

We have been running promos all week for our new fashion slot with Guy Browne which launches on Monday.

'Good work. And how about you, Ziggy?'

Ziggy looked better and has lost that hunted look that she had for ages.

'I like my evening course. We did some digital editing last week. And I'm pleased for Simon,' she said.

Around four Gerry called me, as he so often does these days.

'I've got a cracking topic for next week,' he said.

'Tell me.'

'I want to discuss how different star signs reveal their ambitious side and how they try to climb the greasy pole.'

'That sounds intriguing...'

'You know what gave me the idea? It's this in-fighting in the government at the moment. They're jostling for the succession, aren't they? It's quite unseemly and I thought I could touch on that, you know, mention the home secretary and the chancellor's star signs and the different ways they're staking their claim to the top job.'

Gerry scans the newspapers and he gets a lot of his ideas from news stories. I like it when his forecasts have a topical or controversial edge to them and we never get any comeback because he's talking about astrology.

'That's clever; go for it,' I said.

'I saw the promo for your new fashion man yesterday.'

'Guy Browne, I think he's going to be good. I'll have to introduce you.'

'Please do. But, darling, I need to warn you. I saw Amber last night and she's deeply offended that you're using him to front the fashion slot at StoryWorld.'

'Oh, for heaven's sake!'

'I know; professional jealousy. But be careful because it looks like she and Julius are an item again.'

Chalk Farm flat, Saturday morning

I called Fizzy's room at the clinic and was told she had gone home so I rang her mobile but that went to answerphone.

'Hi, it's Liz. Hope you're taking it easy. I can come over on Sunday if you like and go through Monday's line-up. Call me.'

She lives in Pimlico in a mews house which is built above two garages. I've been there several times over the years when she throws drinks parties and it's a pretty house, the kind of home you would expect a TV star to live in. It's not child-friendly, though, as you enter by a steep staircase to the living quarters above the garages. I wonder if she'll move when the baby comes.

Ben is flying to Dubai today to start his new life and Flo and I said we would see him off. We took the Tube to Heathrow airport. It's a long ride from Chalk Farm, especially when you are not looking forward to the experience when you get there. Flo was subdued. She plugged in her earphones and examined the ends of her hair as we rattled along. I was thinking about Fizzy. That story she told me about her mother's pink wedding dress had made me feel for her. It sounds like she comes from a family obsessed with appearances and I wonder how supportive they are being to her.

I hate airports. I hate the lighting and the recycled air and the miles of corridors. I hate the shops and the overpriced catering that is on offer. But I guess it's mainly that I hate goodbyes. Sometimes just watching strangers saying goodbye to each other at a station or at an airport can bring a great big lump to my throat, which is absurd as I don't know these people. I think it's because I never had a chance to say goodbye to my darling dad.

It is always so difficult to find things to say when you are waiting for someone to leave. But I did my best and Ben did his best and we managed to keep the conversation going and not once did we mention that this Christmas he would not be seeing Flo. They called his flight and he hugged Flo for a long time. As he walked through the barrier and away from us I was willing him to look back, just the once, but he strode forwards until he was out of sight. Flo's shoulders were heaving and then the floodgates opened and she cried without restraint. I realised that she had been holding her tears in, trying to be brave for him. We were both in a bad way and I suggested we go to the cinema and watch one of the Christmas blockbusters.

Chalk Farm flat, Sunday evening

I had left a second message for Fizzy at lunchtime offering to come to her house and work through the briefing notes for Monday's show. I know she is determined to return to work tomorrow. I said she would be interviewing our new fashion expert Guy Browne and that I had his screen test on my laptop if she wanted to see it. Still no word from her and I'm starting to worry. I know she doesn't have many female friends. Her personal life has always revolved around the men in her life and she won't be getting any support from that quarter now. I suppose it's possible she went away for the weekend to convalesce but I had left messages on her mobile as well as her landline. It was odd.

CHAPTER THIRTY-SIX

StoryWorld TV station, London Bridge

I did not get in early enough to talk to Fizzy before we went to air. It was her first day back on the sofa and I had biked the briefing notes of Monday's show to her house. I watched from the gallery as Guy Browne did his first fashion slot for us. He was as lively as I had hoped he would be and he's getting a good response from the viewers. He and Fizzy hit it off at once and I was sure she'd be pleased and say something positive at the morning meeting.

I grabbed a coffee and was the last to reach the meeting room. Julius opened proceedings by making a big fuss of Fizzy.

'Ledley did OK last week but you are the one the viewers want to see, Fizzy. Welcome back and thank you for a great show today.'

She smiled warmly at Julius.

'Yes, it's great to have you back,' I said.

She glared at me then dropped her eyes and said not a word. Later, when we came to discuss Guy's slot, Fizzy addressed her remarks directly to Julius.

'I'm glad we're doing a fashion slot at last. I always said we should do one. And Guy is good.'

'I liked the chemistry between the two of you,' Julius said.

I jumped in here. He was my signing, after all.

'So did I. You looked comfortable with each other and I agree with you, Fizzy, Guy will bring something new to the show.'

She did not look in my direction or acknowledge my comment. Julius and Bob saw what was going on and I knew with a sick feeling that trouble was coming my way.

I held my team meeting and we went through the work schedules for the week ahead. Towards the end Molly and Simon got into a spat about whether or not Twitter was a force for good.

'I like that it's democratic. Everyone can get their opinions out there and we're no longer dependent on the mainstream media,' Simon said.

'It's just an echo chamber. People find their tribe on Twitter and stick to their group and reinforce their existing beliefs. It doesn't change anything,' Molly said.

'I don't agree. I've seen campaigns take off on Twitter, some important social justice campaigns,' he said.

'No, it's all about vanity and getting lots of followers and retweets. And I've noticed that men always have to have the last word in any exchange you have on Twitter,' Molly said.

I knew better than to take sides. They weren't getting on as well as they usually do and I feared it was because I had made Simon my deputy.

I couldn't stop thinking about how Fizzy had been in the meeting and I recalled that she hadn't returned my calls over the weekend. Something was going on so I went down to her dressing room. It was locked and when I tapped on the door Ellen opened it and she looked embarrassed when she saw me.

'I need a word with Fizzy,' I said.

Ellen gave an apologetic shrug.

'She's not up to seeing you. I'm sorry.'

'But we need to talk.'

'She's adamant, Liz. Best leave it.'

Fizzy ignored me for the rest of the day, simply wouldn't

talk to me and I'm hurt by this change in her. I thought we were growing closer over the last few weeks. I know she is very emotional at the moment and Bob is probably still giving her a hard time about the baby, but why have I become public enemy number one?

It was mid-afternoon when Martine called me and said that Julius needed to speak to me. She looked grim as I approached her and when I went into his office he insisted that I sit down in front of his desk. I did so with a feeling of rising trepidation.

'We have a problem,' he said.

'What kind of a problem?'

'You have completely alienated Fizzy.'

I felt simultaneously sick and dizzy and I stared at him, lost for words.

'I went to see her on Sunday and she feels strongly that you are working against her,' he said.

'That's crazy. I have no idea why she's saying that.'

'The important point is that she believes it, absolutely, and you need to sort it out.'

The last time Fizzy and I had talked we had been in her room at the clinic and she had opened up about her mother's miscarriage. It didn't make any sense.

'Did she say anything specific?'

'She says she can't trust you.'

I shook my head in disbelief.

'She's very emotional at the moment. Of course she can trust me,' I said.

'She asked me to get rid of you.'

That shocked me. That winded me.

'You know what I think? I think there's too much fucking hysteria in the station these days and you've got to sort it. We

327

can't have Fizzy feeling upset like this. She's our main asset,'
he said.

I was wretched that Fizzy had not only turned against me
but that she had talked to Julius about it. He had gone round
to her house at the weekend while she was blanking my calls.
The irony was that it was me who had urged her to tell him
what was going on. She had made him her ally again and
made me the enemy.

I grabbed my coat and headed out of the building without
telling my team where I was going. I trailed along by the river
feeling thoroughly miserable. What had I done? I knew it
would come to this one day. I knew there would come a point
when the forces would be stacked against me. I've been
walking through a minefield for years and finally I've made
too many enemies; Julius, Bob, Martine and now Fizzy.
There's a tipping point and I've reached it. I was running
through everything Fizzy and I had been through over the last
few weeks. She has been on such a roller-coaster over her
pregnancy. First she decided to have a termination and then
she couldn't go through with it. That was followed by the
terror of almost losing the baby last week. I walked for thirty
minutes; I noticed the Christmas lights strung along the
perimeter of the river and if anything they made me feel even
more bleak. Ben was in Dubai, Todd was in Sydney and I was
on my own. Standing looking at the silver and gold lights I felt
a moment of profound loneliness.

As I headed back to the StoryWorld building it occurred to me
that I am copping it at the moment because Fizzy confided in
me. I have become her punchbag. I have got to see her face to
face and it needs to be away from the poisonous atmosphere
of the station.

I hurried upstairs and called Janis.

'I need to do something this evening at short notice. Is there any way you can stay later tonight?'

'Sorry, Liz, but I can't, not tonight. Do you want a word with Flo?'

'Yes please.'

Flo came to the phone and I told her I'd be late and she'd be on her own for a few hours.

'It's OK, Mum. Don't stress. I'm fine on my own.'

Fizzy's mews house is tucked away in an exclusive corner of Pimlico. You enter through an arch and the private road is cobbled. These would once have been stables and now they are bijou residences for the moneyed and the well-born. A black Mercedes with smoked windows purred past me as I walked. Her place is halfway along and it comprises two mews houses which have been knocked together with a central entrance between the two garages. Her house is painted white and on either side of her yellow front door there are terracotta pots holding bay bushes. As I approached the house I saw Loida, Fizzy's housekeeper, coming out carrying a bin bag. I've met Loida a few times at Fizzy's drinks parties. I hurried over and she recognised me.

'Hello, Loida. Is Fizzy in?'

She nodded.

'She's resting and I'm just leaving for the night.'

'That's OK. I won't be long.'

Loida looked doubtful.

'She said no visitors.'

'I need to update her on the show tomorrow,' I lied.

'She needs to rest,' Loida said.

'I won't be long.'

I watched Loida put the bin bag into the wheelie bin and waved goodbye to her. As I walked up the stairs I could hear the sound of the TV coming from the sitting room and it was Ledley's voice that I could hear. Her sitting room is long; it stretches the length of the two houses. Fizzy must have assumed I was Loida because she didn't move from her position on the sofa as she lay there watching Ledley's interviews from last week. She was wrapped in a towelling robe and had the remote in her hand and I watched her rewind and start to watch Ledley's interview with Dirk again.

'Hello, Fizzy,' I said.

She jumped as if I had caught her doing something illicit, and turned off the TV.

'What are you doing here?'

Her voice was hostile. I walked further into the room and sat on a chair by the sofa.

'We need to talk. Julius said I had upset you somehow?'

'Loida!' Fizzy called out.

'She's gone for the evening. What the hell is going on, Fizz?'

'I know exactly what you're planning and you're a bitch to do that to me.'

She had spat out the word bitch.

'What are you talking about?'

'You want Ledley to have the main anchor role not just during my maternity leave!'

'That's crazy. What on earth gave you that idea?'

'Julius told me you've got a thing for Ledley. You can't bear to have him criticised and you let him get away with all kinds of things.'

'Oh, Julius said that, did he?'

'Now you think here's your big chance to promote him and get rid of me.'

'That's frankly delusional! He's a chef, for God's sake.'

'Don't tell me he wouldn't jump at the chance of being the main anchor. Everyone wants that.'

'It's *not* what he wants. He's building his food business. This is Julius trying to poison your mind against me. You know how he tries to divide and rule us all.'

She shook her head resolutely.

'Bob told me you were singing Ledley's praises to the roof too,' she said.

'As a good stand-in; at short notice...'

She narrowed her eyes.

'I don't think so. You have your favourites and you've got an agenda.'

'I've tried to support you every step of the way,' I said.

'Oh yes?'

'Yes.'

'You've been *very* keen for me to go through with the pregnancy and get me off air.'

'This is paranoid. You told me you wanted the baby.'

'I can't trust you. I can't trust anyone. Now get out of my house,' she shouted.

I left her because I didn't want her getting into even more of a state. As I travelled home on the Tube a wave of utter weariness was stealing over me. Julius doesn't like to lose power. I got one over on him with the screen test and now he'll be trying to undermine me at every opportunity. I could just imagine how he had worked on Fizzy's fears, fanned the flames of her insecurity over Ledley. This was how it was going to be from now on. I would have to be even more vigilant.

When I got home Flo was sitting at the kitchen table.

'You weren't long, Mum.'

I felt a great wave of tenderness for her. I put my arms around her and kissed the top of her head.

'You are my best and darling daughter,' I said.

'I've been WhatsApping Dad.'

'How is he?'

'His flat is so cool. He sent me some pix.'

She showed me the shots on her phone. Ben had done a selfie by a large window and you could see high-rises soaring behind him.

'He's high up. Look at that view,' I said.

'That's his sitting room.'

There was not much furniture in the room but then he had only just moved in.

'Impressive.'

'He says he'll pay for me to fly there and see him in the new year,' she said happily.

I felt a tremor at that. It would be a long flight to Dubai and she was only fourteen.

'I'm making a cheese omelette. Do you want some?'

'No thanks.'

I broke three eggs into a bowl and as I whipped them I returned to a fantasy I often have of giving up this life of stress and moving somewhere like Folkestone, where Fenton lives, and living a simpler, less demanding life. My salary would be half what I get here, if I could even find a job, but oh the relief to walk away from all the politics and the backstabbing at StoryWorld. I sprinkled the grated cheese over the egg mixture in the pan. I know it will never happen though. Flo is a London girl through and through. She is settled at school and I couldn't inflict such a change on her.

Later I called Fenton.

'Fizzy's turned against me overnight. She thinks I persuaded her to go through with the pregnancy because I was conspiring to replace her with Ledley who apparently I have a thing about.'

'It sounds like she's in the grip of her hormones and not thinking straight.'

'I thought we were getting closer. You know, it's one bloody thing after another.'

'It's a snake-pit but keep your chin up, sweetheart, because you're strong and I know you will prevail,' she said.

'And how are things with you and the sexy Bill?'

She giggled.

'We are trying very hard to keep our relationship a secret at the moment. He works with such a cynical gang and he can't face the ribbing he'll get. Being secret kind of adds to it all.'

She sounded happy and I was pleased for her. As long as I have Fenton in my life I never feel completely alone.

CHAPTER THIRTY-SEVEN

StoryWorld TV station, London Bridge

Straight after the show today we've got the launch of Ledley's marinade *Go Luscious with Ledley* and I had dressed for the occasion in my dark red fitted dress and black ankle boots. The PR team were setting up in the atrium as I walked to the gallery. I sat down next to the director.

'What's up with Fizzy today? She's like a cat on a hot tin roof,' he said.

He was right; Fizzy was keyed up with a hectic flush on her cheekbones as she linked into the first pre-recorded story, about a project in Manchester that has turned an old church hall into a hacker's house, a place where formerly convicted hackers could use their IT skills for social good. She is so volatile at the moment and she wants to get me the sack. I reminded myself that I had the memory stick and that that was my armour with Julius, whatever stunt Fizzy tried to pull. The story ended and she linked into the ad break.

'Be sure to stay. Next up I'm joined by everyone's favourite TV detective, George Walter.'

'You got everything you need there, Fizzy?' I said to her through her earpiece.

She ignored me as she looked down at a sheet in her hand, and she was reading through her notes as Henry brought George Walter in to sit next to her on the sofa. They spoke briefly and the ad break ended but instead of reading the introductory link on the autocue Fizzy leaned towards the camera and said: 'Please bear with me. I have some news I need to share with you all.'

With a sick feeling I knew what was coming. The director did not and he watched in horror as Fizzy looking straight into the camera started to tell the viewers about a pivotal moment she had reached in her life. She was using the words I'd drafted for her almost unchanged. She had reached the bit about how she would never reveal who the father of her baby was and how that part of her life was over for ever. All the time she was talking to the camera George Walter was sitting next to her, looking bemused. The voice of Henry the floor manager came over the system to us.

'I need instructions. Do we take the camera off her?'

'There's no scheduled break for another five minutes,' the director said.

'You have to let her go on,' I said.

I knew her speech was drawing to a close because I had written it.

'Keep the camera on her,' the director said.

Now she was asking the viewers to forgive her transgression and to support her in her decision to be a lone mother.

'Christ,' the director said.

'I feel I have so much love to give this baby.'

She turned to George Walter.

'Welcome to our show, George. I'm sorry for the delay but I needed to share that with our viewers.'

He kissed her on the cheek and said: 'I think that was very brave of you.'

She moved seamlessly into an interview with him about his new series. Two minutes later Julius stormed into the gallery.

'Of all the unprofessional claptrap! Using our show for her personal stuff,' he roared.

He was standing right behind me. He gripped the back of my chair and I could feel the tension radiating through his body and his arms as he watched Fizzy interviewing George Walter.

'Did you know about this, Liz?'

'No.'

'It wasn't your idea?'

'No!'

My stomach did a double flip. I was in deep trouble if he found out it had been my idea, and my words too. I tried to remember if I'd deleted my draft of the words from my system. Fizzy's eyes were unnaturally bright but otherwise she was as professional and as charming as ever as she chatted to George Walter about what made his detective so loveable. She thanked him for coming in and linked into the ad break.

'If the viewers react against her she's out,' Julius said.

I was scrolling through my phone.

'We're already getting a lot of reaction.'

'I want to see it, all of it, every last damn comment. List it and bring it to my office.'

He left the gallery and the director and I exchanged glances.

'Never a dull moment,' he said.

I hurried upstairs to my team who had been watching the show and were standing in a small knot discussing Fizzy's bombshell.

'Come on, there's work to do. I need all four of you to collate the comments.'

Tweets and emails flooded in during the last half-hour of the show and my team recorded every one. I was reading them as they came in.

'Make two columns please, positive and negative, so we can tell at a glance which way it's going,' I said.

Down in the atrium, the preparations for Ledley's launch were going full steam ahead and the smell of roasting meat was wafting up the stairs. Fizzy's dramatic announcement meant we would get even more press coming to the station. I looked across the staircase to the newsroom on the other side of the divide. I could make out Bob sitting in his office with the door closed. I wondered what was going through his head. Betty arrived at the top of the stairs and approached the team desks. She had come in for Ledley's do and was wearing the peach-coloured blouse StoryWorld had bought for her and a rope of pearls at her neck. She looked put-out.

'A quick word, Liz?' she asked.

I showed her into my room.

'I had my suspicions, you know, that she was pregnant. I tried to raise it with you last week. I wish you'd told me.'

'Betty, we're up to our eyeballs collating the viewers' reactions. Can we talk about this later, please?'

Martine knocked on my door and came in.

'Julius has cancelled the morning meeting. He wants to see the viewers' reactions now.'

I hurried out to the team and looked at the long list of comments. There were a few vicious troll messages. One emailer called her a marriage-breaking whore who should be sacked on the spot. Another emailer wrote that she felt sorry for any child born to such a vain, irresponsible and immoral woman. These were massively outnumbered by positive tweets and emails wishing her luck. One woman offered to knit bootees for the baby and a lot of tweets were saying #GoFizzy.

'GoFizzy is trending,' Simon said.

'Good. Give them to me now.'

'They're still coming in,' Molly said.

'Go on tracking them but there's enough here to show Julius.'

Ziggy printed off two sets of comments and I walked down to his office with Martine in attendance. He was pacing around his room.

'I'm fucking seething. Using the station to air her secrets!'

'It's going to be a firestorm and we've got to manage it somehow,' I said.

'I know. Saul called. He's on his way in. Says we need to rush out a report for the board.'

'Early indications are that the audience are with Fizzy,' I said.

I handed the sheets over to him. I stood by his desk and we both read through the comments.

'She's made a fool of us all,' he said.

'The media are downstairs in force so I suggest we put a brave face on it and don't let them know we're angry.'

He looked at me and nodded slowly as the sense of this dawned on him.

'Give me a line I can use,' he said.

I scanned the comments again and was struck by the level of empathy that was being expressed by our viewers and the warmth of their wishes for Fizzy. Most of them felt that a baby was an event to feel joyous about.

'We underestimate our audience. I think you should say we know our viewers are generous people who can understand Fizzy's decision and their comments show this very clearly.'

'And if they ask me if I knew she was going to do this?'

'Tell them yes, absolutely, and you support her one hundred

per cent because that's the StoryWorld way.' I couldn't resist adding: 'Real people, real life, real stories, live.'

I went to find Ledley in the atrium. While I had been upstairs the space had been transformed into a Jamaican street party with yellow and green banners that said *Go Luscious with Ledley* and huge sunflowers in silver pots at the end of the tables. The heating had been turned up and the atrium flooded with yellow light to create the feel of a summer day. The giant barbecue ran along one wall and the caterers were laying out cooked chicken legs and browned sausages onto silver platters. I spotted Ledley talking to the musicians who had formed into a line with their steel drums. He was back in one of his printed pattern shirts with the sleeves rolled up and green jeans tucked into boots. Guests were arriving and there was already a clutch of photographers in the atrium with more arriving as Fizzy's announcement went viral. The senior PR woman was clad in an acid-pink suit and she and puppy woman were handing out press packs about Ledley's marinade. I pushed my way towards Ledley.

'It's going to be a great party,' I said.

Ledley is rarely angry but this morning I could see that he was and that he was just about holding it in check.

'Why did she decide to go public today of all days, my launch day?' he said in a low voice.

'Who knows? She's been so volatile recently.'

'I thought we were mates. I didn't think she'd try to upstage me.'

'I doubt it even occurred to her. She's so self-obsessed,' I said, but as I was saying these words the thought occurred to me that perhaps Fizzy had chosen today to punish Ledley for sitting in for her on the sofa. I spotted Harriet standing at the edge of the gathering and she had a drink in her hand. I felt a spasm of irritation that she'd left the others upstairs to get on with the work while she joined the party. I thought about going over and telling her to get back upstairs until the work was done but Gerry arrived at that moment.

'What a fantastic turnout, Ledley,' he said.

He and Ledley did an awkward high five. The PR woman in pink came over.

'I'm going to have to steal Ledley from you. Capital FM and LBC and the Food Channel are queueing up to interview him.'

Gerry and I wandered over to the drinks table. The choice was rum punch, carrot juice punch and pineapple punch.

'Did you know she was going to do that?' he said.

I reached for a non-alcoholic punch.

'Not today.'

'But you knew she was going to reveal all on camera?'

I needed to backtrack, to distance myself from any involvement in her revelation.

'I knew she was pregnant and something had to be said sooner or later.'

'She's playing for high stakes, but then she is a Leo, of course. They're a courageous sign, willing to take risks.'

He sipped on a pineapple punch.

'The viewers are with her so far,' I said.

'And you've no idea of the father?'

'Gerry! She's entitled to keep that a secret, don't you think?'

He smiled at me.

'You're too good for your own boots sometimes, Liz.'

I saw Julius walking down the stairs to join the party and Martine was behind him. He was smiling as if he didn't have a care in the world and as if it was a normal occurrence for his top presenter to do an unscheduled piece to camera about her personal life. There was no sign of Bob. He would be lying low for the foreseeable. The hubbub in the atrium was building and the steel drums were adding their ecstatic rhythms to the noise.

Saul Relph appeared at my side. It is rare for him to make an appearance at PR events and this was the first time I'd seen him since our exchange of emails. My face got hot as he leaned in towards me.

'Everything all right with you, Liz?'

'All good, thanks.'

'I'm glad to hear it because you are a valued member of the team.'

His words were warm but how he said it was stiff. I could tell he couldn't wait to get away from me and it still rankled that he had implied I was somehow complicit in Julius crossing the line that night. He was about to leave my side as a stir rippled through the atrium. Fizzy had walked in. The guests broke into spontaneous applause as Ledley walked over and hugged her. The cameras were popping. That would be the picture tonight and the big story would be her pregnancy not his marinade.

'And *she* is very important to our continued success,' Saul Relph said as we looked at Fizzy who was smiling at the cameras and looking rather beautiful.

'I agree; our viewers love her.'

She had indeed outflanked us all.

Let me see now: Martine dislikes me; Bob loathes me; Molly is angry with me for promoting Simon; Fizzy doesn't trust me and Julius is waiting for an opportunity to get back at me. He likes nothing better than a good fight and he will relish trying to cut me down to size. But I have a deputy and

I can delegate more to Simon. I can start to put Flo first.

I watched Saul Relph walk over to Julius and slap him on the back. They seemed to be sharing some joke and looked comfortable together. The power relations at the station may not have changed fundamentally but I have learned an important lesson. It's not about doing the right thing at StoryWorld, it's about doing the smart thing. I would never be able to tell Mum that I had resorted to blackmail to get my way at work. Part of me felt horrible that I'd had to stoop to that. But another part of me felt proud that I was finally on my way to being one of the boys. I had put my career and my needs first instead of always thinking about the feelings of others.

Chalk Farm flat, 7 p.m.

Tomorrow I'll get Simon to collate all the radio interviews and press coverage of Ledley's launch. I hope for Ledley's sake that his marinade gets a mention. Fizzy may look soft and pretty on the outside but she has a core of steel. I turned my phone off and tapped on Flo's door.

'Do you fancy doing some baking, sweetheart? I thought we could make cupcakes.'

She got off her bed.

'Oh yeah, and I'll choose the toppings.'

We went into the kitchen and I got out the twelve-hole baking tin and the flour, caster sugar, butter and eggs.

'Can I do it all?'

'Yes please. I've had one of those days.'

I sat down at the table and watched her cream the butter and sugar and beat in the eggs.

'Vanilla extract?' I said.

'Just a teaspoon,' she said.

'Maybe put the oven on to heat up,' I said.

She did and then started to fold in the flour. She has a graceful way of doing things and is more precise in her movements than I am. She placed twelve paper cups into the tin and spooned the mixture into them.

There was a comfortable silence between us as the kitchen filled with the sweet smell of cakes baking and Flo beat the buttercream for the topping. I can do this. I can be an effective boss at work and ruthless when I have to be and a loving, patient mum at home. Television, StoryWorld, is my career and I'm not going anywhere. But Flo comes first and I will set limits on how much of me they get.

COMFORT RECIPES

FOR THE STRESSED OUT

My thanks for the striking cover to Anna Dorfman and to Liz Hatherell for the meticulous copy edit. I'd also like to say a big thank you to the book bloggers and readers who review my books and to The Prime Writers, a terrific support group of fellow writers.

Most of all, thank you, Barry Purchese, for your understanding, your loving support and your masterly feedback.

CAN'T WAIT TO READ THE

NEXT INSTALMENT?

THE STORY CONTINUES

IN JULY 2017

TURN THE PAGE TO READ

A PREVIEW...

PREVIEW

CHAPTER ONE

As soon as we got in Flo started looking for Mr Crooks and started to panic when he wasn't in the flat or our small garden. She got straight on her mobile to Janis who reassured her that he'd been fine when she'd been in to feed him this morning. He had probably just gone for a wander.

I was stuffing dirty clothes into the washing machine, two weeks' worth, some of which were still powdered with sand from the beach at Bordighera. For the first time in years having Simon as my deputy had allowed me to have a complete break from StoryWorld and I had a good tan and a hole in my finances. I was heading back to work on Monday and needed a detailed briefing from Simon. I made a mug of tea, black because I'd forgotten to buy milk, and called him.

'Welcome back. Was your flight OK? Heard there were delays at Heathrow' he said.

'We didn't fly. We were on the overnight train from Ventimiglia and it was brilliant, though I didn't sleep very much.'

'Good holiday?'

'Fantastic. Pasta and ice cream to die for and we swam in the sea most days. How have things been?'

'Fine really, no mishaps to report and Ledley is going from strength to strength.'

'Glad to hear it. Fizz is back next month.'

'He might find it hard going back to a weekly slot' Simon said.

Ledley, the StoryWorld chef, has been sitting in for our star presenter Fizzy Wentworth while she's been on maternity leave and he's been a hit with our viewers. Fizzy had her baby in late May and is only taking three and a half months off. She's determined to be back on the sofa at the beginning of September. She's worried that if she stays away longer Ledley will get too entrenched in the anchor role.

'And Lori Kerwell arrived last week' Simon said and there was something in his voice, the verbal equivalent of rolling his eyes.

'What's she like?'

'She's scary; really scary. All pent up energy and dead eyes.'

'Oh dear!'

''She's insisted on coming to the morning meetings and by the second day was commenting on the output.'

'I hope that's a short term thing. It's an editorial meeting' I said.

'Yeah but she said it will help her understand where she can develop business tie-ins.'

'And is Julius OK with that?'

'Not sure. He put her in her place on Friday.'

The gossip at the station was that Julius Jones, our director of programmes, was not overjoyed at the appointment of Lori Kerwell. She had been appointed by the MD to develop sales and marketing and there is often conflict between the editorial and the business sides in television.

'Can you talk me through the running order for tomorrow' I said.

'Loula is our celebrity interview of the day.'

'That's a good signing.'

Loula was the latest winner in ITV's blockbuster talent show.

'Harry got her for us. And Molly's story is on FGM.'

Female genital mutilation was a challenging topic for my researcher Molly to have chosen.

'How did she cover that?'

'She found a young Somalian woman, Beydaan, very brave. She shopped her parents because she doesn't want her young sister to go through what happened to her. Liz, she was seven years old when she was cut.'

'Bloody hell!'

'I know. Molly had to shoot the interview so you can't see her face. And we've changed her name of course.'

This was making me uneasy.

'And who will Ledley talk to about it?'

'We've booked the officer from the Foreign Office who runs the FGM Unit.

'That's a good call. You sure Ledley is OK with this?'

'Molly briefed him at length on Friday.'

'Well huge thanks Simon for all you've done. Let's both sit in the gallery tomorrow and we can go to the morning meeting together.'

'It's good to have you back.'

I unlocked the French doors and stepped out into our garden. It needed a sweep out there and my beloved hollyhocks needed water. I filled the watering can and gave them a good soaking. Their large pale pink and cream blooms rested against the warmth of the back wall. They are too big really for our small patch but I love them so much and looking at them always lifts my spirits. The washing cycle had finished and I pulled the clothes out and hung them over the drying frame which is a job I hate doing as the frame is not quite large enough. I wondered if I should call Ledley and talk through the FGM story with him. It is not the easiest subject for a male presenter to deal with. But I had left Simon in charge and I trusted him. The cat flap clattered and Mr Crooks emerged blinking into the sitting room. When he saw me he let out an outraged yowl.

'Flo, Mr Crooks is back and he's got the hump' I called out.